PUTTEES AND A PINSTRIPE

MACHINE-GUNNED BY the *Luftwaffe* on his way home from school in the 1940s, growing up in war-torn and post-war Britain, Mike George humorously lets us join in his riotous boyhood romps, teenage gropes, relationships, and army service in Korea and Gibraltar, while offering some outrageous views on life, love and the price of frogs. An absolute must for anyone who fancies having their fancy tickled by hilarious reminiscences, rambunctious belly laughs galore, provocative reflections and graphic, bawdy scenarios from an author who amongst all his other uproarious adventures once even got to dance with the young Brigitte Bardot in a Spanish cellar. You'd be doing yourself an enormous and unforgettable favour to read about all this, and everything else he got up to along the way. Enjoy!

GU00691217

PUTTEES

AND

A

PINSTRIPE

by

Mike George

ONE

TEN MILES INLAND from the chalk cliffs of the Sussex coast nestles my hometown of Lewes, set in the springy greensward of Kipling's much beloved South Downs, about a fifth of the way between Brighton and London. The River Ouse flows through it, an 11th century Norman castle stands o'er it, and on Thursday 9th June 1938 I was born in it. Not in the castle, but in a nursing home in nearby King Henry's Road.

Fifteen months later my elders declared war on Germany.

Over the next five years all the other war babies and I were to grow up in bomb blasts and air raid shelters. While our young bodies struggled to contend with dried milk, reconstituted orange juice and home made birthday and Christmas presents, our fathers, uncles and big brothers were all away settling world affairs with high explosive, bayonets, and the whole horrendous panoply of total war. Despite these privations we turned out to be a robust, resilient and ricketless breed with good strong legs, because we walked everywhere. In blizzard, monsoon or in heatwave, always in shorts, we certainly walked to and from school each day - one of my earliest memories of which, is tar melting in the road.

This is why -

Britain and Germany had been at war for three years.

The RAF's famous Few, young pilots with an average age of 22 and only 12 weeks training under their belts who if they survived a fortnight meant they were veterans, had heroically already reduced the *Luftwaffe's* presence in our skies in the

1

summer of 1940. Standing up there alongside Trafalgar and Waterloo as a victorious feat of British history, of those brave young 3,000-strong Battle of Britain 'glamour boys in blue, with considerable substance' no fewer than 500 of them had been killed from the 35 Hawker Hurricane squadrons and the 19 squadrons that flew R.J. Mitchell's immortal Supermarine Spitfire, that gloriously iconic bird of the air with its famous elliptical wings which was soon to give it a top speed of 462 mph: but the Germans had made more planes since then, and in order to continue to distress Britain's civilian morale Deutschland's *Luftwaffe* supremo, Hermann Goering, had recently started a new series of 'tip and run' terror raids over the south-east's coastal towns of Dover, Brighton and Worthing.

Germany's new single-seater BMW-engined *Focke-Wulf (Fw)190* - known as the *Würger*, or Shrike - also referred to as the 'Butcher Bird' because of that particular raptor's habit of impaling insects and nestlings and other prey on thorns - was arguably even better than the renowned *Messerschmitt 109,* and slightly faster than our own then otherwise world-beating Spitfire.

It was 12.30 on a stinking hot day in May, in the summer of 1942. I was just four-years-old, when I found myself not being mugged, raped or abducted, but machine-gunned by one of the Fatherland's merciless 19-year-old pilots.

Unaware of the *Focke-Wulf's* terrifying pedigree, I was just a tiddly kid and simply threw myself instinctively down in the road, clawing at the gravel while this particular *Fw190* came screaming out of the sun hammering cannon at me as though I was an armoured troop column instead of a care-free British nipper strolling home from kindergarten for his spam and junket lunch.

Germany's Bremen factory managed to produce 20,000 of these beasts during the War: perhaps if they had produced one less I would have been better off.

The black-crossed enemy fighter-bomber's 13 mm shells ricocheted along the road, sending shards of flint whining through tree-bark, foliage, nearby front doors and windows.

Their discarded brass cases clanged and bounced along the pavement. Various splinters of stuff purred, whanged and whacked into my face. It didn't take long. Having shot me up, the raider surged over the roof of Doctor Lonsdale's house at the bottom of the road, dislodging a flurry of tiles that slithered swiftly to smash into the guttering, banked to climb steeply into the wide blue yonder, and made off back towards the English Channel. If he was not intercepted en route by an *'Achtung Spitfeur'* he would reach his home airfield in northern France at St Omer Wizernes near Calais just in time for a celebratory *Bier und Bockwurst* lunch.

This event was not some gilded figment of my Walter Mitty-ish imagination. The swots who plot fighter attacks and bombs that have dropped with little black dots spattered across local area maps have since confirmed that the raid took place. One of them told me I should not have been so paranoid; that particular raid hadn't been planned with just me in mind: also that with a bit more research he would probably even have been able to come up with the name of my *Fw190's* pilot, an option I refrained from pursuing in case it made me switch into belated vengeance mode and I set out to track down his descendants for retribution.

Most commodities during WWII were rationed. To acquire his ration, each person was issued with his own ration book. Clothing, too, was rationed. I had desperately needed and had recently been bought a new pair of grey flannel shorts for school. Tucking my ubiquitous 1940s matching grey shirt into them earlier that morning my mother had sternly admonished me to take great care not to get them torn, dirty, or in any way soiled because they were the last pair I was going to get.

'They're going to have to last you till the end of the war, Michael.

'How long will that be, Mum? Suppose I'm eighteen by then?'

'Don't you be cheeky to me, young man,' she chuckled, lightly slapping the backs of my thighs.

Now the noise of the *Fw190* roaring down from the sky had brought my heavily pregnant mother tearing out of our front gate fifty yards away: 'Lie down Michael; lie down. Lie down; lie *down*,' she screamed, frantically clenching her pinny with one hand and wrenching her hair with the other.

The *Luftwaffe* pilot having departed, smothered in gore and chippings I prised myself loose from the molten tarmac like a homunculus emerging from a black swamp.

Mother screeched down the road, skidded in on her knees and clutched me desperately to her bosom. Thank God she wasn't wearing her one and only pair of nylons, which like my hitherto pristine grey nether wear were going to have to last till the war's end.

'Oh *Michael* . . .' she cried, shaking me with combined anguish and relief: 'I thought I told you to be more careful. Just look, you've gone and got tar all over your lovely new shorts.'

*

Some families had corrugated iron Anderson air-raid shelters dug into their back gardens, alongside the cabbages, cauliflowers and runner beans strung out on wobbly poles, but ours never ran to one of those. We used the large communal job that had been constructed beneath a huge grass bank a hundred yards away down in Prince Edward's Road, which served us well until 1942. Germany didn't change tactics in 1942. But my baby brother Anthony was born.

The Germans used gas in the Great War. My little brother used it in the Second. He should have been a German. He was a sort of fifth columnist baby. He undermined local civilian morale even more so than Goering. Powdered egg was the cause. It was difficult in the confined and foetid space of Prince Edward's Road air raid shelter to accommodate the area's bomb-avoiding populace, my little brother's one a.m. feed and his two a.m. evacuation. Some of the long suffering, nostril-wrinkled neighbours with war ravaged nerve ends who cohabited with us in that underground shelter, decided that enough was enough. By common consent one night they ceased merely glancing intently and muttering to each other

4

and finally drew concerted and voluble attention to their discomfort. Our highly offended 29-year old mother flashed them all a look of withering disdain, huddled in their smelly blankets on bunks in the glow of faltering lamps, and with a superior toss of her head gathered her reeking babe to her arms, snapped her fingers at me to follow *tout de suite* without demur, and together we climbed back out to the deserted pitch black street and scurried off home as if through a cloudburst, which minutes later there was - of hot metal. Fortunately there was no one to see us otherwise she might have contrived a nonchalant saunter with my stinking brother slung on one hip, like Sophia Loren and bairns in some black and white film about Naples.

The droves of *Dorniers* droning overhead through our searchlights criss-crossing the blackness, unleashed their payloads and the bombs came raining down.

With the night sky over Lewes lit like the 4th of July and incendiaries bouncing off manhole covers, mother had to think fast. Ample as her bosom was in peace and however high she thrust it now, unaided it was insufficient to thwart the might of Goering's *Luftwaffe*.

My parents had been married five years and in those days one seldom moved into a ready made home. Extending unsecured credit to *hoi polloi* was not yet the norm. None of us felt especially deprived, but by today's standards our home was spartan. It had bare boards throughout, except for a much handed down and threadbare 'family heirloom' carpet (circa 1880) in the dining room and an only slightly posher one (circa 1920) in the drawing room. Blackout cloths were hung over the kitchen windows which for light relief mother had festooned with morale-raising 'Up Yours, Hitler' type cartoons she had cut out of newspapers and magazines.

The twin centrepieces of my parents' possessions were two heavily upholstered - again inherited somewhere along the way by family defaults and deaths - Victorian armchairs, their navy blue leather buttoned into pockets, like chesterfields. Desperate women have been known to lift motor cars if there is a child trapped beneath. I never got to see my mother in a bikini, which hadn't been invented then, but I'm sure she must have possessed a six-pack to die for. With nothing but two gentle hefts and barely a grunt she was effortlessly able to up-end both these massive chairs to form a little castle. We seemed to spend most of the war crawling in and out of this improvised horsehair-stuffed bomb shelter of mother's in the middle of the drawing room floor, either sheltering from the real thing or rehearsing doing so. Restored to their rightful position and re-upholstered both chairs now grandly await their next call to duty. Originally constructed in 1850 it is too much to expect that having staved off the aerial wrath of 1940's Berlin the contemporary upholsterer's art will enable those good old chairs to face and repel the next war's sci-fi assault, but at least my grandchildren and I will meet the atomising 21st century's laser zaps in style and comfort.

Lewes lay beneath Goering's Berlin-London flight path. It also lay beneath the RAF's flight path to Germany. This way we copped the lot. We did so by accident more than design, although one or two more close shaves before I was seven and the war ended did make me wonder whether Hitler considered me to be some sort of personal threat to the Thousand Year Reich.

At tea time the sky used to darken and vibrate as wave after wave of battleship grey British and American bombers droned overhead en route to their night raids on Germany. As I was being tucked up to sleep it was to the sound of the asymmetric pitch of the German team's engines throbbing over our house for their reciprocal match. A few hours later the RAF and USAAF - not quite so many of them this time - would awaken us as they coughed and lurched their wounded way home again. Some had 'bought it' over Germany. Others would spend the remainder of the war as PoWs. So near and yet so far, some of them would pitch into the gently undulating South Downs to meet their premature million-year sleep amongst the flint and chalk of a proud but sorrowful English countryside. Having dropped their load and evaded enemy flak, the lucky ones would land, relinquish *Bertha, Glenda* or *Foxtrot One-Kilo* to the tender loving care of their ground crews, crash out exhausted in their Nissen huts on their blanketed iron bedsteads, and then with a huge sigh of relief and a grateful prayer enjoy another full English breakfast next morning.

I seldom bothered even trying to get to sleep until after the *Luftwaffe* had vented its wrath on London each night, and flown back over our garden trying to avoid our night fighters and regain German airspace once more instead of joining the others in the wheatfields of the Weald, or that other, watery Channel grave.

These early years of mine in Lewes were heavy going for my recently appointed guardian angel. At the end of Ferrers Road, where we lived, was a beautiful stretch of countryside which formed a magnificent adventure playground. There were trenches to crawl from and bricks to hurl; trees to swing from and an enormous static water tank brimful of green and stinking H_2O to sail homemade things upon and fall into; and there were rusty iron bits and barbed wire with which to sever each others limbs: oh yes, we were war babies alright. Tough years for the parents of young children, but great and exciting years for us youngsters. They were halcyon days in their way, despite the very real fear of death being brought constantly home to us by the twice daily wailing of the air raid sirens; boyhood days which we lived to the full despite the privations of which, never having known anything else, we were blissfully unaware. We had lots of fun.

I had a good war.

TWO

IT WAS NOT EASY FOR MOTHER to bring up two tearaway sons in such a fraught environment. To do so and still retain her sanity she tempered her natural maternal compassion with a strict code of discipline. Doctor Spock might have taken issue with her, but Doctor Spock didn't live with us in Bomb Alley, Sussex, from 1939-1945.

My brother Anthony and I were brought up on the cutting edge of a rattan cane. Neither of us was especially keen on this idea, but it was an inescapable fact of life and the discipline it instilled went a long way to helping us survive those parlous formative years.

It was three hundred yards from our house up to nature's bountiful adventure playground at the end of the road. Still being just a toddler my brother wasn't much use to our gang, but mother ordered that he had to tag along with us anyway, so I was stuck with him throughout the war. During daylight hours either one of us could be anywhere from carving something in the top of a tree to encouraging the loathsome Scots kid from number 32 to drown himself in the water tank. Come bedtime mother was not prepared to flog up there every evening to break us from the gang's embrace and argue, so instead she stood outside the front gate and yelled.

'*Anthony,*' she would holler at the top of her voice. 'It's your bedtime.'

She was ignored.

There was no pending air raid. We had eaten. We were playing. Pauline Smith from number 28 was coming along very nicely for a five year old and had finally agreed to drop her knickers behind the water tank for sixpence to make us let go of her pigtail, and now mother insisted on spoiling our natural development.

'*Anthony,* I shan't call you again,' she yelled.

'Oh Mum, *must* I?' wailed my grime encrusted infant brother, barely out of his rompers: I allude solely to his age here; nothing to do with Pauline Smith.

'Yes, you must,' wafted the delayed response on a current of air from Family HQ down the road, 'and tell Michael I shall want him back here in ten minutes, too.'

'When's that, Mum?' I shouted back obtusely.

'You'll find out soon enough if you don't get here,' she yelled. She knew all the angles our mother, and had each of them licked.

Gladys Ellwright, one of the war ravaged old biddies who had found my brother's nappies so offensive in the air raid shelter, now found this nightly battle of wits a bit disquieting as well. She confided to several of the neighbours that with a war on she felt sure there was plenty of call for CSMs in the ATS, a sentiment which courtesy of another neighbour, mother got to hear about. Ever since the shelter incident she had secretly hoped Gladys might cop a stray ton or two of German explosive over her side of the road. This latest affront coincided with mother having a sore throat. No more did she intend shouting to announce each day's close of play, so from somewhere or other she managed to purloin a police whistle. With the rattan cane swishing like the Sword of Damocles to aid our concentration should it falter, after tea that afternoon Anthony and I were apprised of how mother saw this new system working.

'There'll be four blasts for Anthony; two for you, Michael.'

'What if we don't hear them, Mum?'

'You'll hear them,' she said, twitching the cane meaningfully.

We both knew we'd hear them. Clearer than a clarion call from Hades we'd hear them.

Her system proved effective.

After a few days of Anthony and me fearfully responding to mother's peremptory whistle blasts and us both thundering back home, deprived of my leadership the rest of the gang would disperse shortly afterwards so that the entire street was cleared of kids and locked up for the night in about fifteen minutes flat. It couldn't last though. One afternoon a policeman turned up on his bicycle at our back door to inform mother she'd have to stop blowing her illegal whistle in case some other passing policeman mistook it as a warning of something real. This temporary setback of mother's enabled us to play on unhindered whilst, undeterred, our devil-woman dreamed up an even more powerful system.

A bugle.

She never quite got the hang of the bugle, but the rapidly degenerating old biddy opposite, Gladys Ellwright, so wanted to survive the war to see her 20-year old son Gerald home from Burma, that she thought better of complaining a third time. She had long since pegged mother a notch or two beneath Goebbels in her pecking order, and was fearful lest a further ruction might inspire her to replace the bugle with something even more heinous. She was right, of course. In case her bugle was confiscated, being an adventurous woman with considerable initiative mother had for some time been trying to secrete ammunition for father's revolver. Two shots for me; three for Anthony.

The siren wailed. The bugle blew. Anthony was in bed with 'flu, so the call had to be for me. I took the brick out of the loathsome Scots kid's head, dropped it on his foot, gathered up my sheath knife, penknife, cigarette cards, unusually shaped stone, apple, club, bow and arrow and long piece of garrotting wire, and whipping my imaginary horse galloped homeward back down the road in my Clarks sandals and corduroy shorts to the safety of the upturned armchairs. But on this occasion I was too late. The crafty Hun had managed to beat the siren. As I skidded in through our front door a familiar looking *Fw-190* started to let rip outside. Our large landing window disintegrated in a hail of cannon fire. The wooden bannisters were chewed to kindling, and for the second time in this benighted war young Michael found his countenance being re-sculpted by splinters and broken glass, courtesy of *Krupps of Essen*. I was only five and didn't even have any bum-fluff yet, but was beginning to look like Charles Bronson already. 'Oh, shit,' wailed mother, or whatever the '40's in-phrase was (and there must have been a few) quickly crawling out from beneath the two armchairs and brandishing the by now all too familiar nail tweezers with which she did most things from minor brain surgery to unblocking the drain, and deftly commenced to flick shards from my body.

After that Hitler stopped trying to shoot me in the face. I would soon be six, after all.

*

One dark stormy night in 1943, there came a loud knock at our front door.

'Michael, see who it is will you,' mother called from the kitchen.

I opened the door to find myself staring at a pair of black boots, gaiters, and long legs clad in khaki battledress trousers. With eyes popping from their sockets my gaze slowly climbed to take in a buttoned-up khaki greatcoat, and beneath the black Armoured Corps beret a moustached and suntanned face smiling benignly down at me.

'Who is it, dear?'

'A soldier,' I yelped.

Wiping both hands on her pinny mother protectively hurried out into the hall to see, cast one glance at our caller, and shrieked: *'Arthur.'*

*

I didn't know who or what Arthur was.

It turned out he was my uncle.

Married to Joan, my mother's younger sister, Arthur had been called to arms shortly after I was born, so he'd not yet had the pleasure of meeting me. A 9th Lancer, he had been one of the Desert Rats in their thin skinned Crusaders and later American lease-lend Sherman tanks, fighting with Monty at *El Alemain*, and then along with the rest of the Eighth Army went on up into Italy. To a small boy who had seldom been farther than the end of his road, this seemed like an incomprehensible achievement. At this time of my life and for several years afterwards it was my perception that there were two places in the world each as unattainable as the moon. They were the unimaginably expensive and virtually inaccessible Hollywood, and the *Führer's* lair at *Berchtesgaden.* Whatever magical place did those wonderful moving pictures come from, and how would one ever discover where exactly was the *Berghof,* the German dictator's palatial residence? Years later when I was in Hollywood I found it much cheaper than England. And when eventually I visited *Obersalzburg,* the very heart of Hitler-land, and rode up in Adolph's shining brass, green leather upholstered lift through the 120 metre elevator shaft constructed through the core of *Kehlstein* mountain to reach his renowned Eagle's Nest hideaway at the summit, where the eponymous birds of prey could be seen gliding on thermals past the windows and nearby soaring peaks, I realised the world was shrinking, and that my revised perception was beginning to master the fact; my personal introduction to the Global Village; but meanwhile Uncle Arthur's discarded greatcoat, beret, boots and gaiters lay in a heap on our hall floor while he sat in the drawing room relaxing in one of our now right-way-up for once Victorian leather armchairs, drinking tea.

After exclaiming his name, mother's first remark was: 'You'll be wanting a bath.' To the best of my knowledge she didn't usually make this offer when people came to our door; neither to the postman, the milkman nor the stroppy ARP warden who officiously stopped by occasionally to warn us of a chink of light in one of our curtains, however much they needed a bath, so whether this was some common courtesy extended just to visiting family in time of war, or being taller than me she'd more readily scented diesel, Libyan sand and several days' travel grime I don't know, but while I sat with my chin in my hands and elbows on knees cross-legged on the floor gazing in awe at this wondrous khaki-clad being who was trying to remember how to be dainty about holding a teacup, mother was outside in the kitchen furiously banking up the boiler. One man in our bath. This was certainly a novelty in our house where we only used to bathe every Friday night and in order of precedence, all using the same bath water: father first, then mother, then me (who used to practise peeing upwards) and then my little brother Anthony who subsequently always preferred showers. In those days I would only ever have conceived of anyone enjoying a bath all to himself if they were getting married, going to meet the King, or having an audience with God. Yet here was this virtual stranger fetching up seven-feet tall on our front doorstep being allowed to use up a whole week's supply of hot bath water. In one go. Strange things happened in war.

I only saw my uncle twice during the war; on that occasion, when he came back from Africa to have a bath, and a second time when he was demobbed and he and my aunt came to visit us on their way home to civvy street, but Uncle Arthur had become my instant hero. Every day that he and the Eighth Army were punching their way up through the cold mud, hot blood, the guts, sweat, and tears of Italy and beyond, I used to pester my mother with 'When's Uncle Arthur coming to see us again, Mum?'

That night my hero slept in my bed, while I was relegated without objection to the doubled-up armchairs in the drawing room. At various times during my own subsequent military career, the kernel of which path was undoubtedly embedded during that visit from my uncle, I had cause to appreciate how much the welcome we gave him, that simple cup of tea, the hot bath and clean white sheets afterwards, must have meant to him.

How was the kernel of nascent militarism embedded?

When he came downstairs next morning wearing my father's borrowed dressing gown, he found me admiringly standing guard over his boots, gaiters, greatcoat and the black 1st Armoured Division beret, still lying there on the hall floor.

'You can put my beret on if you like, Mike; let's see how you look in it.'

'Corrrrr; do you really mean it, Uncle. *Can* I?'

'There,' he said, reaching out with his strong suntanned hands, wriggling the beret's Royal Armoured Corps mailed fist cap badge to stay somewhere above my left eye instead of smothering my entire face. 'Sure looks pretty good to *me;*' then as a seeming afterthought: 'Don't suppose you'd like to try on the boots as well, would you?'

Would I!

Without even having to remove my Clarks sandals he lifted me up and lowered me effortlessly into his two big black ammunition boots with their heavily studded leather soles. 'There's only one thing needed now to complete this whole ensemble,' he grinned, and produced his web belt, but even after he'd quickly adjusted its buckles to their maximum reduction it still embraced my tiny waist almost twice.

'Gosh: do you think I could go right outside in them?' I asked, thumbs hooked in the belt while gazing down in wonderment at each manfully shod foot.

'Course you can, old chap. Make sure you come back though won't you, otherwise I won't be able to return to the war and might get shot as a deserter.'

It took quite a while for me to shuffle the three hundred yards up to the top of our road, probably scraping more wear out of the boots' hobnails than they endured for the rest of the war. Sadly there were few people around to see and admire this one-off Churchill Youth, feeling ten-feet tall clad in his embryo fig, out there on parade eagerly prepared to defend single-handedly his neighbourhood should a horde of German paratroops suddenly take it into their mind to drop from the sky. When I did an about-turn at the top of the road and moved forward to shuffle back home again, I ended up on my face with grazed knees and palms. The boots hadn't turned round with me. Quickly standing up I bent down and yanked them about to face the right way, and off we went once more. I was hooked. The war was a way of life and would go on forever. Soon I would grow out of my grey flannel shorts and mother would *have* to let me join the army, if only for me to get something bigger to wear. It couldn't happen quickly enough for me.

My uncle only remained with us that one day. He had stopped off on his way through to Guildford, where Aunty Joan was living and working. A week later he went back to rejoin his regiment in the desert, prior to moving on up into the Italian Campaign.

After the War we saw each other periodically. While I grew taller and fuller he somehow seemed to become shorter and slighter than on that long ago night in 1943 when first we'd met. He and Aunt Joan went on to produce four cousins for me. Arthur eventually died (in 1978) and then Joan (aged 90) joined him up there in 2005.

Having been at the age to yearn for and procreate a son of his own in 1943, and no doubt touched by my early adulation, just after he'd died my aunt told me that she'd found a small photograph of me, aged five, tucked away in the back of Arthur's wallet.

The love and respect forged those 24-hours in 1943, it turned out, had been reciprocal.

THREE

MY FATHER WAS WELSH

When he was a little boy of four a large picture fell off his bedroom wall, the broken glass embedding itself deeply in his head. His distraught mother gingerly wrapped his bleeding skull in a towel before picking him up and carrying him carefully but quickly downstairs. It was a dark, stormy night outside. There were few cars in the Welsh hills in 1914. My grandfather carried him on his back across a brace of Brecon Beacons to the nearest doctor. The Edwardian practitioner plucked the shards and slivers from his tiny noddle, stitched up the rents, bandaged him, and then father and son set out back through the murk together on their return trip.

Nothing to do with his earlier head injury, but two years later my father developed pleural empyema, which in those days was almost always rapidly fatal. His left lung had to be surgically drained of its accumulation of pus. The kitchen table was scrubbed and covered with a clean white cloth, upon which my anxious grandparents laid their six year old son face down for the same family doctor to anaesthetise him with ether and slice him open along the line of his left scapula. By all accounts the release of purulence from my father's lung was so forceful that it hit the ceiling. Miraculously, he was one of the lucky ones. He survived. But for the rest of his life he was to sport what looked like a scimitar scar down his back, as a result of which, much to his suppressed resentment, he was forever exempted from military service.

Both my grandparents and parents are dead now, and I regret never having found out why one day in the 1920s the former chose to move from Pontypridd, in south Wales, to Lewes, in East Sussex; but they did, and that is how I became Sussex born and bred.

Not to be confused with Lewes County Grammar School which started in 1930 and whose pupils wore blue uniforms, from 1921-1928 my father attended Lewes *Old* Grammar School, so called because it had been founded as long ago as 1512, whose pupils' kit was maroon with silver white facings. Because up until then he had been having such a bad time of it medically, much to his mother's consternation he now pulled out the stops to make up for all the mollycoddling and lost time - to excel at sport. He became a useful cricket, hockey and tennis player, an oarsman, and no mean athlete, as well as consistently coming in the top three in academic subjects.

After he left school he joined Barclays Bank and in 1936 went to work at their East Grinstead branch. My maternal grandfather, one Walter Henry Masters, owned a 'By Appointment' butcher's shop in the town (he once sold some pork sausages to King Edward) bang opposite the bank, and - hey presto - guess what? Mother and father were married in 1937 and posted back to Lewes Old Bank (a branch of Barclays) where father spent the war. At school, and during my image conscious twenties, I did little to disabuse my peers of the inference I'd allowed them to draw that along with many other feats of derring-do my courageous commando-trained father had been Lord Louis Mountbatten's highly decorated principal staff officer in South East Asia. In fact because of his empyema he was an ARP warden and a lance corporal in the Home Guard, although on both counts I believe quite a good and conscientious one. As their marital relationship developed a pace he and mother began to discover that they were completely incompatible. Our wonderful but nevertheless still scatty mother was undoubtedly a bit neurotic. For example - if because of affairs of state father ever arrived home late for lunch, she used him as target practice. No sooner would his head appear round the door than, like Jim Bowie in a strop, she'd hurl a carving knife at it. Fortunately it always missed and bounced off the wall by its handle, but mother's behaviour

17

pattern did little to enhance the gaiety of our home life during those dark years.

Eventually the situation was resolved, however.

One spring evening she chanced to stumble upon our 44-year old father intimately engaged with another lady on our tartan family picnic rug just behind the allotment shed, up by the broccoli, so she promptly initiated divorce proceedings. Well, next morning to be precise. This was social suicide back then of course, and meant they would be automatically denied access to the Royal Enclosure at Ascot, but this realisation failed to deter mother one jot. She forged implacably ahead down the road to freedom. Such was the ferocity of her intent that father had no option but to accede to the whole dismantling process, and apart from the initial shocks to their systems it has to be said that they were both much happier afterwards, when the dust had settled and they had finally gone their separate ways. I should like to add that my father was an urbane and charming gentleman who was well liked and respected by everyone. Especially the doxy by the broccoli. But obviously not by mother. They simply could not get along. Mind, this above related incident, when father was found illegally getting his rocks off behind the allotment shed, was not to occur until 1954. I only happen to mention it here - in the middle of World War Two - because it is a convenient juncture to do so. *Much* more was to happen before then.

*

It was the summer of 1944.

For months the build up had been underway for *Operation Overlord*, the combined Allied Forces D-Day landings on the Normandy beaches—the long awaited liberation of German occupied Europe. American, Canadian and British troops had been billeted all along the south coast of England in readiness. It was a six-year old's dream come true. The 19-year-old Land Army girls weren't complaining too much about it either. Strong, lusty, healthy, nubile young fillies, fetchingly attired in their jodhpurs and with blouse buttons straining beneath their green pullies (I was reasonably advanced for six and my memory serves me well) strutted about the place thrusting their wares happily at the heroes of the hour. When men are at war exercising their basic urge to kill, half their womenfolk will cast propriety to the winds for a packet of cigarettes or nylons and the chance to allow free rein to basic urges of their own. It may be argued that as she sees the male lifeblood of her generation spilled in battle, woman is genetically inclined to do her own God-given thing to replenish the breed. The Land Army girls around Lewes may not have been aware that this was their real reason for lying down so readily in the long grass that summer, like dad and *his* piece of fluff a decade later—but it's a reasonable theory and I'm sticking to it.

Many years later a lifelong friend of mine, Michael Ockenden, was to write a successful book called *Canucks By The Sea*, a historically researched account of the activities and dispositions of all the Canadian troops who had been stationed around Eastbourne and its environs during the war. Following a local press mention, what then turned out to become a best seller running to several reprints, was launched in Eastbourne Town Hall in November 2006. Michael thought a few mildly interested people might turn up for the event, so laid on tea and scones for twenty.

The place was packed.

There were hundreds.

Every seat was taken, and there were many others leaning against the walls and standing in the aisles. What especially delighted us was the surprising number of distinguished looking silver-haired ladies of a certain age who appeared. As each one hesitantly entered the hall we observed her slightly shocked and reluctant recognition of the others of her scarcely remembered wartime clique, whom she grudgingly acknowledged with a barely discernible, surreptitious little nod from behind the conveniently designed upturned Medici collar of her coat, which - as with an artfully held fan - for some reason she was discreetly contriving to use to obscure her face. This body language was not some vain endeavour to enhance any fading allure, but a clear statement that at this time of life these ladies would really prefer not to have been seen there at all actually, in case their attendance was construed by the public at large as being an admission of long ago indiscretions committed in the black-out after a joyous succession of wartime dances - yet having read in the *Eastbourne Herald* about this particular book's launch, they had secretly known all week that they and their cupboard skeletons would be absolutely compelled to attend.

My next door neighbour at the time was a darling old girl of 91. Worth almost half-a-million because of its location and size, her house was falling down around her ears from neglect. Her father had paid £1,200 for it in 1917, and Babs had lived there all her life since then. (By 1937 the house had still only been worth £1,300!) During the war, the Canadian troops my friend Michael had researched and written about had been stationed in many of the surrounding houses.

'They used to park their tanks right along the pavement here,' Babs told me once shortly before she died. 'Every night when they returned from practising manoeuvres in the hills everything was so muddy they had to open all the fire hydrants and hose down the entire road. They were *such* great fun and were always throwing dances that we all used to go to. Life's never really been quite the same since then, you know,' she chuckled, and a delightful twinkle appeared in her rheumy old eyes. 'There was a gel lived in that corner house over *there* - her palsied hand quiveringly indicated the house opposite 'who was really rather naughty though. Her husband - a Black Watch orficer - was a PoW in Germany. Much against her better judgement, I'm sure, one night this gel was rather easily persuaded, *I* think, to go orf to the cinema with one of our Canadians. Well, just as you might imagine, one thing led to another and before you could say 'knife' she ended up bigamously marrying the fellow, and going to live with his parents over in Canada, to await his return. And, do you know, at the end of the war, when her poor cuckolded Black Watch husband was released from his German PoW camp and came home here to discover what she'd done - well - he was really quite put out.'

It was Friday 9th June.

D-Day plus three.

My sixth birthday.

My mother and I had been in town shopping. Supermarket trolleys piled high with comestibles waiting to be stacked in the car boot had yet to be invented. Mother's small wicker basket hanging from the crook of her elbow contained our four-strong family's entire food ration for the week.

Our historic little county town was packed that morning.

Something was afoot.

Mother and I stood crammed amongst a lot of other people on the broad stone steps of the Crown Court. She seemed to be doing quite a bit of unnecessary foot shuffling and I noticed that her face was beginning to turn slightly pink. Peering around her shopping basket I could see that a swarthy young man was trying to take hold of her hand. When mother told the story later it turned out he was one of the many Italian PoWs employed as agricultural labourers on the neighbouring farms. Mother was 31 then, suntanned and an unusually attractive young woman. The enterprising Italian had simply been doing what Italians do and understandably trying his luck, hoping to be invited back for a hot bath . . . and extras. (Years later she confessed with half a smile that she'd been quite tempted; but father was still coming home for his lunch in those days.)

This brief romance with her Latin admirer ended when he was edged away by the crowd as it pressed off the steps towards the kerbside. Whatever was about to happen, was just going to take place. Beneath the black and gold clock face of St Michael's church further up the High Street, people were spontaneously cheering, waving and clapping their hands as a convoy of camouflaged khaki lorries came rumbling towards us. Their drive shafts were humming and the enormous tyres *thrummed* over the warm tarmac. Each lorry was packed with laughing, singing, cat-calling Tommies off on their way to the coast. Like a role reversal of girls casting petals before the path of warriors, these soldiers were divesting their pockets of all their left-over small change and lobbing it out to the crowd. Glinting coin-of-the-realm for which they were fighting bounced and rolled into shop doorways, in some cases accompanied by green £1 notes (£30 today) and brown ten shilling notes (£15). The Lewesians spilled gleefully off the pavements onto the road to scrabble for and scoop up this largesse. Mother stooped shyly to retrieve a gleaming half-crown piece (£7) from the gutter and a silver sixpence (63p) for me.

What a birthday it was!

I now know that these lads were 'D' Company of the Hallamshire Battalion of the East York and Lancs Regiment going through to the port of Newhaven for embarkation to the Normandy beaches. The Hallamshire's regimental history later recorded in no mean fashion the great appreciation they felt for our warm Lewesian greeting they received that day.

*

It was 3.0 o'clock on a hot Friday afternoon in 1945.

Thirty other little seven-year old boys and girls and I were sitting in Class One at Western Road Primary School listening to Mrs Cull our form mistress read us our traditional Friday afternoon Enid Blyton story. Sandra Banks who sat beside me on these occasions and had lovely blonde curls but protruding teeth was noisily sucking on a boiled sweet. She had been awarded three gold stars that week for being good. The boiled sweet was prize lolly from teacher. It was also inducement lolly for the rest of us. Children's pleasures were fewer and simpler in those days, plus we were more easily conned.

A bluebottle was buzzing like a small doodlebug against the windowpane. Suddenly I saw a man's lined and tired face appear pressed against the glass from outside, using his hand to deflect the reflection. Class One's curious gaze collectively followed Mrs Cull as she placed our open storybook face down on her desk and quickly strode on those sensible shoes of hers across to the door. It clicked-to behind her as she shook hands and spoke to the stranger. Each of us looked quizzically at the other, shrugging our shoulders and rudely straining our ears in an effort to catch just a snatch of their conversation. Sandra Banks had taken what was left of the boiled sweet out of her mouth to look at, and dropped it on the floor. She was just bending to pick it up when Mrs Cull came back into the room again.

'Sandra,' she called, 'if your desk is tidy dear you can go now. Your daddy's here to take you home. Isn't that nice?'

Sandra left the sweet sticking to the floor, banging her head on the edge of the desk as she sat up again.

'I didn't think I'd got a daddy, Miss,' she said, lifting sticky little fingers to rub at her bruise.

Emitting one enormous sob the soldier strode across the room to sweep his surprised little daughter up into his arms in a bone crushing hug.

Sandra had been barely two when he had gone off to Burma.

This sort of thing kept happening at school in those days.

*

English weather has always been fickle and global warming had not been heard of, yet the recollection of our wartime summers is that they were long, hot and Huckleberry Finn-ish. We lived in shorts and sandals. Winters regularly had deep, white snow, mittens, balaclavas and snowmen. The war our adults waged did not seem to impinge too greatly on our daily lives. We still went to school.

The bane of my life at this time was a seven year old potential thug and public pugilist called Billy Manser. Billy was the undisputed leader of the junior chapter of the school gang. Equally feared as Billy was his lanky, snotty-nosed, bony-wristed, eager and phobia-ridden lieutenant, Norman Luckhurst. He of the mighty squint. Norman lived down Leicester Road; Billy up on the Neville Estate somewhere, and there were other lethal and obnoxious little heavies who constituted the gang's remaining cohorts.

The functional and fashionable footwear at Western Road

Primary School in 1945 - absolutely *de rigeur* if a boy was to hold his head with pride and be counted amongst his peers - was steel-heeled, steel-tipped, multi-studded, junior-size army ammunition boots. Our fathers had already tested and proved their durability. They were definitely kick and scuff-proof. Mud and blood washed off them easily and they were tough. Get up a good enough speed in them and you could slide in a shower of sparks along the pavement, feeling their soles beneath burn friction hot through threadbare socks. The effect was more greatly enhanced by a bomber jacket buttoned at the throat and allowed to flow freely behind in one's slipstream. Needless to say my mother did not go a lot on ammunition boots, nor the Zorro cape concept.

More than anything else in the world I craved a pair of those boots so's I could legitimately ride with the pack, but my intransigent mother was engaged in a toadying programme with Mr. Cull at the time, our school's headmaster, endeavouring to create the impression that I came from a nicer home and finer lineage than the rest of my classmates and so should receive special treatment, should any such special treatment be on offer; which it wasn't, of course. To my everlasting shame she sent me to school each day wearing black elastic-sided dance pumps, a navy blue raincoat and a silly little navy blue beret with a tiggle-taggle-wiggle-waggle-woggly tuft of umbilical felt pig's tail on top, where it hadn't been properly cast off from its loom, or wherever it is berets came from. Other mothers loved me. Their daughters appeared indifferent, except they tended to incline more to Billy Manser's rough and ready mob. Playing not yet with but by myself in the corner of the playground at break times, I came to learn the meaning of ostracisation, feeling myself destined to a life of perceived effeminacy before even knowing what that meant, or that one day it would even become so fashionable that it would seem almost compulsory. It was a wonder Billy Manser's mob didn't lynch me. To hell with Hitler bombing and strafing my face every time I went out - him I could handle - it was Manser's Mafia scared the shit out of me.

Sauntering provocatively booted with his generals about the perimeter of the school's concrete playground, hands sunk deep into the pockets of his grey flannel shorts, Billy resembled Attila The Hun surveying a Teutonic Plain before leaping on it from some Caucasian ridge. Intermittently he would dispatch parties of skirmishers to smash some unsuspecting new kid into submissive allegiance. Belt a hoop here. Throw a rock there. Break Mary Barnard's daisy chain, or make gleeful play for Cheryl Pritchard's knickers.

During these formative years I strove to remain on the periphery of school warfare. Although I lived in constant fear of Billy's bullying and was eminently suited to receive his unbridled persecution, not once in all that time did he get a single minion to bash me, nor did he ever deign to do so himself. Perhaps even darker forces were at work. My mum might have squared up to his mum, and said: 'Listen up, Babe: lay off the Fauntleroy Kid - *capisci*.'

Billy Manser, I feel sure, later grew up to become a Teddy Boy, socked a length of lead piping into the back of some old man's skull and is still doing time. Else he went on to be a plumber. Or maybe even a trendy vicar somewhere. (Sixty years later I learned that what he actually did was to join The Royal Tank Regiment.)

*

One day, in the summer of 1946, my father walked up Ferrers Road brandishing a small, curved yellow thing. Children streamed from their houses as their parents told them what it was. They flocked round my father as if he was the Pied Piper.

He held a banana.

None of us had ever seen a real live banana before.

All evening curious neighbours fetched up excitedly at our open back door to refresh their pre-war memories looking at it. Eventually mother ceremoniously set to peeling back its skin before dividing it with a razorblade into two-dozen finely sliced slithers. My brother Anthony and I and another eighteen children from our road queued up and filed past her one at a

25

time, as if to receive a polio vaccine on a sugar lump. Mother dispensed a mushy sliver of this exotic fruit onto our fingers which we put inquisitively to our lips either to sniff, lick or knock back like a soggy mini-wafer. After five years of privation that symbolic little banana provided the most exotic and tangible proof that perhaps the war really was over now, and there was a whole new world waiting to reveal itself to us beyond the end of the street. Having since learned how crucial bananas and other fruits are to our daily diet to prevent us dying it is amazing that despite the deprivations we endured everyone was so fit during the war. My Uncle Arthur, constructed of sinuous whipcord, went through the North African Campaign on a diet of hard-tack biscuits and bully-beef with no ill effects whatsoever: nor did the searing heat of the North African sun give him skin cancer, despite not having any Factor 13 in his knapsack.

I was eight years old. My grey shorts had now become excrutiatingly tight and were probably doing untold damage to any procreative dynastic ambition, but I was still not growing up fast enough to partake in the hostilities.

This was of no import, because no sooner had one batch of war weary warriors returned home to a land fit for heroes than a new set of 18-year olds would kiss their mothers goodbye, set off for a short back and sides, and then on to do two years spud bashing in foreign climes. Or Aldershot. Or Catterick. This was National Service. The Army had always been there. The Army would always be there. There was still plenty of time for me to take my place at the barber's queue.

*

Another boyhood joy I recall from those times was comics.

The *Dandy* and *Beano,* Korky The Kat and Desperate Dan need no introduction.

Friday night was father's night out, when he would arrive home late from the Bank after stopping off on the way for a few bevies at *The Pelham Arms*. Before that, however, he would have called in at the newsagent.

I would be fast asleep in bed when he got home on those long ago Friday evenings, but then next morning, Saturday, was as exciting as Christmas. I awoke with the sparrows and couldn't wait to scamper downstairs in a ferment of anticipation, barefoot and freezing in my pyjamas, skidding to a halt by the tea trolley in the drawing room where . . . *yes* . . . my luck was usually in, and there I would find waiting for me my very own pristine copies of both that week's *Dandy,* and *Beano.* My little heart pounding with excitement I'd then dash back upstairs to my bed to spend the next hour wallowing in the antics and japes and exploits of all my comic book heroes. They were rare and sad occasions, those days when father had been unable to acquire a copy of either periodical and the tea trolley lay cruelly barren before me.

My brother Anthony and I were healthy boys who in the normal way had grown to hate each other. As a special favour I would occasionally let him read one of my back numbers, but as a general rule this was not the case. My comics were sacred.

'Oh go on, Mike,' he'd wail. 'Let me read just one of them.'

'No, get your own,' I'd retort with malicious unreasonableness, detaching myself from his presence and strolling off to rejoin the members of my newly formed Black Hand Gang at our hideout inside a hollowed-out blackberry bush at the top of the road.

'You let me read one last week,' he yelled at my departing back.

'Precisely,' I retorted, 'all the more reason for you to wait a while before reading another.'

His birthday is 15th April.

At 7.0 o'clock on 14th April 1947, on the eve of his fifth birthday, when mother came into my bedroom to tuck me up that night, she said: 'I suppose you've got something for your little brother's birthday tomorrow, have you?'

I nearly swallowed my heart.

'Birthday? Tomorrow?' I croaked, aghast with innocence. 'I didn't know I had to get him something, Mum. How was I meant to do that. You do that sort of thing.'

'Well dear, now that you're older I feel you ought to give

him at least a *little* something, don't you? After all, you are given sixpence a week pocket money to spend. When I was tucking him up earlier he was so excited, wondering what you might have got him. He's so proud to have you as his big brother, and docs admire you so very, very much. I know his only wish is to grow up to be just like you when he's older. I don't suppose you notice when you're playing together the way he puts his hands in his pockets, just like you do, and tries to copy the way you walk. I know you find him a bit of a nuisance at times, but he *is* your little brother and . . .'

She'd made her point. Tears sprang to my eyes and a lump to my throat.

'Yes Mum; of course I've got something for him.'

'Good boy; I thought you would have.' Smiling, she kissed me fondly and closed my bedroom door quietly behind her.

I scrambled quickly out of bed and bent earnestly to my task, experiencing my first lesson in how focused and concentrated the mind can become in an emergency.

Ten minutes later I opened the door, tiptoed quietly into Anthony's room and placed a crudely wrapped package at the foot of his bed. Pausing only to remove his thumb gently from his mouth for him, and to reflect a little, too, I suppose, I then tiptoed back to my own bed again.

Next morning I was awakened by loud rustlings from his room and heard him eagerly unwrapping his presents. There was silence for a while, followed by a mild thump. He had jumped down from his bed to the floor. A moment later my door slowly opened halfway. Squinting through one eye I could see him hanging on the knob with one hand while clutching his pyjama trousers with the other, gazing at me with bewilderment and awe.

'What do you want?' I growled.

'It's my birthday.'

'I know it is. I suppose you want me to be nice to you.'

He continued to swing on the door for a moment.

'I got some good things,' he said, adjusting the grip on his trousers.

'Did you?'

'Corr, yeah . . . Mum an' Dad gave me a gun an' a book an' a paintin' box,' he exclaimed excitedly. And then in a rush, blurting it out in disbelief, he shrieked: *'An' you went an' gave me all your old comics'!*

Spontaneously erupting across the room he flung his podgy little arms affectionately about my neck. 'Thank you ever so much, Michael. I haven't read hardly any of them, an' I know you've wrapped them up all by yourself in old newspaper an' string an' stuff, an' did me a card from you in writin', an' I didn't think I'd be getting anything so I'm ever so pleased an', honestly, I'll let you have them all back again when I've finished. Every last one of them.'

Ever since then the incident has been such a perennial joke between us that for his 65th birthday I purchased and sent him that current week's edition of *Beano*, which in our day was twopence but now costs £1.20p. Subsequently I have learned that a 4th December 1937 first edition of *Dandy* recently sold for £20,000.

March 1950 was when *Eagle* arrived. I devoured each copy of *Eagle* avidly and retained my collection in pristine condition right through from Volume 1 Number 1, until I left school. Shortly before she died I asked my mother: 'What ever happened to all those old *Eagle* comics of mine, Mum?' 'Oh, I threw those away years ago, dear,' she told me.

A copy of *Eagle* Number 1 in good nick is now worth over £1,000.

Such is life.

*

One Christmas when my own two children were still toddlers I had to cry *'Enough'*.

The base of our family tree that year was festooned with their gaily wrapped 'must have' presents, for which the paper alone cost more than any gift my brother or I had ever received at their age. No sooner had their mother and I blown the start-whistle (*after* breakfast: none of that 4.00 a.m. nonsense for us thank you very much) than each of them dived in to rip their packages frenziedly apart, tearing off and discarding their cards and rummaging dementedly to tug out the contents like entrails being wrenched by ravenous young vultures in some fast-forward feeding frenzy. The thrill was short lived; their excitement receded and they reverted to watching videos while their mother and I bent to retrieve the cards strewn amongst the debris in an attempt to relate them as nearly as possible to whichever present they might have accompanied. In those days, you see, although they carped about it children were still being made to write thank you letters. I am often reminded of the mother and daughter who were overheard discussing the manger in Selfridges' brightly tinselled window one year, and the mother exclaiming: 'Good God, look at that; they're even trying to drag religion into Christmas now!'

I always remember the present I treasured most as a boy in our early post-war years. My father - never a handyman - had made me my first very own gun. It took him three weeks of applied dedication to carve its shape from a piece of wood each evening out in the garage after I'd gone to bed, and then a further week to glue on its foresight, screw on a small door bolt, and fashion a trigger guard from a Lyle's Golden Syrup tin, to shield the nail he'd bent into shape for a simulated trigger. For the sling he adapted a webbing strap from one of his Home Guard ammunition pouches. Lack of funds prevented a paint job, so it was a whitewood rifle with which I proudly spent the next few years fending off Zulus, Indians or any left over Germans who dared to set foot in the games of my imagination.

It was to be a few more years before I received my first big present though.

By now the astute reader will have perceived that each year my birthday falls on the 9th of June.

The hot evening of Tuesday 8th of June 1948 had been spent repelling imaginary marauders who were attacking the gooseberry bush out in the back garden. My mother applied calamine lotion to cool the sunburn and mosquito bites on my body. At 10.0 o'clock I was tucked in bed with cool sheets up to my chin listening to the bird chatter slowly dying in the garden outside. The smell of newly mown grass and pipe tobacco wafted sweetly in through the open windows. On the morrow I would be ten. Almost a man already. What would my present be this time I wondered?

To allow air to circulate, the door to my room had been left ajar. Suddenly I became conscious of a rustling sound down by my slippers beside the bed. Fear clutched at my heart. Most evenings before falling asleep I managed to imagine sounds emanating from the fluff and flick on the floor beneath the springs. I knew there were snakes, crows and hobgoblins inhabited my room by night. They crept up from under the floorboards and writhed in turmoil beneath me throughout the hours of darkness. Each night, too, my bed would become surrounded by a deep green algae-filled moat, teeming with snapping alligators. I was safe in bed, but should I once dare to set foot beyond the mattress I would be snapped by the ankle, dragged down, ripped apart and eaten raw. Obviously either a disturbed or over imaginative child, it was strange that I never wet myself. Came the dawn these nocturnal horrors had scurried back beneath the floorboards to return to whatever other dimensional never-land it was they inhabited by day. These images of mine were so vivid I marvel that I survived until adulthood undevoured and mentally undamaged. *(Shows what he knows: Author's friends.)*

This time, though, the insistently growing rustling from my slippers was definitely real. Timorously I took a wary peek over the edge of the bed, and gasped. My eyes popped like saucers. My heart soared with joy and disbelief.

A puppy.

Wagging its stubby little black and white tail it was wiggling its butt with delight as it snuffled and chewed my slippers.

A real live puppy.

'Hallo. Are you mine?' I asked it.

'Of *course* he's yours.' My beaming parents hurried quickly into my room from outside on the landing where they'd been waiting with barely suppressed giggles to enjoy my reaction. (This was back in the good old days before mother had started using father for target practice).

'But you've got to let *me* have a go on him too,' cried Anthony, getting in on the act, bursting from between their legs, still holding his pyjama pants up with one hand as he bent in vain to retrieve the writhing pup with the other. All thoughts of moats, snakes and alligators dissolved in a trice and I leaped from my bed.

'*I* must hold him first,' I insisted. 'Can he sleep with me, Mum? Can he? Please? Oh, do say yes. Can he? Please?'

Mother looked at father. Father looked at mother. Each shrugged at the other. The room eventually cleared, and I was allowed to snuggle down with my very own warm bundle of sweet smelling fur nestling in the pillow alongside my head.

It was bliss.

But not for long.

Ammonia.

The room stank of the stuff and next morning remnants of my shredded slippers were strewn about everywhere.

Smoky grew apace and while doing so developed a pronounced penchant for ankles and motor bikes. Much to his surprise, one day he caught one, so had to be put down as a result of his shattered spine and the angry motorcyclist's broken limb. He was the only dog I ever had - a sad end but an experience to which I was grateful to my parents. Since those days a globally peripatetic lifestyle and more than twenty places of residence have afforded scant opportunity for me to own another, although I have often dreamed of having a couple of Afghan Hounds (or panthers) (or silver-chained cheetahs) called Whiplash and Spike draped across the back seat of my Aston-Martin (*when* I get one) - or a golden-eyed blue Great Dane with some equally exotic and ridiculous name.

Or an eagle.

FOUR

THE SOUTH DOWNS AROUND LEWES have interesting geographical features. The River Ouse, which flows through and then out to sea at Newhaven, is bounded by flat and fertile agricultural land. This offered invitingly easy access up its valley floor for our Roman conquerors and other marauders of less beneficent ilk. To the south east of Lewes this valley is flanked by two naturally defensive vantage points, the 650' Firle Beacon - and Mount Caburn, which is only 480' but felt like Everest when we first climbed it as boys clad in our ubiquitous corduroy shorts (held up by multi-coloured striped belts with their snakes' heads buckles) and our Clarks sandals.

Mount Caburn was an Iron-Age hill fort. Its one-time inhabitants having long since departed it has more recently become a popular launch pad and playground for the hang-gliding fraternity who when airborne and viewed from the road or a passing railway carriage resemble indolently circling squadrons of thermal-borne pterodactyls gracefully protecting their mythical mountain fastness from some sort of Sword and Sorcerer attack.

To repel more sophisticated fayre, in 1087 William The Conqueror's brother-in-law William de Warenne began the construction of Lewes Castle built on twin mottes arising from the middle of the medieval town. It was completed in the 15th century and from its original battlements today one can still sight one's eye through its stone embrasures and conjure up the martial cries of yesteryear as foe fell to arrow and knight to lance.

Not a lot of people remember this but back in the 13th

century King Henry III was exasperating the English nobility by ignoring the constraints of the Magna Carta, as well as continuously tolerating the unruly behaviour of some of his French relatives called the Lusignans.

Matters came to a head in 1258 when King Henry was forced by his barons to accede to the Provisions of Oxford, a document which laid down that his behaviour should be monitored by a committee of self-styled baronial 'good guys'.

Miffed by the imposition of such restrictions, in 1261 King Henry 'reasserted' himself. The principal militant baron, Simon de Montfort, remained defiant however, resulting (in 1263) in the hotly debated Provisions of Oxford being submitted to the arbitration of King Louis IX of France. The following January, mindful of stirring discontent amongst his own nobility, King Louis vindicated King Henry in the Mise of Amiens, by which the Provisions were annulled. Because of this war broke out between de Montfort and his 5,000 strong supporters and King Henry's 10,000 strong royalist army, their principal conflict taking place at the Battle of Lewes on Wednesday 14th May 1264. King Henry commanded the infantry encamped in the fields surrounding St Pancras Priory and his son Prince Edward commanded the cavalry based at Lewes Castle. Simon de Montfort's baronial army - whose participants wore distinguishing white cross emblems - took up its commanding positions on the South Downs just north-west of the historic little town. Riding out from the castle Prince Edward's caparisoned cavalry bedecked in its clanking armour of the day gained an early success over de Montfort, but then the prince pursued a retreating Montfortian force to the north and somehow forfeited any chance of an overall royalist win that day.

The King and Prince Edward were captured and imprisoned. De Montfort became the de facto ruler of England. Prince Edward then escaped and captured de Montfort's man, Baron Robert de Ferrers, the Earl of Derby, and imprisoned him in the Tower of London. Prince Edward then went on to defeat de Montfort at the Battle of Evesham in 1265 where the latter died fighting, and by then the royalists were so pissed off with him that just for good measure they cut off his hands, feet and testicles and then decapitated him.

With their cause apparently doomed the last Montfortians surrendered in June 1267. King Henry III continued to rule until his death in 1272 when his son became King Edward I, otherwise known as Edward Longshanks, Scourge of the Scots, ably played by Patrick McGoohan in Mel Gibson's *Braveheart* - voted 94th in 2002's list of our One Hundred Greatest Britons, ranking between Sir Walter Raleigh and Sir 'Dam Busters' Barnes Wallis, with Sir Winston Churchill quite rightly coming first, and John Lennon 8[th,] above Baden Powell, The Duke of Wellington and both our Queens Victoria and Elizabeth; but none of those last few pieces of gratuitous information has any bearing on what happened next, despite my having been born near de Montfort Road in King Henry's Road nursing home, living in Ferrers Road and having spent much of my war years in the Prince Edward's Road air raid shelter, which you will remember my brother stank out to high heaven, thereby bringing about our excommunication by the public at large.

What with one thing and another they've had to be quite an aggressive bunch, those sod-bashing Sussex forebears of mine. If it wasn't the Romans or the Normans it was Napoleon and the *Wehrmacht* trying to crash their way up into England via the county of my birth. No wonder my friends and I devoted our alternate Saturdays to practising defence and attack manoeuvres over the soft chalky greensward and flinty pathways of our heritage. It was in our blood to do so. Future generations of Britons may depend upon us even yet.

Al*tern*ate Saturdays?

First this innate aggression of ours had to be trained and honed. The recognised precursor to military service in those days, every boy's rite of passage, was to become first a wolf cub and then a scout. This was in the days when scouts still wore shorts and bush hats, not berets; and didn't carry i-Pods, but with official blessing touted sharpened cold steel around with them. Today's directive from Gilwell Park's Scout HQ is that 'no form of knife is to be part of a scout's uniform. Knives will *not* be worn (halle*leul*ah - perish the very *thought* of it . . . *hrrrm*) but if it is deemed that their use may be required at camp they are not to be carried by individuals but packed in a locked box to be issued only under close supervision' . . . in the event that the Troop should perchance stumble across some little twig or something that really does need to be carefully pruned or sharpened. Axes, hatchets, and saws too, have to be held centrally and only issued to individuals who are known to have been suitably trained in their use - *and* who are wearing 'stout footwear'. Axes? Stout footwear? In my Clarks sandals or daps, aged 10, I used to have my very own tomahawk *and* a Kikuyu spear! 'No one's going to duff *you* up m'lad, are they!' our friendly local bobby would remark from his slowly pedalled matt black bike, grinning down with avuncular fondness at me as I clanked earnestly off towards the fulfilment of whatever that day's mission might be. At this rate the once Great Britain is never going to be allowed to go to war again: Health & Safety regulations would prevent it.

In 1793 Lewes's House of Correction had been built in North Street. A tall, red-brick walled grim and forbidding weathered edifice which sixty years later was considered no longer 'fit for purpose', so when the present Lewes Prison was completed in 1854 the House of Correction was sold on to the Admiralty for use as a naval prison, which then famously accommodated Russian prisoners of war who had been captured in the Crimea. Back in those glorious mid-Victorian days Finland was under Russian jurisdiction and had raised nine sharpshooter battalions to fight alongside their Cossack colleagues, so there were three-hundred Finnish PoWs from one of their Grenadier Rifle Battalions detained in Lewes at that time as well. In the late 1940s, long after the prison had been decommissioned, it became a TA headquarters and the venue on alternate Saturday mornings for meetings of the 1st Lewes Wolf Cub Pack under our dear old pipe-smoking Skipper Hankin who lived on the Neville Estate and drove a small green electrician's van for a living.

Russian and Finnish names and the historic dates of their owners' incarceration had often been carved into the prison's solid stone-walled cells and heavily grilled doors. The building's iron and concrete stanchions would echo to the reverberating clang and clatter of our youthful feet as we pounded up and down its stairways yelling, scrapping, and playing murder-ball. We beat the dust of ages from those stone floors, which interested eyes could sift for memories as swirling motes arose and resettled in the iridescent sunshafts probing their curious beams through the thickly grimed and mossy iron-barred 19th century prison windows, installed long ago by long deceased glaziers and craftsmen. Demolished in 1963 to make space first for a pay-as-you-stay car park and more recently a new police station, would that that old prison still stood today: oh to be able to re-visit and sit once more in one of its cells to dwell upon some of the thoughts and emotions to which it must have been privy. To think that the Anatoly Borzakovsky whose name had been so painstakingly and enduringly inscribed with a knife across the door lintel of Brown Six's cell might have seen the fateful Charge Of The Light Brigade or personally shot some British soldier who would then have fallen to the tender ministration of Florence Nightingale or Mary Seacole fills me with wonder now - yet in 1949 we covered Anatoly's name with a large chart depicting the semaphore alphabet.

So on our alternate non cub-meeting Saturday mornings, laden down like embryo Indiana Joneses with ropes, knives, cudgels, spikes, and anything else we could muster that seemed potentially lethal, like a miniature band of partisans our 'gang' would set off for the hills - to meet-up in our field headquarters, inside another blackberry bush, its secret entrance concealed by a vicious clump of stinging nettles - and that particular part of the hills known thereabouts as the Chalk Pits.

The quarrying of chalk and lime in this area in the 18th and 19th centuries had produced some sheer chalk cliffs, which coincidentally and quite dramatically marked the position of the Montfortian forces' left flank in the 1264 Battle of Lewes, a site which – excitingly - remains largely unchanged to this day but aged ten we didn't pay much heed to that sort of thing at the time.

So there we were, me and my gang, garbed out in our Saturday morning rig, setting out towards the Chalk Pits, heads intently bent on adventure and brave feats of derring-do. To the east of us lay the Offham Road and a sweep of Tarzan-like foliage descending sharply down a steep muddy bank thick with nettles, brambles and rusty tin cans, to the valley of the River Ouse. To the west of us lay the 18th century Lewes Racecourse where horse racing had been taking place since 1727. The course a two-mile horseshoe with a climb of 100-feet up the Sussex Downs in its first half-mile - acknowledged in its day as one of the loveliest courses in the country, had enjoyed a colourful track record. But racing there had also had its uglier side. During the inter-war years race mobsters and razor gangs were often in evidence, terrorising race courses and dog tracks throughout the land with a series of blackmail, extortion and protection rackets, levying tolls on racecourses and greyhound stadiums and bookmakers, in the latter case using damp sponges to erase the odds from their boards if they didn't pay up which may sound funny and kind of childish but wasn't if you were a bookmaker. Octavius Sabatini, aka Charles Darby Sabatini, alias Frederick Handley, was the founder and senior member of the infamous Sabatini Gang, otherwise known as The Italian Mob who preceded the violent Kray Twins by 30 years in inflicting their reign of terror on society. A 1950's teenager, I remember how the very name Kray used to strike such fear into everyone's hearts that we were convinced they were going to arrive in our town and be waiting for us at the corner to carve us up on our way home from school one afternoon, or that they would fetch up and batter in our front door demanding payment from our parents to prevent us becoming bottle-scarred for life. Mind you, I wasn't a million miles from the possibility. Out of the whole of England it was Lewes Prison to which Reggie Kray was transferred in the late '80s which was about the time I found myself - rather foolhardily as it turned out - chatting up a woman in a bar one evening, when her very large, tall, big, handsome and personable partner came across to introduce himself and join us. Shaking his affably proffered ham-like fist I then found I was enjoying a most pleasant interlude with an entertaining and seemingly charming Charlie Kray himself - the notorious twins' big brother. An undoubtedly bad lad himself by all accounts, but good fun to be with, although I do seem to recall making a conscious effort not to mention anything too contentious. Before I was born though, before the era of the Krays, it had been the Sabatini gang fielding players not named Mad Frankie Fraser, Jack 'the Hat' McVitie or George Cornell but characters such as Battles Rossi and Johnny Rico, all of whom were to become the inspiration for Graham Greene's *Brighton Rock*. Sabatini himself was eventually arrested at Hove dog-track and subsequently imprisoned in April 1940, but on another occasion, prior to that, back in the 1920s, it was his notorious Sabatini Gang which had fought a pitched razor battle with the police one day up on lovely old Lewes racecourse. *Plus c'est la même chose:* today's Sabatinis are now Yardies, armed and dangerous teenage inner-city street gangs, and militant Islamists.

In 1963 this dear old venue featured on a Levy Board hit-list of courses scheduled to have their financial support axed. Sir Gordon Richards and the Australian jockey Scobie Breasley had each enjoyed a good record at Lewes, but in September 1964 the town staged its last race. A year after its closure the track became a training centre. The former Tote buildings were converted into a yard and the weighing room turned into a house. The grandstand, which for decades had been such a prominent white landmark up there on the crest of the Downs - resembling the silhouetted barn on the bucolic horizon of Andrew Wythe's painting *Christina's World* when one cast one's gaze at it from down in the town - was redeveloped, and houses now stand on the site. But the view from up there on the Downs through to the English Channel still remains magnificently unchanged. Meanwhile, back to the Chalk Pits . . .

. . . only one of the three pits was still being quarried back then in the late 40s. The other two were disused. Unfenced, they were conveniently situated as Beachy Head nursery slopes for those who, still not yet entirely sure about their suicidal inclination, perhaps felt they would like to think about it a little and attempt a non-committed dry-run first. The pits also served as ideal adventure playgrounds for the various boyhood gangs which roamed there. Such as ours. Most of our parents strictly forbade us to go there. That way they always knew where we were.

Health & Safety?

Pah!

There were only ever two fatalities during our formative years of occupation. The first was Freddie Brown who plummeted to an early demise when the branch of an overhanging tree he was climbing snapped. Outraged and understandably screaming with flailing arms and legs motoring wildly he plunged and bounced down the cliff-face to land with a clearly audible smack across a large sacrificial chalk slab below. The second was his Jack Russel, Pinky. Emitting one short sharp anguished squeal Pinky went scurrying after him so eagerly that when he reached the cliff-edge and realisation kicked-in it was too late to arrest his skid. Finding himself involuntarily launched into mid-air with tiny paws churning he performed an exquisite quintuple somersault on *his* way down. Pinky was probably the more popular of the two but each was a sad loss and I remember Mrs Brown was pretty cross and upset with us when she found out. She'd adored Pinky.

An Eastbourne based pathologist friend of mine told me that two-thirds of those who jump off Beachy Head and fail to end up as fatalities but bounce on the way down and have their descent arrested by a bush, say that although they regret their torn skin and bruising, before they were even half way down they'd regretted more their decision to jump. Whether it was their change of heart and a lot of back pedalling that then prevented them meeting a terminal *splaaaat* one doesn't know, but it's an interesting statistic.

For months afterwards Freddie and Pinky's passing marred the enjoyment of our weekly forays to the Chalk Pits on account of none of us was allowed to go there anymore. It all happened such a long time ago though. None of us was quite so flippant at the time of course at this our first encounter with tragedy. Freddie died not in vain. He still lived on as an adventurous and up-for-it nine-year-old boy in many a memory and means different things to each of us who knew him. A couple of weeks before Freddie fell out of his tree his father had been executed; beheaded by the Japanese in Burma. They weren't having much luck as a family really. On the eve of her 28th birthday two months later the attractive Mrs Brown was herself found hanging by a length of flex from a garage beam. Somebody none of us knew came to pack up their house and sell it for them. I think it went for £900. It was a telling introduction for us all to those particular aspects of life. Later that year a nearby neighbour, Mr Wolf, shot himself dead in the head with his WWI service revolver. Why? He had been declared bankrupt. Probably for about £500 but such was the dishonour of bankruptcy in those days that suicide was the only noble mode of egress whereas today it has almost become an expected and acceptable rite of passage for most aspiring businessmen.

It was up at the Chalk Pits that I experienced my first encounter with a handgun.

Brian Middleton and I had detached ourselves from our main group to effect a flanking movement and lob rocks at a rival gang. While Brian and I crawled off through the long wet grass to encircle them our main body was busily engaged with a ten-foot ash-plant endeavouring to wriggle loose and dislodge like a bad tooth a large chalk boulder from the cliff-face above. The idea was to unleash upon the unsuspecting foe we had espied below as large a rock fall as possible, but which usually only resulted in an inoffensive little trickle of scree. We were quite nice and well adjusted boys at heart so our activity could hardly be rated with the hurling of bedsteads over motorway parapets. Or could it?

Nearing the completion of our pincer movement Brian and I slithered into a clearing, and froze - as our fathers might recently have done if unexpectedly encountering an enemy patrol. Japs we could have handled, but we were fearful of

41

what confronted us there at the Chalk Pits that day.

Huddled in an intense group not fifty yards away from us stood three Bigger Boys. Strangers to our parish. Aged at least 13. Aloof. Detached. Senior. Like wandering Samurai camped outside the village waiting for something to happen and imbued with the mythical prowess sufficient to deal with it when it did.

Brian and I were of the opinion that perhaps we might turn out to be the 'it'.

Then we heard faint intermittent *plopping* sounds emerging from their midst . . .

. . . and saw a glint of sunlight reflected from the blueing of a real-live-*gun* barrel.

Bigger Boys - with a *gun!*

This was major league.

It was unlikely that Brian or I would be seeing out this day alive.

We glanced at each other like cornered rabbits.

Should we remain frozen to the spot? Turn and creep rapidly away? Bolt? One of the trio turned and saw us quaking in our posture of cramped indecision at the bole of the large oak by which we had come to rest, which at the time seemed as good a place as any to relinquish our mortal coils.

'Want to see something good?' he yelled across to us. 'Come and take a gander at this.'

There was no metallic timbre to his voice. No hint of any death-knell ring.

But -

. . . 'It's a trap,' I hissed at Brian. 'They'll murder us.'

'I don't think so. Anyway, we've got to go over. If we don't, they might shoot.'

'Come on then,' I muttered. 'At least we might get a chance to look at that gun.'

Adjusting our accoutrements - bow, arrow, rope . . . you've read the checklist and know the inventory - tooled up like Rambo (who hadn't actually been thought of yet) (perhaps we were his unwitting inspiration), hooking our thumbs with macho bravura into our snake's head belts, we sauntered

42

nonchalantly across the clearing towards them. This was in the days of Dick Barton Special Agent (transmitted by the BBC daily Mon-Fri at 6.45 p.m. *waaaaay* back before The Archers) when even the embryo Teddy Boys scheduled to become the flick-knife-wielding scourge of our '50s High Streets were at this time wresting with nothing much tougher than nappy-rash.

'What do you want to show us?' I asked, hitching my shorts' belt higher and tighter. Drawing my sheath-knife with studied insouciance I started to pare my dirt-filled nails. It was a psychological ploy I'd picked up at the *Odeon's* B-feature only the week before. It was meant to strike cold forboding into the hearts of protagonists, but no one in this group seemed to give a damn or even to notice.

'Syd here's got this Webley air pistol for his birthday,' one of the Bigger Boys chirruped excitedly, 'and just look at what we've found.'

He pointed at a pile of slimy grey rocks his accomplice was prodding with a stick. Syd stood detached, his podgy arms folded, pistol barrel at the port, pointing 45-degrees skyward, like the jacket illustration to Ian Fleming's *Goldfinger*, although 007 was another one who'd not been invented yet, either. Okay - so it was only an air pistol - but for the future famous *Goldfinger* photoshoot, apparently, so was Bond's, yet he still managed to create a considerable degree of respect holding it.

A gun is a gun is a gun after all.

A greasy patina shone slickly across Syd's clammy white forehead. His lips curled in foul expectation. I didn't like Syd. But he had the gun. I drew my gaze away from him to focus on what was taking place. That's when I grasped the awfulness of what we had unwittingly stumbled upon. The sharpened ash twig manipulated by Syd's lieutenant was being used to poke a family of toads reluctantly from their lair beneath the rocks. Grandfather toad's slug-pulverised carcass already lay smashed and quivering atop some wet leaves, a pulpy mass of bloody green suppuration, the colour of a mandarin's robe, welling forth rejected lead pellets from its dying flesh. Now Syd's beater was lining up the rest of the miffed, toothless, tail-less amphibians for their mindless slaughter. Blinking unsuspectingly they waddled into the sunlight. Syd stepped from his mossy plinth and sauntered across to survey the sacrificial horde. Syd had to be some lousy rich kid: the first I had encountered. Tugging at Brian's sleeve, I turned away. He followed me keenly back the way we had come.

Receiving no hail of hot lead to the backs of our hurriedly retreating legs, we managed to live on after tea to experience many another character-building boyhood adventure. So did the gun-toting trio. Having completed their massacre we glanced back to see them strolling away from the killing field, just after our knoll-top 'B' team successfully managed to entomb the vacated site with a finally dispatched massive rock fall.

Well, an inoffensive little trickle of scree, anyway.

FIVE

GEORGE FORMBY'S RENDITION of *When I'm Cleaning Windows* used to tickle me pink as a kid so for my 12th birthday (on 9th June 1950) my parents gave me a ukulele. Concurrently this was the day chosen for us to leave our family home at 10, Ferrers Road in Lewes and go to live at 54, Milton Road in Eastbourne, only seventeen miles away, but at that age it felt like the far side of the world.

The sun was shining and the maw of the Pickfords van readily consumed our meagre household effects.

The removal men must have been relieved when the loading was done. Grinning indulgently to conceal their restrained malice, throughout their exertions they had been incessantly and tunelessly serenaded by me, my cracked falsetto and my ukulele with the only three chords I knew to accompany the only three lines of the only song which I knew - *Carolina Moon.*

By 11.30 a.m. we were on our way to live at the seaside.

It was sad leaving our dear old house behind with its twelve years accumulation of childhood and wartime memories. When we got to our new home in Eastbourne, which had been acknowledged as the most heavily bombed town in the SE of England, I cried myself to sleep with homesickness that night. Fate allied to father's career progression had decreed the commencement of Phase Two of my life when at that stage all I desired was the indefinite continuation of Phase One. I hate upheaval and yet when years later I was to choose the Army as my profession it became a recognised part of my lifestyle every two years. The various phases since that first family move of ours from Lewes to Eastbourne have been numerous, each of them creating either some sort of landmark or turning point and all of which have been occasioned by Fate or Circumstance putting in its oar. I always wanted to be the pro-active captain of my fate and master of my soul but a family and a lifelong lack of disposable income or sufficient funding seemed to prevent me from being either. I was shifted about like lightweight flotsam in the maelstrom of life with my goods and chattels yawing along behind in the wash.

Our new house at Milton Road in the heart of Eastbourne's Old Town never appealed. It was a grey place on the wrong side of the road that seldom got any sun. Mother and father entered the final stage of their ill-fated marriage there and on my thirteenth birthday I got an airgun.

'Yes, Dad,' I assured my father, having been sternly cautioned about the constraints governing my new present. 'Of course I'll only fire at the target nailed to the garden tree.'

Father went off to work, mother ensconced herself in the kitchen, and Birthday Boy secreted his gleaming new airgun upstairs to his bedroom. From my open window the field-of-fire up the street opposite was magnificent. Behind the security of my half-drawn curtain I was provided with the perfect sniper's vantage point. By angling the airgun a certain way I could ricochet its little lead slugs off the pavement 30-yards away with a puff of red brickdust to send them whining off into the trees, shrubs and surprised pedestrians just like the real thing *whanging* off rocks up an Apache-infested canyon or John Wayne firing his Winchester in *Stagecoach;* or just about any Boy's Own hero I cared to think about really.

The be-capped septuagenarian contentedly puffing the shag in his much chewed briar squinted into the sun as he obliviously free-wheeled slowly down the road with his string-bag of meagre groceries slung across the handlebars of his black sit-up-and-beg Raleigh bicycle, blissfully unaware that he was having a laser-like bead drawn on him from a nearby bedroom window through the Lee Van Cleef eyes of an embryo assassin.

I squeezed the trigger.

There was a *ping* as my pellet bounced off the old man's rust-mottled chrome bell. Pipe-dottle and pipe shot from his mouth as he wobbled from his buckling bike like a rodeo rider whose pony has pitched onto its front knees. He scrabbled to embrace the harsh bark of a kerbside elm, slithering unceremoniously down its shagreen trunk on his stubbled chin to subside in a pile of mucky rubbish at the bottom while his bike's front wheel span erratically in the gutter. *Mickey The Kid* cackled . . .

. . . but then he gulped.

A black Wolsely police car with its bell on the front had pulled into the kerb beside the old man in his now torn and yoke-splattered raincoat. A magisterial figure in blue climbed out. With hands on hips and silver pips glinting on his epaulettes he stared intently up at my suburban eerie. Exaggeratedly breaking open the weapon's barrel and blowing down it ostentatiously to clear its spiralling whiff of imaginary cordite I admitted culpability to myself, apologised both to God and to Jesus, expiated all previous boyhood pranks, foreswore any more future ones and quickly threw a nervous but respectful 'fair cop' acknowledgement to the policeman who was pointing his finger up at me and waggling it just ever so slightly. He was an Old School copper whose breed as we know is now long gone. Clambering from the windowsill I hurried to lock myself in the loo to run a reappraisal of my life. The doorbell never did ring. There was no need. The policeman knew I knew he knew I'd never try anything so stupid as that again. I'd got the message. Loud and clear.

Or had I?

When I ran out of slugs I thought firing darts would be fun. They were sharp and lethal with pretty little kingfisher-hued flights to them. If you could retrieve them they could be re-used. When the sap was running freely from the liberally peppered fruit trees in the garden and I had impaled much of the rest of the area's still-life I decided to aim for the sky. Lying on the garden lawn on my back to enable my eyes to follow the dart's trajectory I squeezed the trigger to send one winnowing skyward . . . and lost it. Ten seconds later there

47

came an anguished howl from next door. '*Jeeezus* H. *Christ*' bellowed Colonel (Retd) H.C. Percival who had been bending down in the sun re-potting a pink begonia on the terrace outside his French windows. A minute later he came roaring round to our kitchen door frantically massaging his right buttock to return the proffered little bloodstained dart which he held quivering aloft between a soil begrimed thumb and forefinger, and to harangue mother. A minute after that she removed my airgun and cuffed my ear. I moped off into the shed to sulk and started to clean my bike. Then I noticed father's discarded set of circa 1926 golf clubs slewed away in the corner amongst the dried paint and creosote tins and cobwebs and garden implements. At random I selected one of the set's iron-clubbed hickory shafts. Trailing it disconsolately back out onto the lawn I proceeded to use it to drive a tennis ball relentlessly against the garage wall. I was young and supple. The swing of the club in my grip felt good and satisfying. Moving further back from the garage I drove the ball harder and even harder still against the brick wall. All of a sudden the club's tired and neglected leather grip unravelled. The club shot from my hands. Flying from my grasp it went snaking off like a greased wraith to sail straight over old Percival's freshly creosoted lapboard fence. Fortunately it was summer and his French windows were open. Unfortunately he was entertaining a coterie of elderly ladyfriends to tea. Their subdued and conventional conviviality, genteel conversation and Boer War reminiscences were suddenly rudely interrupted by the sight of my father's unaccompanied number-nine iron still trailing its cobweb behind it as it came sailing swiftly but gracefully in through the window like a Scud missile to land with a *splosh* in the sponge cake.

My mother had instilled in me 'the form' for such occasions. Walking sheepishly round to Percival's house I bravely rang his doorbell. A shadow fell behind the glass. The door was flung open by an almost apoplectic Percival with a crumb-laden napkin at his neck proffering the club to me like King Richard The Lionheart handing down a small ceremonial sword to a squire. 'I believe this is yours,' he intoned gravely.

Give him his due. The old boy certainly possessed grace under pressure.

'Thank you, Sir,' I said, trying not to let my relief appear as cock-suredness. 'I didn't do it on purpose.'

'Didn't you?' He sounded surprised, and arched one eyebrow. 'No - I suppose you didn't.' And I thought I perceived just the hint of a tear in the corner of the old man's eye. Or . . . or . . . could it possibly have been a twinkle?

Licking off its residue of strawberry jam and crumbs I slung the club back amongst the rest of the paraphernalia in the shed just as my younger brother Tony came in through the gate from school. Leaning his bike against the wall he unstrapped his cricket bat from the crossbar.

'Fancy a knock-about, Mike?' he shouted.

'Yeah - okay, may as well,' I agreed, helping him drive three stumps into the lawn.

'Toss you for bat,' he cried.

'No, you've been playing all afternoon. I'll go first.'

I was four years older than Tony and besides it was my birthday.

I took the bat and adopted my stance before the wicket, taking scant heed of father's words as they flashed subliminally across my mind: *'If you're going to play with a hard ball in the garden, then for heaven's sake keep your shots low.'*

Tony bowled.

It was too good to miss. I was last bat for England at The Oval on the closing day of the Australian Test. My 'all' went into that delicious stroke. It was power-poetry in motion. Leather and willow connected like a firing-pin on a nuclear percussion cap . . .

Mindful of the number-nine iron and the comfort of his guests, Percival had now closed his French windows.

My ball took out a pane about nine-feet square, showering the ladies' laps and trifle with more broken glass than a Baghdad explosion and coming to rest like a small red cannonball just a hair's breadth from the *Capo-di-Monte* on the sideboard.

'Oh *no*,' I heard Percival roar, slapping his thighs like aghast pistol shots of disbelief.

'Oh Gawd,' groaned Tony quickly drawing stumps and scarpering off to clamber up the apple tree in one fluid movement.

'Oh Lord,'I muttered feeling my overworked young heart take off yet again on its well known circuit round my ribcage.

I shuffled towards the kitchen trailing my bat behind me. Mother was in good cake-baking mode that afternoon, preparing my birthday tea. 'Hallo darling,' she said, all fluff, smiles and powder as I went in. 'Are you having a nice game?'

'Er . . . Mum - you see it's like this . . .'

Upstairs in my bedroom where I had been sent after Colonel Percival had come belting round full of foaming froth to return my cricket ball and institute his justifiably furious Board Of Enquiry with mother in the kitchen, my gaze roamed about my early adolescent artefacts adorning the walls. My eyes immediately lit upon my bow suspended over the fireplace. I hadn't played with my bow for ages. Lifting it carefully down from its nail I tautened the string till it twanged and then rummaged through the wardrobe for the quiver of arrows I could remember having stashed there the previous autumn.

My lately vacated sniper's window was still open onto the garden. I had never fired my bow from up here before. Placing the nock of the first arrow against the string I drew it back and let fly. It *whooshed* from the window to embed itself deliciously four-inches into the lawn. This is rather good sport, I thought, nocking another arrow.

'*Corr,* that was t'rrific,' yelled Tony, running out into the garden from downstairs. 'Why don't you aim at the tree?'

It was a good and faithful old family tree. It had been shot at with pellets, stabbed with throwing knives, hung on, swung from, been carved upon, had bodies tied to it with rope, had Catherine wheels whizz scorchingly round its gnarled knots and crannies and was now about to be socked in the slats by a steel-tipped arrow. A second time I aimed and let fly. Unerringly the arrow thudded into the tree's bark to quiver with satisfaction, shivering its recipient's timber.

50

'Corr, that was *great*,' Tony yelled again, and I had to agree with him - it had been good.

'Why don't you aim between my feet this time,' Tony shouted keenly, a trifle foolhardily too perhaps, standing there with his legs exaggeratedly apart and his hands on his hips like a miniature Colossus of Rhodes just begging to be . . . 'Like we do with the throwing knife.'

'Okay,' I said, taking careful aim and drawing back the third arrow on its string.

'I know - tell you what'd be much better . . .' he cried a bit too late, quickly having thought of something else after I'd already released the lethal barb and sent it streaking from my grasp . . .

Downstairs the Mother/Percival cricket ball negotiations were still underway in the kitchen when Tony traipsed in resembling an uncooked shish kebab. I'd missed his eye but the blood-dripping arrow hung limply from his cheek like a broken limb twitching in the breeze.

'Mum - I think Mike's shot me,' he mumbled through a mouthful of arrowhead and dislodged molar.

'Oh, my *God*,' mother cried. Having coped well with all those visits from the *Luftwaff* she was a tough old bird but still clasped her hand to her mouth in that involuntary way women do.

'I think, Mrs George, that I shall have to leave you now and return to my guests,' said Percival loftily, rising to his plus-foured legs and placing the cricket ball gently on the dresser. 'You seem to have had quite enough on your plate for one day so perhaps we could continue the discussion of this matter later?'

'I didn't do it on purpose Mum, honestly,' I hollered as I thumped up the stairs again to my room.

'I don't believe you can imprison minors, deport them to the colonies or have them put down,' Percival growled, letting himself out through the kitchen door as mother plucked the arrow from Tony's cheek and wrapped his head in a tea-towel . . . 'But I do think you should consider securing him to a length of chain . . .'

51

'I've only got three arrows left,' I yelled down through the ceiling, 'so make sure I get that one back, won't you Mum?'

One way and another it was a helluva day.

Old Percival died shortly after that but my father assured me it had not been septicaemia from the dart or in any other way really associated with my behaviour that day.

By then, though, I was a year older and into girls . . .

SIX

ALONG WITH MANY OF MY AGE who are still alive I seem to have been spawned at the dawn of pre-history (now it's been dropped from school curricula as being extraneous to requirement), brought up as a war baby and then - ill prepared to cope - deposited on the doorstep of the groping and luckless early fifties. Not so long ago a recently qualified and rather self-important young man tried to explain to me why it was impossible for my - the older - generation to understand his generation.

'You grew up in an entirely different world', he informed me: 'actually an almost primitive one. Today's young people grew up with television, jet planes, space travel, and man walking on the moon. Our rocket ships have visited Mars. We have nuclear energy, electric and hydrogen cars, computers, and light-speed processing.' When he paused for breath, I broke in. 'You're absolutely right, old lad. 'We didn't have those things when we were your age. So what did we do? We invented them. Tell me, if you will, sir - what are you going to do for the next generation?'

Wherewithal money in my day was acquired doing newspaper rounds; on our bikes, not in cars. 'With it' gear was jeans and a check shirt purchased from Millets and sex was something a lot of people muttered about but had neither nous, know-how nor car seat with which to be able to actually *do* anything about. As if our natural adolescent ineptitude was not a big enough burden to contend with the fifties also threw up another bogey against which to pit our pubescent wits. The first influx of Foreign Students.

I never could understand how a pimply-faced, buck-toothed, wire-haired 16-year old French boy with glasses and thick rubber-soled shoes was automatically meant to be imbued with more sex appeal than his similarly endowed English counterpart, but apparently where our girls were concerned he was. As good old George Formby once so famously sang: *If women like that like men like those then why don't women like me?*

Not that all this foreign opposition suffered so from the ravages of adolescence. One or two of the bastards were inordinately handsome and prematurely masculine with thick tight curly black hair, Mediterranean swarthiness and Greek profiles and proportions. What chance did the 16-year-old ink-stained, black-headed Eddie Smiths and Mike Georges of this world stand against that lot?

And these were just the Gauls.

The really big guns, the hunter/killer sharks of the circuit, well - they came in the guise of Medes and Persians. Oh, didn't they just!

Deep in the confines of Drago's Bun Lounge several of our era sat huddled over our demonic hot lemon drinks ogling the stocking-topped lass of seventeen summers seductively clambering up to straddle the red plastic-topped stool opposite. Like the burgeoning exotic fruit that she was she seemed to be filling out and blossoming before our very gaze.

After much muttering about what we would like to do with her interlaced with references as to how far Tony Higgins was meant to have got with Liz Browne when they saw *Annie Get Your Gun* at the *Picturedrome* the previous evening—one of us eventually managed to suppress his adrenalin enough to get (albeit shakily) to his feet and stroll nonchalantly across to ask Legs if she would care for a *cappuccino* when suddenly the whole carefully rehearsed scene was shattered by the roar of something unmistakably big and fast and colourful arriving alongside the kerb outside.

Legs uncrossed them rapidly, patted her hair, gathered her handbag and assumed the poised position. We thus precluded oiks lifted our palms and eyeballs to heaven and sucked noisily on our straws to register our weak and disregarded disapproval at the pending rape of English maidenhood while Drago's Bun Lounge hung in its pall of fag smoke like a scene from *High Noon* (due at the *Picturedrome* the following week).

The flash fiscal onslaught of silver Porsche (or Ferrari / Lamborghini / Maserati) usually heralded the arrival of some red-shirted, black-leathered-haired-eyed Ishmail the Beautiful swaggering into Drago's because thanks to Dad's bountiful bit of oil producing desert he had it made . . . Turk, or Persian or Saudi, or any other damn' thing but down-at-heel, callow, sallow Brit.

Aged seventeen to twenty-five these former day Omar Sharif type coffee bar cowboys just could not lose. For some unaccountable reason blonde-haired Mary Jones in her final year with the VIth Form at the High School seemed to prefer being taken to wine and dine along the coast in a Jaguar XK120 drophead coupé with a perfumed, sloe-eyed Ahmed and later (or sooner) dispensing her fondle favours with him than she did going Dutch to sit with me in the *Picturedrome*'s stalls and riding home (upstairs) on the number 9 bus afterwards. Her loss you'd agree.

Memorable and typical for example was one Friday evening in the Spring of '54 when our St John's Church Youth Club Annual Social & Dance (admission sixpence) was raided by half a dozen Persians. They had heard our gramophone music grating through the window of our church hall as they prowled past in their multicoloured fleet of Mercedes, Alfa-Romeos and . . . oh, the hell with it.

All was going smoothly inside (girls in one corner, sugar and spice and giggling; us morose and attitude-riven blokes all bunched and huddled in another) and Jack Revell was just changing the record (Pat Boone probably) when the door swung open to reveal the gold toothed leer of the slim hipped Magnificent Six just in from Mecca.

'Oh, yes,' said twelve Islamic eyes, flashing.

'Oh, sir,' said the male contingent of St John's Church Youth Club edging warily towards our vicar.

'Oh, look,' squealed our pubescent womenfolk, fluffing

their frills and falling over themselves feigning disinterest.

'Oh, Christ,' said the vicar, meaning it.

'Oh, *no*,' said Miss Dives our hardy perennial harmoniumist striding forward purposefully in her sensible shoes in St John's hour of need to do her thing for England and The Cross against these Saracen invaders. 'Good *evening*,' she boomed commandingly. 'And how may I help you young gentlemen?'

The Persians misunderstood and thought she was just some other perennially flighty British piece belatedly offering herself on a plate to be danced with and adroitly seduced. Looking at each other and shrugging their shoulders at this formidable female infidel they easily ignored her, broke ranks and started to sidle across separately to address all-of-a-flutter clusters of our cooing girls. Undeterred, brave little Miss Dives adopted a memsahib stance before the leader of the tribe and said: 'I'm afraid I shall have to ask you and your friends to leave, you know. This is a private dance and you have to be a youth club member and attend three meetings before you can come. And besides you haven't paid your sixpence.'

Persian Leader deftly handed her a fiver from an alligator skin wallet, Jack Revell accidentally dropped his needle arm and Bill Hayley and The Comets (not Pat Boone, apparently) rocked to life for the umpteenth time that evening. Raising his eyes to Allah, Persian Leader took Miss Dives's hand and with experience born of much natural talent and practice got the old thing reluctantly tripping the light fantastic like she hadn't done since the tennis club dance at Maidenhead in 1923. Her tweed skirt flipped at its hem and our invincible vicar who had harboured fantasies about her since childhood cowered behind the stage under the pretence of putting the kettle on.

The rest of our coterie of girls coyly rose to accept the gold ringed, brown sinewy fingers being gently proffered to them and diffidently (at first) proceeded to do their own frenzied little bit for England.

Us? Well. We skulked, didn't we! Into our plastic beakers of squash and muttered. And felt impotent, weak, inadequate, and wanting. And cross. And chicken. And as the sons of our fathers, wondered how we'd only so recently managed to put

56

WWII in the bag.

My girl – Karen - whom I'd been eyeing up for a whole month now and had actually nodded to earlier on our way in that evening, which was the accepted way in those days of letting her know you had marked her out for your next kill and thought she had smashing 15-year-old tits and looked great now that she only wore her flatties to school and had got her first pair of black high-heels for weekends and evenings was also dancing with one of the well-heeled stiletto pushers whose gypsy princess mother had married an oil well.

Hitching the (still) snake's head belt onto the hips of my heavy duty, baggy, grey, shapeless trouser-tubes I glanced manfully at Mike Ockenden who was making the same Gary Cooper-like adjustment to his own nether garments. To no avail. We were bitched and knew it. Glowering through hooded lids at the back of one of the Arabs as he flashed past with Maureen Sanderson in his arms, Mike hissed: 'One day I'm going to go to Persia and slowly work my way through the female populace of that chap's father's camp . . .'

We glanced admiringly at Mike who knew that we knew he knew that we knew he didn't really mean it. But he had spoken bravely on all our behalves and thereby offered us some respite from decision making. There was now no immediate call for us to take up arms to do anything about this latest affront to our dignity. We would await an opportune moment.

The only other form of immediate retaliation would have been to send a small raiding party outside to let their tyres down, but even to us this seemed a bit childish. We might get knifed or even thumped.

So we did nothing. The thought of confronting even the smallest of the gate crashers invoked a hot flush of presentiment - but why? Why at that age (and sometimes even now) did we immediately credit everyone whose mettle had not even been tested, with being vastly better in prowess, physical strength, justification, guile and ability than ourselves?

Would that I could have ruminated longer on the situation. Would that I could report our having solved it with a swashbuckling grin, a gory Persian head and a kiss of pride from our girls. But it was 9.30 p.m. and even though it was Saturday tomorrow I knew I still had to be home by my allotted curfew.

Fishing my cycle clips from my tweed jacket pocket I shuffled stern-facedly out of the back with the rest of my mob and banged my knee swinging it angrily across my drop handle-barred turquoise Philips Kingfisher (with Derailleur gears) upon which I did my paper round and then cycled to and from school each day. The fastest bike in the street, I had been quite pleased with it up till then. Now as I pedalled desultorily homeward with my tail getting caught in its spokes I swore that on the morrow somehow I would have to find out the secret of attracting women.

As though to strengthen my resolve the surrounding neighbourhood suddenly erupted with the shattering roar of a Persian-revved Ferrari. Eighteen-year-old Abdul (may curses be upon him) was absconding with the obviously more than willing, eager, big-titted 15-year-old Angela Parsons and was racing her peaches and cream off towards the open-till-midnight coffee bar where *I* was not allowed to go. But while I sat there in the gutter with my front wheel still spinning Angela at least had the grace to look the other way as they shot past enveloping me in a shimmering haze of clear exhaust and the impressive sound of niftily changed, wrist-flicking gear shifts. Although I never said so I was always grateful to Angela for averting her gaze from that humiliating moment in my life.

So were the male sexual awakenings in the fifties constantly thwarted. Condoms were the most terrifying and embarrassing things to acquire and our pusher in the changing room at milk break at school was accorded all the respect he deserved. It could have been no fun assailing the bastion of the rubber goods store behind the station and ordering them by the gross from the formidable harridan within. Especially in your school cap. But at least since enterprisingly earning himself this concession 'Smudger' Smith was spared the toil of having to do an early morning paper round to earn his living.

Packets of three were carried in the wallets of our generation like sacred talismans without which one rarely ventured forth. It seldom, if ever, of course, *did* occur - but our chance might just come anywhere at anytime and there were too many ghastly stories then told (well, one or two anyway) of peers who had actually had it finally offered to them by some lass whose hormones were equally at boiling point but had temporarily misplaced their packet of three. In my experience such a packet might last from the Lower IVth right through to the Upper VIth without ever being opened once in combat. But it was bad for the image for the imprint of the rubber ring to show through one's wallet like a concealed half-crown indicating that there had been a long sojourn within. Similarly if opportunity did present itself and one gleefully ripped the top off a much faded purple packet only to crumble perished rubber into her lap one's name would not rate too highly in the local girls' High School underground bulletin-board that week and one might be advised to cycle home another way for a few days. Hence most sensible lads used to have dry runs on self occasionally just to keep the hand in. Checking the shelf life and turnover of one's stock ensured that should occasion one day present itself (it must, it *must*) - then one would be up to meeting it.

So there we were bursting to express ourselves and thanks to 'Smudger' Smith possessing the means whereby to contain that expression—yet nowhere to put it. All our girls were off up the road sharing it out with the Persians while we were left with their 10-year-old sisters. For some reason the Persian female students of our own age weren't interested in us either. Being young English was turning out to be a bit of a drag all round really: and for absolutely ages afterwards too, in fact; because throughout maturity whenever I've seen an attractive woman whose chemistry ignites my own I have cringingly and insecurely assumed that she would probably consider me too young and immature for her to bother becoming involved with. I still do, dammit, even now after I've long been allowed to wear suede shoes and am eligible for a bus pass. I mean, how mature does an attractive woman of 60 need a prospective beau to be? Common sense suggests that over the years I must have been in with a chance once or twice yet I have always almost invariably (well, nearly always) baulked at pursuing things further. Mind you at my age I've probably left it a bit late to be a toy-boy as well now. All the women I find attractive these days are too young and any of the few who find me attractive have either got Alzheimer's or wigs.

In fairness it must be said in the final analysis that very few of our Eastbourne '50s girls ever went off completely to rear little Persians of their own. With knowing looks and a glint in their eye most of them returned to the staid old British fold fairly soon to settle for one of us pig-skinned gentry who - depending upon our GCE results - were by now either articled clerks or trainee shoe salesmen. The appeal of a semi-detached and the kids near Mum seemed to be more commonsensical to Glenda in the long run than dashing off to live in an air-conditioned palace in the desert even though it meant trading a Cadillac and pool for a Ford Anglia and an allotment.

Thus it was not on the morrow but many hard-won years later I discovered that the secret of success with women had little to do either with muscles, looks, money or self. Oh, sure - they were good for starters and tight buns help quite a lot too apparently but they are really only a bonus to good old basic chemical attraction and familiarity.

All you have to do is be yourself and inevitably (or not) some women will loathe you and the vast majority will remain blissfully unaware of you - but one or two might actually come round to thinking you are quite pleasant and throughout your life one or two of those might even come around to falling in love with you. And that's nice. Or can be.

And who knows - one day you might even get to go and live in Persia where you can slowly get your own back for my entire generation. Out there though I've been told they don't just ask you nicely not to molest their property or say nothing as we did and skulk off home to let the girls sort it out how they like. Out there I've been told they make their point with knives and slice stuff off from your body, lash you several times, throw stones at the remaining pulp and then sometimes quite often even cut off your head afterwards as well. And for good measure y'tackle and bollocks too of course.

*Hell*uva price for a bonk.

SEVEN

NOT EVERYONE TOOK ARTICLES or became trainee shoe salesmen; in any case, unless one was of the select few - *la crème de la crème* who had been deferred by having gained a university place which in our day only about five percent seemed to manage - the rest of us knew that as soon as we left school we were going to have to go off and complete our two years compulsory National Service as an anticipatory prelude to which most of us had joined our respective school cadet forces as a matter of course.

I couldn't wait to join the cadets and loved it when I did.

Diminutive and moustachioed Eustace Ford MA used to assume far away wistful expressions as his mind meandered reminiscently along the poplar lined highways and gaily bedecked bistros of the France of his long ago youth. While he stood thus purportedly imparting the language to the Lower Vth the Lower Vth would whiz elastic-banded paper-clips at each other and watch Thomas in the desk by the window by the radiator undergoing a manual voyage of self discovery inside his trousers pockets.

It was only recently that Thomas had started discovering himself. With not even a vestige of self-conscious surreptitiousness he openly lavished his affections on his new found friend beneath his desk, the duality of whose role fascinated him beyond measure. Seemingly oblivious to the nudges and giggles going on all around he must have thought he was the only one thus blessed as thrice weekly (at least) he transported himself briefly to erotic realms beyond the confines of our classroom.

The barely suppressed amusement suffusing the class, the whir of projected paper-clips and the rhythmic rasping from Thomas's pockets would eventually permeate Eustace Ford's consciousness. Looking a trifle bemused by it all he would say: 'Come along now boys, this is all very silly behaviour don't you think.'

He then seemed mildly hurt that as an immediate result of this stern admonishment the entire class didn't look instantly abashed. Poor old stick. He only ever wanted to teach his belovèd French and be liked. We callous brutes interpreted this as weakness.

Paradoxically however . . .

. . . Eustace Ford MA (like Thomas's new found friend) also enjoyed a dual role in life. Every Wednesday afternoon he had been empowered to grow six inches in stature by donning boots and khaki battledress when for a few brief hours he once again became Lt-Col Eustace Ford and the paper MA was replaced by an equally hard won and very real MC. Assisted by the new English master who had been a National Service subaltern in tanks and the Art master who had been a World War I subaltern and only came in twice a week, Eustace commanded the school's Army Cadet Force.

Hopeless at maths (I once got minus-three in Algebra, because I'd also misspelled my name at the top) and barely able to pull myself up the gym ropes, it was nevertheless as a soldier that I was to excel. (*Hardly! Author's ex CO*). I could scarcely wait for my 14th birthday to arrive. That was when I would be deemed old enough and eligible to report to CQMS Donovan's stores above the Geography room and draw up my too large or too small battledress and my blue beret with its brass Gunners' badge to which august fraternity our cadet force was loosely affiliated.

My khaki shirt and size-five ammunition boots (I'd finally got some) already possessed pride of place in the wardrobe at home. They had been proudly purchased from Millets with my hard-earned paper-round money. Oh yes - we had to earn our Queen's shilling in those days. She wouldn't have just anyone as a cadet. Worth had to be proved from the saddle of a bike on a rainy mid-winter's early a.m. paper run.

Having thus earned my junior spurs the day finally dawned when I arose to take the khaki ensemble from its bag in the wardrobe, and don same. The gaiters proved frustrating.

Gaiters were doubtless designed after it was discovered that puttees didn't prevent the bloody mud of Paschendale from seeping through to your socks. On men they conveyed a sense of reality and urgent purpose. On me they span round uncontrollably and looked daft but they did manage to keep one's trousers out of the bike chain. As for the uniform proper the late Spike Milligan aptly described it as being a most suitable mode of attire in which to convey soup. With my navy blue Kangol beret swivelling around on top endeavouring to secure purchase on the Brylcreemed teenage mop - I was ready for war.

Feeling like the vanguard of an armoured thrust I wheeled into the gravel of the school courtyard, parked up in the bike sheds, and adjusting my satchel slung it across my shoulder and clumped off loudly to morning assembly and prayers. The same as fish on Fridays we always had Christian Soldiers on a Wednesday but whereas hitherto it had been just a hymn today I was inculcated with the cause and awash with emotion as my voice thundered (and squeaked) forth the stirring words accompanied by Edward Pinkney (Upper Vth Music) on the school harmonium.

It was a stinking hot summer's day and my concentration waned as the morning buzzed desultorily on. I itched and perspired and fidgeted and had a plimsole hurled at me by the Latin master and twice asked to be excused so that I could go and glance undetected at myself in the main hall mirror as I passed.

'What are you doing there, boy . . .?'

'Admiring myself . . . oh . . . sorry, sir. Cramp in my leg, sir.'

15.00 hours: (3 p.m. to laymen)

'Get *on* . . . . *Parade*!' bellowed our 17-year old CSM, Nevil

Barber. Then as an afterthought: 'You new recruits go and fall in by the bins outside the kitchen.' (***Pretty much where his military career remained:*** *author's CO again.*)

My God. This was for real. It had started happening. As the Upper Vth (apart from a few Conscientious Objectors who did extra Latin and subsequently had a worse time of it doing their National Service which was harder to get out of than the ACF) strolled out onto the hockey pitch and shuffled into some semblance of a line, we recruits clasped our hands behind our backs and spent a lot of time self-effacingly considering our toe caps. We knew our place. Those bigger chaps out there had already seen some service. They knew how to come properly to attention, slope arms *and* march properly in step. Well, sort of.

Our 17-year old CSM mouthed a few more tame oaths of command and the 1st Battalion (we didn't then have a second) relaxed and waited. Standing over there by the bins we expected an enemy air strike or at least a para drop to darken the azure skies above the bike sheds at any moment. And then suddenly as if on cue the air really was shattered by a burst of machine-gun fire. I flinched. We all ducked. We rose sheepishly. It was the grounds man's *pop-pop* mowing the cricket table. The silence was resumed. The Armistice was signed. We were unscathed heroes.

Then the ranks stirred for real. We all sensed an eminence. Every eye swivelled to the direction of the woodwork shop. The door was swung majestically open by an aide (the new English master with his one cloth pip straining at its seams) to reveal a knot of colour. Monty? Lovat? Wingate? Flanked by his two subalterns Lt-Col Eustace Ford MC MA imperiously emerged clutching an antique colonial fly-whisk and surveyed his troops. Casting a cursory glance at us recruits huddled over by the kitchen bins he lost his balance on the first step down. Regaining it, and his composure, realigning his toupé and replacing his peaked Service Dress cap as if nothing had happened he proceeded to inspect his command.

The main inspection over he came over towards us new boys, flicking his leg with his whisk, which wasn't a bad thing to do in the vicinity of our bins. He considered us disdainfully for a while before speaking. This was because although he'd done it many times before he couldn't think of anything too inspirational to say but when he did it was: 'Well now. This should be a very proud day for you chaps, wearing your country's uniform for the first time.'

'There's room for half the country in mine, an' all.'

'Yes, Higginbottom. You're only fourteen though and so that's there to allow for growth.'

It wasn't very often Eustace said a funny. When he did it was usually by accident and took him as much by surprise as it did the rest of us. The result was that when we'd stopped laughing he was still fighting to compose himself, couldn't, and stood chewing his lip like *On The Buses'* Inspector Blakey.

'There is no reason for you to treat the school's cadet force lightly as no more than just a jolly prank to get you off Wednesday afternoon lessons you know. During the last war boys of your age were defending Berlin against the Russians.'

'Boys from this school, sir?'

'Use your intelligence, Short. Of course not boys from this school. This school wasn't here then.' He coughed. 'You will now be broken down into squads,' he went on, 'and start to be taught the basics of foot drill. After a few weeks, depending upon your performance and progress, you will be issued with rifles and taught arms drill.'

Just then the fall-out area was shattered by a deafening clash of cymbals, the wet *thwaboom* of a very sick old bass drum, the slack *thwock thwock* of the tenors, and the staccato machine-gun rattle of a mini-battery of earnest snare-drums. This was followed immediately by the death scream of twelve bull mooses as the bugles let rip with their version of *The British Grenadiers.* From behind the bike sheds came the school band hoving into view. Oh what a magnificent sight to behold. What panoply. What Gods.

As the columns swayed past onto the hockey pitch only Cleopatra's palanquin and a Nile backcloth were missing. Every bandsman wore a glistening white belt and gaiters and miniature shiny brass replicas of his particular instrument glinting on his arm. Wearing loops of blue, red and yellow-plaited lanyards with tassels bouncing from their ends like potentates' dressing-gown cords the buglers marched along hurriedly behind their runaway bugles drooling and spraying spit as if they were restraining Rottweilers.

The drummers marched proudly erect and looked fixedly ahead, seemingly oblivious to the cumbersome equipment bouncing and swinging along before them like some ghastly African disease.

The right hand drummer in the front was even more proud and more erect than his fellows. He wore a magnificent red sash. He wore it with justification. In the Band's hierarchical pecking order he ranked on a par with the Vice President of the United States. *He* was the *solo* drummer.

And there - strutting before them peacock-like and superb - was the Drum Major. Sergeant Roy Fielder of the Upper VIth. Blond hair on his chest, and a girlfriend. With the same megalomaniac exhibitionist paraphernalia as everyone else girt liberally about his person the Drum Major additionally possessed his own particular baubles of office which left the Crown Jewels in the shade.

Apart from his red sash which was even bigger and broader than the heroic solo drummer's and *festooned* with badges he wore a pair of - white gauntlets. Alright, so traffic police and bus drivers wore white gauntlets too. Not like our school Drum Major they didn't. All he lacked was a flashing neon sign declaring I AM THE GREATEST; a sentiment which would have attracted little or no dissent.

But if there had been any doubt about who the Drum Major was, any chink of dubiousness in his armour, this was irrevocably countered by . . . *the Mace*. It was on their ability to wield their Mace that Drum Majors lived or died. To be able to twirl, flash, toss, whirl, hurl and control completely that five-foot, crown-topped mahogany stave with its silver chain snaking round it like a serpent down a tree was a feat only allowed God's chosen few.

The Band marched, countermarched, wheeled and halted.

Roy Fielder effected an impossibly magnificent final flourish with his Mace and the world waited with bated breath. Even the Headmaster gazing out of his study window waited. The Mace made a secret 'in' signal to its devotees and as one man the Band then slowly marched disdainfully off parade.

If I had been submerged in the deep end of a swimming pool I would have heard more than I did of the remainder of that afternoon's activities. A seed had been sown and was already gestating at a galloping pace. *I* - all five-feet two of me - was going to become the next Drum Major. Gene Krupa aspiring to be President of the United States stood more chance of success in his mission than I did in mine. For a start I couldn't even join the Band as one of its lowliest buglers for another six months. Before we could 'specialise' we had to learn the rudiments of killing. These were acquired by smudging shoe polish on our faces, hiding behind a bush out on field manoeuvres down at nearby Rodmill Farm (now long since become a housing estate) and sitting in cow pats out in the rain. But the six months did duly elapse and I applied and because Hamner and Ellerby had left and they were short that term I was issued with and signed for a well worn and dented converted copper cocoa tin that might well have sounded early morning muster at Mafeking and very probably did. Mind you, a brand spanking new Ferrari could not have brought with it more pure joy to its owner or more anguish to his parents. Suburbia obviously offers limited practice facilities for aspiring buglers so I was banished to the hills to learn my craft.

Any old gentlemen who think they recall hearing the plaintive notes of a fractured and ghostly *Last Post* wafting discordantly over the Downs Golf Club on Sunday mornings weren't imagining it and I'm sorry if their game was ruined by the expectancy of a Zulu massacre pending at the eighth tee.

And so six months later and six inches taller the erstwhile nonentity went on parade on Armistice Sunday and party now to Roy Fielder's 'in' signals with that magical Mace took his cue and played solo bugle as we gave our 'eyes right' at the Town Hall. I was on my way. The next step to Mace-dom was to become a drummer. So I became a drummer.

For the next six months the Sunday morning golfers now teed off to pure Gene Krupa, who was still drumming and not yet presiding. Attendance at the Downs course depleted sadly that season as word spread about the haunted bunker and members defected by the score to adjoining clubs. But - proficient at last - I eventually stood silhouetted on the horizon one day and saluted the remaining members with a haunting farewell roll while all over the course they stopped putting, doffed their bobble hats, and raised their number-nine irons in salute. To this day they have played on unhindered.

At this juncture in my rise to fame there came an obstacle in the form of competition. A renegade upstart called David Wheeler who turned out to be just as good a drummer as me and some (especially him) thought even better also aspired to claim the Mace. The result of this confrontation was that the school now possessed two of the best drummers the world had ever seen. We even gave demonstrations at local youth clubs, playing together, complementing each other's performance, and then with glazed eyes and fixed grins endeavoured to play each other off the stage and into a state of nervous collapse and resignation. To no avail. We simply improved our drumming even more with the result that for the first time in the Band's history we had *two* solo drummers.

Highlights of course were the various parades in the town in which we took part during the year. How incongruous they were. The Band of The Royal Marines professionally and staidly setting the pace followed sedately by the TA and the Police and St John Ambulance and the Boy Scouts all shuffling past the Church of St Thomas or the Mayor or a flagpole or whatever - and then - coming along behind flanked by the Girl Guides and the Wolf Cubs, a motley contingent evocative of a New Orleans funeral procession. Lt-Col Eustace Ford proudly headed his khaki muddle, all the time trying to keep a quick tempo step with his frenetic bandsmen up front.

The new solo bugler Bob Payne had taken a page from my book (although it was another golf course he'd practised on) and his triple-tonguing technique was well up to the craziest intricacies of the breathtaking performance going on in the front rank. David and I juggled our sticks, turned our drums around, changed step in mid-march and generally transformed our part of the parade to the level of a carnival in Rio. But it was magnificent.

And then - one day - the Old Lion stood down. Roy Fielder was almost eighteen then and going up to Oxford. The time had come for him to take off his white gauntlets and hand the Mace on to the next generation.

Me?

The entire school walked the corridors with eager anticipation and whispered chatter. With our adrenalin pumping David and I studiously avoided one another. Eustace and his subalterns went into daily conflab with the Headmaster and little knots would gather at the main gate to await bulletins. The press hounded us for a release. (Well - Howard Spencer's big brother did ring up once from the *Gazette* offices) but still no decision was forthcoming.

It was one autumn lunchtime. The school grounds man was sweeping up the leaves on the gravel drive. I stopped to exchange a few *bon mots* of puerile banter with him. As I did so Fate contrived to knock the head off his bass broom. Stooping to retrieve the handle for him I heard distant music and experienced a strange feeling beginning to course through my veins. The blood pumped through my temples. My shoulder blades turned cold. I experienced a liquid flutter in my colon. This was it. Someone upstairs was nudging me. Why not? For the past two years I had done nothing but prepare for this moment, with one of my mother's brooms out in our back garden. Today providence had blown the leaves into a pile outside the Headmaster's study window. Like Fred Astaire with a cane I limply broke into a routine with the grounds man's broom handle. My apprehension receded with each successive and successful twirl that I did. Each whirring flourish brought with it increased confidence. The bell rang and the school poured out for lunch. The broom handle flashed and as it shot into the air and performed a triple somersault faces appeared at the Headmaster's window and beamed. The handle bounced down onto the ground and leapt obediently back into my outstretched hand. The school cheered. The grounds man cheered. I hurled the handle once more skyward and left it arcing over the telephone wires. Before it landed with a clatter I had retrieved my books and strolled off unconcernedly towards the library. The Mace was mine.

David burnt his sticks, his bridges, buried his drum and threw himself off the gym roof. It wasn't very high so he only sprained his left ankle but he'd made his point and then went and locked himself in one of the lavatories. He was understandably disappointed, but the best man had won.

It was another stinking hot summer's day. My ankles were beginning to swell and my uniform itched like hell. The white gauntlets felt clutchy inside and I knew I should have had the foresight to have offloaded last night's curry.

We were drawn up on parade expectantly awaiting Eustace's word of command. Down the hill - down there in the town through the High Street and along the seafront waited Mother and Father and my little brother and the girls and the cheering waving crowds and the cameras and the Mayor on his plinth by his flagpole and that other band, the Royal Marine one, and fame and glory and the realisation of my young life's ambition . . .

'Carry on please, Drum Major.'

Drum Major! *Moi!* I'd made it. I controlled the quaver in my voice and with a recently acquired *basso profundo* commanded: 'School will march off - by the right . . . QU*IIII*CK . . . *MARCH*.'

Oh the music played and the people swayed and there I was at last . . . and as we marched into The Avenue a ripple went along the sea of faces:

'Is that 'im, Mum? Is that the greatest Drum Major the world 'as ever seen?'

'Ohhh, look: i'n't 'e smashin'. I like 'is kit. Is 'e meant to be smilin' like that when 'e's marchin'?'

''E's not smilin,' - 'e's bitin' 'is lip.'

'Nar, 'e ain't; 'e's just so made up wiv 'imself 'e's wettin' 'isself, i'n't 'e?'

'Oh, shuddup Syd. I fink 'e's luvly.'

By the time we came within sight of the Mayor the crowd was *agog* with my mace work. The previous week I had removed its finial crown and poured molten lead into the hollow. Although the wristwork required to get it started was phenomenal, once it was going there was no stopping it . . . it-was-going.

The parade drew closer to the Mayoral plinth. This is where the crowd was at its most dense. I had done a reconnaissance the previous evening for what I was now about to do. The overhead telephone wires were stretched tautly across the street just at the right place. They shone like spun gold in the glaring sun. Almost time now. Nearly there. The cymbals clashed. My heart thumped. Almost . . . ready . . . *NOW!*

Just as I launched the Mace skyward the head flew off one of Ernie Hollamby's tenor drumsticks and smacked me in the back of the neck. The crowd gasped. Hollamby, I'm sure, blanched. I faltered, teetered for effect, and bravely carried on. As we gave our 'eyes right' the Mace would be whirring in a graceful arc over the wires. As we gave 'eyes front' I would casually retrieve it in its descent. I could do it - really I could. I mean, you know I did it with the broom handle outside the Headmaster's window didn't I. It was a cinch.

Bloody Hollamby's drumstick. As we gave the 'eyes right' the Mace got itself all tangled up in the two telephone wires. They juggled it back and forth like a dog shaking a rat and then re-launched the lead-filled missile straight at His Worship. He had the presence of mind to duck when he saw it coming but it still crashed onto his foot. In acute pain he emitted an enraged yelp and drop-kicked it eastward, during which trajectory it removed four hats and an ice cream before screeching like a banshee straight through a plate glass window where it came to rest after slithering along the sweet counter. The parade concertinaed. I concertinaed. After some degree of order had been restored my Band marched on without me. I dragged myself soulfully into the shop to retrieve my Mace and someone asked if I wanted it wrapped and suggested not eating it all at once because it was a big one. One glance at the shattered window told me it was back to the paper-round again in the morning. Shouldering his way through the highly amused crowd outside a police inspector wanted to know if I had planned the Mayor's assassination on my own or were there any accomplices?

The formalities of acquiring shame and infamy now over I skulked off along the back streets and caught a bus home. No one was in of course. They were all down on the seafront with their cameras waiting to witness my debut and were apparently most perturbed when the Band marched past without me. 'Mum, why'd he desert so soon?' my little brother asked. Our relationship hasn't improved much since.

Next day at school wasn't too funny either. How are the mighty fallen? David Wheeler grinned at me when we passed each other in the corridor but I managed to weather the humiliation and a few days later the heat lifted when one of the masters conveniently had a stroke and died. I was always very grateful to him for that.

EIGHT

DESPITE THE DÉBÂCLE of my debut with the mace and my burgeoning love-life being impeded by Arabs it seemed that things were slowly but finally beginning to fall into place a bit. The mace having been retrieved and repaired and my position as drum-major re-ratified, on subsequent public appearances I even managed to twirl the thing with sufficient élan on one occasion to catch the eye of an attractive girl called Kerry whose parents were the licencees of a successful local pub.

Kerry was a chirpy, vivacious, more or less highly principled, pert little 14-year old blonde number and we had lots of exploratory fun together for the short period that we were 'going steady'. While her parents tended their raucous clientele downstairs in the bar Kerry and I would while away our evenings doing our homework in their flat upstairs, playing the piano, endlessly discussing life's problems and discovering various other little ways to amuse ourselves until one evening when with well controlled steam emanating from her teenage ears she took me aback somewhat by blurting out: 'I will if you will.' I was sixteen and mother had always suggested that when the time came and the offer was first made I shouldn't, so I didn't, fearful lest parental wrath from both sides and that of an outraged society at large should descend upon me. My heart took a momentary turn for the worse in so instinctively rejecting Kerry, a different sort of knee-jerk to those we'd been experiencing so far together, but back in those days *every*one knew - it was simply a given - that that sort of malarkey *al*ways made the girl pregnant and gave you VD. This was the evening that Kerry realised life had more to offer her than me, thanked me for our practice and went on to negotiate solace from a new beau, a school friend of mine whom she married shortly thereafter, although he never thanked me for my honourable behaviour in having left her intact for him. I endured an hour or so of emotional turmoil but then gleefully forced myself to re-enter the merry-go-round, this time determined to hit The Big Time.

There used to reside in Eastbourne back then an accommodating and most bounteous lass of sixteen scrumptious summers called Brenda. Brenda was possessed of a charming nature and an excitingly sensuous face but it was not for these attributes that she was so popularly known by all and sundry as 'Bumpers'. Brenda had been endowed with unnaturally large breasts (probably before even Jordan's mother was born) which not just for their curiosity value alone she was not averse to putting out on a fairly regular basis for most of us to fondle: sometimes one and more often than not both of them, but always *some*thing. She seemed to have become conditioned to considering this altruistic act something of a public duty on her part and so had we. My genes and wimpish declination of Kerry had told me that I must now be biologically 'old enough' to step properly into this freshly exciting arena of young adult life so it was Brenda who became The Big Time to which I aspired. Most of the older guys had already had a go on her and eventually it became my turn to wriggle on to her list of suitors for an hour or two's rite of passage. We went to the *Picturedrome* together one Saturday night to see a Jimmy Cagney movie. I remember I got cramp from excessive contortions and too much surreptitious writhing but also a remarkably memorable and substantial handful. Brenda had also earned for herself and enjoyed the soubriquet Penny Wank but such was not to be my fortune that night, after which event she moved on to accommodate the next on her packed appointments list while I sought new and less fleeting conquests, my brief and happy experience with her leaving me an avowed tit man for life.

*

Although quite an accomplished drummer, and possessed of sufficient rhythm to knock out a pretty syncopated tune on the piano I was unable to dance a single step. If we were to become well rounded chaps who wished to enjoy successful careers and social lives, in those days it was expected that we should become acceptably proficient at ballroom dancing. This meant learning to do the waltz, the foxtrot and the quickstep. The girls whom we knew all seemed able to glide gracefully into any of these dances perfectly naturally, as though the manual had arrived tucked under their arms post-partum, whereas we clods in our grey flannel bags found them extremely difficult to execute. But unless one was prepared to drop out of society completely the acquisition of these dancing skills was yet another rite of passage that simply had to be mastered. No two ways. Unlike today we couldn't just make up the steps as we went along but had to be taught the formalised moves. One Saturday afternoon Tony Higgins and I did bite the bullet and take ourselves off to a dancing class in the Church Hall together but one session of that was sufficient to push the whole idea even further onto my back burner, until . . . over a *cappuccino* one day I happened to mention my shortcoming to a burgeoning terpsichorean artiste of fifteen, a popular member of our crowd called June Wilkinson. A stunningly attractive girl June had already set the VIth Form and half the male teaching staff agog by becoming so frenzied with the beat at one of our school dances that her skirt had swirled up round her waist like a lariat to reveal our first ever real-life glimpse of stocking tops and just about the fairest pair of pins in town. June's career path was set. She left Eastbourne and went to London's Windmill Theatre and from there straight on to Hollywood and thence *Playboy* to become a popular and well known showbiz pin-up and performer in the '50s, '60s and '70s.

'*I'll* teach you,' she cried, clapping her hands eagerly at the prospect. 'It's really *so* easy. Come round to my place on Saturday afternoon at three.'

Specially bathed and with a purloined dab or eight of my father's Old Spice sloshed behind each ear I rang June's doorbell at 2.59 p.m. She lived with her brother and their parents in a flat behind a then WWII bombsite where today's Eastbourne branch of Marks and Spencer now stands. By 4.00 p.m. I had learned to waltz, foxtrot and quickstep and whenever over the years I have had occasion to execute those steps it was fondly to recall the tuition I received over half a century ago, for which I thanked June with effusive gratitude and imagined I was Fred Astaire tripping my way lightly home for tea. And sadly it really was just the waltz, foxtrot and quickstep that June taught me that afternoon. Honestly.

My first tender love affair was with a pretty little redhead called Joey Rowsell. Joey and I felt warm and soft and nice together from the moment we first met and walked hand-in-hand through the park and past the daffodils to enjoy our first prolonged kiss behind a bush up near the golf links. I can still see the green dress and shoes she was wearing that day. It was to Joey that in my best writing I felt moved to compose my first ever love letter and post it to her home to which I had not yet even been invited. Joey was the sweetest thing I had ever known and all I wanted to do was to look after her. Then one day she wasn't on the bus to school and I didn't know why because she hadn't said anything about being away and I didn't know what to do about it because mobile phones and texting hadn't been invented then, so I had no means of contacting her all day and fluffed my Latin test.

My recent girlfriend Kerry was in the same class as Joey and it was she who came round that evening to tell me that Joey had been rushed off to hospital with something called leukaemia.

Shortly after that Kerry came to the house again to tell me that Joey had died.

'Oh; well, thanks for letting me know,' I said, having no idea how I should react to such unaccustomed news of such magnitude, so trying to play if cool, yet feeling an overwhelming need to take myself off for a thoughtful walk alone somewhere.

With hunched shoulders and my hands sunk deep in my pockets I slammed our front door behind me and kicked an undeserving tin can up the street. Unsure whether it was permitted or if I was being overdramatic I allowed impulse to draw me inside our neighbourhood's St John's Church where I slumped bereft into one of the pews and started to whimper. I felt it might have been a time to do more than just whimper but being young British and inhibited the echo within the empty tea-time church precluded my doing so. Holding my emotions in check I clattered from the pew and out of the church to run home, crash up the stairs and hurl myself across my bed. My bewildered mother swept efficiently into the room after me, braced and ready to face either a belated German attack or some deranged axeman on a spree. Seeing no blood on my face, no protruding bone, and that both arms and legs were still intact it was with only the merest hint of panic in her voice that she asked what on earth the matter was with me.

'Joey's dead, Mum,' I wailed clawing at the blanket.

'Oh, *no*,' she gasped. 'Darling, I am so *very*, very sorry.'

Instead of fussing, she left me there to grieve, smoothed my brow once before leaving the room and said: 'We'll talk about it when you're ready.'

It was then I felt able to let go.

For the first time in my young life I emitted a protracted howl of anguished desolation, followed by great racking sobs. Every pent up adolescent emotion unleashed and exploded from me.

After such a premature cataclysmic purgative and sobbing myself dry it was a relief to find I was undamaged. Dehydrated, yes, but my still intact emotive marrow felt as cleansed as a bamboo shoot after a tropical storm. I had not then heard Beethoven's Pastoral Symphony but subsequently realised that he had been inspired to compose it purely to express my innermost awakenings after the event of that day. If ever I've hit a cumulative sticky-one since then I've opted for tears rather than an ulcer every time. The cleansing power to the soul of a good old blub is phenomenal. It flushes the system and clears the ground for a fresh unimpeded run at whichever six-foot wall's so frustratingly been blocking you. You may still graze your knees and bang a shin or two going over but the chances are that this time – refreshed - you'll do it. Never be afraid to have a good cry. It's not cissy. Try a snuffle. Have a sob for England some time. You'll enjoy it!

There was no system in place at school whereby I could ask to leave early to attend Joey's funeral. In any case they would have raised an eyebrow or laughed at me. I was only sixteen and I am sure I wasn't officially meant to be in love at that age. It probably wasn't allowed. Besides, I didn't know what to do at a funeral. I'd never been to one before. My school uniform hardly seemed sombre enough for such an occasion but it was the most formal attire I possessed in my wardrobe. Also I would be far too shy to try to intrude on the private grief of Joey's family, none of whom I had ever met, and as far as I knew didn't even know of my existence.

Tough call for a kid.

In the event, after school I propped my bike up against a wall, went into the florist next to the newsagent opposite the cemetery gates and paid one-and-sixpence of my hard-earned paper-round money for a small sprig of mauve flowers. Carefully crossing the road I entered the cemetery and sidled furtively through it from bush to bush until I could see the impressive funeral party gathered about the graveside. From my distance I was unable to hear the words of the clergyman but eventually Joey's committal drew to its close and the grown ups slowly dispersed and filed forlornly away. Waiting until the last black vestments had disappeared I moved quickly to the hole in the ground that was already being filled with the good earth by two old Sussex retainers. I stood there as bowed, humble and inadequate as some small alien on the edge of a strange universe, confronted by the mountain of wreaths, flowers, cards, cellophane and ribbons which surrounded my little friend. Hesitantly I proffered my own pathetic one-and-sixpenny posy of wilting purple pansies and dropped them into the hole along with the next shovelful of dirt. Perhaps my flowers' true rate of descent was confused by blurred vision at the time and the lapse of it since but I do believe that instead of simply dropping they floated down and came to alight and settle oh so gently atop her spiralling mound.

When I got home from school next afternoon it was to find that my mother had been crying.

'What is it, Mum?' I asked hurrying to place a comforting hand on her shoulder. She dabbed at her nose, sniffed and smiled.

'I had a visitor this afternoon,' she said. 'Your little Joey's mother came to see me.'

I was clutched by nervousness. No one had seen me at her funeral. I couldn't think what I had done wrong.

'She came to tell me that when she was going through Joey's things she found a letter you'd written. Having read it she said she just wanted to come and share with me, as one mother to another, how beautiful she thought it was and how very pleased she was to know that although Joey was only fifteen she had received at least one secret love letter in her life.'

Nearly swallowing my heart I smiled gratefully up to God who stood with His arms embracing a smiling fifteen year old Joey, who is still fifteen for me over half-a-century on.

NINE

I WAS NOW well into being sixteen.

I had practised shaving, nicked myself, was now onto my third girlfriend, and had legally bought my first ninepenny packet of cigarettes, but still my father insisted that I had to be home by 9.30 p.m. on Saturday nights.

It was a drag.

I wasn't even beginning to feel tired by 9.30 p.m. but still I had to report in or suffer the consequence . . .

. . . which was ?

A rattan cane.

The cinema didn't finish until 9.00 p.m.

Dances didn't hot up until 10.30 p.m.

Dad was misinformed.

He wasn't being beastly on purpose, he just hadn't appraised the situation correctly.

All the same, I was the one bearing the brunt of his unreasonableness.

Somehow he had to be apprised of reality.

The situation had to change.

I wheedled; I cajoled and I whined - but to no avail.

I assured him that I wasn't intent on embarking upon a career of rape and pillage or smashing shop windows after dark.

It was no good.

He remained adamant; 9.30 p.m. it was and 9.30 p.m. it would remain.

Each week I eked it out closer to 10.00 o'clock and each

week I received consistent and salutary bamboo cuts across my buttocks for my trouble.

It was silly; it was undignified, it was quite unnecessary and I was becoming increasingly annoyed.

It was Armistice Day 1954: a most auspicious and appropriate occasion for what was to take place early next morning . . .

Immaculate in my blancoed whites and razor-creased battledress, my position as Drum Major now fully restored, I had wielded my mace like a dervish that day as I led the band up Grove Road past the mayoral plinth. That corpulent civic worthy had flinched and naturally tucked one foot anxiously behind the other at my approach but I'd grinned and given him a broad wink during the 'eyes right' and I could swear he'd relaxed and winked back at me.

Flushed with self satisfaction afterwards a group of us khaki-clad bandsmen met up with a willing clutch of new groupies and persuaded them to come for a coffee with us. By now it was 6.00 p.m. Playing with their coffee spoons the giggling girls then suggested to us that they might quite like to be taken to the cinema: Nudge, nudge; wink, wink. A quick flick through a mental process told me that we should be out by 9.00 p.m. which would allow me a good half-hour window in which to hurry home before being subject to my father's regulation forty lashes.

The film was awful: it broke down and we didn't leave the cinema 'til 9.30 p.m. Then the girls wanted another coffee. The two guys with me were buglers in my band. *I* was the Drum Major; El Sup*remo*. How was *I* going to be able to say: '*Sorreeee* but I've got to be home by 9.30 p.m.'?

Wimp.

The hell with it.

Statement time.

After all, I was sixteen wasn't I.

Discretion went to the four winds.

Foolhardy valour prevailed.

Albeit only a cut down version but was I not wearing the Queen's uniform? According to Lt-Col Eustace Ford our school cadet force CO, Hitler's Youth - several of them, in fact - had died defending Berlin against the Russians at my age. And younger. *Dear Herr Hitler; Please to make sure Heinz is home by 9.30 p.m. this evening as usual, won't you. Vielen Dank: seine Mutti.*

I shall now digress for a moment . . .

One day in 1962 while I was having a pub lunch in Soho I was roaring through a thrilling and true book I was reading about a WWII RAF navigator who'd been shot down over Holland in 1941 while returning from a bombing raid over Berlin in an attempt to destroy Goering's headquarters. The author had become a PoW who'd escaped and been recaptured several times, on one occasion being tortured by the Gestapo. Eventually he'd made it back to England and promptly set off on another raid in which he was shot up and burned, then having become one of the famous Doctor Sir Archibald McIndoe's Guinea Pigs at East Grinstead's Queen Victoria Hospital where he'd had his face rebuilt. The name of the book's author was Richard Pape. There was a photograph of him on the back cover. Taking another hurried chunk out of my bar-lunch sandwich and quickly turning the page I was rather miffed when a blazer'd gentleman sipping a pint on the adjoining bench disturbed me, saying: 'I hope you're enjoying reading that.'

'I am; very much indeed thank you.'

'That's good - because I'm the chap who wrote it.'

Imagine my amazed double take to find that I was serendipitously sitting next to none other but the author himself, Richard Pape.

Not so reluctant now, I closed his book and we enjoyed an enlivened conversation for twenty minutes before leaving the pub together and going our separate ways. The point is that his book was appropriately called *Boldness Be My Friend . . .*

So, back in 1954's Eastbourne the giggly girls and my two bugler friends and I went for a coffee followed by a walk along the beach afterwards. Later we huddled in a windswept bus shelter fondling and pecking each other, after which we saw the girls back to their homes at the far end of town. The time now was 11.30 p.m. I sensed that my colleagues in this escapade weren't in the same degree of trouble as me. Perhaps they came from the wrong part of town so their parents didn't love them as much. I was beginning to wish mine didn't, either.

I bade them farewell and hurried off home.

It was now midnight.

Opening our front door as quietly as I could I tiptoed apprehensively up the stairs in my studded ammunition boots. Silly thing to do I suppose but it wouldn't have made any difference if I had taken them off. I knew my father would be waiting up there for me just the same.

I didn't have to put the switch on.

My room was bathed in moonlight.

Romantic?

Some hope.

I was just loosening the buttons of my battledress blouse beginning to wonder whether by some miracle I'd got away with it when the door opened. He hadn't wasted any time. He came in and stood there with the cane at the ready. We regarded each other. Midnight *was* a bit beyond the pale, perhaps, for a sixteen year old virgin (yes honestly) whose official bedtime was still 9.30 p.m. As a blow for rebellious self expression though I felt I had made my point.

'So what happened?' my father asked. He was nothing if not fair.

I told him.

'It sounds to me as if you got a bit carried away with yourself young man,' he said sternly. 'Come along then. Over the bed please.'

The die was cast.

'I don't think so Dad. Not this time. No.'

'What on earth do you mean?' he demanded, taken aback. 'I suggest you do as you're damn' well told.' I could sense his quivering, white lipped prescience. 'Over that bed please at once young man, or I'm afraid it will have to be a double dose.'

'Dad, if you ever raise that cane to me again . . .'

He lifted his arm . . .

I caught the bamboo's downward cut right across my palm. It stung like blazes but I clenched the cane, wrenched it from his surprised grasp and snapped it smartly into four across my knee. Its broken yellow ends shone dully like dry and brittle bone.

I handed the four pieces back to him.

There was a ruminative silence.

'Alright,' he said. 'We'll say 11.30 p.m. from now on then shall we?'

He shook my burning hand and made to leave the room. Pausing at the door he turned and even in the moonlight I perceived a combination of slight nervousness, incomprehension and pride in his expression as he smiled and said: 'Well done son.'

It was hell bringing up parents.

TEN

TO ENABLE ME TO BUY MY ROUND of lemonades at Drago's Bun Lounge - and up till now it seemed like I had been doing so all my life, and also because it was good character-building discipline to rise at 5.30 a.m. both summer and winter - I continued to do a paper-round each morning. Right up until I left school. It wasn't too pleasant a pastime in snow, sleet, and driving rain but at that time of day in summer, when I look back on it now, I realise just how pleasant it all was.

Vinall's, the now long defunct newsagent was just across the road from our front door. I had only to glance out of my bedroom window opposite to see if the distributor's van had deposited the morning's bundles in the shop's doorway and three minutes later I was dressed, on my bike and out on the road with the tautly packed canvas *Daily Express* bag full of that day's deliveries slung across my shoulder. The thought never occurred to me as I dashed from house to house in my T-shirt, jeans and plimsoles that twenty years later I would be seeing feature articles of my own published on the centre pages of the self same publication.

Meads today, overlooking the sea to the west of Eastbourne has become cramped, run down and tired. Its one time magnificent multi-floored mansions have all either been knocked down and had flats built in their place or been converted into bed sits, mostly for the undergraduates of Brighton University which despite understandably strong opposition from local residents successfully commandeered some of the beautiful buildings in the area to convert into part of their overspill campus housing their Health, Podiatry, Physio, Sport and Cooking courses. In the days when Eastbourne used to be the salubrious watering hole for which it was renowned, Meads then was the town's genteel, red-bricked Nob-Hill, its populace a gallimaufry of retired gentlefolk; judges and generals and their ladies and entourages, all living splendiferously in the palatial single-family Victorian and Edwardian houses that lined the sylvan roads. Edwina Mountbatten and others of similar ilk had been to school here. In those days a more idyllic setting in which to do a paper-round could not be imagined. Today a newspaper round pays £35 a week. Doing my job from six to eight a.m. for seven days I earned nine shillings and sixpence a week, which in today's money would be about £10. Exploitation - or what! *Naaah*; we never even thought about it. There was still then a certain *noblesse oblige* for the retired admiral's widows - who in the light of changing times were no doubt beginning to struggle a bit to hang on to their respective family piles - still to supplement our annual income by tipping 'tradesmen' like us at Christmas.

So ingrained by rote did my repetitious daily route become that I believe I could go out today on the self-same run and still deliver everything to the correct house, even though the occupants at the time would long since have turned to dust. The number of steps, stairways, door-handles and passageways are as familiar to me as I write as the stairways were at school or the ones at home. I can still run up and down them all in my mind's eye without missing a single step or bannister hold.

The most recurring adolescent fantasy I enjoyed as I delivered my papers in those far off summers was that one bright sunny morning the door to one of the flats would be opened by the young actress Janette Scott, fresh faced and flouncing in a crisply starched white gingham dress, who would say: 'Hallo, you're a nice, good looking paper boy. Won't you please come in and make love to me?'

From where I acquired my obsession with Janette Scott, the late actress Dame Thora Hird's daughter, who later married and divorced the American singer Mel Tormé - I have no idea;

she was the same age as me, and although I suspect that by then I was probably just getting into older women, I still fancied her like crazy. It was silly really because I was pretty certain that a sixteen-year-old film starlet from Morecambe would hardly be living incognito in an Edwardian flat in Eastbourne, and even if she had been and I had said yes, it would have made me awfully late for school but for two whole summers my testosterone-charged fantasy persisted unchecked. And certainly unrealised. It was seldom that I ever saw a resident anyway. As I have now learned to my pleasure not many retired folk had occasion to be up and about at that time of day, especially in order to satisfy the fanciful curiosity and burgeoning need of a newspaper boy with bubbling sap.

Today, the same as most of the rest of Britain, dear old Eastbourne has unfortunately 'had its day' and become something of a tip.

Along with the sure conviction that some Divine Power had understandably exempted Great Britain from uprisings or natural disasters - events which were normally only experienced by the world's less fortunate peoples - we had always harboured the quaint notion that the mainstream of English life would pass Eastbourne by, leaving us to continue enjoying our elitist conservative lifestyle unmolested in our own special backwater. But inevitably 'new society's' spread sought us out, infiltrated our boundaries and the resultant trickle soon became a constant stream of unstoppable traffic. Slowly at first but then with gathering momentum we began to receive more than our fair share of DSS dropouts voluntarily deciding to graduate from their inner city ghettoes to the delights of the seaside; immigrant workers and African AIDS victims, all were foisted upon or fetched up in our parish for sustenance and free medical treatment.

When I was a teenager my mother would not have gone shopping down Eastbourne's main thoroughfare - its aptly named Terminus Road - without wearing a hat and gloves. Although the South Downs, Friston Forest, and some of the town's remoter environs still remain quite glorious and 'nice people' with proper values still exercise their dogs there, one

88

hesitates to go down into the town's same Terminus Road today without a knuckleduster. It is as if the decrepit, sub-human contents of some failed medical experiment, or an asylum, have been emptied into the Arndale Centre and stirred; or that the Star Wars cocktail bar clientele have taken over the town. Tattooed yobs and slobs with metal face furniture abound. Sartorial degradation and lack of personal grooming are rife. English has become almost a foreign language. There are no decent pubs. There is only one restaurant in town that works, and that's run by Italians who quite rightly refuse to employ a single Brit on their staff. The roads are lined with parking meters impeding trade, and the town no longer has any heart or soul, both of which have been torn out of it and uncaringly discarded. Eastbourne today has become a very, *very* sorry town.

Back in the 1950s though, when it still possessed charm, it was a clean town and one that started to gain increasing popularity with foreign students who wanted to come over to England to learn English. Burgeoning language schools abounded and many local families made a few pounds putting these students up under the guise of broadening the minds of their own children while enabling them to pick up some French or German into the bargain. Our family was no exception. We jumped on the band wagon along with everyone else.

My mother's first venture was to house quite a nice little chap, the sixteen-year-old *Comte* Alain de Bartillat whom she thought was a charming lad. Next time round she slipped up a bit though. Jean Lefèbvre, an industrialist's son from Roubaix in Northern France was a buffoon, a great galumphing galoot of a fellow after whose stay mother reverted to needlework for her pin money.

Despite having these two boys to live with us throughout their respective summers I acquired no particular proficiency in French - until the following year. That is when I met and fell in love with sixteen-year-old Monique Cecile Boyer. Monique came from a then little known fishing village in the South of France, called St Tropez. Monique - who against tremendous odds successfully managed to retain her virginity that summer - would be about seventy now, and quite possibly either divorced or widowed. Perhaps I should have stayed in touch. But the result of her six week sojourn in the south of England that summer (I regret to say with another family, not ours) is that I then came top in the whole of Sussex in the GCE French oral exam, whereas today I can probably manage just about sufficient French, German and Spanish to land me in gaol but not enough to get me out of it.

The same as then, the mass of foreign students who now invade the town each summer still flock in from their lodgings every evening to meet and congregate outside the railway station. Many of them are undoubtedly the *grand*children of the very girls who used to wait for us in the self same spot. Many are the international relationships that were spawned on those railings. Often when I have been overseas on a Sunday and bored with nothing to do and/or homesick I have found myself wandering down to the harbour to watch the big ships and think of home. All over Germany I noticed during off-duty hours the *Hauptbahnofs* had groups of *Gastarbeiters* standing lonely and aimless around the various kiosks, such points of arrival and departure having a compelling focalisation about them for strangers in a strange land.

For very many years my previously mentioned lifelong friend, Michael Ockenden, who wrote *Canucks By The Sea,* ran a very successful Eastbourne Language School with his friend David Ashdown. This I am sure was because he had a desire to 'communicate'. Michael was a radio nut at school and so gravitated quite naturally into the ACF's Signals Section. While I was banging away on the back field working up a storm with my bugles, drums and The Mace, he and his cronies would sit up in the Signals Room in the attic huddled round a radio set like the Gaumont organ intoning: *'Hallo Dirty Dog One, this is Charlie'* to some Yugoslavian fishing smack up the Amazon. The complexity of static and atmospherics left me baffled but it appealed to Michael big time. He passed all his exams and became a radio officer in the Merchant Navy. Later he joined the RAF and then with his attractive German wife, Micki, returned to Eastbourne to open his language school. At one stage the roof of his house used to resemble a BBC relay station with all its different masts and wires. There was nothing more fascinating than to see him sit down, twiddle his knobs, tune in, and start talking about the weather to that other well known radio ham King Hussein of Jordan whilst concurrently clapping one earphone to his head and tapping out a quick-fire message in Morse to the signals officer of a Liberian tanker in the Caribbean while at the same time stirring his coffee with a pencil.

*

Looking at our 1954 school photograph recently - 300 young blades on the threshold of life - I reckon that even now, over half-a-century later, so strong are the impressions made during our formative years that I could still name two-thirds of those five ranks of tousle-haired peers, young hopefuls kneeling on the grass or seated with those behind standing on raised tiers of gym benches and chairs, sporting their varying degrees of sartorial inelegance.

Eastbourne Grammar School wasn't East Moulscoomb Secondary Modern, nor was it Eton or Harrow, so we represented a pretty good middle-piece cross section of Young Britain at the time. Unlike today a much smaller percentage of the nation's more academically gifted youth managed to get itself up to university back then, but several of ours did. We had still others make it through Sandhurst, Cranwell and Dartmouth - one of us even going on to become a vice-admiral and one time Surgeon General of the armed forces. We also produced several vicars, scientists and professors, musicians, and assorted entrepreneurs, as well as our own fair share of crooks, vagabonds and dropouts, social misfits, cranks and British Rail ticket collectors. Oh - and me.

My own particular 'Gang' at school was about twelve strong - pubescent young guys who found they rubbed along fairly well together, fancied the same groups of girls, laughed at the same jokes and situations, and all came from pretty much the same family backgrounds. There were Denis and Eric, the Leroy twins; Pete Hoadley, Dickie Fountain, Dickie Moon, Robin Frost, Brian York, Jack Revell, 'Squiz' Squires, Michael Ockenden, and my special chum - Colin Wright - and although today we enjoy a widely publicised and thriving 600-strong old boys' association which lunches together every November my friend Colin has never yet been located or re-emerged from the mists of time, so whether he still lives or has sadly departed I know not.

Whilst I had been bugling, drumming, and working my way up through the ranks of our ACF band to become the greatest Drum Major the world had ever seen, our bass drummer was an extremely pleasant VIth former called John Franklin. John was also a senior prefect and for our varnished and gold-lettered school notice board he used to sign his official prefectorial pronouncements with rather a distinctive and flourishing signature.

Fifteen years later when I was in the army and serving as a corps troops' adjutant in Germany a missive landed on my desk in Bielefeld one day whose signature was instantly familiar to me. This time it was not the usual notice bidding the IVth Form Thespian Society to report to the music room tomorrow lunchtime for play rehearsal, but still the unmistakeable signature's author unquestionably had to be one and the same. With an excitedly palpitating heart I could hardly wait to do something about it, to trace and locate the unit and re-establish contact with the writer; but before then - as so often happens - Fate herself contrived to intervene.

When I was leaving 1st British Corps Headquarters at lunchtime that very same day a well known figure with a familiar gait and face strode jauntily across the road and came bounding up the HQ steps towards me intent on entering the building. Wearing BAOR's summer shirt-sleeve order he was no longer carrying his bass drum with him, just his bamboo swagger cane and the shiny gold pips and red-backed crowns of a lieutenant colonel on his epaulettes. *'John Franklin,'* I loudly hailed him. He skidded abruptly to a halt and did a series of amazed double takes, and then once the recognition and mental processing had clicked into place much hand pumping and back slapping ensued. It was just like Monty bumping into Alexander on the steps of GHQ Cairo, although it is unlikely they would have got quite as pie-eyed as John and I did together later that evening. Now both in our seventies we still see each other at our school annual reunion occasionally and happily relive this experience.

Another reunion I had is the one that never was. This was with our school's freckle-faced carrot-top, one 'Ginger' Courts. 'Ginger' used to clash cymbals in the school band. It was a Saturday night in 1957 in Hong Kong when I was staging through on my way up to Korea. Nathan Road was so packed with teeming humanity that it made Oxford Street at Christmas look like some village lane. Bobbing above the milling crowds of Chinese I suddenly saw the unmistakeable head of 'Ginger' Courts being hurriedly swept along towards me like a log in a mill-race. The nearer he drew I was hardly able to contain myself with excitement, until at last we arrived abreast with one and other. *'Ginger'* I cried, anticipating his amazement and joy when he saw me, and so reaching instinctively out towards him.

'Oh, it's you; hallo,' he said, stern-facedly acknowledging me just once before disappearing off towards China never to be seen or heard of again. With my hand still outstretched I stood open-mouthed with pain and disbelief. Perhaps I should be charitable. Maybe he was being chased by the police or some tong or other.

*

On Friday nights, after a hard week at school my (sometimes) doting mother would kindly indulge my three essential whims: clean sheets, a bath - and a steak for supper. Then on Saturday mornings it was on with the glad rags and off down the town to meet The Gang at Drago's Bun Lounge to plan the day's activity by sussing out what parties were on that night. That was in autumn, winter and in spring. Long before Thailand had become so popular or Alex Garland had even been thought of, in summer we would foregather on The Beach. *Hoi-polloi* or mixing with the trippers round the pier were not for us; oh, no - instead we elected to move westward to one of the secluded and infinitely more refined pebbles of a beach along at the posher Holywell end of town in Meads. Eastbourne Borough Council had allocated each beach a number, screwed on a small plate to its breakwater. We lot opted to frequent beach number six, thereby appointing ourselves The Beach Six Society and promptly setting about ensuring in various subtle ways that there was seldom anyone but us on it. Here we romped and jostled, sunbathed and swam, posed and practised flirting with our young womenfolk who were struggling alongside us with all the hormonal changes of their own burgeoning sexuality to contend with. We also pretended to be studying for our GCE exams.

From Dewsbury, in Yorkshire, at this time there arrived in Eastbourne the town's new Chief Constable, a gentleman called Dick Walker who as well as the rather formidable Mrs Walker brought with him their two daughters, Elizabeth and Susan. Elizabeth was way out of our league, being almost twenty, but her younger sister Sue was the same age as us and one of the most graceful and eye-catching of creatures young blood could ever hope to behold. Seeming to me to be a cut above our other girls and making me feel quite gauche and inadequate in her presence she excited me enormously with her aura of unavailability. She was like a princess who seemed to want to play with us village kids, without either side really knowing how to bridge the gap. Sue was an enigma. Hence a challenge. I did venture to walk her home from a party once and later took her to the cinema a couple of times but never would I have dreamed of trying any sort of clumsy grope such as those experimental grabs I'd enjoyed earlier with 'Bumpers' in the *Picturedrome*. Hitherto my birds had all been stalwart beer mugs, whereas I felt Susan to be more like a Dresden tea-cup. (Later she told me that she'd wanted to be treated like a beer mug all along, but was shy).

Out of the blue one Thursday afternoon (studying for GCE)

Beach Six was taken over by a busload of happy holidaymakers, all down on a works' outing from the Midlands. Assuming an air of sullen affront at this invasion the Beach Six Society and I huddled by the breakwater, a morose group of seething resentment idly lobbing rocks intermittently at the sea while the interloping visitors rearranged our pebbles and ruined the whole day for us.

Eventually they packed up and went home but Enough was Enough. Although several ideas were bandied about, none of us really had any idea what could actually be done about it but it was decided that a recurrence definitely could not be tolerated. Besides, it might affect our exam results.

Da-da-dee-dum.

Along came our two Superheroes to the rescue.

That evening Denis Leroy and I set about acquiring two stout brushes and a gallon of red paint from somewhere or other, returned stealthily to Beach Six at dusk and across a 30′ stretch of its extremely absorbent concrete wall commenced to daub in three-feet high capital letters the message:-

RESERVED FOR RESIDENTS ONLY: TRIPPERS GO HOME

Possibly not a terribly contentious sentiment by today's standards of graffiti but for us it was quite exciting . . .

. . . and so it proved to be.

The dehydrated and porous concrete hissed and sucked the paint thirstily to its core. Denis and I cackled hysterically over what we had so daringly done, thinking what a terrific wheeze it was and how impressed all our friends would be when they saw it next day.

Tired and paint-stained we set off home like two abattoir employees at the end of slaughtering day.

That night I had bad dreams.

While processing the day's events my subconscious was having second thoughts about what we'd done.

Great scarlet banners leaped across my brain.

At 5.00 a.m. I got up, hurriedly dressed and tiptoed quickly downstairs to let myself quietly out of the door, climbed onto my bike and cycled as fast as I could – time was of the essence

- round to Denis's house. He was up too. We conferred.

'Suppose we'd better do something about removing it,' we agreed.

Yes - but how?

'What the hell with, though?' we asked each other, desperate for ideas.

'Soap and water won't do it. It'll have to be some kind of spirit,' suggested Denis.

'Yeah, but it's only 5.30 a.m. The shops don't open till 9.0 a.m. and we've got school today in any case.'

'*I* know what we can do,' said Denis suddenly, and tiptoed back inside his house.

Two minutes later he re-emerged with a duster and a five-fluid-ounce bottle of Cutex nail varnish remover purloined as if by a thief in the night from his mother's dressing table while she still slept.

With hope springing eternal we jumped onto our bikes and pedalled furiously off back to Beach Six again.

The English Channel looked like a gunmetal millpond.

The horizon was etched the colour of a blood orange.

The sky was an eggshell blue.

It was going to be one stinking hot summer's day again.

Denis was first down the wooden steps onto the beach with me close behind.

We both groaned - *'Oh, my God.'*

By daylight it was clear to see the enormity of what we had done.

It had seemed like a good idea at the time.

Now we weren't so sure.

Our friends would certainly be impressed alright but how many of them would prove their mettle by visiting us in Young Offenders' Custody we didn't know.

Enormous red letters shrieked from the beach wall. They were so stark and compelling that their dappled reflections in the gently lapping tide looked like the glowing flames of a sacked city. They were probably visible in France. From outer space they might even have upstaged the Great Wall of China. We viewed our handiwork in dumb silence, like a couple who had just paid an artist £5,000,000 for a commission which when unveiled is considered appalling.

'Come on,' said Denis, unscrewing the five-fluid-ounces of Cutex and wrapping the duster round his right finger. 'We'd better make a start . . .'

Hardly surprising, it only took about half of one frustrating minute for us to realise and accept the fact that with only one bottle of ladies' nail varnish remover the whole Sisyphean task was utterly beyond us.

We gave up resignedly and skulked off, me to do my paper round and Denis to complete some unfinished homework before breakfast and going off to school.

It was W.C. Fields who once said: 'If at first you don't succeed, try again; but then give up. There's no point in being a bloody fool about it.'

Sufficient unto the day the evil thereof.

We would worry about the consequences of our foolhardy action as-and-when.

After all, no one had seen us.

It was quite possible we might even get away with it.

When I came home from school at 4.30 p.m. that day my mother was standing inside the door waiting for me.

'Bath; hair wash; best clothes; five minutes,' she commanded.

I got the message.

We'd been rumbled.

When I was ready she inspected me and said: 'I understand that you indulged in a bit of vandalism last night.'

In her inimitable fashion she had found out.

'I've telephoned the Chief Constable,' she went on, 'and as a special favour to me as a hard-pressed single-parent mother struggling to survive he has agreed to grant you an interview before you most likely go to prison. (*Cheeeze*, I thought: we were right: it *was* serious). You and that Leroy boy have both got to be in his office at 5.00 p.m. so you'd better get a move on hadn't you. *MOVE.*'

I moved.

Slinging my bike up against the Police Station wall I presented myself sheepishly (for the first time ever) at the front desk where a whey-faced Denis was already waiting. 'Your mother?' he asked. I nodded. 'Mine too,' he said.

The Duty Constable told us to stand by the wall, against a background of clanging cell doors and crackling radio messages. After a short wait a burly shirt-sleeved sergeant came to take us up to the grandest office in the building and opened the door to usher us in. We entered. There like a moustachioed Solomon at his desk by the window sat Susan's father, Eastbourne's commanding and all-powerful Chief Constable - Dick Walker. This was in the days when our police force was still revered and respected and earned these sentiments.

'Hallo Michael,' he said severely but pleasantly enough given the circumstances. 'Hallo Denis. Won't you please both come in and sit down?'

He was firm, fair and fatherly. The upshot was that Denis and I were invited (!) to report to the already informed Borough Engineer's Department within the next half-an-hour seeing as it was Friday, where we would draw up the necessary stores and equipment needed to remove the results of our unappreciated first foray into the art world. We were given until sundown the following day to complete our task. Thank God it would be Saturday.

The Borough Engineer's Yard was a heavy-duty DIY man's paradise. Denis's bike was laden down with a large bucket and two vicious wire brushes, while my own cross-bar was festooned like a tinker pony's pannier with several industrial cans of paint remover. By the time we had trundled this lot into storage for the night my best clothes were plastered more gungily about me than my new grey shorts had been when hauling myself out of the tar after getting machine-gunned by the *Focke-Wulf* back in the summer of '42.

Next morning, Saturday, we awoke to a rose-pink Egyptian dawn heralding another blistering hot day ahead. By 8.00 a.m. Denis and I were already on the beach hard at it. Clad only in our swimming trunks, plimsoles and filthy protective leather gauntlets like those worn by WWII tank drivers, we had already sloshed paint remover into the bucket and were attacking the first three-foot high R of RESERVED FOR RESIDENTS ONLY: TRIPPERS GO HOME like zealots with a cause. By 8.30 a.m. we were sweating like piglets. Our cramped and weakening grips loosened on the coarse handles of the wire brushes. Our bodies were soaked, smudged with grime and stinging from spirit splashings. Our arms and back muscles screamed at us. The sun beat down across our shoulders like an iron bar. Not so much as a blur had dispelled either the deep penetration or the glaring clarity of RESERVED FOR RESIDENTS ONLY etc., the permanence of which was obviously going to realise the hopes of the Third Reich and the reality of the Pyramids. The two wire brushes dangled listlessly from our wrists. We looked at each other with utter helplessness. Violins whimpered in the soundtracks of our minds. We were two whipped kids.

Word had somehow spread of course.

By 9.30 a.m. most of The Gang had arrived, with our female support group in tow, i.e. a full turn out of The Beach Six Society. Seemingly in their hundreds the two dozen or so of them tumbled noisily down onto the beach. Their tumult instantly ceased at what they saw. They were awestruck with our handiwork. Like an inscrutable sphinx RESERVED FOR RESIDENTS ONLY etc. stared immutably down at them, over the beach and out across the Channel to France. They shuffled with respect at what Denis and I had done but then perceiving our spent and abject forms they grinned with relief that it was not they who had been socked in the ear with the banana. With Denis and me still the focal point of their attention they then left us to our misery and dispersed happily to swim, sunbathe and lounge along the beach wall coining witticisms at our expense. Denis and I felt like court jesters under pain of death to perform. The girls' presence spurred us to renewed effort but the effort was to no avail. We were both done for. After Dawn Hickman (principal groupie) had sidled over in her black bikini to bring us a very welcome tomato sandwich and a slug of orange squash each, we collapsed onto

1. The dear little chap who on several occasions Hitler tried to machine-gun . . .

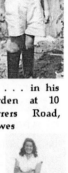

2. . . . in his garden at 10 Ferrers Road, Lewes

3. A part of the Beach 6 Society: and about half the wall that was later emblazoned with **RESERVED FOR RESIDENTS ONLY** . . . some of the post-cleansing striations of lettering can still faintly be seen

4. Those were the days . . .!

5. Sue

6. Monique Boyer (aged 16 – now 70) who helped me pass my French oral

7. Eastbourne Grammar School Cadet Corps Band (1952) - Sgt Roy Fielder (Drum Major - *centre*) with L/Cpl John Franklin next to him wearing his white leather bass-drum apron – later a Lt Col with whom the author served in BAOR. The author? The 14-year-old bugle-boy standing *(R)* behind and between them. 'Ginger' Courts (chased by Hong-Kong tongs) *3rd left centre row*

8. Just passed my French oral

9. Dad

10. My brother, Tony,
Cape Town - 1957

12. From young
drummer boy, to . . .

13. . . . the greatest Drum
Major in the history of the
world – EGS ACF -1953

11. Mum, Cape Town - 1957

the beach and accepted defeat. It was 9.45 a.m.

At 10.00 a.m., as if by magic three council operatives suddenly turned up with sand blasters to do the job properly for us.

Dick Walker knew his stuff alright.

We had paid our penance with a vengeance.

We would not err again.

When I returned to Eastbourne twenty years later, I took a nostalgic stroll down to Beach Six to see how much of it had changed. It hadn't, not very much. What's more, struggling for expression through the concrete wall like weeds growing through the runway of a disused airfield I was still able to perceive a blurred and indistinct dull red outline suggesting that once upon a time this beach had . . . almost . . . been RESERVED FOR RES . . . (etc).

My name may not liveth for evermore but it seemed that some of my misguided teenage handiwork might.

Despite my professional brush with her father the reticence I felt over the possibility of initiating some sort of relationship with Susan dissolved over the ensuing months. We became quite 'an item' and grew extremely fond of each other. I became an ever more regular visitor to her parents' house in Old Orchard Road. Mrs Walker used to feed us delicious fruit cake and coffee while Susan sat like the princess she was, playing me classical music on their drawing room piano. I was hooked. For the first time in my life I felt the pangs of true love and enjoyed the whole silly feeling of it enormously. Dick Walker gave me the impression that he wasn't too keen on the arrangement, but my courting of his daughter had commenced the week he initiated the Doctor John Bodkin-Adams murder enquiry. The media was just about to floodlight the whole case for the world so he was understandably slightly preoccupied. It wasn't until I met Susan again years later that she told me it was her mother who had not really been in favour of our relationship but had decided not to not oppose it in the hope that it would run its course (which it did) and that I would soon leave to seek my fortune in the Maldives, or even further afield than that - whereas her father had apparently been quite tickled by my painting venture and had told her it was just the sort of thing he would have got up to as a boy.

*

By now it was Christmas 1955.

Despite the distractions from our Beach Six Society Study Group I had managed to acquire five GCE 'O' Level passes. I had just left school and was kicking my heels wondering what to do until my eighteenth birthday in six months time when I was due to be called-up to do my two years compulsory National Service.

Remember these lines?

There's a breathless hush in the Close tonight
Ten to make and the match to win
A bumping pitch and a blinding light,
An hour to play, and the last man in.
And it's not for the sake of a ribboned coat
Or the selfish hope of a season's fame,
But his captain's hand on his shoulder smote
'Play up! Play up! And play the game!'

The sand of the desert is sodden red —
Red with the wreck of the square that broke
The Gatling's jammed and the colonel's dead,
And the regiment's blind with dust and smoke.
The river of death has brimmed its banks,
And England's far, and Honour a name,
But the voice of a schoolboy rallies the ranks —
'Play up! Play up! And play the game!'

Sir Henry Newbolt's famous poem 'Vitaï Lampada' (Light of Life) refers to how a future soldier learns about stoicism by playing cricket on the famous nineteenth century Close of

103

Bristol's Clifton College. What is less well known are the facts that the Square that broke, the Gatling that jammed (was poetic licence: it was actually a Gardner gun) and the Colonel who was dead (when in fact he wasn't: artistic licence) referred to The Royal Sussex Regiment fighting at the Battle of Abu Klea, which took place on 17th January 1885 in the Sudan - a battle at which during one critical point there was furious hand-to-hand fighting with bayonets, many of which were substandard and bent on impact. (Sound familiar?) The regiment was part of Gladstone's and General Sir Garnet *'The Very Model Of A Modern Major-General'* Wolsely's 10,000-strong Desert Column, transported up the Nile in 800 small boats shipped out from England to supplement the steamers that had been provided locally by a then fledgling travel company called Thomas Cook, in its vain attempt to relieve General Gordon, besieged by the Mahdi's jihad-crazed dervish warriors at Khartoum. Exciting stuff for me to reflect upon before I too went off to don my woollen khaki battledress and by a whisker catch some of the tail end of the Raj as Great Britain commenced withdrawal from her Imperial commitments and the last embers of our once glorious Empire finally flickered and died.

Between its commencement in 1945 and its cessation in 1963 when the last National Serviceman was discharged (2/Lt Richard Vaughan of the Royal Army Pay Corps on Thursday 16th May that year), at a rate of 6,000 reporting for training at various military (and to a lesser extent RN and RAF) establishments every second Thursday throughout the 18-years of its existence, over two-million young men between the ages of 18 and 26 'participated' in National Service - 35,000 of them becoming commissioned officers - in 26 different theatres of operations. Alphabetically these either had been or would be Aden, Austria, China, Cyprus; Egypt, Eritrea, Gambia; Gibraltar; Gold Coast and Hong Kong; India, Indonesia, Japan and Kenya; Korea, Libya and Malaya; Nigeria, Palestine, Pakistan and Sarawak; Sierra Leone, Trieste and USSR, West Germany - and the West Indies. By 1956 most of these locations were shutting down like deleted computer icons but perhaps there would still be just time for me to realise the long-cherished image of myself springing down the gangway of a gleaming white troopship, a lean, mean fighting machine, fit as whipcord, sun-tanned from serving in one or other of these exotic climes, homeward bound at last with my worn but rugged kitbag slung manfully on one shoulder and a colourful parrot squawking in its cage for my mother.

In January 1956 I decided there was no point in hanging about kicking my heels so I pre-empted the event.

Catching the train from Eastbourne over to Brighton one day - when Brighton was still a town and not yet the self-styled city she has since become - I walked into the Army Recruiting Office there and signed on as a three-year regular. This was a scheme designed to appeal to and attract the more aimless of us early, whereby we could do six months service this side of our eighteenth birthdays and then six months at the other end, meaning they would get three years sweat out of us instead of two for just a little bit of extra dosh each week.

My childhood days and schooling were now over.

I was seventeen-and-a-half.

At last my time had come to take the Queen's shilling.

TOMMY

Rudyard Kipling (1865-1936)

I went into a public-'ouse to get a pint o' beer,
The publican 'e up an' sez, "We serve no red-coats here."
The girls be'ind the bar they laughed an' giggled fit to die,
I outs into the street again an' to myself sez I:
O it's Tommy this, an' Tommy that, an' "Tommy, go away";
But it's "Thank you, Mister Atkins", when the band begins to play,
The band begins to play, my boys, the band begins to play,
O it's "Thank you, Mister Atkins", when the band begins to play.

I went into a theatre as sober as could be,
They gave a drunk civilian room, but 'adn't none for me;
They sent me to the gallery or round the music-'alls,
But when it comes to fightin', Lord! they'll shove me in the stalls!
For it's Tommy this, an' Tommy that, an' "Tommy, wait outside";
But it's "Special train for Atkins" when the trooper's on the tide,
The troopship's on the tide, my boys, the troopship's on the tide,
O it's "Special train for Atkins" when the trooper's on the tide.

Yes, makin' mock o' uniforms that guard you while you sleep
Is cheaper than them uniforms, an' they're starvation cheap;
An' hustlin' drunken soldiers when they're goin' large a bit
Is five times better business than paradin' in full kit.
Then it's Tommy this, an' Tommy that, an' "Tommy, 'ow's yer soul?"
But it's "Thin red line of 'eroes" when the drums begin to roll,
The drums begin to roll, my boys, the drums begin to roll,
O it's "Thin red line of 'eroes" when the drums begin to roll.

We aren't no thin red 'eroes, nor we aren't no blackguards too,
But single men in barricks, most remarkable like you;
An' if sometimes our conduck isn't all your fancy paints,
Why, single men in barricks don't grow into plaster saints;
While it's Tommy this, an' Tommy that, an' "Tommy, fall be'ind",
But it's "Please to walk in front, sir", when there's trouble in the wind,
There's trouble in the wind, my boys, there's trouble in the wind,
O it's "Please to walk in front, sir", when there's trouble in the wind.

You talk o' better food for us, an' schools, an' fires, an' all:
We'll wait for extry rations if you treat us rational.
Don't mess about the cook-room slops, but prove it to our face
The Widow's Uniform is not the soldier-man's disgrace.
For it's Tommy this, an' Tommy that, an' "Chuck him out, the brute!"
But it's "Saviour of 'is country" when the guns begin to shoot;
An' it's Tommy this, an' Tommy that, an' anything you please;
An' Tommy ain't a bloomin' fool -- you bet that Tommy sees!

ELEVEN

'GET YER BLEEDIN' 'AIR CUT,' roared the florid-faced Provost Corporal 'Buster' Bates, barely ten seconds after I had entered the portals of the Royal Sussex Regiment's Roussillon Barracks dépôt on Broyle Road in Chichester for the first time and stood shell-shocked in front of him there on the Guard Room verandah with my small suitcase of meagre belongings at my feet while he eyeballed and snorted saliva at me like a Channel swimmer *in extremis.*

A Sussex man by birth it was naturally my 250-year-old County Regiment of 'South Saxon' foot-soldiers to which I instinctively gravitated with whom to serve.

By opting to do 22-years (with a recurring three-year demob option) instead of just doing the usual mandatory two years I was going to receive the princely sum of seven-shillings a day remuneration as opposed to the poor old National Serviceman's meagre four-shillings - and an extra dollop of jam on my bread at tea-time.

The now vaguely remembered inducement definitely seemed worthwhile at the time but would doubtless appear derisory today. My seven-shillings a day (£6 today when the minimum wage is £5.20 *an hour*) amounted to £2.50 a week or £10 a month (£127 a year) which today would equate to getting £42 a week (£182 a month) or £2,184 a year. You may have to read that bit again. What it means is there were not many soldiers in my day driving Ferraris, whereas these days a 'still *under*paid' private soldier picks up . . . not £2,184 . . . but £16,000 a year. The equivalent amount to this in my day would have been £930 a year . . . not the £127 we *did* get; or £17 a week – *then* - rather than just those measly £2. And I was a Regular. A National Serviceman only got four-shillings a day; £4 a month (£96 today); £48 a year = £1,159 at today's value. *And* we had to pay for our own haircuts and Brasso . . . but because we knew no better and everyone was in the same boat, although we were always short of money and whinged about it we were cheerful enough about our lot.

It was Monday 30th January 1956. I had caught the train from Brighton and walked the mile-and-a-half through pouring rain up from Chichester Station to the famous Broyle Road barracks. Back in those days taxis were a luxurious non-option utilised only by lords, ladies and the super-rich.

'You are 'an *'orrible* little man,' went on the persistently obnoxious Corporal Bates. *'What* are you?'

'I rather thought that I was a new recruit, reporting for training. I . . .'

'Don't you DARE fuckin' answer me back like that you smart-arsed little git. Whaddya trying to be? Some fuckin' comedian or sunfink?' he screamed, banging his heavy provost corporal's cane and stamping his right boot so apoplectically onto the concrete in time with his meaningless tirade that I was concerned lest he self immolate or otherwise expire on the spot. He looked like an overweight Adolph Hitler doing a jig. *'I told you: You are an 'orrible little man.* Now — *WHAT are you?'*

I still hadn't caught on.

If you are confronted by a screeching drunk you don't comply with his demands. You humour him.

'I am a three-year regular reporting for . . .'

'Jeesuz H. Fuckin' CHRIST . . . I will fuckin' *KILL* you if you don't fuckin' . . .'

'What seems to be the trouble here C'orl Bates?'

Speaking with a languid public school drawl and with one solitary pip straining for self expression on each epaulette, my saviour, a real, live second lieutenant, the duty officer, had at that moment come strolling round the corner of the guardroom, the cuffs of his battledress blouse affectedly turned back to reveal a red polka-dot snuff rag tucked into the wrist of one of them. Flicking his leather-clad swagger cane indolently against the outside of his immaculately creased right calf, at three-o'clock on a Monday afternoon he was probably bored and with nothing better to do had fortuitously appeared like my knight on a white charger to save me, another virgin squaddie.

'I was just telling this man 'ere to get 'is 'air cut *SAH,*' screeched Corporal Bates, smacking his cane smartly up under his left arm, smashing himself to shuddering attention and flinging up one *snorter* of a quivering salute. It was a ridiculous charade which we've all of us either experienced or read about or seen at the cinema many, many times since those days and it is absurdly amusing to write about it in retrospect but at the time it wasn't funny. If someone addressed you like that today, flaming eyeballs protruding on stalks, their face puce with simulated and completely unjustified indignation, the cords, sinews and carotid arteries in their neck straining and pulsating fit to explode, it would usually presage the administration of a vicious head butt from a deranged psychopath. But back then in the days of National Service it was the perfectly normal and expected manner for NCOs to address their underlings. There *was* no other way. No other language. It was the parlance of common currency. The only medium of communication.

'It already looks pretty short to me,' the delightful officer remarked, briefly taking me in and managing a quick little smile. 'Very well C'orl Bates. Well done. That'll be all thank you. Carry on please. This chap needs to report to the Orderly Room doesn't he. I'm going that way myself so I'll take him across.'

'Very good - *SAH.*' (Crash; bang; wallop). Salute.

'Whereabouts are you from?' the young officer asked, indicating that I should pick up my case and walk with him.

'Eastbourne – er - Sir.'

If one was possessed of a modicum of intelligence it didn't

take too long to tune-in to the requirements of army-speak.

'Oh really? I think my grandmother lives somewhere down there.'

'Lots of them do. Er - Sir.'

'Sir' was probably no more than a year older than me and like me with indoor watercress was obviously having great difficulty growing his moustache.

'Quite so,' he smiled. 'This is the Orderly Room.'

We had walked only a few yards and were now standing outside a clutch of green painted Napoleonic-era wooden huts. 'You'll need to report to Colour Sergeant Griffiths, the Chief Clerk. I'll take you in . . .

'. . . Afternoon Chief: Here's another new boy for you. Feel like processing him?'

'Very well Sir,' said a dapper little chappy, each sleeve of his khaki battledress blouse bearing the three gleaming white stripes surmounted by a crown denoting the rank insignia of a colour sergeant, plus a colourful chestful of ribbons of course. 'Leave him to us Sir; we'll get him shoved through alright.'

'Thanks Chief.' Then turning to me he said: 'Best of luck. I expect we'll be bumping into each other again sometime later.' And with that he saluted, leaving the office to go and wander off round the camp to try to find something else to do between then and tea-time.

'Why on earth did he salute me?' I asked, flattered and rather surprised by the extremely pleasant gesture.

'He didn't salute *you*, you bloody idiot,' the Chief Clerk snorted with derisive disbelief. He saluted the office. Don't ask me why but whenever an officer enters or departs from an office he salutes. It's some sort of formal courtesy that originated way back when in the mists of time somewhere, probably spawned from something funny that was meant to have happened in history sometime, like King Alfred burning his cakes, or the soles of his feet, or whatever it was he was meant to have done. Although what that's got to do with anything, I wouldn't have a clue. I'm Colour Sergeant Griffiths. And you are - ?'

'I'm a horrible little man.'

110

'I'm quite sure you are sonny,' he continued unperturbed; 'but now I would appreciate it if you would hand over your documents if you would be so kind.'

I fished in my jacket pocket to produce for him my Attestation Papers from Brighton's Queen's Road Recruiting Office where earlier that day, Monday 30th January 1956, I had been 'sworn in' as a 22-year regular with a tri-ennual demob option by one retired Lt Col Flower, with a bristling moustache and cigarette ash down the front of his brass-buttoned blazer: my Marching Orders and Medical Certificate, confirming that among other indignities that had been foisted upon me three weeks previously in a drafty room over in Brighton's Preston Barracks' Medical Centre I had stood naked and managed to cough successfully without any further troublesome ado - and the stub of my travel warrant.

'Right; well now: I'm afraid we're going to have a bit of a problem with you my lad. You see, you're not your normal run-of-the-mill National Service recruit what we're used to, who's been called up in a batch and told to report here at a specific time ready to be processed through our still slightly rough-at-the-edges but nevertheless well-honed sausage machine production line. You've signed on as a three-year reg'lar. We don't get many of your sort. You're a one-off. An individual; which rather suggests to me that this is prob'ly what you're going to be like for the rest of your life, isn't it, 'spectin' special treatment an' that. The best table wherever you go. A plush velveteen box wiv crimson broffel-fittings at the featre . . .'

The term gobsmacked not yet having entered the lexicon it is fair to say that I was nonplussed. Where was this man coming from?

Subsequently I divined what might have been coursing through C/Sgt Grifiths's mind. The array of medal ribbons denoted that he was a wartime soldier. With a long memory.

Back in January 1942 a 21-year-old actor by the name of Peter Ustinov had been called up and posted to the Royal Sussex Regiment here in Chichester. When he appeared before the War Office Selection Board to undergo assessment for officer hood, the verdict had been: 'On no account is this man to be put in charge of others'.

6411623 Private Ustinov P. appeared surprised that the Army failed to recognise his talents, though he later extracted much comic material from its foolishness. 'I can tell you frankly that I loathed every minute,' he said of his military career, 'and would not have missed it for the world.'

Ustinov's first play *'House of Regrets'* - a Chekhovian evocation he had written about elderly White Russians in London - opened to favourable reviews at the Arts Theatre in October 1942. Unfortunately his Royal Sussex CO at the time had been short sighted enough to refuse the young author his formally requested permission to attend his own Opening Night. This debatably wrong decision being completely unacceptable to him Private Ustinov naturally went AWOL for a few hours to attend the event.

Later that evening to the cries of 'Author; author . . .' the young Ustinov appeared on stage to receive the public's acclaim and plaudits which theatre critics of the day duly printed - along with photographs of him - in their next morning's editions.

Having thus cocked a snoot at authority Ustinov was scarcely surprised to find himself hauled up in front of his CO a couple of days later to receive his expected roasting and to learn the extent of his retribution. The punishment he was awarded would have been recorded on his documents somewhere at the time but is otherwise not recalled. What is remembered is the actor/author's surprise when his CO said: 'I am not awarding you this punishment solely for disobeying my order but for the blatant committal of your other offence. I simply will not *tolerate* a private soldier of mine having the temerity to appear in public on a West End *stage* wearing suede shoes with battledress. March the prisoner out S'Arnt Major.'

Sir Peter might well have received his award in this same office I was standing in now; and quite probably did. A pathetic coke fire flickered in a miniscule black iron grate. Trestle tables piled with toppling pink and buff files lined the walls. Three pasty looking clerks sat hunched and pecking over their black sit-up-and-beg Remington typewriters which clacked and *thunked* as they struggled to select and rearrange their QWERTYs into some correct semblance of order. Over in a corner a L/Cpl was struggling to wrap a waxed stencil round the drum of an ink-filled Roneo machine prior to hand-cranking off a requisite number of the following day's Part One Orders, the daily unit bible which detailed where everyone should be and what they should be doing at any given time during the day. *God* - it is unbelievable . . . the privations we had to endure in the way we used to live back in those pre-technological times before photocopiers!

'Alright George? No need to stand there like a tit in a trance,' C/Sgt Griffiths admonished me. 'We've finished with you in here. You can now go across to the QM Stores and get yourself issued with your kit.'

It was an undignified balancing act.

Think of a housewife folding a pastry pasty containing a variety of meat and veg items to pop in the oven and then magnify the size of that considerably. A tough, almost unbendable straw mattress was the pasty, its meat and veg being two pillows and pillowcases, two bed sheets, a mattress cover and three rough grey blankets; two pairs of hobnailed boots and gaiters, two sets of battledress, two hairy shirts, vests, pants, and socks; two pairs of denims, belts, braces and pouches; a small pack, large pack, and a water bottle; two pairs of pyjamas, two khaki towels, a tin mug, mess tins, knife, fork and spoon; a set of tin plates, a small canvas holdall containing needles and thread (called a 'housewife'), a button stick (used to slide behind buttons to keep Brasso off your uniform when polishing) and a navy-blue beret with its accompanying Roussillon Plume cap badge; a coarse, coir bedside mat; a tin hat, a waterproof groundsheet (called a poncho), a necktie, and a soap dish with a lid - much of which (and there was more) had to be crammed into a kitbag, all of which was rolled up in the mattress and staggeringly carried buckle-kneed for a couple of hundred yards across the square from the

Quartermaster's Stores towards a 1938 brick-built Sandhurst barrack block. I was being shown the way by a sniffling hunchback with Bell's palsy and a rictus who at some time or other must have received a head wound, an aging regimental retainer called Private Tomlinson shuffling along beside me picking, inspecting and flicking bogies, prepared to offer no assistance whatsoever. Various items of kit kept popping out of this unmanageable bundle of mine so that my path was strewn with a trail of discarded militaria that I would have to come back to retrieve again a.s.a.p. At least I hadn't yet had to draw a rifle and bayonet from the armoury to balance on top of it all.

Oh - the indignity of it.

After breathlessly humping everything up iron-bannistered concrete stairways and along echoing corridors I almost fell into my first ever barrack room, collapsing my stuff onto the nearest bare-springed iron bedstead I came across. His duty done, gratuitously having gravely imparted the intelligence that the daily tea ceremony would be taking place in the cookhouse at 17.00 hours, Tomlinson departed morosely on his way to spread gloom, despondency and germs elsewhere. Placing my hands on my hips to aid inhalation I then turned about and quickly retraced my steps to pick up all the bits and pieces I'd left littered along the way. Back then aged 17½ I hacked it quite well. Today I would have suffered a myocardial infarction after the first minute of such an effort.

The wooden floored barrack room had sixteen beds and sixteen green tin lockers in it, and that was it. I am a pretty neat and tidy individual by inclination but even so it took me a while and a half to sort everything into any semblance of order, to make my bed, hang and stash stuff in the locker and generally get myself organised.

C/Sgt Griffiths had told me that the next 90-strong recruit intake was not due to form up for another two weeks. As far as he was concerned the Brighton Recruiting Office had 'goofed' by sending along me - a volunteer, a fortnight ahead of all the others - the conscripts. It meant I would be living alone with the barrack block all to myself for a while and with nothing to do except fill in time but that he would be giving some thought about how best to help me do this.

As it was now 5-0 o'clock I thought I'd better try to find my way down to the cookhouse which I had been told was somewhere in the same block. Clutching my two plates, mug, knife, fork and spoon I went back down the stone staircase and outside the entrance onto the pathway where for a moment I thought I must have stepped onto a railway station platform.

A steaming squad of distressed denim-clad soldiers was chugging down the road towards me like a clattering train with packs and rifles bouncing and clanking on their shoulders, their clothing awry, tin-hats juddering about their skulls and sweat bouncing from their soaking brows. Staggering to a ragged halt like some dishevelled mob in front of the barracks they loosened the chinstraps of their tin-hats and removed them, gratefully unbuckled their belts and equipment and with their shoulders heaving and mouths agape bent over double blowing and gasping to suck in more air. Several of them were retching. This was the previous intake of recruits just having completed their final 10-mile march and run in two hours in full battle order prior to the completion of their 12-weeks' basic training and imminent passing out parade as fully trained soldiers, the week before which they would be given a pass-out party where groups of giggly young reasonably eager and interested ladies from Woolworths would be invited and bussed in from the town to come for a dance that evening.

Phew!

When my turn came - would I be up to it?

Course I would.

I think I can; I know I can; I will, I will I will.

The cookhouse was a clattering barn of a place full of plastic-topped four-man tables and chairs with a long hot-plate running along the right hand side leading off to the kitchen behind where, as I was soon to learn, many a spud had been bashed and greasy pot washed in dirty luke warm water. Tea was tea; sausage and mash and two slices of white bread and marge with a dollop of jam spooned out of an industrial-sized tin of the stuff. Being alone and shy I sat by myself in my civvy shirt and trousers and was just finishing my tasteless repast when the thundering horde of squaddies I'd seen came crashing in for their own far harder earned replenishment. The cacophony of their raucous camaraderie even further excluded one but I knew that before long I would be part of an identical such group as this. Walking down to the end of the cookhouse I scraped the residue of my meal into a bin, rinsed my plates and eating irons in a bowl of water and returned upstairs to my barrack room. Stashing my new culinary implements on a shelf in my locker I could think of nothing else to do for the rest of the evening but to seek out the Naafi and find out what *that* was all about.

The Naafi was situated at the far side of the camp - a timber framed shack built on brick stilts with iron-bannistered stone steps leading up to its entrance. At that time of day I was the only person there. The recruit squad was all back in their barrack rooms furiously bulling their kit, while the permanent staff would have gone home to their families. I ordered a cup of tea and a dried out current bun from the pleasant enough lass behind the counter and sat down on a beaten up old sofa to flick through some scruffy magazines that were lying around. Then I had a go at indolently tinkling the sticky ivories of the sit-up-and-thump Naafi piano but then gave up and wandered back to my own empty barrack room to read a book, turn in, and have an early night.

Next morning it was raining.

Having been in the cadets at school (the best Drum Major in the history of the world remember) I knew how to put on my khaki shirt, denims and boots although garbed thus I looked like some shaven-headed East European political prisoner rather than the gloriously be-sashed and brass-badged young bird-bait peacock I'd been in my previous finely-tuned cadet outfit. After a greasy breakfast I strolled over to what appeared to be some sort of timber-built administration wing to find out if somebody there might be able to suggest what I should do for the rest of the day.

'WHERE'S YOUR FUCKING BERET, SOLDIER?'

Moustache bristling, the stubble of his ginger crew cut standing on end as if electrified, the single crown sewn to each lower sleeve denoting his fearsome rank a CSM had suddenly appeared breathing fire and brimstone in the doorway.

'Er – I left it in my room; I didn't know I had to wear it.'

'I am Company S'Arnt Major Blenkinsop and you call me SIR, you 'orribly scruffy, idle little oik. I suppose you're the new young reg'lar who turned up yesterday are you? Done no basic training yet, don't know left from right or whether your arsehole's been punched, bored or drilled, eh? So what are we going to do with you for the next two weeks before the rest of your mob turns up, eh? Well, today young man, you can help out on Coal Fatigues. When you've finished that, which will be about three-o'clock this afternoon, you will report back here to me. Understand? DO YOU UNDERSTAND?' he screamed in case I hadn't.

'Yes,' I nodded, quickly then remembered to add 'Sir' before he either hit me, shot me or ripped off my head and drop-kicked it out of the window.

'TOMLINSON.'

The previous day's regimental retard came shuffling in on cue from the wings.

'Tomlinson; today I want you and the new Private George here to get yourselves off down to the Motor Transport Park and pick up the coal truck. After that you know what to do. Same thing you did last week. And the week before that. Then report back here to me again when you've finished.'

Leering like an emaciated Quasimodo wearing broken-down size-12 boots, Jed - for this, it was to transpire, was his name - Tomlinson, who, it was also to transpire, having had a bullet ricochet off his skull whilst serving recently with the Regiment's 1st Battalion out in Egypt's decidedly unsavoury Canal Zone, had been RTU'd here to the Regimental Dépôt to await a medical discharge, shuffled me out of the Alaskan lumber-camp offices into the rain and - now officially appointed comrades-in-arms together - we headed off towards the MT Park to do coal fatigues for the day.

Coal is not used so much domestically these days. If used

nowadays it is usually purchased gift-wrapped from supermarkets in reinforced little brown paper bags and doled out to the hearth with tongs, like dainties. At the time of which I speak there was still a breed of labourer known as Coalmen. Coalmen wore understandably filthy back to front cloth caps on their heads like Norman Wisdom, the peaks swivelled to cover their necks in some ludicrous imitation of the sunshade on the back of a French Legionnaire's *kepi*. Coal Merchants' offices were located in every high street, where one placed one's order for delivery a few days later which would arrive in one hundredweight (1 cwt) tarpaulin sacks on the back of a flatbed lorry. To prevent his spine becoming too bruised or dented from humping these sacks (and to stop his collar getting dirty: ha-ha) the coalman wore a leather apron down his back attached to a headband, with a thick leather pad strapped over his preferred shoulder. He would heft the sack off the lorry by its corners and onto his back and wobble forward on overworked knees to empty it over his leather-padded shoulder down the receiving coal chute, where it *whooshed* and roared to settle in a cloud of dust in the bunker below. Twenty sacks to the ton. Coalmen were strong, and dirty. They usually smoked and had congested lungs, along with black lines etched into their craggy faces. Even those who persistently came bottom of class at school in absolutely everything did not really want to grow up to become a coalman. I - I who had five 'O' Levels and had joined the army to enjoy the sound of bugle, fife and drum, creaking saddlery, the jingle of spurs, camaraderie, glory and sunlit shores - in one day had become appointed nothing less than . . . a regimental coalman! And it was raining, which made it doubly mucky. I didn't care so much about Jed Tomlinson who had long since been regimentally broken-in and had obviously been somewhat backward even before that Egyptian bullet with his name on it had bounced off his noddle. He was used to this sort of thing, but I came from a *nice* home. Elastic-sided pumps, a blue raincoat and beret, and a mother who had curried favour with my primary school headmaster, remember. I wasn't cut out for, nor was I meant to be performing such a menial task as this;

specially on Day One of my glorious new career. There *must* have been a mistake. Or this time had mother got through on some hot-line to CSM Blenkinsop and demanded: 'Please will you make a point of toughening him up a bit for us please S'Arnt Major?'

When we got there the MT Park was a predictably dismal looking place that damp grey January morn. Syd Burgess our lorry driver looked equally miserable. He heaved himself into the cab up front while Jed and I clambered onto the back. We pulled out of the MT Park and sloshed round to the camp coal-yard. Jumping down into the black slush Jed picked up a couple of coal shovels leaning against one of the wooden-sleepered walls and handed one to me. 'Get shovelin', he said, grinning as he started to heft his first load of sopping wet coal up onto the back of the lorry. Strange to think that as a kid I had enjoyed splashing about in pools of water and making mud pies. This not entirely dissimilar chore did not seem as enjoyable.

As the now coal-laden 3-ton Bedford truck ground its way laboriously round the barracks' perimeter through the January puddles and persistently demoralizing drizzle, the only slight consolation we had was that we were delivering the stuff to the Officers' Quarters, a pleasantly arranged row of 1930's redbrick residences. Reversing into the driveway of each one we would shovel our coal into two buckets at a time which we would carry through the gate and down the side of the house to deposit into the wooden coal bunker outside the kitchen window. At about 11.30 a.m. one of the jolly-hockey-stick wives actually flung open her kitchen door and invited us in for a cup of tea which Jed, Syd (the zit-riddled lorry driver) and I accepted with cautious alacrity. She was a bubbly and charming sort and the tea was hot, sweet and wonderful (as were her accompanying chocolate bourbons) but Syd suggested later that as 'er 'usband was away on some military mission somewhere, 'e reckoned she 'ad just bin soundin' us out to get some more nutty slack dumped in 'er chute.

After lunch we returned with Syd Burgess to the coal-yard to shovel the unexpended portion of the day's deliveries off the back of his lorry before going back to the MT yard with him to brush and hose the vehicle clean. Because it was now 3.00 o'clock we then trotted dutifully back to report to CSM Blenkinsop as ordered.

'Here you are lad,' he said, and handed me a small piece of buff coloured paper.

'May I ask what it is Sir?'

'Leave pass.'

'Leave pass'?

'You heard me correctly. Leave pass.'

'I'm afraid I don't understand Sir. I've only been here a day. How can I be entitled to leave already?'

'Because we don't know what the fuck else to do with you, that's why. The next National Service intake of which you will be a part won't be forming up for another two weeks. You haven't been trained. You don't know even know how to salute properly yet. You're no good to man or beast. You're a liability. How do you think we are going to keep you occupied in the meantime eh? It's far better that you piss-off out of the way, then come back again when you're wanted. Any complaints?'

'No Sir.' I grinned at him happily.

'Very well. Now - here's a rail warrant for you, and ten bob (£8) advance of pay to see you through. Go and get cleaned up. Stash and lock up your kit and get yourself back here by Monday 13th February. Right? Now *GO.*'

TWELVE

BEFORE I HAD ACTUALLY SIGNED ON the dotted line to join the Army, while I had still been 'considering my options' one Leslie West, an RAF Squadron Leader friend of my mother's, had arranged for me to undergo three days of potential aircrew selection tests at RAF Hornchurch, in Essex. On the morning that I left our house with my small suitcase to walk to the station to catch the train, an extraordinary occurrence took place. Having been so memorably shot-up at the age of four in Lewes by that *Luftwaffe Fw190* in the war, I instinctively took cover by a tree as a very large grey RAF Gloster Javelin flew over so low and so slowly that it must have been almost at stalling speed. I could see its pilot waving to me before he gracefully banked and flew off again. It was as if he had been sent down specially by Zeus, the God of Thunder and the Sky, to seek me out, as a reassuring omen that I was making the right choice and had already been pre-selected by greater powers for a meteoric rise to Air Marshaldom. But it was not to be. Our three days at RAF Hornchurch were spent operating batteries of things like fruit machines on the pier, designed to judge our powers of coordination required for landing fast jets in fog, strange places, or even on a regular airstrip. The outcome of my endeavours indicated that I would have crashed. It was a shame. Blue is a nice colour and suits me rather well, but I failed the tests.

Later I learned that the pilot who had waved at me from treetop level had been severely reprimanded for having flown home to show his mother (two doors down from us) his new plane. Although he had waggled his wings several times, it had all been in vain because he'd overlooked telling her that she was part of his flight plan and he might be dropping by that morning, so she'd gone shopping.

About this time, too, there was the story of the freshly trained Armoured Corps driver who had gone AWOL with *his* new toy. He hadn't really gone AWOL. In fact he had simply driven proudly home to show his mother his tank. Slightly anxiously, perhaps, his mum said: 'Very nice dear, I'm sure,' before taking him in for a cup of tea and a biscuit. When he came out again half-an-hour later to get back to work, it was to discover that a crowd had gathered round his tank. There were quite a few policemen about the place too. *And* the local press. Photographers also, of course. (No TV crew; this was back then, remember.) Quite a kerfuffle ensued when the '15 minutes of fame' squaddie had to reverse his tank back down the street and out onto the main road again without squashing something. A fleet of police cars and motorcycle outriders fell-in to escort him the 20-miles back to camp. There was quite a reception committee waiting for him at the main gate when they got there. Afterwards, apparently, he spent quite a long time performing menial tasks about the place.

On another occasion, aged sixteen, I was walking down Eastbourne's Terminus Road one Saturday morning with nothing better to do, when there emerged from a shop doorway beside me one of the most magnificent creatures I had ever seen in my life. A freshly minted second lieutenant in the British Army. Better equipped for a catalogue or catwalk than a trench, he was wearing an immaculate brand-new service dress and Sam Brown belt, brown shoes gleaming like conkers, gloves and a swagger cane, and over his arm carried an officer's British warm overcoat, presumably in case there was a sudden change in the weather, it being well into August by now. Agog with curiosity about this young officer's mission, I followed him. I followed him all the way down to the far end of Terminus Road, where we both turned round, and then I followed him all the way back up again. He didn't do a thing - except stroll. I believe I caught him glancing interestedly into the plate glass windows of certain shops as he passed, but other than that I couldn't imagine what duty he could possibly be engaged upon.

But I knew that when I grew up I wanted to be one.

THIRTEEN

'IT'S SIMPLY NOT *FAIR*; I haven't budgeted for this at all, Michael,' my surprised mother cried. 'Two days ago you went off to join the army - and now without so much as a by-your-leave, here you are back again. I can do you toad-in-the-hole and a cup of tea, but other than that, there's nothing. And you'll have to sleep on the sofa. I've already let your room to a student, and you're not turfing your little brother out of his, that wouldn't be fair. How long are you here for?'

'Two weeks, Mum.'

'*Gawd;* well you'll have to get a job, that's all. I can't have you hanging around here all day. Do you think you could get your old newspaper round back again?'

'Don't know, Mum. I don't know that I'd be allowed to, now that I'm serving my Queen and Country.'

'But you're not serving your Queen and Country, are you. All you've done is turn up for a day, delivered a few buckets of coal, and now they've sent you home again. Did you screw-up big time or something son? What?'

'Course not, Mum. It's like I explained to you. They can't start training me until the others turn up. Simple as that.'

My ten-bob (£8) advance of pay allowed me the equivalent of 50p a day to spend, which in those days was about ninepence, or the price of a beverage. I chilled. I hung around Drago's Bun Lounge, and drank coffee.

Then after two weeks I went back and had another bash at re-joining the army.

FOURTEEN

'GET YER BLEEDIN' 'AIR CUT,' roared the florid-faced Provost Corporal 'Buster' Bates - but this time it was not me he was yelling at. He was pacing up and down furiously addressing a gaggle of woebegone and bedraggled oddments that had just been unceremoniously debussed from the back of a Bedford 3-ton truck, now doing a U-turn outside the Guardroom to return to Chichester railway station to pick up its next load of incoming recruits.

'You there!'

This time it *was* me he was addressing.

'You're an old soldier. March this lot across to dump their kit on the beds in your barrack block, then take 'em over to the QM Stores to draw their kit. *MOVE.'*

Having just arrived back myself I was wearing a sports jacket and grey flannels and carrying my own suitcase of things, but Corporal Bates having publicly acknowledged me as an old soldier, I certainly had no difficulty reverting to my days as the best Drum Major in the history of the world.

'SQUAD. Squad . . . *wait for it* . . . Squad - Atten-*SHUN.* Pick up your kit. Leeeeeeft . . . *TURN.* Quieeeeek . . . *MARCH.'*

They were a shambles. Understandably. Why wouldn't they be? But I was delighted. No sooner had I begun to herd them away like sheep, shuffling along completely uncoordinated and out of step, than I noticed a group of khaki-clad figures had emerged to stand on the balcony just outside the Orderly Room. Amongst them I saw the nice young second lieutenant who had temporarily befriended me on the day of my arrival a couple of weeks earlier. I knew it would be a complete travesty, but as the draft of new recruits and I drew abreast of the group I could not resist the folly of yelling out: 'E*YEYES* . . . . *RIGHT'* and at least snapping my own head over smartly to acknowledge the officers and senior NCOs assembled there on the balcony. I caught a couple of approving grins, nods and *sotto voce* enquiries as to 'Who the hell's *that* precocious young upstart, then?'

When we reached the spot where two weeks earlier I had seen the previous platoon gagging-in from its 10-mile forced march, prior to its recent passing out parade, I cried: 'SQU*AAAAD* . . . *HALT* . . . That means . : *STOP*.'

They got the second bit alright, mostly careering into each others backs.

'You can now follow me with your kit, and I'll show you the barrack rooms. When you've selected your bed and dumped everything, make your own way back down here, and report to that wooden building over *there*. That's the Quartermaster's Stores where you'll draw up your army kit - and may God have mercy on your souls. Tea will be in the cookhouse . . . over *there*, at 1700 hours. That's five-o'clock. Right. Let's go.'

Goodness, but I was getting into my stride. At this rate I'd make General in no time.

*

If lads of eighteen can be called grown men, that night for the first time I heard grown men cry. Not sobbing, but snivelling and whimpering, into their pillows. Not all of them, but a good few. First time away from home? Missed their mums? The prospect of the rigours to come? The physical and emotional ordeal that was going to be imposed upon them, and the fear that they may not shape up? Yes - all of these. Waiting for your First World War platoon commander's whistle to blow, ordering you out of the muddy trenches and over the top into the barbed wire and hails of machine gun bullets for the first time, or even the fiftieth, would have been utterly dreadful; far worse than the unwelcome novelty and discomfort of having to sleep in a strange bed for the first time - but everything is relative, and some, not many, but a few were for some reason so traumatised by the transition from their home environment to the army they even went on to hang themselves; usually in one of the ablution blocks during the hours of darkness, where we'd find them strung up all blue with their tongues hanging out just before breakfast, which made for something of a talking point over the bran-flakes.

By reveille next morning the whole platoon knew that I was no more an old soldier than they were, although having washed and shaved alongside everyone else in the cold ablution block, my cadet background did enable me to help several of them get dressed for breakfast, in their strange new items of kit.

The rest of that day, and for the rest of the week we were paraded, marched, run about, given instruction in how to fold our sheets and blankets into bed blocks for inspection each day; shown how to blanco our webbing equipment, bull our boots, polish our bayonets; strip, clean and pull-through our .303 Lee-Enfield rifles &c - and then at eleven o'clock the following Wednesday morning Bob Day, Roger Broadbent, Dan Salbstein, Mike Nelligan, David Baker and I were called out of the platoon and ordered to report to the PSO (Personnel Selection Officer) in the Orderly Room. What's all this about, we wondered? A puzzled sextet, we marched as smartly as we could across to the Orderly Room, frantically trying to think what was up.

PSO's were a specially selected breed at the time who rather than direct *cordon bleu* chefs into the Army Catering Corps, for some perverse reason would send them off to drive a tank for two years; it has always been familiarly known as the square peg / round hole syndrome. One of the most unusual encounters was between Captain J.S. (Jack) Fakley of the Buffs, and the Kray twins. In retrospect rather appropriately, this was done in a dungeon in the Tower of London. Having interviewed Ron, put him down as 'a professional boxer', and already written him off as beyond redemption, Fakly then encountered Reg, and experienced a profound feeling of *déjà vu*. Eventually the twins absconded and sent a saucy postcard to Captain Fakly from Southend. Both of them were then finally arrested, court-martialled and sent to prison.

The outcome of our own interviews with the PSO that day was quite straightforward. Being either public or grammar school boys who could talk reasonably proper and had a few GCEs under our belts, we all went up a notch by becoming designated as POMs. Potential Officer Material. All of us who were identified as such from each National Service intake in each regiment within the Home Counties Brigade, which were The Queen's Royal Regiment (West Surrey), The Buffs (Royal East Kent Regiment), The Royal Fusiliers (City of London Regiment), The East Surrey Regiment, The Middlesex Regiment, The Queen's Own Royal West Kent Regiment - and of course us, The Royal Sussex Regiment - would not undergo basic training at our respective regimental dépôts with *hoi polloi*, but would all combine to complete it at the historic old Wemyss Cavalry Barracks, Canterbury, the Home Counties' Brigade Dépôt (long since become just another housing estate, of course) in Kent.

On a bitterly cold and snowy Friday 24th February 1956, reeling groggily from a raft of injections hastily administered in the MI Room by a RAMC corporal (probably all of us with the same needle: what a cocktail), cocooned in our greatcoats and staggering under the unaccustomed weight of FSMO (Full Service Marching Order, when you carried everything you possessed, plus an entrenching tool) in one of that winter's days of sub-zero temperatures Bob Day, Roger Broadbent, Mike Nelligan, Dan Salbstein, David Baker and I went from Chichester to Canterbury by train via every known frozen south coast 'Halt' on the way, sustained en route by a packet of army-issue Smith's Crisps, two corned beef sandwiches and an apple.

At Wemyss Barracks, Canterbury we formed part of 83 Squad, comprised of fellow Home Counties Brigade aspirants for the coveted Second Lieutenant's pip - Mike Gale, Mike Lovick, Keith Trevett-Lyall, John Buchanan and Peter Gray all of the City of London Royal Fusiliers, and Roger Culpin, Joe

128

Cadiz, Terry West and Geoff Page of the East Surrey Regiment. L/Cpl Keith Adams (The Buffs) was our Permanent Staff minder, and Sergeant Bateman, a ferocious little Royal Fusilier with boots you could shave in, was our platoon sergeant.

'When'd'you lot 'ave your jabs?' he demanded with unaccustomed solicitousness in our barrack room that evening, having observed an encroaching lethargy creeping up on his new charges as the medicinal juice began to kick in and take its toll. We informed him that it had been earlier that morning.

'You better make sure you sleep with your shirts on tonight then, 'adn't you,' he said strangely, and left.

Curious but unquestioning, we did as advised. Next morning we were grateful that we'd done so. Tautly encased within their sleeves our left deltoids had swelled to the size of grapefruits, our arms so stiff it was impossible for any of us to raise them above waist height, our only consolation being that we were presumably now immune to rusty nails, lockjaw and dengue fever.

For the next twelve weeks we were to undergo exactly the same basic training as our short-lived acquaintances left back in Chichester, but we would be doing so Business Class. It wasn't in the least Cor' Blimey, and at times some reasonably intelligent conversations took place. We sweated just as much, but it was arguably a better class of sweat. It was also my introduction to some form of elitism, which I have to say I quite enjoyed.

Sergeant Bateman ruled our lives. Only 5' 4" and aged no more than about 25, he tore about the place like a demented little old man on speed. Whatever we were doing or wherever we were, he would always be there, suddenly appearing beside us from nowhere. It reached the stage where we half expected to wake up in the middle of the night and find he was in bed with us too, which was a terrible thought and put many of us off our breakfasts, but for the whole of those twelve long weeks he was undoubtedly the officially appointed custodian of our very bodies and souls. He was responsible for teaching us everything the army had decreed that we needed to know.

Under his auspices we stripped the bren, and fired the sten, handled our rifle like our wife, and learned to throw live grenades. Emitting blood-curdling roars we thrust our bayonets into straw, gave them gut-wrenching twists, withdrew them with the aid of a firmly implanted boot, and moved swiftly on. We burned over the obstacle course like Olympic athletes, successfully completed our ten miles forced march and run in two hours in full kit (I thought I could; I knew I could; I did, I did, I did) - and spent many, many hours square-bashing; pounding the parade ground learning to drill, that essential vehicle that allowed access to the installation and embedding of all future discipline. Screeching at us like a banshee Sgt Bateman would tear through our ranks berating us as useless scum, and at times becoming really quite hurtful.

'George,' he screamed into my face on one occasion, bouncing up and down whilst eyeballing me like a spitting mongoose, 'your trouble is . . .' he needed to pause for no more than a nanosecond to think up something sufficiently insulting, but then, whether an original or plucked from his own repertoire, he got it, and jubilantly roared: 'You look as if the best part of you ran down your mother's leg. Now - Stand up straight man.'

I shuddered at such effrontery, and that it should be allowed, but political correctness, curse it, was still a long way off in those days, and the belief at the time was that abuse like this used to put hair on our chests and hone us to face all future events.

Eventually, however, the day came - Friday 4th May - when having bulled ourselves stupid, we fell-in on the square for our passing out parade as fully trained infantry soldiers, but rather special ones (no truckload of Woolworths girls for our party) who after a spot of leave would all be meeting up again at Barton Stacey Camp, near Andover in Hampshire, to attend a WOSB.

What was a WOSB?

The Regular Army's officer training programme at the Royal Military Academy Sandhurst traditionally took two years to complete. Came World War Two, though, and the

Army quickly found it needed to recruit and train a larger supply of supplementary officers more expeditiously. It wasn't so important that they should be immaculate at sword drill, know how to eat peas properly, or be completely *au fait* with all the usually recognised graces, but that after 16 weeks - subject to their possessing at least a de*gree* of social acceptability - they were sufficiently trained and able to hit the ground running in any theatre of war, and kill people.

After the Second World War, National Service and Short Service commissions were granted to provide the large numbers of junior officers required by a large army, but as both categories were only engaged for a limited period, the time available for Officer Cadet training was restricted to a few months. The war-time OCTU system was adopted for this purpose and two Officer Cadet Schools were set up. One was at Mons Barracks, Aldershot, previously used by 161 Inf OCTU (RMC) and the other was at Eaton Hall, Cheshire. Officer cadets of the Royal Armoured Corps or Royal Artillery went to Mons, while those of the other arms and services went to Eaton Hall. When National Service was abolished in 1960 it was decided to retain the Short Service system, as this improved the long-term prospects available to career officers. Eaton Hall OCS was closed and Mons OCS was to become responsible for training all Short Service Officer Cadets, as well as all those joining the Regular Army as graduates.

As a preliminary to attending either training establishment an 'initial interview' selection process was devised, called a War Office Selection Board - or WOSB. This was a three-day series of tests designed to assess a potential officer's physical and moral stamina, leadership qualities and all round suitability to be commissioned. In turn, the system was to remain in place after the war to determine National Service candidates' suitability for commissioning as well. It was to continue right up until the end of National Service in the early sixties, when WOSB then became replaced by a RCB (Regular Commissions Board).

The RCB, located at Leighton House, Westbury, in Wiltshire, was to conduct the same series of selection tests for applicants for a regular army commission as the earlier WOSB at Barton Stacey had done.

Meanwhile, however . . .

Back in 1956 . . . on arrival at WOSBy on Sunday 6th May, my lot and I were shown to some steel Nissen huts, allotted beds for the three nights, and were then taken up to a large room in a rambling old-fashioned mansion. It was grand to sit down at a table, to eat lunch with proper cutlery off decent plates, and to be waited on by WRAC girls. The Board Members sat with us, and we knew only too well that they were all eyes and ears. If one of us really had eaten our peas with a knife it might not have helped a whole lot. We each wore a numbered tabard, to enable us to be recognised and referred to anonymously over the following three days of our attendance there.

That afternoon we sat at desks answering various written tests and question papers, a lot of which seemed quite pointless to us. We were then given individual sessions with various staff members who read out fifty nouns at thirty second intervals, and told us to record on paper the first idea that came into our heads about each one. Next we were shown some indistinct photographs and were asked to write a paragraph on the idea each of them conveyed to us. We toiled at these papers till the evening. Then we went back to our ante-room, sat, talked, and read, generally trying to appear at ease despite what fear and trepidation each of us was really feeling.

The following morning we were divided into teams to carry out a variety of 'group tasks' timed against the clock. Designed to sort the men from the boys and draw out the natural born leaders among us, these consisted, for example, of getting a heavy sand-filled wooden crate through a steel scaffold, most of which was painted red and so could not be touched. We could only touch the green bits. Or swinging a concrete-filled petrol drum across a 'crocodile and mine-infested canyon' with the aid of three lengths of rope and two planks, each of which was too short to be of much use. There were sufficient tasks for each team member to have a go at being the leader, hopefully in control. The rest of us were loyally expected to support him, while he was expected to listen to, take on board, sift and either accept or reject whatever crazy idea any of us might come up with in our anxious attempts to be seen as a useful team player and contributor.

Next up, we were split into two groups to manhandle a 100lb log which with thumping hearts and bursting lungs we had to lug round an obstacle course. A twelve-foot-wide stream was the first obstacle. There were also tyres hung from beams through which we had to clamber, windows to dive head-first and somersault through commando-style, high walls to clamber over, and - worst of all - a canvass tarpaulin pegged and roped down to the wet ground. The examining officers took great delight in standing on this sheet, thereby making it more difficult for us to crawl through or to keep any sense of direction as we struggled for light and air.

It was not all beef and brawn though.

We did tick-tests, wrote essays, and had a discussion at which the President of the Board was present (a red-tabbed full colonel), as well as the usual retinue of corps and regimental captains and majors clasping clipboards, and either hurriedly or with seemingly disinterested languor, scribbling notes about us. We had to discuss various articles in the room, one of which was a horrible oil painting of a gloomy looking forest. This resulted in a wildly eclectic input of views about Picasso, Turner, and several others I had still never heard of at that age. My own earth-shattering contribution to the discussion was the memorable observation that I didn't really know too much about art, but that I liked what I liked, a remark duly noted on several millboards - probably annotated with just the single word Prat!

The real ordeal, though, was our individual private interview next day with the same colonel. We had been briefed over the grapevine that he asked many general knowledge questions, so that evening we took turns to pour over the *Daily Telegraph* in a belated attempt to bone-up on that day's current affairs, but when it was my turn to confront him all he asked me was what I had done last summer and my views on capital punishment, the previous year's case of Ruth Ellis, the last woman to be

133

hanged in Britain, still then being of great interest to everyone.

For me the worst part of the three days was the five-minute lecturette. Most of the others - the public school lads, obviously - were able to speak ably about huntin', shootin' and fishin'; their recent climb up Kilimanjaro, skiing at Klosters, or bob-sleighing. Me? I was seventeen-and-a-half and had never done anything. Certainly nothing to talk about. I had never joined the school debating society, so the only self-confidence development I had undergone had been playing Pindarus, a Roman soldier in the previous autumn's school production of Julius Ceasar. All I could recall of my few short lines, was: *'Oh Cassius, Pindarus will run far from this country, where a Roman will never notice him.'* After I had failed to marshal any coherent thought and stuttered, waffled and gurgled my way through five minutes of stumbling ineptitude at WOSBy's five-minute lecturette - thus it proved to be.

Later that day we split up and all went back to our respective barracks.

A week later I received the buff-enveloped notification that I had not been deemed quite up to it on this occasion; but maybe some other time. Naturally I was disappointed, but callow youth that I was, even I was prepared to acknowledge that at that stage I was nowhere near ready to be a leader of men. If I *had* passed, there would have been something drastically wrong with the system.

Bob Day (Eastbourne College), Roger Broadbent (Gordonstoun) and Mike Nelligan (probably somewhere like Radley) were selected as suitable candidates, and were to go off to Eaton Hall for sixteen weeks training, being the next step to their elevation to the near god-like status of second lieutenants. Mike Nelligan, who was extremely ginger and freckled, when he was commissioned, was sent off to join the King's African Rifles.

Bob and Roger I was to bump into again.

FIFTEEN

AT THE COMPLETION OF OUR THREE-DAY WOSB we returned to our regimental dépôt at Chichester to do odd jobs about the place, and to discover the true meaning of the words 'meaningless drudgery'. The Battalion proper had already made its way from its two year BAOR tour stationed over in Germany, at Elizabeth Barracks, Minden, via Brentwood, by train to Southampton Docks onto a 17,000 ton former German liner which had become the troopship *Empire Orwell*.

At 5.15 p.m. on Thursday 5th July 1956, destined to be the last trooper to pass through the Suez Canal before Eden's ill-fated upcoming war there, they set sail for Korea, where The Royal Sussex Regiment was to be the last British regiment to serve in that still active service theatre. In the fulness of time a supplementary draft of us would be sailing out to join them there, but somehow that time had to be filled in the interim.

It was another transition period.

On a Saturday morning four weeks later, my 18th birthday - (9th June, remember?) - Bob Day, Roger Broadbent and Mike Nelligan departed with much anticipation and only slight trepidation to undergo their officer training at Eaton Hall. Dan Salbstein had been selected to go off to do a Russian course, and whilst awaiting *our* fate the rest of us settled in for a long round of spud-bashing and a fair selection of those other mindless duties for which National Service was so infamous.

Concurrently, at any given time the Army has always been either cutting back, or recruiting.

On the occasion of which I shall speak, the local chapter had decided to do some recruiting.

On 1st January 1956, British Lion was to release a film adapted from the book by Max Catto, called *A Hill In Korea*. For the benefit of movie buffs and aficionados this wartime action movie starred a young George Baker (who was eventually to become TV's Inspector Wexford), and co-starred Harry Andrews, Stanley Baker, Ronald Lewis, Steven Boyd, Victor Maddern, Robert Shaw, and a 23-year-old wannabe with a bit-part in this, his first movie - someone called Michael Caine. Three years after the actual Ceasefire, this was to be the first major feature film to portray British troops in action during the Korean War. Based on real events, the film followed the fortunes of a small fighting patrol composed mostly of National Servicemen - 'old enough to fight, but too young to vote' - in what started out as a routine sweep through a quiet village. As the British troops moved out, they found themselves cut off from their own lines by a huge force of Chinese soldiers. The patrol attempted to break out, but the enemy seemed to be everywhere. Faced with the prospect of either capture or certain death, the survivors made their final stand in a deserted temple, where they fought to the last bullet. It is of interest that only three years previously Michael Caine had actually been fighting out there in the Korean War himself. As a National Serviceman Fusilier Maurice Micklewhite (as he then was) fought with his regiment, The City of London Royal Fusiliers. In his autobiography *What's It All About* he describes a night patrol he was on when he came within a few feet of a Chinese patrol. He said the Chinese wore tennis shoes and were very quiet, but you could always tell when they were about because they consistently chewed garlic, the way we chew bubblegum. There was no ambient light whatsoever in the dead of night, and the nearby smell of garlic was all that prevented Fusilier Micklewhite from experiencing an uncomfortable encounter with the enemy, and - instead of emerging triumphant - perhaps the ghastly prospect of the South Wales Borderers later having to be wiped out by all those Zulus at Rorke's Drift!

Because of his Korean service experience, Michael Caine delightedly found himself being paid £150 a week for his dual duties as novice actor *and* technical director.

Critics of *A Hill In Korea* questioned how masses of Chinese soldiers would charge across open ground to try and overtake machine-gun nests, but it is known that during the Korean conflict the Chinese army would smoke opium before a charge, working themselves into such a frenzy that they would be almost oblivious to the danger of such an attack, or even the pain of wounds - although all our brave chaps in Flanders' Field ever had to steel their nerves with were Capstan Full Strength or Woodbines, oh . . . and just the occasional tot of rum too, perhaps.

At a cost of £400,000, on the site of the historic 1597 Unicorn Inn on the corner of Brighton's Queen's Road and North Street, on 27th July 1927 a 2,000 seat cinema called *The Regent* had been opened. After reigning there supremely for 40 years, it became a Bingo Hall in 1967, and then in 1973 it was closed to make room for a flagship branch of Boots the Chemist.

So what was my significant involvement in any of this?

Nothing exciting at all, really. Big fleas having little fleas, is all. It was simply that for the three days Thursday 11th to Saturday 13[h] October 1956 a Private Wildman and I had to dress ourselves up in appropriate 'Korean' summer kit and be lorried over from Chichester to Brighton at teatime each day, just to stand in front of a hastily erected camouflage net in the foyer of *The Regent* cinema every evening while it screened *A Hill In Korea*. The purpose of our mission? To attract new recruits.

The result?

Need you ask . . .?

Apart from delivering coal on my first day, this was my most noteworthy contribution to Queen and Country to date.

The whole of that May and June were spent kicking around at Chichester peeling potatoes, polishing floors, enduring innumerable kit inspections and constantly being told to get our haircut. But then on Monday 25th June, for no apparent reason at all it was deemed expedient that a small detachment of us should be posted to Connaught Barracks, adjoining Dover Castle, to supplement the ranks of the City of London Royal Fusiliers (Michael Caine's old lot) who were stationed there. To what extent the seven of us - Ray Allen, Don Holman, John Baxter, Kevin Flynn, Fred Sparrow, Bob King and I - were effectively expected to supplement the Royal Fusiliers is anybody's guess, but there it was.

We were only there for six weeks. But this all had to do with one Colonel Gamal Abdel Nasser, the then President of Egypt.

Having swept leaves, polished more floors, and by toting a pick-helve round the perimeter wire at night repeatedly guarded Connaught Barracks against invasion, I was back in Eastbourne again on a few days' mid-summer leave. I had only been clomping round my home town in my hairy battledress and best boots for a few hours, when a telegram arrived ordering me to report immediately back to Camp, at Dover. It was a nuisance, but an exciting one. What was afoot? Was my nation in peril, and my training to be put to the test at last? *Phew! Quel* stuff.

It was now Sunday 5th August. The reason we had been re-called was simply to pack our kit up in order to return to Chichester, because ten days previously, on 26th July, Egypt's Colonel Nasser had nationalised the Suez Canal.

This action was unacceptable to Sir Anthony Eden, Britain's then Prime Minister, so he was planning a joint Anglo-French assault to reclaim the Canal. Known as *Operation Musketeer*, this was to be launched on Wednesday 31st October. Because of this, all manner of khaki and tri-service stirring was occurring in the meantime, of which my colleagues and I constituted one extremely insignificant part. The City of London Royal Fusiliers, to whom we were attached at Dover, had been ordered out to the Cyprus staging post in readiness. I suppose at the time it was deemed administratively more convenient for the Fusiliers to issue us with a rail warrant to rejoin The Royal Sussex, our parent regiment back at Chichester, rather than go through the more complex rigmarole of transferring us permanently to become City of London Royal Fusiliers.

To support the invasion, large air forces had been sent to Cyprus and Malta by the UK and France, and many aircraft carriers were deployed. The two airbases on Cyprus were so congested that a third field which was in dubious condition had to be brought into use for French aircraft. Even RAF Luqa on Malta was crowded with RAF Bomber Command aircraft. The UK deployed the aircraft carriers HMS *Eagle*, *Albion* and *Bulwark* and France had the *Arromanches* and *La Fayette* on station. In addition, HMS *Ocean* and *Theseus* acted as jumping-off points for Britain's helicopter-borne assault (the world's first). Meanwhile the Israel Border Police militarized the Israel-Jordan border (including the Green Line with the West Bank) which resulted in the killing of 48 Arab civilians by Israeli forces on 29th October (known as the Kafr Qasim massacre).

For those who were there and care to remember, or simply for historic interest, the unfurling events were obviously well documented.

On the morning of 30th October the United Kingdom and France sent an ultimatum to Egypt. This was followed by the initiation of *Operation Musketeer* on 31st October, with a bombing campaign. On 3rd November, 20 F4U-7 Corsairs from the 14.F and 15.F Aéronavale, taking off from the French carriers *Arromanches* and *Lafayette*, attacked the Cairo aerodrome. Nasser responded by sinking all 40 ships present in the canal, closing it to all further shipping until early 1957.

Late on 5th November, the 3rd Battalion of the British Parachute Regiment dropped at El Gamil Airfield, clearing the area and establishing a secure base for incoming support aircraft and reinforcements. At first light on 6th November, Commandos of Numbers 42 and 40 Commando Royal Marines stormed the beaches, using landing craft of World War II vintage (LCM Landing Craft, Mechanized). The battle group standing offshore opened fire, giving covering fire for the landings and causing considerable damage to the Egyptian batteries and gun emplacements. The town of Port Said sustained great damage and was seen to be alight.

Acting in concert with British forces, 500 heavily-armed paratroopers of the French 2nd Colonial Parachute Regiment (*2ème RPC*) were hastily redeployed from combat in Algeria and jumped from Noratlas Nord 2501 transports of the ET

(Escadrille de Transport) 1/61 and ET 3/61 over the al-Raswa bridges, together with some combat engineers of the Guards Independent Parachute Company. Despite the loss of two soldiers, the western bridge was swiftly secured by the paras, and F4U Corsairs of the Aéronavale 14.F and 15.F flew a series of close-air-support missions, destroying several SU-100 tank destroyers. F-84Fs also hit two large oil storage tanks in Port Said, which went up in flames and covered most of the city in a thick cloud of smoke for the next several days. Egyptian resistance varied, with some positions fighting back until destroyed, while others were abandoned with little resistance.

In the afternoon, 522 additional French paras of the 1er REP (*Régiment Étranger Parachutiste*, 1st Foreign Parachute Regiment) were dropped near Port Fouad. These were also constantly supported by the Corsairs of the French Aéronavale, which flew very intensive operations: for example, although the French carrier *La Fayette* developed catapult problems, no less than 40 combat sorties were completed. In total, 10 French soldiers were killed and 30 injured during the landing and the subsequent battles.

British commandos of No. 45 Commando assaulted by helicopter, meeting stiff resistance, with shore batteries striking several helicopters, while accidental friendly fire from British carrier-borne aircraft caused heavy casualties to 45 Commando and HQ. Street fighting and house clearing, with strong opposition from well-entrenched Egyptian sniper positions, caused further casualties.

It was a short war.

This operation to take the canal was highly successful from a military point of view, but was a political disaster due to external forces. Along with Suez, the United States was also dealing with the near-simultaneous Soviet-Hungary crisis, and faced the public relations embarrassment of criticizing the Soviet Union's military intervention there while at the same time avoiding criticism of its two principal European allies' actions. Perhaps more significantly, the United States also feared a wider war after the Soviet Union leader Nikita

Khrushchev threatened to intervene on the Egyptian side and launch attacks by 'all types of weapons of destruction' on London and Paris.

Thus the Eisenhower administration forced a cease-fire on Britain and France which it had previously told the Allies it would not do. The U.S. demanded that the invasion stop and sponsored resolutions to this effect in the UN Security Council. Britain and France, as permanent members of the Security Council, vetoed the resolutions in the UN Security Council. The U.S. then appealed to the United Nations General Assembly and proposed a resolution calling for a cease-fire and a withdrawal of forces under the terms of Uniting for Peace (UfP). The General Assembly held an emergency session and passed the UfP resolution.

Britain and France withdrew from Egypt within a week.

Part of the pressure that the United States used against Britain was financial, as President Eisenhower threatened to sell the United States reserves of the British pound and thereby precipitate a collapse of the British currency. After Saudi Arabia started an oil embargo against Britain and France, the U.S. refused to fill the gap, until Britain and France agreed to a rapid withdrawal. There was also a measure of discouragement for Britain in the rebuke by the Commonwealth Prime Ministers, St. Laurent of Canada and Menzies of Australia, at a time when Britain was still continuing to regard the Commonwealth as an entity of importance, as the residue of the British Empire and as an automatic supporter in its effort to remain a world power.

The British government and the pound thus both came under pressure. Eden was forced to resign and announced a cease fire on 6th November, warning neither France nor Israel beforehand. Troops were still in Port Said when the order came from London. Without further guarantee, the Anglo-French Task Force had to finish withdrawing by 22nd December 1956, to be replaced by Danish and Colombian units of the United Nations Emergency Force (UNEF). The Israelis left the Sinai in March, 1957.

Before the withdrawal, Canadian Lester B. Pearson, who

would later become the Prime Minister of Canada, had gone to the United Nations and suggested creating a United Nations Emergency Force (UNEF) in the Suez to 'keep the borders at peace while a political settlement is being worked out.' The United Nations accepted this suggestion, and after several days of tense diplomacy, a neutral force not involving the United States, Britain, France or most of the Soviet Bloc was sent with the consent of Nasser, stabilizing conditions in the area. Pearson was awarded the Nobel Peace Prize in 1957 for his efforts. The United Nations Peacekeeping Force was Pearson's creation and he is considered the father of the modern concept of 'peacekeeping'.

Eden's resignation marked, until the 1982 Falklands War 26 years later, the last significant attempt Britain made to impose its military will abroad without U.S. support. Harold Macmillan was every bit as determined as Eden had been to stop Nasser, although he was more willing to enlist American support in the future for that end. Some argue that the crisis also marked the final transfer of power to the new superpowers, the United States and the Soviet Union.

The imposed end to the crisis signalled the definitive weakening of the United Kingdom and France as Global Powers. Nasser's standing in the Arab world was greatly improved, with his stance helping to promote pan-Arabism and reinforce hostility against Israel and the West. The crisis also arguably hastened the process of decolonization, as the remaining colonies of both Britain and France steadily gained independence over the next several years.

After Suez, Aden and Iraq became the main bases for the British in the region, while the French concentrated their forces at Bizerte (Tunisia) and Beirut.

Meanwhile, I'd cut the top of my finger off in a bread slicer.

Let me tell you about that.

Packed and ready to go to play their part in the foregoing hostilities, before they embarked for that then latest Middle East hot-spot, the City of London Royal Fusiliers' Last Supper was tea. Rattling their irons and gabbling, well nigh a thousand

142

of them were queuing up for it. Because we were not going with them Ray Allen, Don Holmwood and I had been detailed off to slice loaves in the bread store. At 10 slices per loaf we had 100 loaves to get through. Fortunately there was an electric slicer. I pushed while Ray stacked, and Don delivered. After loaf number 76 had just *zinged* its way through the hatch it occurred to me that in order to break the monotony some light relief might not go amiss, so I pretended to have cut off my finger.

'Oh, my *GOD*,' I yelled, reeling back from the slicer and clutching both fists to my groin, screwing my face into a contortion of simulated agony, and staggering back against a tableful of loaves.

'Chrissakes Mike, what the helluv you done?' Don hurried over concernedly to pat my shoulder and investigate.

'I've taken my finger off,' I croaked, trying to look ashen.

Ray looked at Don, Don looked at Ray, and they both looked at me; but I couldn't sustain it.

'Ha-ha-dee-ha-ha,' I chortled, slapping my thigh and returning to my task at the slicer. With Ray and Don both likening me *sotto voce* to that special part of the female anatomy, a further 500 Fusiliers outside were still jostling forward for their tea.

It was then I cut my finger off.

No; really I did.

'Oh, my *GOD* - <u>Nooo</u> . . .,' I shrieked again, aghast that retribution for my prank had been meted out quite so quickly and severely. I thought you were meant to wait a while: have it creep up on you. Take you by surprise years later when you least expected it. Not to be instantaneous like this. It must have been that with this up-coming Suez thing an' all, God was in a hurry that day. He didn't have time to mess about.

'C'<u>mon</u> Mike,' for God's sake stop pissing about like this, will you. We'll never get finished.'

'Honestly,' I hissed through clenched teeth. 'I really have taken it off. I'm not kidding. Honestly. Look, I'm . . .'

Don nudged Ray. With an ill-concealed grimace he indicated what until seconds previously had been a virgin slice of bread but was now turning pink. Emerging from it like the Lady of the Lake's fist clutching *Excalibur*, or an embryo toad-in-the-hole, alone and solitary, was the tip of one of my fingers. It appeared that I had only removed a little piece, but it was enough to do the job, lying flopped over there like an artist's poking through the palette of bread, or something small having a tight squeeze coming out of an open manhole.

'Jesus,' said Ray, and quickly picked the slice up on the palm of his hand to bear semi-aloft like a crown jewel before him for all to see. 'Hey - look at this,' he yelled ill advisedly up the dining hall at the 400 Fusiliers still clamouring for their scoff. 'George has taken his finger off in the bread slicer.'

A groan filled the air. Sullen faced Fusiliers broke ranks and shuffled off back to their billets, reluctantly forsaking their last meal on the merest off chance they might encounter a stray piece of my gristle. Men of war? Big girls' blouses, more like.

Back inside the bread store meanwhile, I thought I was quite probably going to bleed to death. My fist had involuntarily clenched itself tightly closed. My knuckles had gone white. I could feel the remaining three nails biting into my palm. So tightly was it bunched there was not even a sign of seepage through the cracks, but I knew my life force was pumping away inside my left fist there. All I had to do was unclench it and everything within a 10-foot radius would become instantly incarnadined. But at the same time I was concerned lest I was causing a build up, and that like two simultaneously erupting sideways volcanoes there would suddenly be a violent expulsion of blood from each ear.

'For God's sake Ray,' Don yelled. 'Give him back his finger, will ya? The medics might be able to do something with it.'

'There's not a lot I can do with that,' the RAMC captain said half-an-hour later, after I'd rolled up in the back of a 3-tonner at the Folkestone medical centre and piled wanly into his 'surgery' just as he was hoping to get away to play golf. 'It's too small,' he said. 'Where's it come from, anyway?'

'It's the top of my finger, sir,' I whimpered as we both

144

surveyed the sorry thing nestling forlornly in my grimy handkerchief.

'Which one?'

'One of those: in there.' I nodded at my clenched left fist.

'Well, open up your hand and then I can have a look.'

'I can't,' I said. 'I've tried, but it keeps staying shut all the time.'

'Trauma, eh,' he said, whopping a little bottle onto the end of a syringe and dexterously sticking it into my arm. 'Now try.'

While the muscles relaxed, my fist began uncurling of its own accord. From where the tip of my second finger had been, blood was pumping quite nicely from the fleshy pink meatus that remained.

'Not a pretty sight, is it,' said the young doctor, now beginning to take some interest and hurrying it up a bit as my blood splashed onto his highly polished lino. 'Would you mind bringing it over here and dripping into the sink please? Grinning boyishly, as though just about to attempt some jape or other, he said: 'Now - I've never actually done this before, so I don't know if it's going to work, but in theory it should.' Wielding a fresh hypodermic needle he grabbed my wrist and held it tight. Slowly depressing the plunger he directed the egressing drops of liquid straight onto the still suppurating finger-tip, which immediately stopped bleeding.

'Well now - that's nice to know, isn't it,' he said triumphantly, apparently chuffed at having pushed back yet another frontier of medical science. He lobbed the syringe into a dish with a crash like a discarded *assegai*. 'I thought it would work. It's a coagulant which is normally stuck into you, but it seems to have been just as effective my way, doesn't it. There's no need to stitch it,' he said. 'It'll heal over alright in a day or two. Try not to knock it about too much though. I'll bandage it up, and I think you should wear a sling for a while. But you'll be okay.'

Ten minutes later I came out with the finger looking like a misshapen bobbin of cotton suspended from my neck by a sling. After just six months service for Queen and Country I had sustained my very first wound. If I had been American I might have got a medal for it.

Three days later the City of London Royal Fusiliers departed for Cyprus, and the seven of us returned by train back to our regimental dépôt at Chichester once more.

What would happen next, we wondered?

SIXTEEN

THEY SIMPLY DIDN'T KNOW what to do with us.

No-one did.

A fashionable cliché at the time was 'spare pricks at a wedding', and that is exactly what we felt like. The Battalion was on the high seas, aboard the troopship *Empire Orwell* en route to Korea. New intakes of National Servicemen were fetching up at the front gates fortnightly to undergo basic training, and others kept filtering through individually or in penny packets, back from various theatres around and about the place for their demob, while like loose change down a grating our little lot was being chivvied about from pillar to post performing a plethora of meaningless chores *à la* painting coal white, stuff like that. Filling in time. Waiting for what? In those days you had to be 18½ to serve in active service theatres, so we had been left behind in temporary limbo because we were officially still a few months short of being the right age to go and soldier alongside our more mature peers. We knew we were due to form the nucleus of the first draft to be shipped out to Korea to join the Battalion there as soon as the time was right, but meanwhile . . .

. . . our days were filled more or less thus:

A chain-smoking, clip-moustached Scot - Sgt Jock Walker - was appointed our luckless mentor, to guide us through a period of our lives which became expediently entitled at the time Advanced Training. Advanced Training consisted of one hilarious drill parade at which Jock must have expended the full extent of his military knowledge, because thereafter for several weeks we lay on our beds reading comics all day, when we were meant either to be 'tidying the place up' or 'getting on with bulling our best boots'. A place can only be so tidied, and a pair of best boots polished only so far before they begin to wear thin. Even our masters realised this, and after a while took to making only the occasional token forays into the rest home environment of our barrack block, where we did constitute a convenient and readily available labour pool; one or other of us was always being grabbed piecemeal off our beds and having to rush off to perform some menial task or other for someone of higher rank, which meant anyone and everyone.

One day John Baxter and I had been detailed to tidy the OC's office when he was away for the morning. In the process of doing this I happened to glance at his open diary on the desk to see that he had pencilled in a Fire Drill, due to take place at 12.30 p.m. that same day. Nipping quickly back to our barrack room I delightedly informed all the others of this, with the result that at 12.25 p.m. there were thirty squaddies properly accoutred in tin-hats with happily grinning faces pressed to the barrack room windows, eagerly awaiting the call. Confident that he was going to be able to berate all of us for our tardy turnout, when the OC returned to his office and pressed the fire alarm button he was amazed to see 30 squaddies immediately come pouring out of the barrack block onto Number One Square, humping hoses, slopping buckets of water and sand, and tripping over clattering stirrup pumps.

Reaction time?

Ten seconds.

Realising he'd been bested he easily got his own back by deciding that his imaginary fire had broken out on the far side of the camp, so bearing our inconveniently weighted appliances we all had to double, clanking and cursing for quarter of a mile before honour was satisfied and we were stood down for lunch.

That afternoon there was a Pay Parade. Having just returned from our short stint with the City of London Royal Fusiliers at Connaught Barracks, Dover, some of us had several kit deficiencies to pay for. Bob King had been so careless with his

148

stuff that it seemed he'd come back with only the clothes he stood up in, and a toothbrush. When he tabbed up to the pay table, saluted and expectantly put out his hand to the Paying Officer to receive his just descrts, his just deserts are what he received. One-and-sixpence. (86p.) Bob looked down bemusedly at the two shiny little silver coins nestling in his palm, and asked: 'What's this for, then?'

'*That* King, is for being a good soldier and having worked hard all week bumping your barrack room floor to near perfection. *Next.*'

'*You should learn to take better care of your kit in future, shouldn't you, King,*' roared CSM Blenkinsop as Bob listlessly saluted the Paying Officer and turned away crestfallen from the table, tears of incomprehension and hurt mounting in his eyes.

That evening Kevin Flynn and I were detailed for guard duty, so I asked Bob if he would like to do it for me for three-shillings. He leapt at the chance. But then Kevin, who I suspected was working up to bonking some girl down in Chichester, offered him seven-shillings (nearly two days pay) instead - which offer Bob accepted with even more alacrity than he had mine.

I am glad in a way that I did do guard duty that night. We have spoken of people crying themselves to sleep, and some even topping themselves in the latrines: and then occasionally we had the likes of Private Hinchcliffe to deal with. Hinchcliffe was a self-proclaimed artist. He considered any form of soldiering or discipline to be a complete waste of his time and energy, all totally beneath him. As a result, he refused to soldier. Because of this he was automatically banged-up in the guardroom. To while away the hours of confinement and vent his frustration while the hierarchy debated what to do with him, he used his dinner plate as a palette. Rather in the style of the 44-year-old paint-sloshing American artist, Jackson Pollock, who had died in a drunken car accident only two months earlier, Hinchcliffe daubed several abstract but interesting murals on his whitewashed cell wall with gravy. When people gravely arrived to consider these artistic works, most of which Hinchliffe purported to be of Christ, he took to smiting them severely over the head with an iron bar he'd managed to prise loose from his cell window. This unusual behaviour confirmed his position as a nut. He was medically discharged as 'unsuitable' a few weeks later, and then quickly became sane again. I believe he then went on to build a very good career for himself.

Speaking about off-duty Chichester, groups of us used to go down to the local *Odeon* a lot. Purely for the nostalgic recollection of movie buffs, some of the films we saw over those few short weeks in 1956 were the late John Wayne's *The Searchers*; Esther Williams' *Unguarded Moment*; *The Iron Petticoat* with the late Bob Hope and Katherine Hepburn; *The Ambassador's Daughter* starring Olivia de Havilland and John Forsyth; *Slightly Scarlet* with the late John Payne, Rondha Fleming and Arlene Dahl; *Storm Centre* with the late Bette Davies, and *Huk* with the late George Montgomery, all famous stars at the height of their glory back then over half-a-century ago, most of whom readers today will never have heard of, yet were household names in their time.

One afternoon Sgt Jock Walker got us fallen-in (strange terminology, isn't it) on Number One Square, and marched us across to the Education Centre.

'Listen in,' he rasped, standing before us on the aromatic wooden balcony of the freshly creosoted Napoleonic hut. 'This afternoon you're going to have a lecture on Keats, so I suggest you pay attention, 'cos I don't suppose many of you even knows what a Keats is.'

In the event, whoever dreamed up the idea that we should have a lecture on Keats had omitted to mention it to the lecturer, Sergeant Kimby of the RAEC, who had gone off to play hockey that afternoon instead. After we had been sitting fidgeting for fifteen minutes, the door was exasperatedly thrown open and in strode a rather flustered Major Keith Tucker, one of the dépôt's company commanders.

'Right,' he said, adjusting his moustache. 'Slight change of plan. This afternoon we are going to have a regimental history lesson. You were all issued with the Regimental Handbook during Week One of your training, so you've had plenty of time to swot up on its content. Now then; first off . . . who can stand up and tell me when and where our Regiment was first formed?'

He was met with vacantly averted stares, and the stir of shuffling boots.

'Surely at least *one* of you is able and prepared to tell me? After all, it's *your* regiment. You're now serving in it, proudly sporting its cap badge, and should be prepared to go out and gloriously die for it . . .'

I don't think any of us had thought it through quite that far.

Suddenly Ray Allen spoke up. 'I think I might know the answer to that one, sir.'

'And you are?'

'Private Allen, sir.'

'Very well, Allen. Spit it out.'

'Sir; the Royal Sussex Regiment was formed by the Earl of Donegal in Belfast in 1701 . . .' and then, as an afterthought, he added: ' . . . at three-o'clock on a Wednesday afternoon.'

'Three-o'clock on a Wednesday afternoon: what on earth do you mean, three-o'clock on a Wednesday afternoon?'

'Sir; they were going to have it in the morning, but it was raining.'

Major Tucker had a sense of humour. Ray was not court-martialled, but the remainder of our first regimental history lesson was short lived, because ten minutes later we were stood down and yet again told to go and get on with our best boots.

*

Throughout its proud history the Royal Sussex Regiment (35th/107th of Foot) was known by various *noms de guerre*. One of these was The Orange Lilies. This name derived from the gold *fleur de lys* on the Colour we captured from the French Roussillon Regiment at the Battle of Quebec on 13th September 1759, combined with our uniform's orange facings. These orange facings originated from an historic association (another story) with the Dutch House of Orange. (Queen

Juliana of the Netherlands and later her daughter, Beatrix, were successively the regiment's Honorary Colonels-in-Chief). Because of our county's soil oriented association we were also, rather less romantically, known as The Sussex Swede Bashers; as well as being called The Haddocks, a late Victorian distortion of Brighton's famous dolphin emblem Lowther's Lambs was another one of ours. Colonel Claude Lowther (1872-1929) was a Liberal Unionist MP who purchased Herstmonceux Castle in 1911. In keeping with the mood of the time, in 1914 he opened recruiting offices all over Sussex and personally financed and raised four battalions (11th/12th/13th and 14th) of South Downs' lads, who became affectionately known as Lowther's Lambs. Rather than being some allusion to the renowned South Downs sheep, this had to do instead with the name of Colonel Lowther's pet lamb, Peter.

On Friday 30th June 1916 these battalions of Lowther's Lambs were to mount a diversionary tactic at the Battle of Richebourg, one hundred miles north of the Somme, at which they were terribly damaged by German machine guns and artillery. One thousand were wounded that day, and of the 365 killed, a hundred of them came from Eastbourne. It became known as The Day Sussex Died. Then after the First Battle of Ypres, suitably impressed and vanquished WWI German PoWs gave us the hard earned sobriquet by which we were also to become known - The Iron Regiment.

During the Great War, in addition to Lowther's Lambs the regiment raised twenty battalions of men, and then next time round went on to field fourteen battalions for World War Two: but by the time I had come along to join them in 1956, we were down to just one battalion.

In 1956 South-East England's Home Counties' Brigade consisted of The Queen's Royal Regiment (West Surreys); The Buffs (Royal East Kent Regiment); The Royal Fusiliers (City of London Regiment); The East Surrey Regiment; The Middlesex *"Diehards"* Regiment - and Captain Mainwaring's Queen's Own Royal West Kent Regiment, with its well known *Dad's Army* connection.

The Royal West Kent Regiment's prancing horse cap badge

with its *Invicta* motto lends itself to an interesting historical aside. A chap called Vortigern, meaning Overlord, was our country's 5th Century leader of the then Romano-British administration. Most of the country was quiescent, but Vortigern was having a bit of trouble quelling the Picts and Scots. To enhance his manpower and assist him in subduing the upstarts, be brought over three boatloads of German mercenaries from Jutland, under the leadership of two brothers - Hengist and Horsa; each of their names being alternative words for 'Horse' in Saxon. After the Scots and Picts had successfully been sent packing back to the hills, Vortigern rewarded Hengist for his trouble with a parcel of land known as Thanet. Through the marriage of Hengist's beautiful daughter, Rowena, to Vortigern - combined with various other medieval machinations - Thanet was soon to become the Saxon Kingdom of Kent, with Hengist at its helm. Hence the subsequent adoption of a 'horse' as the county's symbol.

Its motto - *Invicta* (Unconquered) - is better yet. It is associated with the story of the Treaty of Swanscombe in 1067, when according to local legend, a year after seizing the English throne William the Bastard was travelling to Dover one day when he was confronted by the tough and warlike Cantware (the People of Kent). They demanded from him the reinstatement of their ancient laws and rights, in which case he would receive their loyalty, or else be obliged to 'battle most deadly'. Apparently William didn't fancy his chances much that day, so acceded to their not entirely unreasonable request, thereby negotiating trouble-free and safe passage for himself and his entourage, as a consequence of which William has never been styled 'Conqueror' by anyone native to the County of Kent.

That's the story behind just one of our country's good old regimental cap badges, which now no longer exist.

But then on 31st December 1966 all these fine old Home Counties' Brigade regiments were ordered by decree to relinquish our hard-won county regimental cap badges (the Royal Sussex officers' silver badge for long having been acknowledged as one of the most beautiful in the British

Army) for an artificially contrived Saxon crown pierced by a blunt sword, which none of us liked at all. This had to be worn to facilitate communal recognition after we'd been reduced, disbanded, mixed up and amalgamated to form 1, 2, 3 and 4 Battalion(s) The Queen's Regiment.

As though *this* wasn't enough, 'they' then set about cutting us back even farther. On 9th September 1992 - under the Ministry of Defence's much vaunted Options For Change 'rationalisation' programme, 1, 2, 3 and 4 Battalions The Queens Regiment were all conveniently merged with the equally proud and long-lived Royal Hampshire Regiment, to form the new PWRR (Princess of Wales's Royal Regiment - or *'Camilla's Marauders'*).

This shrunken, concocted hybrid became the new community regiment for Kent, Sussex, Surrey, Middlesex and Hampshire, finding fortuitously bestowed upon it the bountiful largesse of all these counties' earlier fine regiments' combined traditions, battle honours, and the history of nearly two thousand years of soldiering which came rolling in for their protection and safe keeping. For example, originally awarded to the erstwhile Queen's Royal Regiment in 1662 (for its service on behalf of King Charles I) PWRR inherited what is recognised as being the oldest battle honour in the British Army - Tangier. For good PR measure it also found itself now nicely and neatly packaged and presented as being England's 'senior' infantry regiment - which the now subsumed Queen's Royal Regiment had been: established in 1992 remember! Game, set and match, British Government.

I will not malign the PWRR, which consists of a fine body of men who have quickly built new achievements and traditions for themselves, the most notable example, perhaps, being that of the outstanding bravery displayed in Iraq in 2004 by their very own badly wounded Lance Corporal Johnson Beharry, to whom on 18th March 2005 Her Majesty The Queen graciously had the pleasure of presenting the first Victoria Cross in 25 years.

If in order to prevent them being sold off, laid-up or lost for ever, the hard-won scarlet and gold of all these disbanded and amalgamated regiments had to go somewhere, then arguably it was perhaps perfectly right and proper that they should have been inherited and continue to be borne by their mutual successor, PWRR. But it was a prolonged and deeply saddening affair that such substantial chunks of our nation's military history should have been dissipated in this cost-cutting way. Imagine if after 500 years of pride and mutual self support your own family, and its unique coat-of-arms, had to be changed to accommodate and incorporate six other families and their altered escutcheons. And it continues unabated today, until the time will soon be upon us when - almost certainly with limited overtime and less pay than that awarded to our Police Force - Britain's military representation will purely be as a token 9 to 5 section of some spiritless new European paramilitary defence force.

As well as containing most of Sussex's 18-20-year old males - those who hadn't joined the Navy, the RAF, or been deferred, medically excused, registered as conscientious objectors, or done a runner - The Royal Sussex Regiment also hosted quite a few of Eastbourne Grammar School's old boys, so the rite of passage of living in Chichester barracks had been a natural continuum for me.

The barracks' site had been occupied by the military in tented accommodation since the mid-1700s. In 1795 the barracks proper began to be built, at what turned out to be a final cost of £76,167. In 1803 French PoWs started to construct the additional wooden-hutted outbuildings that remained there for many years, some of which were still in use when my 1950s intake and I had arrived to commence our induction and basic training there.

Throughout the nineteenth century the barracks were occupied by various cavalry and infantry regiments, but then in 1873 they became the dedicated Brigade Dépôt for the 35th/107th (later Royal Sussex Regiment) whose home it was to remain for the next hundred years, until in 1964 it was then decreed that the Corps of Royal Military Police should set up shop there and claim it as *their* physical and spiritual home for the ensuing half century.

In 2005 the Government then saw fit to close these famous old barracks down completely.

At the time of writing it has not yet been fully decided whether the historic site will become a shopping mall or a housing estate. My readers' guess is as good as mine!

Newsflash· I have just today learned that it is planned to build 1,200 houses there, plus a school and a medical centre: however, we are currently suffering a massive downturn in the UK economy when many already approved major building projects are being shelved for the duration, so - who knows?

*

As I was striding out with purposeful self confidence round the camp's internal perimeter road next morning on my way for a coffee and bun at the Naafi, I saw three incredibly smooth looking figures proceeding gracefully towards me, switching at their calves with their barely broken-in officers' rattan swagger sticks, while playing verbal frizbee with each other's brand new halo. Fresh down from Eaton Hall and two weeks leave, newly commissioned 2/Lts Broadbent, Day and Nelligan - my erstwhile comrades Roger, Bob and Mike - had returned to the regiment. By virtue of their new rank they had now become elevated upon very high indeed, and it was expected that they should be approached and addressed with deference at all times. Yet why should each of us be feeling embarrassment at this encounter? I saluted them, as required, delighted to do so but thinking that there but for the grace of having failed my first shot at WOSBy I would be strolling insouciantly along beside them, four musketeers instead of three. They each returned my salute, wanly smiled, nodded, and continued on their way, although good old Mike Nelligan did have the courtesy and consideration to pause for a few moments to enquire what I had been up to since we had last seen each other. We were all the same age and had shared much during our basic training at Canterbury, but fifty years later when we were to meet again and reminisce nostalgically over a reunion lunch Roger Broadbent told me that when they saw me coming towards them that day, since the newly imposed wedge of this massive social distinction had been governmentally jammed between us, taken unawares on the spur of the moment like that, none of them could think how they were expected to react towards me.

I wondered if life would ever bestow upon *me* the authority symbolised by the right to bear a malacca or leather-covered swagger stick. It is possibly one of the most useless pieces of military equipment ever devised, primarily used by empire-building Victorian officers to rap knuckles as salutary on-the-spot reprisals to indigenous personnel for malpractice, or to continue repelling revolting tribesmen after their revolvers had run out of ammunition. Probably the best description of the swagger stick's true function may be quoted from a British regimental sergeant major's instruction to a group of newly commissioned young officers. 'Now gentlemen, your swagger stick is not for rattling along railings, cleaning out drains at home, or swiping the heads off poor innocent little flowers. Nor is it for poking into stomachs or for fencing duels in the mess. No, gentlemen, it is to make you walk like officers and above all to keep your hands out of your pockets'.

During World War One walking sticks were often carried by officers. Such sticks came to have a new and greater use with the introduction of tanks which often became 'bogged' on battlefields, particularly in Flanders. Officers of the Tank Corps used these sticks to probe the ground in front of their tanks, testing for firmness as they went forward. Often the commanders led their tanks into action on foot. To commemorate this, Royal Tank Regiment officers have subsequently always carried an ash plant instead of the short cane customary to other arms.

Cavalry officers carry a riding crop.

Male tour guides at Disneyland use swagger sticks as pointers.

More interesting perhaps, the girl tour operators use crops!

SEVENTEEN

AT LAST!

With a considerable degree of interest, the following day we saw that our names had finally been published on Orders as constituting the first draft for Korea. What we had all been waiting for. A palpable undercurrent of excitement pulsated round the camp and went coursing through our veins. We began marching about the place with a more sprightly spring to our step and our lives assumed purpose once more, although maybe we wouldn't have been quite so keen if the war had still been going on out there. The nominated draft consisted of Corporal Johnny Butler, Kevin Flynn, Pat Holman, Don Holman, Pete Holmwood, Sam Sampson, Jim Davidson, Christian Emms (with whom I had been at school), John Hammond, Bernard Granville, Paul Botcherby, Pat Patterson, 'Bumper' Bailey, John Baxter, Fred Sparrow, Ray Allen, Bob King, Derek Cresswell and a few other stalwart lads who have long since outgrown my memory. Next morning we all reported to the MI Room to queue up for our cholera jabs, which took the edge off things a bit; but we survived.

On Friday 2nd November we packed our kit and handed in our bedding. I drew £13 (£224) from the Pay Office and left Chichester to set off back home to Eastbourne to enjoy two weeks embarkation leave . . .

. . . and also to become love struck, all over again.

The attentive reader might recall the name Susan Walker, the Chief Constable of Eastbourne's daughter with whom I'd enjoyed 'a bit of a thing' during my last year at school.

The 'thing' I'd had, was about to be resurrected.

The lemons in the fruit-machine of life became chemically aligned, setting my love-bells clanging Big Time.

Con*currently* . . .

. . . don't get your hopes up *too* much, but we'll come back to Susan again pretty soon —

. . . a WWII RAF fighter pilot by the name of Basil Wright had a son called Colin who was one of my best friends at school. Basil Wright was a test driver for the then Rootes Group at Coventry. Every Friday evening there seemed to be a brand new Sunbeam Alpine parked outside the Wright's residence in Eastbourne's Grove Road. One evening during the summer Colin 'borrowed' his father's current car, and we went for a drive together. Somewhere up near the top of Beachy Head (there's no need to worry) he let me take the wheel. It was a thrilling rite of passage. I had never driven a car before, and was briefly learning to do so now by dint of Colin in the co-driver's seat telling me fairly anxiously what to do with my hands and feet as we went careening round bends at 40 mph. The term 'crash course' sprang to mind. There were definitely one or two adrenalin-charged moments before, weak-kneed, we eventually took the beast home to berth. Following his father's footsteps Colin then went off to Coventry to attend the Rootes Group Training Course. He had bought himself a motorbike and, fortuitously, he too had appeared home in Eastbourne for a while during my embarkation leave. So we had transport. Again, Colin let me have a go on that machine too, but I wrapped it round a tree with him riding pillion and bruised his knee. Better the bike than one of his father's cars - but even so. We soon had it fixed though, and were back on the road again by tea-time.

The following day I caught the train to visit my father and say farewell to him, prior to departure for my upcoming two year stint abroad. Mother and he had been divorced for two years now, and dad was living on his own in a bungalow he'd bought at 32, Stoney Lane, Southwick. Southwick is a small seaside town in the Adur District of West Sussex. It was mentioned in Domesday Book and in 1956 had a population of around 8,000, but it is difficult to find much more than that to say about it. No - wait a minute; apart from the famed contralto Dame Clara Butt having been born there in 1872, there *is* an unlikely tale to tell about the place. For some amazing reason best known to herself, in 1995 the acclaimed American singer, Whitney Houston, let it be known that for a reported £3M she wanted to purchase Southwick Green. She had plans to build some sort of a *palace* there, similar in design to George IVth's Royal Pavilion, over in nearby Brighton - but when she saw the proposed site, apparently changed her mind.

Making him endure a period of professional and social penance for having had the temerity to get divorced, Big Brother Barclays Bank had 'punishment posted' dad to Southwick, appointing him manager at their tiddly little local branch there, as much as to say 'There - now let that be a lesson to you'. By subsequent dint of considerable charisma, quite a degree of applied professionalism and a pretty intensive whack of social engineering, dad managed to re-climb the ladder, achieve two more upwardly mobile promotions for himself back into the mainstream once more, and enjoy a successful re-marriage before retiring quite nicely, but in 1956 both father and son were still in their respective states of flux. So we caught a train up to London together, and that evening went to St James's Theatre to see Max Wall and Elizabeth Seal in my first ever West End show, *The Pyjama Game*. Dad went back home to Southwick again afterwards, but - big boy now - I stayed on, checking in to Room 231 of the Kenilworth Hotel in Great Russell Street. On my own. Golly; but life was beginning to become *so* grown up lately.

Now from the pinnacle of my great age I think sometimes how wonderful it would be, for example, to be able to hear again *Beethoven's Pastoral Symphony* for the first time. Throughout his life my father was an opera buff. During my early years I lay in bed listening to the strains of Puccini's *None Shall Sleep* from the gramophone, wafting up the stairs of our lately Hitler-blitzed home. With sublime contentment I would drift off to sleep to the lilting strains and crystal top-C of Madam Butterfly's *One Fine Day*, without really hoisting in

160

what I was hearing. I was more used to humming along on 1955's radio programmes to The Platters singing *Unchained Melody* and Fats Waller's *On Blueberry Hill,* Ottilie Patterson and Chris Barber's jazz, Tennessee Ernie Ford's *Sixteen Tons* and Elvis Presley's *Blue Suede Shoe.* But then one day a radio DJ was to play someone's request that made my skin prickle, my hair stand up on end and tears spring to my eyes. *Wow!* What stirred me to the innermost core of my being? It was the soaring operatic duet *Your Tiny Hand Is Frozen* from Puccini's *La Bohème.* After dad and I had seen *The Pyjama Game* I had decided to stay on overnight in London, just to take myself to Sadlers Wells next day to see the whole opera for real. It was the first most truly wonderful and memorably moving experience of my life, after which I became hooked on the stuff forever.

It is lovely how it is passed down the generations, too.

Before Japan entered the market the ultimate musical acquisition when I was seventeen was a piece of kit called a Pye Black Box. In Europe it was the last word in acoustic reproduction equipment, and probably cost a staggeringly unattainable £25 (£452) or something. Post 78s, we used to play things called LPs (long players) on it at 33 rpm, as well as 45s. (You'll have to ask your grandfather). Military service, marriage and a career all combined to prevent me from ever acquiring one. It was then not until the late 'sixties that I was finally able to lash out to buy a Bang & Olufsen stack for myself, which in those days was the equivalent of a Rolls-Royce. When my daughter was seventeen, *her* 'music' (as she used to call it) came packaged on obligatory teenage life-support facilities, called cassette tapes. Her persistent repetition of *Zebediah Zonk And The Westwind Wild's Thumping Song* didn't used to grab me too much I recall, and fruitlessly I would rail nightly at her ecstatic and dedicated enjoyment of such raucous cacophony. Then one summer she and *her* seventeen year old daughter, Hannah, came to stay. Of course I didn't have a *clue* what 'sort of music' my granddaughter Hannah liked (sadly I was widowed at the time), but I did have sufficient street-cred to know that it (then) came on something called a CD, and that an appropriate piece of kit upon which to play one of those shiny discs would hopefully impress her with the fact that there were some old fogeys around who could still be cool, man - what? (God, I feel breathless already, trying to keep up with myself).

When they both arrived, the proudly acquired CD player in my granddaughter's room seemed to be taken as much for granted as her washbasin and bed, but according to my daughter was duly noted and appreciated, and over the next few days enabled Hannah to introduce me gleefully to some interesting new sounds, noises, names, concepts, migraine . . . none of which I had experienced before, so that in itself was novel and created an even greater appreciation of a) the generation gap, and b) what had once been peace, quiet and our own good old-fashioned cultural icons of yesteryear.

After three nights' non-stop action, when even *her* energy-charged young body cried '*enough*' and Hannah decided to turn in early for some recuperative therapy, my daughter went out to a flower-arranging party and I was left to my own devices. I sat down with a small whisky/soda and started to tinkle the ivories of my baby grand. Encroaching rheumatoid arthritis notwithstanding I am still able to impress myself occasionally by ripping off a few fistfuls of dexterous arpeggios for openers, which my wife disparagingly used to refer to as 'Michael having a quick burst on his banjo.' To me it was more reminiscent of a quick burst on my bren-gun, but having got 'the burst' (of whatever it was) out of my system, invariably I would then settle down to play a version of my favourite Rachmaninov's *Rhapsody on a Theme by Paganini*.

Like a cruising barracuda, through a hurried mouthful of toast at breakfast next morning, one of Hannah's eyes caught mine, and with quickly dismissive disinterest, she enquired: 'Gramps - what was that you were playing on your piano last night?'

It's amazing what shops can produce, when coerced to acquire something 'this instant' by a persuasively demanding teenager - especially if that teenager is my 'instant gratification' granddaughter in a hurry.

That evening my home was suffused by an inexplicable and all pervasive calm. Grand-daughter Hannah had decided to stay in for a second night, to 'wash her hair'. My daughter and a friend of hers were exchanging recipes and big girls' talk about my prostate in the kitchen (no that's not where it's kept, but you know what I mean) and I was allowed the chance to finish reading *Captain Corelli's Mandolin.*

I did not then wear a hearing aid, but it still took a while for some sounds to register. I was on page 270 - where Captain Corelli is declaring his undying love for Pelagia - when I became aware of something rather lovely wafting like brandy flame on a Christmas pudding from beneath Hannah's bedroom door to writhe its way seductively down the stairs and wrap its musical arms endearingly around me in my armchair . . .

. . . the dulcet strains of a professional rendition of Rachmaninov she had acquired, emanating from the CD player I had bought her.

With great pleasure and a warmly encroaching grin I realised that *Zebediah Zonk & the Westwind Wild's Thumping Song* (or whatever Hannah's equivalent was bloody well called) had possibly 'had their day' where my granddaughter was concerned.

Wahay!

What an investment for the future that little CD player proved to be.

*

After a cracking good full-blown English breakfast, I checked out of the Kenilworth next morning, having paid the mind boggling sum of £1.2s.6d for my one night's B&B (£20) - whereas today the Kenilworth would *actually* charge £140.

The remainder of my leave was spent in Eastbourne. Like pre-migratory starlings on a telegraph wire it seemed that all my teenage friends were in town at the same time, each in the process of opening his or her oyster of life prior to departing to follow its directions. Most of us would never see each other again. One or two of us were to stay in touch; while in late maturity others of us would gravitate back to the town to settle, play golf and attend annual reunion lunches and funerals together.

It was at this juncture that cupid twanged his bow in my direction.

Re-enter Miss Susan Walker.

I called at her house.

We went for a walk together. And young love had a new lift-off.

The problem was that having suddenly now developed the very serious hots for each other, she confessed to me that she hadn't realised I was going to be away for two whole years. She thought it was only going to be for about six months. She was attractive, ripe and now well into the arena for plucking. While I was away *hordes* of admirers were going to be lining up for a shot. If her parents thought they had problems shielding her from me, God knows how they were going to cope when her scent really got out. God knows how *I* was going to cope, lugging a bleeding heart round the world with me in my kitbag. Meanwhile we went to the cinema a lot; hung out at our favourite coffee bar(s); visited friends' houses again - and again and again; bought a £6 camera (£100) and took lots of black and white snapshots of each other; attended dances; held hands; kissed and cuddled; practised all manner of stuff without actually 'doing it', and then, inexorably, it was Monday 19th November - the day my leave was over and it was time for me to report back to camp. My mother and brother walked to the railway station with me where one of my good friends, Robin Frost and an earlier girlfriend of mine, Dorothy, who Robin subsequently married, and Sue, were already there waiting to see me off. Lots of introspection from Mum and Tony; lots of firm hand pumps, bonhomie and back-slapping from Robin; lots of sniffling and eye dabbing from Sue; lots of suppressed eagerness to be off, from me.

I arrived in Canterbury at 10.30 a.m. and several of us made our way up to Wemyss Barracks together. Only six months previously I had completed my basic training here as a potential officer, and now here I was again, returning as a semi-hardened squaddie on the eve of departing to live in some snow filled ditch in Korea.

Funny old life.

We were billeted in Wemyss Barracks' run-down 'B' Block, with a solitary Crimean-era wood-burning stove to keep us warm. That afternoon was spent drawing our Korean-issue winter kit and equipment; thick rubber-soled cobbly-wobbly boots, innersoles, long-johns, string vests, pullies, reinforced combat jackets and trousers, gloves and of all things two pairs of pale blue silk pyjamas: And an amazing piece of kit called a parka. This was a padded all-weather outer coat with a strap that did up between the legs like a parachute, and had a hood with a malleable wire frame to shape it close round the face to keep frost-bite at bay. It was to prove a God-send in the minus 40° Celsius temperatures we were going to encounter; several of our number retained theirs, and still use them today for snow clearing, over fifty-years on.

It was so cold there in Canterbury the two weeks we transited through that we would happily have worn our Korea kit, but weren't allowed to. We dressed up for each other and stomped around the Victorian cavalry barrack rooms like Shackleton's advance party to the Antarctic, but then the whole caboosh had to be repacked in a kitbag, and that's when I began to miss my mother.

By contrast, next day we were issued with our Korean summer kit, the same olive green (OG) stuff I had worn in the foyer of Brighton's Regent Cinema, back in May when promoting *A Hill In Korea.*

This time round my abiding memory of Wemyss Barracks was toting a pick-helve round with me on guard stag and the pungent smell of the coke-burning boilers we had to check, stoke and keep topped up all night so that our colleagues wouldn't freeze to death in their sleep and might get hot water some mornings.

The rest of the time all we did was work in the cookhouse by day and wait to be told when we were going to sail - in the middle of which boring routine I got a boil the size of a golf ball come up right in the middle of my forehead. When it was finally ripe enough to burst the puss erupted across the room with the force and trajectory of projectile vomit, leaving a gaping crater in my brow like a bullet hole.

After three days – *halleleulah* - I received two letters; one from my mother - and one from my darling Sue. It was a Friday, and we had just been issued 18 hour passes. I telephoned Sue and arranged to meet her, for a change, at 11.00 a.m. next day, halfway between Canterbury and Eastbourne - in Hastings.

The following morning L/Cpl John Butler and I went down to the railway station in a truck to catch the westbound train. John was also a regular 22-year man who had joined a year before me. We were to go through Korea and then Gibraltar together, after which John went on to become a CSM. Retired these 20 years he is now a firm stalwart of the Eastbourne Branch of the regimental association, and a star turn each year when he commands the town's annual Armistice Day parade, when it is easy to locate him in his beret and blazer, pace-stick under his arm, by his stentorian voice calling the disparate parade members to order. When they hear John calling them up to *'ATTEN-Wait-For-It . . . SHUN'* they know there's a professional in their midst alright.

Sue was waiting for me outside Hastings station, from where we went round to a pub called *The Cambridge* for a drink. *The Cambridge* had been run for years by a Mr and Mrs Davidson. Their son, Jim, one of our Korea draft, and I were soon to become close lifelong friends. Jim was most definitely quite awestruck with Sue that first time he met her.

That afternoon Sue and I had lunch in a restaurant called *The Star,* did a bit of window shopping, and then went to see Marlon Brando, Jean Simmons and Frank Sinatra in *Guys and Dolls* before going back to Eastbourne together on the train. Sue lived in Old Orchard Road, just up from Eastbourne railway station. The closer we drew to her house we realised that something unusual was happening. Both the road and the pavement were jam-packed with clamouring photographers. Not yet eighteen, and celebrity status already! I could handle it

I thought, as we pressed through the milling throng to reach Sue's front door. All was soon revealed to us over a cup of tea in the kitchen with her mother. 'Today your father initiated the arrest of Doctor John Bodkin-Adams,' she explained. Hitherto Dr Bodkin-Adams in his Rolls-Royce and black homburg hat had been a revered figure in Eastbourne, but now - as the beneficiary of their wills - he was suspected of having bumped off a string of about 160 wealthy widows between 1946-56. After the alleged serial killer's resounding trial at The Old Bailey (until then to be the longest murder trial in British history, to hold the nation in thrall for seventeen days) he was considered (by the jury) to be Not Guilty of murder: but I found it interesting to have been 'there' at the start of the whole thing.

Next evening Sue came to see me off at the station. Half our Korea draft seemed to be there on that train, all hanging out of the windows with their eyeballs on stalks and tongues lolling. I felt proud as a peacock to have her with me; this long before the description 'trophy wife' had ever been coined. My new friend, Jim Davidson, reckoned she was a girl he could even be persuaded to give up fishing for.

This time we were only performing menial chores back at Canterbury for four days (receiving letters from Sue on three of them) before they sent us off on, yet another, 72-hour pass. I went home with Jim to stay with him at his parents' Hastings pub, *The Cambridge*. Next day we motored over to Eastbourne to meet Sue from work, and a clutch of us ended up in Drago's Bun Lounge discussing life, frogs and the cost of butter before Jim and I dropped Sue off at her home and drove back to Hastings for the night. The following morning I caught the train straight back over to Eastbourne again to go straight back round to Sue's, bearing with me a bunch of chrysanthemums. That morning we went out shopping. She bought herself a pair of low black high heels at Saxones and I bought her a locket, a bracelet and Pat Boone's record *I'll be Home*. Gulp: *Aghhhh*. That evening we went to someone's party. When I called to collect her she was wearing a white dress, sitting playing the piano; she looked so fragrant I had never felt so emotionally

167

choked in my life. Her father drove us to the six-o'clock drinks party, and at 8.30 p.m. we were back with our friends in town at our favourite coffee bar again. Jim had come over from Hastings once more in his father's car (it appealed to him to be a party to our romance, and as the fish weren't biting in his local pond . . . what else did he have to do?) and when we had dropped Sue off, we again drove back to his place for the night. Next afternoon he nobly drove me back across to Eastbourne yet again to collect Sue and take her back with us to Hastings for tea. We were hardly jet setters, but were certainly living life in the fast lane, wouldn't you say?

Our 72-hour pass now over, that evening we had to catch the train back to Canterbury from Hastings. Again, the train was packed with the rest of the Korea draft all returning from its 72-hour pass. Sue, by now, had become a sort of draft mascot, and I wasn't the only one who got choked up when she broke down and wept in my arms. Not an expletive was to be heard through any of the open train windows as the boys all respectfully kept their lips buttoned for a change. The guard blew his whistle and waved his flag, the boys yanked me aboard the train just as it started to pull out of the station, and we all hung out the windows waving to the forlorn figure of my lovely Sue standing bereft and lonely on the platform, clutching a soggy hankie before catching a train on her own back to Eastbourne.

We were back in our Wemyss Barracks 'B' Block beds by midnight.

I didn't know it then, but that was the last time I was to see Sue for two years . . .

. . . by which time it was all to be too late of course.

She had only been working at Eastbourne's Dental Estimates Board a short while before moving on to become an assistant matron at Newland's boys' prep school in Seaford and then a nanny in Malta, before marrying, producing her children, becoming divorced, working in the American Studies Department of Sussex University, and then going to live out her retirement in Devon.

At four-o'clock next afternoon, Monday 3rd December, it was confirmed that at two-o'clock the following morning we would finally be departing for Korea.

The rest of the afternoon was spent packing and writing to Sue, and then we all hit town on a bender. At six-o'clock the *Seven Stars* was heaving. By ten-o'clock I could see three of everything, so Ray Allen, Don Holman and I decided we needed to leave the celebrations for some fresh air and a coffee. Once the cold night breeze stung his face the myopia cleared from Ray's gaze, that promptly lit upon a pretty little open topped green MG parked at the kerbside beneath the lamplight's glow. The temptation and convenience of its leather bucket seat to a man in brimful dire straits was too great for Ray to withstand, so if the owner of that waterlogged MG should ever read this please may I apologise to him on Ray's behalf.

As Ray readjusted his dress I realised I had left my beret back inside on the bar, so returned to retrieve it. There was rather an intense darts match still in progress, and the devil was in me. I was now eighteen. On the morrow I would be on the high seas en route to foreign climes. Hesitantly I fingered the hard bulge in the left breast pocket of my battledress blouse. Knives had always held an abiding passion for me. Today they are about as politically incorrect and frowned upon as it is possible to be, but although I was never a Teddy Boy, back then I did usually used to carry an Italian flick-knife with me, for nothing more than affectation, really; and opening letters, peeling fruit, that sort of thing.

I unbuttoned my blouse pocket and surreptitiously withdrew this sleek piece of cutlery of mine, palmed it and depressed its switch. The blade flew open. Without any thought of consequence I drew back my arm and threw it at the board. Talk about hit or miss. Its razor-sharp steel blade glinted in the light as it arced across the bar. With a dull *thwunk* it embedded three inches of itself within the cork bull. I had never thrown a knife so unerringly in my life before. It was one of those very few short, sweet, sublime moments in life when the God of whatever-it-is momentarily deigns to indulge and smile benignly upon Michael George. If the wretched thing had bounced back by its haft onto the floor, which my more usual self would have expected, I would have accepted the consequential egg on my face for such a foolhardy action - but by that zillion to one chance it had stuck straight into the board. Smack in the bull, no less. *Pwhooaarrr.* Arms still poised in mid-air the darts players and the rest of the bar's incumbents stood in a stunned silence. Nobody challenged me. The cavity in my forehead left by my recently burst boil began to suppurate and trickle down my face a bit, but I disregarded that because of my overwhelming desire to grin at them all, and cry: '*Hey* - d' y'see *that*?' But I was showman enough to know it would ruin the effect to have done so.

Instead, I did it another way.

Fancying that I looked a tad like James Coburn in *The Magnificent Seven* (to be filmed four years later, in 1960) I sauntered across the open space to retrieve my implement. The board was fairly high up. I have always been fairly low down. The leverage required to extract the blade was in excess of my ability to apply. Shamefully I had to remove the board from its nail (thanking the good Lord above that it wasn't screwed to the wall), place it on the floor and apply the steel-shod heel of my ammunition boot against it. I tugged at the knife haft, and wiggled it, like a gardener with a half brick stuck 'tween the prongs of his fork. I heaved. The blade snapped. I staggered backwards clutching the haft. 'Shit,' I muttered, tossing it into the corner with a fit of embarrassed pique. There was only one thing to do.

'Night all,' I said, leaving the haft where it lay and the blade still sticking out of the board like an Apache arrow from a corpse. Turning at the door on my way out, I gave them a half-bow. 'I'm sorry about that. Off to do my stint in Korea tomorrow. Send y'a postcard.'

Ray had finished pissing in the MG, but now Don was throwing up over a dustbin.

'Where've you been?' they slurred.

'Playing darts,' I replied. 'Come on; let's go and get some kip.'

Reveille was at 02.00 hours.

The thirty of us loaded our kitbags and each other into the backs of five three-ton Bedford trucks and departed Wemyss Barracks forever at 04.40 hours. It was a crisp, moonlit morning as the small convoy thrummed its way through the deserted streets of Canterbury to the station where a special train had been laid on to transport us to London. Sitting ill prepared and exhausted on a British railway station platform at 05.00 hours in winter with a hangover and no food or drink, was a most memorable and salutary experience in suffering. We all had a short nap on the train before changing at Gillingham for the onward journey to London Bridge. From there we shuffled onto the Underground to get across to Euston where we had a couple of hours to wait. While doing this we were joined by 2/Lts Broadbent, Day and Ayres (another recently commissioned chap freshly arrived from Eaton Hall OCS). Eventually we entrained. Most of us had never been so far away from home in our lives before, and we hadn't really even started yet. Having quickly devoured the starchy contents of our so called 'happy bags' with which we'd been issued, we then slept most of the way as the train's wheels *clickety-clacked* us on the five hour journey up north to Liverpool.

Dusk was falling when we detrained at Liverpool Docks and gazed in awe at the great, white 517-feet long, 12,000 ton MV *Devonshire* moored in waiting at the quayside.

What a chequered career.

Launched eighteen years earlier, in 1938, she was exactly the same age as me, but *look* what she had achieved in the meantime. Completed as a troopship to carry 250 passengers and 1,500 troops, she had left Southampton and did not return to the UK for four-and-a-half years. Although under RAF management she was mostly to carry soldiers, and from 1939 to 1942 sailed to Marseilles, Dakar and Durban; Basrah, Bombay and Singapore; Fremantle, Tripoli and Naples. In 1942 she became an Infantry Landing Ship and carried assault craft to the Salerno and then D-Day landings. Post WWII she served in the Malayan Campaign, and then Korea. In 1953 she was refitted with permanent berths and cafeteria catering, able to accommodate 320 passengers and 825 troops. In January 1954 she returned to trooping to the Far East from Liverpool until 1957, and then from Southampton, which from Canterbury would have been far easier for us to get to, but was not to be. In 1962 she was sold to the British East India Steam Navigation Company for £175,000 (£2.5M today) for conversion to educational cruising. After 110 of these cruises she was finally sold to Cantieri Navali in Genoa to be broken up, and demolition began at La Spezia in January 1968. With our kit bags on our shoulders (no parrots in cages for our mothers just yet a-while; they were for the homeward journey) we now filed slowly up her gangway to become acquainted with the dear lady, embarking on the first most exciting adventure of our young lives.

We were not the only ones aboard. There were all sorts: Green Howards going to Hong Kong; Gunners and Sappers; RAF and the occasional RN personnel, all dropping off and slotting in en route to relieve other, brown-kneed young men who, two years older now, had completed their bash for the Crown and were due repatriation. And there were loads of families; wives, children and girlfriends, these latter being accommodated upstairs in the posh bits, while we squaddie-type oiks were herded down below in berths. My crowd was on E2 Starboard Deck where our 2' x 6' bunks, called standees, were tiered three-high, with only 18" of headroom between each of us. Folded by day but let down on hooked chains by night, they were pretty chronic but not bad.

We stowed our kit and fell-in up on deck for the obligatory fire drill before going off for our 'tea'. At 18.00 MV *Devonshire* weighed anchor and an eager little brace of tugs pulled us more deeply out into the open reaches of the Mersey Estuary. I went up on deck by myself, to be alone and relish the moment, being extremely reflective and logging the novel experience for personal posterity. It was very windy as I watched the Liver Building slide past and the lights of Birkenhead winking and bouncing across the choppy water.

The tugs disengaged and returned to port while the Old Country began to slip away behind us into the distance.

It was Tuesday 4th December 1956, and we were on our way at last . . .

EIGHTEEN

NEXT MORNING the Irish Sea claimed most of my breakfast, and Ray Allen's left boot the rest of it.

In 1997 Leonardo DiCaprio's and Kate Winslett's wind-ruffled hair was not matted with vomit as they stood lovingly entwined on the mock-up *Titanic*'s prow while Celine Dion sang *My Heart Will Go On* - but ploughing down the Irish Sea in 1956 in MV *Devonshire* we had no such facility. No Celine Dion: no orchestral backing. But there was definitely loads of puke flying about the place. Most it would seem, coming from me, although many others were contributing their fair share of the stuff as well. Ray Allen especially. Leaning as far out as we could from the rail together we groaned in unison with each heave, but everything we discarded the wind lashed straight back at us. The entire ship's port rail, starboard rail, hatch covers, companionways, heads, nooks and crannies were also littered and strewn with retching squaddies, all praying for a premature exit from life. Seasickness has never been much fun.

Other than insisting that we should brave the rigours of compulsory lifeboat drill (little of which sank in) 'they' knew that until intestinal fortitude was restored it would be fruitless trying to get anything sensible out of us that day, so we were allowed to repair to our pits to curl up in a variety of foetal positions, bemoaning our birth as the brave ship conveyed us down through St George's Channel and out towards the North Atlantic.

At 7.30 pm we passed the Scilly Isles, which made me think

that if it had taken all night and a whole day of unremitting misery for us just to pass Wales, Devon and Cornwall, I would be an old man long before we reached Korea, especially as we would not be going along the Med for the short cut down through Suez (closed since the war a couple of months before) but as a consequence were to be the first troopship since WWII to go all the way round the Cape of Good Hope and South Africa - the *long* way round.

Next morning it was overcast, but we awoke to find ourselves crossing a dead calm sea towards a razor-sharp horizon. Beyond? The fearsome Bay of Biscay. Fearsome? We were lucky. For us, it was a doddle. After the Irish Sea it was kids' play. No doubt with a surprise chuckle or two still up their sleeves for later, the gods had chosen to be kind to us while we ploughed across the Bay.

Up on deck that evening we watched Virginia McKenna and Peter Finch in the recently released *A Town Like Alice.* Romantic, or what? Until then I'd been more used to groping 'Bumpers'' Brown's tits for one-and-ninepence in Eastbourne's *Picturedrome,* not sitting cross-legged beneath the stars like this amongst a horde of khaki-clad *compadres.* We were like chicks breaking out of our shells with the new experiences, sights, sounds and smells of life all piling up to excite us.

Next morning we were scheduled to pass that rock-bound peninsula off Spain's Galician north-west coast - Cape Finisterre.

The ship's navigator got it right, we didn't bump into the thing, and then spent the rest of that day cruising down the coast of Portugal, all the while becoming aware of the fact that it was getting warmer.

In December.

Next day we were ordered to change into our PT kit because up on deck it was now like an English summer. We lay sprawled about on hatch covers swapping yarns, playing cards and arguing, or huddled amongst the breeze-eddied fag butts at the head of various companionways. Seagulls lazily circled our funnels. Sparse clouds scudded across an ever deepening blue sky. Our bows gracefully heaved their creamy waves to join our stern wash behind us, our wake forming a foam-capped highway trailing back across the deep, dark depths of the Atlantic. Porpoises and flying fish abounded thrillingly all about us.

Up on the First Class decks there were officers and their ladies, and other officers' ladies with other officers, all trying to behave terribly nicely but no doubt finding it difficult to do so in that invigorating sea air and with so much time on their hands, it being a recognised fact that the motion of a ship at sea has always created a disturbing effect on women's gonads: makes 'em susceptible to outrageous amounts of extremely focused and productive flirting apparently. Up in First Class too, they had piano recitals and suchlike stuff, while down below we lower orders only had pontoon, Naafi fruitcake and warm beer.

That evening we sailed past Las Palmas, the capital of Gran Canaria, where twenty years later I would take my wife on our first winter holiday to the sun, but this, as were most things, was still way ahead of me at this stage of life.

Two days later, escorted by schools of dolphins joyously surging and bounding along beside us through our hissing port and starboard bow waves, we approached Dakar, in Senegal, which was to be our first port of call. After we had docked and gone ashore at this French colony, we found its dusty boulevards, bars and sidewalk cafés alive with languidly lolling and insouciant off-duty French paras, each with a Gauloise adhered to his lower lip, their presence being greatly enhanced by their garb. Presumably the same age as us, they seemed to cut much more of a dash in the fashion stakes. For a start they wore long trousers, smartly tucked into laced-up, rubber-soled para boots. They wore romantic looking, distinctively angled large maroon para berets with their Gallic badges positioned *louchely* above their left ear, instead of the way ours were worn, straight and tight over our left eye. Thick webbing belts were slung round their hips like gun belts, from which were suspended lethal looking bayonets, loosely holstered pistols and the occasional esoteric lucky charm.

Their faces and forearms were sun bronzed and swarthy. Silver pendants and personal artefacts hung on chunky silver chains around hairy necks. They looked tough and rugged enough to *be* tough and rugged.

The most practical and attractive form of working dress ever devised by any army in the world is probably the British Army's beige whipcord trousers and khaki-drill shirt, as worn with crepe-soled desert grey chukker boots in the Middle East and Cyprus. Decked out in that little lot, with pips glinting in the sun and a natty regimental side-hat perched colourfully atop one's sun bleached hair, with a pair of twinkly blue eyes and tropical manila skin tone, you made an extremely tasty dish to set before the Queen but this, too, for me was not to be until a few more years down the line.

By comparison, we had now discarded our thick serge battledress and were sporting our jungle green jackets and stiffly starched baggy shorts, which when we walked sliced at our kneecaps like fruit knives through peaches. These had been yanked like crumpled entrails from our kitbags to be laundered and pressed in the ship's dhobi. With our puttees and the Regiment's orange and blue garter tabs fluttering from our woollen hose tops like those of boy scouts, we hardly seemed much of an advert for the killer potential of our nation's land forces.

Puttees came in contemporary colours: well - two, actually; black for Gurkhas and The Royal Tank Regiment, and khaki for the rest of us: smooth light khaki, made at a place called Coldharbour Mill in Devon, by a firm called Fox, for officers, and dark rough khaki jobs run up in one of the world's backstreets somewhere, for everyone else. The word puttee comes from both the Hindi word *patti*, meaning bandage, and the Sanskrit word *patta,* meaning a strip of cloth. During WWI and up until the outbreak of WWII puttees consisted of 9' strips of khaki serge broadcloth, wound spirally round each leg from ankle to knee, and then secured with an adjoined length of cotton tape wound round and tucked into itself. Puttees too tight? - loss of circulation. Puttees too loose? - came unwound, making you go arse over tit into the nearest muddy trench, dislocate your jaw and knock your front teeth out on its corrugated iron shoring.

During WWII these 9' knee-length jobs became shortened to 3' items, which merely wound around the ankles. These continued to be worn until the post-Falklands advent of boots-combat-high, which not yet having been invented down there in Dakar in 1956, our ankles were still being bevelled into our boot tops and bound into place by the bog-standard puttee of the day. Pitted visually against *les paras* we felt less like boy scouts and more like wolf cubs than trained warriors. In Korea later that summer I was similarly attired when I wandered unsuspectingly into an American army club one Saturday night. The place was heaving with well-laced soldiery. Trying to appear unobtrusive, which at that time of my life, being 5' 8" and 9 st 3 lbs of adolescent fright was not difficult, I had no sooner ordered myself a Coke (in a dirty glass) than I felt an enormous hand drop heavily onto my shoulder.

'*Men* . . .' boomed 6' 4" and 250 lbs of coloured bass-baritone master-sergeant, who spun me round to face a clubful of enquiring Americans. 'Men - I want y'all to look at mah good frien' here . . .'

I clasped my hands gingerly across my fly and regarded my booted feet like a bashful virgin at her first dance. My knees quaked in my starched shorts and I felt extremely embarrassed. These were full grown men. I was still a boy. No way did I know how to deal with such a situation. Billy Manser and 'Buster' Bates would have done, though. They would have just stood there looking tough, and claimed their due.

'When I was in Europe in '44,' the big American negro hollered to those at the far end of the crowded bar, 'I was priv'l'g'd to be able to serve alongside men such as this. I want y'all to take a good, long, hard look at this little fellah, as he stands before you now. What you see here is one of the roughest, toughest, rootenist, tootenist fightin' men this world has ever seen.'

It was very nice of him, but - wot: me?

I groaned. He must have mistaken me for a Gurkha, or something. I prayed that I would not be asked to demonstrate some martial party-piece, such as decapitating one of his Navajos or crushing a beer can. I had only gone there to get some photographs developed at their PX. If I'd thought he was joking I might have been able to summon some mild riposte, but he was serious. Long pants might have helped too, but with those wretched little green shorts flapping about my knees how was one possibly expected to maintain dignity? I wriggled free of his affectionate embrace, blushed, gulped down my Coke, and fled. Those fulsome British shorts might have 'done for' Rommel and the Afrika Korps at *El Alemain* and helped forge an empire, but for my money they also contained the seed of its demise.

It was to take me a few more years to discover that it was not always those who looked the part, who delivered; that in real life action almost invariably speaks louder than words. I would have been more reassured if back then I had known about the two French paratroopers seconded to the British SAS for special training. After the first day they met up in the bar. 'Ah, Pierre,' asks one. ''ow 'ave you been doing?'

'*Merde*,' replies Pierre. 'I 'ave 'ad ze most terrible day. *Terrible*. At seex these morning I was awoken by zees beeg 'airy sergeant. 'E dragged me out of my bed and on to ze parade ground.'

'And zen what 'appened?' enquired his mate.

'I weel tell you what 'appened! 'E made me climb urp zees silly leetle platform five-feet off ze ground, and zen 'e said: "Jurmp".'

'And did you jurmp?' asks his mate.

'I did not. I told 'im - "I am a French paratrooper. I do not jurmp five-feet. Eet is beneass my dignity.'

'And zen what 'appened?' asks his mate.

'Zen 'e made me climb urp zees silly leetle platform ten feet off ze ground, and 'e said: "Jurmp!"'

'And did you jurmp?' asks his mate.

'I did not. I told 'eem: "I am a French paratrooper. Eet is beneass my dignity to jurmp ten-feet".'

'What 'appened zen?' asks his mate.

'Zen 'e made me climb urp zees rickety platform a 'undredfeet above ze parade ground. 'E undid 'is trouseres, took out zees enormous willy, and said: "If you do not jurmp, I am going to steeck zees right up your burm".'

'*Oooooh,*' exclaims his mate. 'And did you jurmp?'

'A leetle, at ze beginning.'

NINETEEN

THE REPUTATION CREATED BY OUR FOREFATHERS lay like a protective shield around us. Rather like the Americans in Korea later, the colonial French paras at Dakar surveyed us much as sharks might consider a shoal of whiting, not sure if they were piranha. We, the whiting, played happily on the while, unaware that apparently we were meant to pack one hell of a punch when roused. As it was we caroused, sent postcards, got sunburned noses and went back to the *Devonshire* for our tea. That evening we set sail for Cape Town.

For some incredible reason the following morning Jim Davidson, Paul Botcherby and I awoke to be informed that we had been made up to acting / local / unpaid / unwanted lance corporals. The bestowing of Field Marshals' batons could not have imbued more pride in us trio of lads than those single stripes, denoting our ascent onto the first rung of the military hierarchy's long, tall ladder. We spent the rest of the day with our 'housewives' open beside us, painstakingly sewing our new stripes of office as neatly as possible onto our sleeves before going warily up on deck to strut our excited stuff on our first public appearance.

It was 78° and that evening there was an amazing sunset, the likes of which none of us had ever seen before. The perfect end to an eventful day.

We had now been at sea for ten days. Sailing round the world was quite a long winded, leisurely affair back then. Next day - day eleven . . . somewhere off the Ivory Coast while heading for the Gulf of Guinea towards Gabon WE CROSSED

THE LINE. In these days of interplanetary space travel perhaps not so many people get to cross the Equator for the first time any more, or if they do it is not of quite such significance, but it used to be an eagerly awaited and exciting rite of passage, being dunked in a salt-water pool and smothered in seaweed, flour and other noxious substances; like getting your first erection; you felt you were one step closer to worldly-wise-ness and being allowed the ability to commune with fully grown men. You even received a certificate for it. Mine read like this:

A PROCLAMATION!
TO ALL WHOM IT MAY CONCERN

Know Ye that on Saturday 15th December *Michael A. George* at Latitude 00 Longitude 9° West entered into our Royal Domain and being inspected and found worthy was initiated into the Solemn Mysteries of the Ancient Order of the Deep.

We do hereby declare and publish abroad that it is Our Royal Will and Pleasure to confer upon him the 'Freedom Of The Seas' and to exempt him from the necessity for further homage. And We also direct all Seamen, Landlubbers, Airmen, Travellers and Globetrotters who have not yet visited Our Domain to treat him with the respect due to one of Our Loyal Subjects.

And further, should he ever be found in the sea we decree that all Sharks, Dolphins, Whales, Jellyfish, Crabs and other dwellers of the deep are to abstain from sniffing out, nibbling, harassing, eating, bullying or otherwise maltreating him.

Given under Our Hand at Our Court on board MV *Devonshire* on the Equator: *Neptune Rex*

Early on Monday 24th December we sighted Cape Town's definitive symbol, the Ordovician quarzitic sandstone Table

182

Mountain, appearing over the horizon about forty miles to our fore. The Portugese explorer Antonio de Saldanha had been the first European to enter Table Bay and climb this 3,563' high mountain, in 1503. Of course I already knew this at the time, didn't I.

Here in the southern hemisphere the closer we drew to land, the higher the temperature climbed. Cape Town appeared smaller than I had imagined it would be, nestling beneath the bronze backdrop of the mountain range's Lion's Head to the west and Devil's Peak to the east.

At 12.30 p.m. we were almost beside ourselves with disbelief, the ship listing heavily to port with us all crowding the rail.

Why was this?

It was because the entire quayside was crammed with large, white American cars, their sun bronzed and healthy owners leaning against their open doors or sprawling across the bonnets, all beaming, laughing and waving to us. Burly farmers who had helped General Montgomery and his renowned VIIIth Army (The Desert Rats) drive Rommel and his *Afrika Korps* from Africa's northernmost shores, were now endeavouring to assume some couth as they stood with folded arms and watched their flaxen haired teenage daughters twirling and squealing ecstatically about in flouncing white dresses and high-heeled sandals, having been brought along to see, be seen, and to help in the selection process. It was 'bring a soldier home for Christmas' time. The bright sun glinted off the surrounding red rooftops of Cape Town and all the gleaming white bonnets of the open-top Cadillacs, Chevrolets and Buicks lined up along the waterfront as this gorgeously ripe and nubile parade posed like a scene from the cover of *Picture Post* or models at the opening day of the Earls Court Motor Show. Delirious with amazement at such a miraculous turn of events, eager hordes of rampant and cackling young squaddies streamed down the gangplank to be swept up willy-nilly and conveyed out to the farms and the foothills for Christmas turkey – hopefully, with trimmings.

Being an hour late and a dollar short as usual, I had drawn

the short straw and had to remain on board as Fire Picquet for a couple of hours, so when finally I did get ashore it was on my lonesome. Being last off the ship there hadn't even been a wall-eyed Slack-Alice reject left waiting on the jetty to take *me* home for Christmas, so I had to make do with a one-eared, slightly pink, rugger and cricket-playing, WWII fighter-piloting, 30-year old, £2,000 a year Cape Town surveyor called Bill, who ferrying me from one bar to another, bought me several drinks in several of them and among other things tried to explain Apartheid. Everyone I met was overly friendly. Our unusual arrival - the first trooper since the War -had been forecast with a degree of fanfare in the local press, and being in uniform meant it was impossible for us to buy a drink. Wherever we went *every*thing was found. Bill had an American Ford V8 in which he drove me up to the top of Table Mountain to enjoy its fantastic views before dropping me back at the docks at 10.30 p.m. I hasten to add, completely unharmed.

Unbeknown to the hospitable Cape Towners, sadly we were scheduled to sail that night.

Apocryphal tales abounded for a while that some thirty or more of the guys had failed to return on board, having decided to stay in South Africa and get married instead. One such was Paddy, one of our Army Catering Corps cooks who had gone ashore in his blazer with the ACC badge emblazoned in glorious technicolour across its breast pocket, by which ploy he had successfully managed to convince one accommodating lass that despite his spotty face he was in the Army Commando Corps. Needless to say, Paddy scored - big time.

(It was not until thirty years later I learned that I had a whole horde of South African cousins living in Cape Town at the time, all of whom - as well as being dear family - have since become close friends; right at the top of the Christmas card list).

Christmas morning we awoke to see half the South Atlantic Ocean (as we sailed out of it) and half the emerald green Indian Ocean (as we merged into it) slapping against the glorious coastline of South Africa proper, while we closely hugged its southernmost coast along our port side on our way round Danger Point, up towards Port Elizabeth and Durban en route for our next port of call - Mauritius.

And I had a Christmas present.

The greatest morale-raising gift any soldier can receive, is a letter from home. In the forces the safe delivery of mail rates with as much if not more importance as food, ammo and medical supplies. Forces' mail was handled by the Royal Engineers Postal Section operating out of Mill Hill Post Office, in Middlesex. Our Regiment's postal address in Korea was *BFPO (British Forces' Post Office) 3*. Our shipboard draft's postal address, in transit, was MV *Devonshire At Sea*. Mail from home was meant to be there waiting for us us at every port. At our first port of call, Dakar, we had watched excitedly as great sacks of the stuff was swung aboard on gantries for - as it turned out - every other member of the ship's complement but us. It seemed the poor old Royal Sussex draft had been completely forgotten, or were the victims of some dreadful cock-up. I was then and always have been a copious correspondent. Already I had spent hours at sea writing to anyone I could think of (especially my still dearly beloved Sue) but so far had received no response from anyone, anywhere. But now, here, in Cape Town, on Christmas morning itself, my guardian angel had managed to filter me through a letter from Sue. It was numbered **two** and had been posted on 12th December, but I was ecstatic and read it fifteen times before breakfast.

The rest of the day turned out quite nicely, too. Along with our turkey and trimmings we received from a munificent government a free bottle of beer and 25 Players cigarettes.

For a while there had been a suggestion that after Cape Town we might have been putting in to Durban as well. In the event we never did, and this omission was the cause of rather a sad little incident.

During WWII, hundreds of ships used to sail from and arrive in Durban *en route* to or from various active theatres, their decks invariably packed with servicemen. And Durban at this time had produced South Africa's very own Vera Lynn.

She was a beautiful soprano called Perla Sielde Gibson, who became known as The Lady In White. The story goes that one day, in April 1940, Perla Sielde Gibson was on the jetty when some soldiers on board a troopship goaded her to sing: 'Hey Ma, sing us a song. Come on Ma, be a sport. Ma, give us *Land of Hope and Glory*, Ma.' Not in the least perturbed, spontaneously rising to the occasion like a true trouper Perla cupped her hands to her mouth and broke into song. There was an amazed and appreciative silence. Then the troops joined in, their voices rising jubilantly above the hustle and bustle of the wartime Durban docks. It was the start of a pledged ritual, and after that day Perla would continue to turn out to perform for as long as there were troopships to welcome or send off. As soon as the ships undocked she would start singing her patriotic songs, often with the aid of a megaphone. Then, as the ship turned in the harbour basin to leave she would move to the North Pier, waiting for it to appear there. As it passed slowly through the channel, she would continue to sing, her voice carrying across the water to the men on board, saying her goodbyes in song, singing till long after the ship had crossed the bar and was out of earshot. Dressed all in white and wearing a white hat, she sang patriotic songs for more than a thousand troopships and over 350 hospital ships. There is no doubt that this 54-year-old mother of three made a morale-raising difference, as was testified by so many soldiers, sailors and airmen who were on board those vessels and remembered her lump-forming renditions with such fondness. She never allowed the grief of having lost one of her own sons to stop her singing to the troops. The sad part of the story - for us - is we were told that the 68-year-old Perla and her nostalgic entourage had excitedly turned out in full-fig, white hat and gloves etc., delightedly expecting to sing again, to us, her first troopship since the war, and she was so disappointed at our not stopping that as we sailed by, a dark little speck far out on the horizon, she stuck to her guns and sang to us anyway, but with such gusto that she lost her balance, slipped, and fell off the North Pier into the sea.

Possibly a tad apocryphal, but quite sweet.

Perla, The Lady In White, passed away in 1971, just before her 83rd birthday. Official recognition came slowly. A stone cairn with a bronze plaque was completed in June 1972, erected on that same North Pier where she used to stand singing to her boys. It reads:

To the memory of Perla Gibson
'The Lady In White'
Who sang to countless thousands of
British Commonwealth and Allied Servicemen
as they passed through Durban over the years
1940 to 1971
This tablet was presented by
the Officers and Men of the Royal Navy

In 1995 a statue to Perla was unveiled by Queen Elizabeth II. Today it stands in a prominent place next to the Emtateni Centre, which is part of the Ocean Terminal Building on the T-Jetty.

*

It took us six days to sail from Cape Town to the 40-miles long and 30-miles wide, sugar producing, tropical volcanic island of Mauritius, that tiny (then still pink) dot in the Indian Ocean just north of the Tropic of Capricorn, 500 miles east of Madagascar. With the island's green hills and entrancing harbour approach to Port Louis, its north-western capital, Mauritius is surrounded by beautiful white sandy beaches, blue lagoons, palm trees and coral reefs. Once home to the famous Dodo - that big bird whose wings were too short to fly, which became extinct in the 17th century - the beauty of the place is overwhelming. The author, Mark Twain, noted in *Following the Equator* - a personal travelogue about his 1895 lecture tour round the British Empire - 'You gather the idea that Mauritius was made first and then heaven, and that heaven was copied after Mauritius'.

Anyone and everyone would feel at home in Mauritius.

Port Louis was so called in tribute to King Louis XV of

France, in whose name one Capitaine Dufresne d'Arsel took possession of the island in the early 18th century. Its harbour was built on a marshy expanse and became an important naval base for the French fleet, before - inevitably, back in those good old days, it seems - then coming under British rule, in 1810.

Today (having become the Republic of Mauritius, since its 1968 independence from Britain) most airlines will transport you there, to what has now become an extremely up-market holiday resort, for about £600.

Mauritians comprise an overall population of 1.5-million Indians, Africans, Europeans and Chinese. The Indo-Mauritians are divided into three groups: Hindus, Tamils and Moslems. They are all united and live in peace with each other. The people are full of charm, very courteous and helpful. The official languages are French, English, and Creole, which make the place sound a bit like New Orleans, and yet although there are newspapers published in French, the rule of the road is to drive on the left. God - what Great Britain and our forbears didn't do for the world in their day, eh.

Of Mauritius's 1.5 million population, 150,000 of them inhabit Port Louis. Pollution from the capital's horrendous daily traffic jams blends with the heat, humidity and dust to make one feel quite dizzy, an experience exacerbated by the city's intense activity along its boulevards and in the streets, where one can be overwhelmed by overloaded motorcycles, backfiring old bangers, and buses spluttering their nauseating fumes all about the place. Mauritian women are dressed either in the latest fashion or in traditional saris, and along with veiled Muslim women, men, children, stray cats and dogs, all stroll happily about the place's narrow lanes. Mauritian youths clad themselves in trendy gear and tote mobiles. The sun darkens still more the already tanned and moist skins, translucent halos appear round people's gleaming white or adorned clothes, and the statue of Queen Victoria still sternly and perennially surveys these daily scenes. This is today.

On New Year's Day, 1957, the quayside and jetties of Port Louis were thronged with dusky children wearing crisply starched white cotton frocks or shorts, accompanied by their merrily grinning parents, who were living either in their ancient structures made up of basaltic rocks, or in wooden Creole houses with small tropical gardens sheltering glorious mango trees, pawpaws, hibiscus and bougainvillaea. They had all donned their best clothes and turned out in force to greet our arrival, yet the Union Flag and fly-blown shop window portraits of Princess Margaret, who had recently visited the island as part of her 1956/57 East African and South African tour, were the only apparent indications to us that the place was still a British colony at all.

A couple of hours later, taking the air ashore and enjoying the experience of having my nostrils assailed by the new aroma of alien tropical spices, and my senses pleasurably invaded by even more exciting new sights and sounds, I was strolling along a dusty street back towards the harbour where MV *Devonshire* was berthed, when I succumbed to some small urchin's charmingly insistent plea to become the recipient of the loose change from my pockets. No sooner had I obligingly dispensed to him my albeit rather meagre largesse, than I became immediately besieged from all sides by a chanting mob of coffee-coloured children, who flocked frighteningly from nearby doors and alleyways to grab greedily at my pockets and demand similar remuneration. Hurling a handful of pennies into the air one way, I quickly turned tail and fled the other.

Little bastards.

TWENTY

LIFE ON BOARD A TROOPSHIP was something of a tedious affair, really.

There is only so much that one can pack into a day to make it seem fruitful.

The majority of people – civilians - who go on cruises, do so to be pampered. It was not like that with us soldiers on our cruises. We had to be seen to be occupied the whole time, until either the hierarchy or seaboard drill manual had both run out of ideas, then things were sometimes allowed to relax for a bit.

Sometimes, when it was stinking hot we would sleep up on deck, the grunts, farts and belches emanating from the many less than angelic forms fortunately being swept away on the night air, but normally we would sleep below on our fold-down, chained standees, with about an 18" gap from the man next to us. He, too, would almost invariably be emitting gas, snoring, or enjoying some noisy dream involving his barely remembered girlfriend. In the wee small hours, in such close and torrid proximity, in the depth of sleep, conveniently mistaking her for you and unable to keep his hands to himself, he would often reach out for something to grab, which at the age of 18 was a bit disconcerting. It can still be a bit disconcerting when you're older too, but that's another story.

Desperate to find something to rub up against, at that age we were all of us lugging permanent great erections around with us wherever we went. These were very hard to ignore, and harder still to conceal. Especially at night. With all the understandably fevered and colourful thoughts you can imagine, unleashing themselves to course through our subconscious adolescent minds when we were asleep, these burgeoning reproductive appendages of ours were constantly bursting free to assume separate life forces of their own. With unfettered unselfconsciousness they would strut their stuff, flex their new muscle and . . . preening proudly . . . pose for each other - bragging.

Wandering a troop deck during those tropical nights would have been any nymphomaniac maiden or gay boy's dream, with several hundred of these deliciously tumescent items standing rigidly to attention, all weaving and bobbing like charmed cobras in the air and up for grabs. Like a substantial army of succulent phallic stalagmites - or Privates on Parade, this fecund harvest of turgid teenage todgers were all seductively twitching out their individual dance routines there in the twilight zone, created nightly by the electric hum fuelling the dimmed security lighting system.

Those who did get to wander the troop deck, throughout the night, were the fire picquets. Other than being bombed, shelled or torpedoed, fire on board ship is the sailor's worst fear. Consequently, the performing of fire picquet duties was a given part of our life at sea. It was a constant and incredibly boring task, which we all had to do on a regular rotating- roster basis.

The picquet was merely required to prowl his allotted troop deck for the two hours of each stag, carrying with him a clipboard of orders detailing (in fairly large print) what to do in the case of fire, while sniffing the air for tell-tale signs of smoke. The nocturnal aroma on a troopdeck of sleeping soldiers in the tropics is infinitely more pungent than any tell-tale whiff of smoke could ever be. To humorously alleviate the tedium of their task, or else vengefully redress some slight which they thought they might have been subjected to during the day, with their clipboards raised at the ready the picquet would delight in either selectively (if at all envious) or willy-nilly whacking many of their *compadres'* aforementioned nocturnally paraded involuntary erections into submission, as they strolled past. Rather like swotting flies - sort of. This resulted in a constant groaning and rearranging of bodies as the disturbed recipients of said whacks readjusted themselves, and turned in their sleep. It also allowed respite for those of us whose turn it had just been to be mistaken for a girlfriend. They were now enabled to remove the alien hand that had unwittingly been clutching their thigh, and get some kip of their own before their own erection kicked-in again, and they themselves got sadistically whacked into submission by the next picquet to come on duty.

Another jape was for the picquet gently to remove the thumb from the mouth of one of his sleeping friends and awaken him with a light little tap on the shoulder. In response to the blearily enquired *'Wassamatta?'* he would then whisper into his friend's ear *'Do you want to buy a battleship?'* This was to be avoided though, because when it befell his turn for retaliation, the off-duty picquet could almost guarantee being similarly gently awakened himself three nights later by his now on-duty friend, to be asked *'What colour?'* To which his response, when it was again his turn three nights after that, would be *'Grey.'* And so it went. The joke soon wore thin. It was thought best never even to get started on this one.

Those of us who managed to survive the nights un-neutered, or without buying a battleship, would get up at any time between 0600 and 0730 hours, and queue to ablute in a washroom that was running with a mixture of soapy liquids and various other noxious forms of waste. Curiously, one of the most offensive of these used to be soggy razorblade wrappers. Burnishing ourselves with our stinking, always damp khaki towels, we then clambered into whatever had been decreed as shipboard dress of the day, usually PT kit, before making our way up to the canteen for breakfast.

The standard shipboard breakfast in those days consisted of one long-dead egg, with a cardboard sausage, beans, tinned tomatoes, fried bread, a doorstep of white bread and margarine, with a dollop of jam spooned onto it from an industrial size tin of the stuff, and a mug of Nato pattern tea. We didn't do napkins. We 'washed' our plates and eating irons afterwards in large bowls of disgusting greasy water, and either dried them on our buttocks or aforementioned stinking damp khaki towels. We used to experience the occasional outbreaks of diarrhoea, of course. And intermittent death. But other than that our immune systems never seemed to become too compromised.

The rest of the day was spent in various ways. We usually had to undergo an hour of PT, nicely timed to be held immediately after breakfast of course (while it was still cool) so that the majority of us could throw up. This helped us to remain slim, whilst easing the strain down in the heads.

Our bren guns had been stripped and reassembled more times than the Folies Bergères' chorus line, and for years afterwards there was many a girl about the place whose crucial body part would be mistaken for a released safety catch.

Although all at sea, we were still infantrymen and had to keep our hands in with our stock-in-trade. To do so we would troop up top to expend ammunition firing our rifles, shooting at batches of coloured balloons let loose from the stern deck, and used to pop more of them than addicts did pills.

On some days we were given talks about the 88-radio set, and on others received instruction about knots and splices.

One day an RAEC sergeant stuck the world map on a blackboard-and-easel and asked each of us to come up and point out to him where we thought Korea was. Apparently it might have been either just next to the Pyramids, or else in the Falklands, although the consensus of opinion was that it was probably somewhere in the heart of the Amazon rainforest; thus it transpired that there were very few of us who had even the remotest idea where the hell we'd already been, let alone where it was we were actually heading for.

Then once a week some poor officer or other would be deputed to give us all an on-deck lecture, which was a sweat for him, but made a nice, restful break for us. Officers, by divine selection, were imbued with a superior knowledge, and the natural ability to impart it; or so we were led to believe. It was only later when I was to become one myself that I learned what agonies some of those guys must have gone through, knowing that by the content and delivery of their hastily prepared obligatory talk they had to retain and enhance our respect, and impress us with the breadth of their learning.

We also squabbled a bit.

Lance Corporal John Butler mislaid a gold chain one day, which shortly thereafter he somehow or other found in one of our party's pockets, whereupon he laid into the culprit and gave him a right royal duffing-up for the misunderstanding. Nursing his split lip the aggrieved offender looked a bit sheepish for a while, knowing he'd had it coming to him, but no one ever heard of him nicking anything again, and nor did anyone ever think of reporting John Butler, not even the bloodied recipient of his ire, for the illegality of so justifiably and effectively having bashed a subordinate.

With our thick woollen battledress now stuffed into the bottoms of our kitbags, our Far East and troopdeck summer uniform (which we had first worn ashore at Dakar, vying with the French paras in the sartorial stakes) consisted of lightweight Olive Green (OG) bush jacket, OG shorts and/or trousers. In keeping with the rest of our kit, it was usually ill-fitting. One of our number, John Hammond - a slightly built chap who in compensation had been blessed with a disproportionately large dick, so was known as 'Tonka', and found himself being dealt merciless blows from the lower-deck's nightly clipboard brigade as a consequence, but that's beside the point - was a pretty poncy type who liked things just-so, so he paid a shipboard craftsman to taper, or 'peg' his OG trousers for him. It must be said that the finished job did look very nice indeed. John's bags could have graced the pages of any society magazine of the day, when tight trousers were fashionable. He was the epitome of sartorial elegance as he minced about deck in his peg bottoms and plimsoles, but Corporal Williams took serious umbrage at this unauthorised departure from the military norm. Corporal Williams - 'Willy' - was an 'old soldier', a war time regular whose countenance suggested that his natural role in life might more properly have been tractor driving or turnip picking. His reaction to John's tight trousers was not dissimilar to that of Lord Queensbury's to Oscar Wilde, when the former discovered that the latter had

194

been buggering his son. 'You've been tamperin' wiv the Queen's clobber, and you mustn't do that,' 'Willy' expostulated, showering 'Tonka' with angst-ridden spittle from a puce complexion. 'If I sees you wearin' 'em again, you'll be on a charge.' Thereafter, determined to continue exercising his independent streak, John spent the remainder of the voyage darting furtively about in his tight trousers trying to avoid 'Willy', who in turn spent the rest of his voyage creeping about trying to find him.

We had not stopped in Mauritius long enough to take on water, so on-board water rationing had now had to be introduced. This exacerbated everyone's aggravation, and tensions continually mounted. Hefting those permanent erections around in our pockets the whole time didn't help much either, and with our hormones in turmoil as well, more and more fights were beginning to break out all over the place. To hell with diarrhoea and the occasional death, it was a wonder we didn't have outbreaks of murder too.

*

We had left Mauritius on 2nd January for the six days' 2,500 miles bottom-left to top-right diagonal traverse across the Indian Ocean up to Colombo, in Ceylon - as was; which is now Sri Lanka.

Same as Rhodesia - as was, is now Zimbabwe.

It's a shame: the only thing in life that's permanent these days, is change.

*

In 1505 the Portuguese named the island *Ceilão*, which eventually obviously became *Ceylon*. In 1817 Ceylon came under the annexation of Britain, from whom she gained her independence in 1948. Then in 1972 she changed her name to *Sri Lanka*, which comes from the Sanskrit word *Lamka* meaning *Resplendent Land* - and you can't get more of a potted history of a place than that.

Lying just twenty miles south of India, this pear-shaped (in the nicest sense of the word), also teardrop-looking 250 miles long by 150 miles wide island, is known as the Pearl of the Indian Ocean, and almost 300-years ago it became the inspiration for the invention of a new word. In a piece of his copious and erudite correspondence (written in 1754) the august English author and politician, Horace Walpole, a cousin of Admiral Lord Nelson, famously coined the word *serendipity* - meaning 'the faculty of making happy and unexpected discoveries by accident' - which is said to have been derived from the fortuitously advantageous adventures of the protagonists in a 'silly 5th century Persian fairy tale' he had read, called *The Three Princes of Serendip,* Serendip being the ancient Persian name for Ceylon.

Buddhist since ancient times, Sri Lanka is now a multi-ethnic, multi-religious society, wherein nearly a third of its 20,000,000 populace today follows Hinduism, Islam or Christianity. During WWII it was one of the British Empire's most important Asian ports, with Lord Louis Mountbatten - the Supreme Allied Commander, South East Asia Theatre - having his HQ there, from 1943-46. The wonderfully named northern Tamil province's deep water harbour, Trincomalee, (meaning *Sacred Hill Of The Lord*) continued to be a Royal Navy base until 1957, and still today is a Sri Lankan naval and airforce base.

Sadly, since 1983 there has been an ongoing and to date unresolved civil war between the Government and the Liberation Tigers of Tamil, a militant separatist organisation who wants the formation and acceptance of an independent Tamil state.

On Boxing Day, 2004, the south and east coasts of Sri Lanka were devastated by the dreadful Asian tsunami, but since then the island's tropical forests, beaches and landscapes were successfully restored to once again being the culturally rich and famous tourist destination that Sri Lanka had previously become.

*

Awakened by the clanking rush and roar of MV *Devonshire* dropping anchor about five-hundred yards offshore, at 02.00 hours on Wednesday 9th January 1957 I piled out of my sweat-soaked standee down on E2 Starboard, and hurried up on deck to view the night lights of Colombo. Ceylon (as she was then) wasn't going away, but still I hurried - just in case. Interspersed with the tedium, everything was all so exciting, you see, so that you never knew what was going to happen next. As well as the novelty of this latest experience, I might also have been witness to something else memorable, like a shooting star hissing into the harbour; or missed something extraordinary, like I can't think what at the moment, but it could have been good. After a few minutes wonderment, though, I realised that all I had to marvel at, really, was one purple TWA neon sign winking at me from afar (Trans World Airlines; defunct since 2001). That being pretty much it, I made my way to the guardroom to cadge myself a gratuitous corn beef sandwich (stale and curly) off the night picquet, and then went back to bed.

Reveille was at 06.00, and at 08.30 we were being ferried ashore via a shuttle service of passenger launches. No sooner had we set foot on dry land than Jim Davidson, Derek Cresswell, John 'Tonka' Hammond and I were immediately pounced upon and escorted directly to a jewellery store, where for far too long John embarrassingly endeavoured to negotiate the downward price adjustment of a 10-rupee ring. It was our introduction to that time-immemorial worldwide system of haggling, which any true-blue Brit has always found difficult to deal with, unless he's an instinctive or died-in-the-wool crook - which condition wouldn't necessarily detract from his otherwise being true-blue, of course.

Much to the jeweller's chagrin, we prised John loose and left the ring where it was, sadly rejected and dejected on its black velvet cloth. Outside we clambered aboard a taxi and got the happy chappie to drive us all over the place, savouring the sights and sounds of this new fairy wonderland.

Full of its old colonial homes, the European residential area was just as my Boy's Own imagination had always envisaged it would be. The whole place dripped with lush verdant foliage, and I was tickled pink to see my first ever fruit bats - or flying foxes. There were hundreds of them festooning the branches of all the tall trees. Flying foxes, which can have a wing-span of 5' and weigh more than 2lbs, feed at night and roost in the trees by day. Hanging upside down from branches, rather than sheltering in caves or other cooler roosts, leaves them exposed to the sun in the daytime. Whereas once they could cope, nowadays, flying foxes have been dropping off trees and dying in their droves. Other than humans, they are the first large mammal to be shown to suffer mass mortality as a result of global warming-associated heat waves. More than 30,000 of them are estimated to have died in this way since 1994. The bats commence their demise as temperatures approach 42C. As temperatures increase, they begin to make desperate attempts to cool down, first by seeking shade in the trees, using their wings to fan their little bodies, and then by panting and rubbing spittle over themselves. After several hours in the baking sun they fall to the ground, and are dead within 20 minutes. But the ones we saw that day in Colombo, in 1957, were still a bunch of happy bunnies, or fruit bats, whose unimagined apocalypse from global warming still lay fifty years away.

Our taxi trip cost 15-rupees, the equivalent today to about £15, which is a fair indication of what 'Tonka's' 10-rupee ring was worth, and what an unwitting cheapskate he was in trying to reduce the price.

We were dropped off back in the centre of Colombo, beside an ornate Buddhist temple. After inviting us to remove our boots first, a sandaled, shaven-headed, saffron-robed priest who had been allotted the task that day, showed us round this amazing edifice. At the end of the tour it was indicated that it was expected and would be appreciated if without any trouble we would please put five-rupees into their offertory box (seven-shillings) which today would be about £5. Fair enough. As Buddhist temples go, it was a nice one, and our monk-guide pleasant enough, PR-wise, and probably quite adept at kung fu too.

Although we were all young and healthy, our fitness was being steadily reduced by slothful shipboard life, so that now, after several hours ashore, we had become pretty well creased with Colombo's clamour and excitement, its heat, dust and noise.

After buying ourselves a curry lunch, some pineapples, bananas, and small ebony elephants as souvenirs, and a cluster of moonstones for my mother, we made our way back to the *Devonshire*, and went gratefully aboard. Three others of our draft, who instead of pineapples and bananas had apparently managed to discover for themselves a fairly serious source of Asian beer, staggered raucously up the boarding ramp beside us. Rather than go on a cultural taxi ride and feign interest in some Buddhist temple, Pat Patterson, Bob King and Dave Sommerford had gone and got themselves tattooed instead.

After supper that night we cast off for our onward journey to Singapore.

*

Colombo to Singapore was another six-days' sail, taking us across the Bay of Bengal and the Andaman Sea, then down through the 500-mile long, pirate infested Malacca Strait, through the core of the South East Asian Archipelago. The 1,000 mile long, sixth largest island in the world, the exotic Indonesian island of Sumatra, presented a palm-fringed coastline off our starboard bow. A warm, gentle rain fell on deck, and we heard the sound of intermittent gunfire rolling across the calm sea, which there shouldn't have been, so perhaps it was electrical atmospherics. It certainly wasn't pirates. With 1,000 soldiers on board? Even though at that stage most of us were still only cream-puffs, they wouldn't have stood a chance. In any case, what could they have purloined? Our supply of Naafi fruitcake and lemonade?

Off our port bow the thinly etched green of the Malaysian

Peninsula's dense jungle became clearer and clearer the nearer we drew to its shoreline. We could now distinctly 'smell' the coalesced fragrances of Asian spices and wood smoke wafting out to us from land, making me feel just like one of Joseph Conrad's seafaring Victorian adventurers

When we went up on deck next morning it was to find that we had already reached Singapore, during the small hours, and were now navigating our way through its close-knit network of surrounding offshore islands.

This time there is to be no *real* introductory potted history of Singapore, because the place and its story are already so well known, however . . .

. . . in October 1956, barely three months before our arrival, a major milestone in Singapore's history had taken place when Communist-instigated riots engulfed the whole of the island. The situation was deemed serious enough to call out troops to quell the civil disturbances. The subsequent military operation that achieved this has since been recognised as constituting a textbook example of how military forces should be employed in aid of the civil power. When the call for activation was made, most military units arrived in Singapore within 14 hours. The longest response time was 44 hours, involving the 6th Queen Elizabeth's Own Gurkha Rifles, which was only activated in the late morning of 26th October and was, incidentally, the furthest away, at 470 miles, up in Malaya's Cameron Highlands. By the conclusion of the riots a week later, on 2nd November, an infantry brigade headquarters, six infantry battalions and two armoured car squadrons had been withdrawn from active military operations upcountry in Malaya, to quell them.

In view of all this, and the possibility of a certain amount of 'simmering' still going on, we were delighted to be told that we were to be allowed to go ashore, which we did at 09.30 that morning - after the others had disembarked first. The others? Yes - Singapore was our first disembarkation point, and - their seaborne trip now over - half the ship's complement of troops and families had finally arrived at their long awaited destination, the latter to be met by husbands, fathers and fiancés, while for the former it was more likely to be the sarcastic bite of some awaiting CSM, all geared up to get them swiftly installed in local barracks, or convoyed safely on their way up-country to man the more hairy bits.

A line-up of Bedford 3-tonners was waiting down on the jetty to take the rest of us, the transitees, to the Britannia Club, the home from home for all British servicemen in Singapore, where you could get a steaming hot plate of fried egg and chips and fried bread smothered in lashings of Daddies Sauce, and a nicely brewed cuppa. Plus it had a large Nuffield swimming pool that was frequented by the most awesome *girls; girls; girls*. Well, awesome wasn't a word in such common use in those days, and perhaps in any case they weren't *really* that awesome; but after life on a troopship . . .

Jim Davidson, Derek Cresswell and I had our tea and chips and left the club to try to pack in as much sight-seeing as we could before reporting back to the ship. The shops blew our socks off, they were so different to anything we had ever seen before. For a pittance I bought myself three little paper-knives in the form of miniature samurai swords, their blades made of beautifully tooled steel, sheathed in hand-painted wooden scabbards with red tassles on. One subsequently broke, one I gave to my mother and she kept it in her handbag for years, and the third I still have here on my desk before me now, as I write.

After shopping we each took each other's obligatory photograph standing outside Raffles Hotel, and then returned to the ship again at 14.30, prior to upping anchor an hour later for the penultimate leg of our journey.

Short stay, Singapore.

Just a nip up the road now, to Hong Kong.

Things were moving.

*

The following morning we were heaving our way through the largest waves I have ever seen, battling a passage up the South China Sea. It seemed like our sunshine cruise was over. We were ordered to cram our lightweight OGs back into our kitbags, from whence we pulled out and recommissioned our good old heavy-duty woolly battledress once more. These all had to be pressed, which was quite a performance with so many of us and so few irons to be had.

Five days later, at 16.30 on Sunday 20th January, we sailed into Hong Kong's so called *Fragrant Harbour*, and what wonderful scenery it was to behold, with its high, brown, rugged hills and peaks and every conceivable variety of craft and colourful Chinese junk, either moored or busily scudding about its choppy waters.

Hong Kong was MV *Devonshire's* final port of call this trip, where she would pause, cool her mighty engines, take a breather, and enjoy some substantial replenishment before turning round and setting off to ply the high seas back to the more familiar west once more, with a fresh passenger manifest; this time a predominantly carefree load of guys who had completed their two-year stint of National Service for Queen and Country and were now eagerly high on happiness, embarking to enjoy her facilities on their homeward-bound run to demob and their long awaited freedom.

TWENTY-ONE

THE OVERALL TERRITORY OF HONG KONG lies on the eastern side of the Pearl River Delta, bordering Guangdong province in the north and facing the South China Sea in the east, west and south.

Hong Kong consists primarily of Hong Kong Island, Lantau Island, Kowloon Peninsula and the New Territories, and additionally encompasses a collection of 262 islands and peninsulas in the South China Sea.

To the north the Kowloon Peninsula is attached to the New Territories, which span northwards to connect eventually with mainland China, across the Shenzhen River.

While Lantau is the largest island, Hong Kong itself is the second largest, and most populated.

The narrow body of water separating Hong Kong Island from the Kowloon Peninsula is known as Victoria Harbour, and is one of the deepest natural maritime ports in the world.

The name 'Hong Kong', which literally translates to mean *Fragrant Harbour*, is derived from the area around present-day Aberdeen, on Hong Kong Island. This is the place where fragrant wood products and aromatic incense were once traded.

Beginning as a trading port in the 19th century, Hong Kong long since developed into a leading financial centre.

Hong Kong was a British crown colony from 1842 until the transfer of its sovereignty to the People's Republic of China in 1997, when officially it became known as the Hong Kong Special Administrative Region, one of China's two special administrative regions, the other being the one-time renowned international Portuguese gambling Mecca of Macau Island, just 37 miles out to sea, to the west.

It was at that moving, rain-drenched handover ceremony at midnight on Monday 31st June / Tuesday 1st July 1997 that our once Great Britain effectively, and once and for all finally 'lost' her empire. Shortly after the ceremony Prince Charles and Chris Patten, the colony's last British governor, boarded the Royal Yacht Britannia on *her* last foreign mission (Britain's Labour Government decommissioned her six month's later as being unjustifiably too expensive to run) and to the strains of Rule Britannia and Land of Hope and Glory- waved a final farewell.

Today the population of Hong Kong is touching seven-million.

*

In 1957 it was less than four-million.

During January and February of that year, our presence, staging through the colony, was to increase it by a good few dozen.

Having disembarked and said our farewells to MV *Devonshire*, for which we would all of us retain a lifelong fondness, at 18.30 a small fleet of Bedford three-tonners took us and our kit from the harbour up to Kowloon's Granville Road Transit Camp, a fenced, hutted, no-frills establishment whose purpose in life was exactly what it said it was - to provide temporary accommodation for troops passing through the colony en route to or from somewhere else. It consisted of hangar-like prefabricated huts containing serried ranks of two-tiered metal beds, sleeping about 150 blokes to a room, their kit festooned on bed heads, hooks, windowsills, and generally strewn about the place like the aftermath of a tsunami. It used to be 'earthquake', but in recent years tsunamis seem to have become more fashionable.

We dumped our kit on the first bed that came to us, and hurried off, starving, to the cookhouse. Too late for tea, we had to settle for what had been left of that day's pudding, a delicious plate of banana custard ladled from a tureen and devoured by spoon; a memorable introduction to what was now to become a staple part of our new oriental style cuisine: banana custard. Now there's a dish. Never to be forgotten.

Wiping custard residue from our mouths we moved quickly across to check out the Naafi, and felt like a bunch of city slickers entering a Wild West saloon . . .

. . . the war in Korea had finished three years previously, but it was still classified as an active service zone. Our regiment was the last British regiment to serve there. By all accounts our Commanding Officer, Lieutenant Colonel R.B.de F. Sleeman, OBE, MC, was doing everything in his power to ensure that all and sundry would remember that fact. Kure, the renowned Japanese R&R (rest and recreation) hot-spot had recently been closed as a venue for Korean service personnel, and Hong Kong had now assumed that undertaking. Every fortnight a new batch of swarthy Royal Sussex men were flown down to clean up, sleep up, beer up, feed up and shack up . . .

. . . there was a group of them now, sitting there in the Naafi when we went in . . .

. . . wearing haunted expressions, they resembled the ranks of some mythical East European penal battalion clothed in barbed wire, with fists like claws, scowling villainously, clutching their beer glasses, and just one look at them would sure as hell have scared the pants off those French paras back in Dakar. Would we be like that soon - a lean, keen, and mean fighting machine . . .!

We edged warily towards one of them who was sitting separately on his own over by the window, uncaringly dropping ash from his lip whilst nonchalantly paring what remained of one of his finger-nails with a clasp-knife, and timorously sidled up to try to engage him in conversation. 'What's it *really* like up there, mate?' we asked.

'Christ, man - don't *ask* me,' he mouthed, playing the psychopathic hard man something rotten. 'I'm here for a few days to try to forget. You'll find out soon enough. My advice'd be to enjoy yourself while you can. Now piss off, and let me get stocious.'

Thus we envisaged the most horrible imagery of corrugated iron, sub-zero temperatures, subsisting in frozen, snow and rat-infested trenches, and having to endure hardship, privation and utter misery. I missed Eastbourne, and for a moment or two thought of making a run for it, but Hong Kong was a long way to get back from with only a fiver, and not being devious I would be bound to get caught and probably shot. Hell, I thought; I'm eighteen. I volunteered. I've looked forward to this all my life. I need to be made into a man. I've joined the System, so now let the System do what it will with me. I can take it. I'm ready.

*

At 19.30 Jim, Derek and I stepped out into Kowloon on an initial recce. It was a fairyland of surprises. Sadly, we were skint, but next day, Monday, was pay-day, *wahay*. But the *women*; and the sights; the smells; and the *women* . . .

That night we were to discover that army transit camps are seldom constructed in the most salubrious of areas. Behind the bushes outside our windows, only three feet away, was a railway line. Only happened it was the main railway line to China. Great big green-panelled diesel trains, like space craft, clanked, hooted, shunted or thundered their way by our hut all night long, just 36" from the windows.

Next day we were glibly informed that we would not now, after all, be getting paid until Wednesday.

I had 40¢ to my name (seven old pence = 51p) with which I was unbelievably able to finance a 50-mile coach trip up into the New Territories, just for a look-see and to be able to say I'd been to China, but as I recall there was nothing particularly memorable about the bits of it that I saw that day.

We were to remain at the Granville Road Transit Camp for seventeen days, kicking our heels and marking time. In case we became too slovenly or suffused with ennui, one or two half-hearted attempts were made to 'get a grip' of us, but they did not amount to much. Most notably we were 'got aboard' by one RSM Maskell, MBE, of the KOYLI (King's Own

Yorkshire Light Infantry - another great regiment now long since defunct, of course) who put us through the rigours of an inspection one morning, but then even he gave up at the futility of it.

In October 1956, just three months before our arrival, the celebration had taken place of the Qing Dynasty's downfall in 1911's October Revolution. It was an important Nationalist festival, but unfortunately some administrative bureaucrat had ordered that a number of Nationalist flags should be removed. Because of this, mobs spread out from the settlements to Kowloon, looting shops and attacking property known to belong to communist sympathizers. The authorities refrained from firm intervention, hoping that the disorder would die out with the festival, but by the next day a full-scale riot had developed.

The most violent incidents took place in the town of Tsuen Wan, just five miles from central Kowloon. A mob stormed a clinic and welfare centre there, killing four people and ransacking the building. Prisoners were taken to the Nationalist headquarters and beaten. Communist-owned factories were attacked, and some people were brutally killed. Foreigners were not especially singled out for attack, but inevitably a number of them became involved. The worst such case occurred in Kowloon, when a car was fired upon and a passenger, the Swiss Consul's wife, was burnt to death. Well, that was the official story: in fact she was rather unpleasantly crucified on a tree, but that never got out at the time.

The British now decided to take decisive action. Armoured cars of the 7th Hussars were brought in to reinforce the police, who were instructed to fire without hesitation. Communists were given sanctuary in the police compounds, and by the 12th the riots had subsided, leaving 15 killed by the rioters, and 44 dead by police action. In total 59 were killed, 500 were injured, and property damage cost was estimated to be US$1,000,000. Two months ago we'd been eating fish and chips in Canterbury High Street. Now here we were in the zone of globally historic colonial flare-ups and rumbles.

Hong Kong's resident British infantry battalion at that time

14. The real army: *L-R* the author; Bob Day; Roger Broadbent; David Baker *(1);* David Baker *(2);* Dan Salbstein and Mike Nelligan – The Royal Sussex intake attending potential officers' basic training, Wemyss Barracks, Canterbury, Kent - 1956

15. The author: arrival at Inchon, Sunday 17 February 1957

16. *L-R* The author, Richard Farrar and Jim Davidson all set for a nippy night's guard duty at Kohima Camp

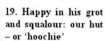

17. The best address in town!

18. Ready to stem the commie hordes: trench-mate, Kevin Flynn, all 'tooled up'

19. Happy in his grot and squalour: our hut – or 'hoochie'

208

BHQ, 1st Bn. Royal Sussex Regiment – Kohima Camp, Korea 1956

20. Snowbound Kohima Camp, Korea, with the forbidding Kamak-San soaring behind

21. The gentle approach to *Easy Block*, the summit of which housed the trenches of our defensive positions overlooking the River Imjin

22. Full board and lodging: inside our 'hoochie'. Author's bunk is the neat one above the two boxes; Jim's is the messy one above

23. The author *(L)* making like a Boer War PoW

Royal Sussex cap badge.

Two-leaf shoulder flash of R.S 24th Division, worn by Royal Sussex Regt in Korea 1955-1957

26. Our insignia

24. If all the hills in Korea were flattened they would cover the Earth . . .!

25. RIP – the last resting place of the author's pet earwig - Eric

209

28. Smarter than Guardsmen . . .

27. The Royal Sussex Regiment's Queen's Birthday and Farewell to Korea parade on 13 June 1957: Captain Steve Ellwood *(L)* – author four to the right of him. Major J.A.B. Glennie (later Brigadier) commanding the parade

30. Part of 'A' Coy

Sgt Boyd

Lt. A. J.Prebble

29. This photo shows about half the Bn frontage: note the Colour Party in No 3 Dress Whites, left-rear

31. The last British regiment to serve in Korea marches off parade, and . . . away - (Author's presence indicated with a small cross)

32. Next stop – the Rock of Gibraltar

was the North Staffordshire Regiment. They had been the first regiment into Korea at the cessation of hostilities in 1953, and had come down to Hong Kong from there. They were now leaving the colony, and so were staging through our transit camp prior to their departure back to UK, and then Germany, where they would amalgamate with the South Staffordshire Regiment to become part of the Defence Review's new Mercian Brigade. This was particularly sad, because it had only been there in Hong Kong a few months earlier that the regiment had celebrated its 200th anniversary.

Over the next two weeks a kaleidoscope of events all seemed to roll into one phantasmagoria.

I drew HK$39 on pay parade (£2, or £34 today) so Jim and I were able to go on a shopping spree, and were amazed when without even buying anything yet, one gleeful shop owner insisted on giving us an introductory small cup of tea, a cigarette, and a scented handkerchief each. We assumed this was because he liked us.

Back at camp later that evening one of our number - an old Eastbourne College boy - burst happily into the room beaming from ear to ear with barely suppressed pride and ecstasy, conveying the news that having deliberately sought out and willingly allowed himself to be successfully seduced by the exotic charms of some local nightclub hostess, he had at last become 'initiated'. Talk about a young man's rite-of-passage. A few weeks later he was to return from Korea to England to attend OCS at Eaton Hall, from whence four months after that he duly emerged as a newly commissioned subaltern; not for having surrendered his virginity in Kowloon that night, but for quickly pulling out the stops and impressing his company commander from the first moment he arrived in Korea.

That night the cookhouse was broken into, so next morning we all had to tumble out on parade, like disgruntled and rebellious characters in some black and white World War Two PoW film, to enable the Military Police to inspect our hands for cuts, which impressed us as being a pretty sophisticated crime detection technique.

That same afternoon John Butler decided enough was

enough, so in his official capacity as a lance corporal he took it upon himself to send a telegram up to the battalion in Korea asking if someone would please be kind enough to arrange for our long overdue backlog of mail to be sent down to us. At Dakar, Cape Town, Mauritius, Ceylon and Singapore the sacks had tumbled aboard the *Devonshire* and air-mail letters and parcels galore had been dished out to everyone, except the stoic but wilting little Royal Sussex draft. But - now, at last, some bright spark at Battalion responded positively to John's telegram, and on Friday 1st February, seven weeks after we had left England, a great sackful of the stuff duly arrived at around teatime. This was way-back before the Internet, mobile phones or texting had even been dreamed of; snail-mail was all, so our jubilation was unbounded. I received 23 letters; seven of them from Sue, nine from my mother, two from my father, cards from my grandparents, and a brief note from Françoise, a gorgeous, flaxen haired French girl who had been part of our 'student gang' that final summer back on Beach Six, in Eastbourne. It took me a whole blissful hour to read them all, and then an additional half-an-hour to read them all again. Recalling that there were those among us who hadn't even been able to point to Korea on the map, I suppose I shouldn't have been at all surprised to realise that quite a number of their nearest and dearest, their friends and relations could scarcely read or write either. As a consequence many of them had received no mail at all. When the rest of us glanced up from our euphoric state and saw them sitting there dejectedly cross-legged on their beds with puzzled, hurt expressions, while we grinningly chortled and devoured our correspondence and all the news from home, those more fortunate of us charitably took it upon ourselves to read out some of our own letters to them.

Bit like taking on orphans, really.

*

Once upon a time, in China - at a place called Xinyang, in Henan Province, on 12th September 1917 to be precise - there was born to a Belgian lady and her European educated husband, who was a Chinese engineer - a daughter; Rosalie Elisabeth Kuanghu Chow. In 1931, when she was 14, Rosalie Elisabeth Kuanghu Chow began to work as a typist at Beijing Hospital. In 1933 she was admitted to Yanjing University. In 1935 she went to Brussels to study science, before returning in 1938 to China, to work in an American Christian Mission hospital in Chengdu. At this time she married Pao Tang, a Chinese Nationalist military officer, who was later to become a general.

In 1944 Rosalie Chow went back to London to study medicine at the Royal Free Hospital, from where she graduated MBBS (Bachelor of Medicine & Surgery) with Honours, in 1948. In 1949 she went to Hong Kong, to practice medicine at the Queen Mary Hospital. Her husband, Tang, meanwhile, had died in action during the Chinese Civil War in 1947.

In 1952, Rosalie married Leonard Comber, a British colonial officer in the Malayan Special Branch, and went with him to Johore, where she worked in the Johore Bahru General Hospital, and also opened her own clinic.

As well as being a practising physician, writing under the pen name of Elizabeth Comber, Rosalie became the author of several books on modern China, novels set in East Asia, and autobiographical works. Mainly because of the perceived anti-British bias of her novel *And the Rain My Drink,* her husband felt obliged to resign from his position as Acting Assistant Commissioner of Police Special Branch. After their subsequent divorce, she later married Vincent Ratnaswamy, an Indian colonel, and lived with him for a time in Bangalore, India. Later, they resided in Hong Kong and Switzerland, where she continued to live after her husband's death in 2003.

Don't some people have interesting lives?

For several months in 1949 Rosalie enjoyed a deeply moving relationship with Ian Morrison, the *London Times'* Hong Kong based English foreign correspondent, whose tragic front-line death whilst on assignment during the opening phase of the Korean war, tore her apart.

Writing under her now better known *nom-de-plume* Han Suyin, in 1952 she produced her famous best-selling novel based on their affair, called *A Many Splendored Thing*.

Inspired by her book, in 1955 Hollywood's 20th Century Fox released the movie version *Love Is A Many Splendored Thing*.

Set in the turbulent days of Hong Kong in the build-up to the Korean War, dealing candidly with themes of racial prejudice and the dangerous political climate, the story concerns a dashing, macho but married American war correspondent Mark Elliot (William Holden), and the drop-dead gorgeous widowed Eurasian doctor Han Suyin (Jennifer Jones) who, while coming from completely different walks of life, meet and fall deeply in love. One scene builds beautifully upon the next, accompanied by dialogue that often sounds like poetry. As you reach for the Kleenex the movie even leaves you with its hum-able Academy Award-winning title song.

During the film, some of the lovers' romantic meetings occur beside a lone tree on a dramatically high, grassy, windswept hill, just above the Queen Mary Hospital, on Hong Kong's Peak. The setting makes the song's lyrics intensely romantic, as they are sung to the main theme.

Once on a high and windy hill,
In the morning mist,
Two lovers kissed,
And the world stood still.

Ahhhhhh . . .

Which is where I come in -

I had seen the movie at home, at the *Picturedrome* in Eastbourne, just a few months previously. My impressionable teenage heart had welled-up near to bursting, wondering when something even half as wonderful as this was ever going to happen to me. Well; there was Susan, of course - but we hadn't slept together: as suggested somewhere earlier, one didn't so much those days, so although I adored her to distraction, I couldn't say I was awash on a tidal wave of passion.

Then one afternoon John Butler and I caught the Star Ferry from Kowloon across to Hong Kong, where we went walk-about for a few hours. During the process we chanced to come

215

upon Queen Mary Hospital and walked to the top of the windswept hill just behind, and - now set on a pilgrimage to the lovers' trysting place - we arrived at the very self-same lone tree (I'd swear) where Ian Thompson and Han Suyin in real life (I'm sure), *and* in her book, and then William Holden and Jennifer Jones had been filmed, engaging in one of the movie's most passionate embraces. In modern parlance, I found this 'hard to get my head round'. But there it was; the real thing, the same tree, in the same location, a whole half world away from Eastbourne. What I didn't know, standing there beneath the tree in question, is that one of the very first films I would be seeing (again) at the camp cinema up in Korea, would be . . . *Love Is A Many Splendored Thing.* Remember . . . *the faculty of making sudden and unexpected discoveries by accident*, summed up by that word from Sri Lanka - serendipity?

TWENTY-TWO

OUR D-DAY ARRIVED.

Up until now we had been killing time in the Granville Road Transit Camp, waiting for our transport details to be ironed out. The plan was that we would fly up to Korea in batches, but then everything went awry. Cheese and tomato sandwiches were the culprits.

They were delicious.

Bearing a large tray slung on a leash round his neck, at about 10-o'clock on the night before we were due to leave, a Chinese char-and-sarni-wallah had come round the accommodation block selling us the soggy, scrumptious and wonderfully filling things.

The groaning and retching had kicked-in just after midnight.

Next morning half our number was ferried off to hospital for tests.

All this mucked-up the flight schedules, so an enterprising Movements Control Officer arranged that we would be transported to Korea by sea, instead. Those of us still upright were driven down to one of Hong Kong's many quaysides, where we waited around in the drizzle for an hour before piling our kit onto lighters and being ferried out to the LST *Frederick Clover*, lying at anchor just a few hundred yards off shore.

No sooner had we boarded and got our kit stowed than another bunch of the guys went crock and had to be shipped off to hospital. Then next morning, three more. Mid-morning a medical officer came aboard to sniff round for a bit, but we all knew it was those rogue cheese and tomato sandwiches that had done the trick. Their effect was so virulent that it was a mystery how some of us had remained unaffected; but I was

217

delighted that I had been one of them.

Later that day, fully purged, wan, and several pounds lighter, the first batch of guys was returned to us. Not wishing to miss the tide, we had to cast off and set sail at 08.15 next morning, so those blokes still left languishing behind in hospital, would have to fly up later.

It was a damp, dank and grey day; but me now tough and a hardened Old Salt. As Hong Kong receded and we went beating out into the East China Sea, the craft pitched and rolled so irregularly that the water came crashing in over our boughs. Some gigantic waves confronted us head-on, one of them in particular stopping us in our tracks with a terrifying shudder more stunning than if we had hit a continent. Me not quite so tough Old Salt now. All the portholes had to be closed, so the thick air soon became blue and foul from tobacco smoke, fug, and the reek of us 24 honking squaddies, all cooped up in our 30' by 10' rusty old whitewashed steel-plated cabin.

Our beloved MV *Devonshire,* now gliding her way gracefully homeward to England, by comparison had been 12,000 tons of luxurious safety. This new beast, within whose dubious confines we had involuntarily come to be incarcerated, weighed in at a mere 2,000 tons.

LST's (Landing Ship, Tank) were designed during World War II to transport and deploy troops, vehicles, and supplies onto foreign shores, for the conduct of offensive military operations, and disembark them without the use of dock facilities, or the various cranes and lifts necessary to unload merchant ships. The vessel was powered by two diesel engines, and had a maximum speed of 11.5 knots and a cruising speed of 8.75 knots. When at sea, the LST took on water for stability, and when conducting landing operations, the water was pumped out to produce a shallow-draft vessel. The lower deck was the tank deck, where 20 Sherman tanks, or the equivalent, could be loaded. Lighter vehicles were carried on the upper deck. An elevator was used to load and off-load vehicles, artillery, and other equipment from the upper deck. Built into the bow were two hinged doors that opened outward to a width of 14', and an extended ramp that made it possible for vehicles to disembark directly from the ship to the beach. These vessels gave the Allies the ability to conduct amphibious invasions at any location on a foreign shore that had a gradually sloped beach. This permitted them to assault poorly defended sectors, thereby achieving operational surprise and in some cases even tactical surprise. These specially designed landing ships were first employed by the British in *Operation Torch,* the invasion of North Africa in 1942. They had long anchor chains. At a certain distance from the shore the anchor was dropped astern, and its chain played out. When the assault troops and *matériel* hit the beach, the LST then winched itself back along its own securely entrenched anchor chain to disengage from the sloping shingle, and refloat.

LST's were in great demand in both the Pacific and Europe. They were used in the invasions at Sicily, Italy, Normandy, and southern France. At Normandy, the Americans' employment of LST's enabled them to meet their off-loading requirements following the destruction of their Mulberry artificial harbour in a storm. In the Southwest Pacific theatre, General Douglas MacArthur employed LST's in his 'island hopping campaigns', and the invasion of the Philippines. In the Central Pacific, Admiral Chester Nimitz used them at Iwo Jima and Okinawa. LST(2)'s served as troop ships, ammunition ships, hospital ships, repair ships, and numerous other special purposes. A number of LST(2)'s were even fitted with flight decks for small reconnaissance aircraft. During WWII 26 LST's were lost in action, and 13 more were lost in accidents and rough seas. During the Korean War, LST's were employed in the Inchon Landing.

Whilst serving on LST 366 in the Mediterranean, in 1947, a gentleman called Les Roberts composed this fitting lament:-

This tale of woe commences
On the day we lost our senses
And we thought it would be fun to go to sea,
From now on we'd be in clover
We'd have girls the whole world over
But instead they stuck us on an LST.

In harbour it is taught us
As laid out in Captains Orders,
In a language that's as tough as tough can be-
' Lock your doors before the Blackout,
Put milk bottles and the cat out;
No, it's NOT the navy —You're in LST's!'

When the gale is howling madly
And she's rolling really badly
And the pounding's simply horrible to see,
Then you think 'Why bother to grow up
Just to stand out there and THROW up?'
Oh how you wish you'd never seen an LST.

With the engineers all paling
At both diesel engines failing
And the steering gear beyond all prayer and plea,
Then, no matter how you pad it
You can't hide the fact you've HAD it,
When they picked you out to serve in LST's.

It's a golden rule for sailors
In both battleships and whalers
That you always have sufficient depth of sea,
Going aground is really wasteful,
Not to mention quite disgraceful,
Yet we do it all the time in LST's.

Then, forgetting all your teaching
You make a mess of beaching
And her arse is where her bows are meant to be,
You just pray that Heaven blessed you
When the Navy dispossessed you

220

And stuck out of sight in LST's.

So. If you're mad enough to join us
You're at liberty to coin us
A motto to inspire both you and me-
Something Latin, maybe Greek,
Like 'FOREVER UP THE CREEK!'
Which is what we are, who serve in LST's.

*

Our old tub, in which we now found ourselves, LST(3) 3001, had been built by Vickers-Armstrong's Naval yard, High Walker, Newcastle-on-Tyne and engined by Hicks and Hargeaves. She was launched on the 15th January 1945. In 1946 she had been transferred on charter to the War Office, and became named *Frederick Clover,* operating as a troop carrier managed for the War Department by the Atlantic Steam Navigation Company. She was later managed by the British India Steam Navigation Company from 1961 until 1966, before being sold to Panama in 1966 and finding herself renamed *Pacific Pioneer.* Eventually she was sold to Leung Yau in 1968, and was then finally scrapped in Hong Kong.

But - just at the moment - she was ours.

*

The following day found us punching our way up through the Strait of Formosa, hoping that the painted Union Jack prominently displayed along each side of the ship would successfully deter any misguided or over-zealous communist mainland Chinese pilot from loosing a 250kg bomb onto us. He might also have tried strafing us with his MiG-19's 30mm cannon as we made our run past Generalissimo Chiang-Kai-Shek's Nationalist Republic of China's Kuomintang government's hotly contested island of Taiwan, in what - if it *had* occurred - would have just been reported as yet another 'regrettable Cold War incident'.

But in the meantime I had other, far more pressing issues to worry about . . .

. . . at this early stage of my life I was 5' 8" and 9st 3lbs of adolescent fright, ill versed in face-to-face confrontation, an artistically inclined young man who generally preferred to seek pleasure in the gentler things of life. When I left the Army after three years, I took up weight-training and powdered high-protein drinks in an attempt to try to slap on some muscle and a six-pack, and years after that I even got to run an Army unarmed combat display team, but three days out of Hong Kong, sailing up the East China Sea in *Frederick Clover*, although considered to be a fully trained infantry soldier, I was still pretty easy meat. I was a weed.

'Bumper' Bailey and Pat Patterson were genetically programmed aggro merchants of the first water. Our draft's equivalent to the Kray twins. They were bullies, having systematically worked their way through the faces of most of their platoon during basic training. Their very existence and presence rendered me tremulous, but, as yet, unscathed. The situation was not dissimilar to the one with Billy Manser back at my infants' Western Road Primary School in Lewes. My deterrent safeguard seemed to lie in my contrived ability to appear disinterested in them or their shenanigans, when, in fact, all the time I was just waiting for them to get around to me, to get it over with, and then leave me in peace until such time as they thought it my turn for another beasting. This apparent detachment of mine both puzzled and annoyed them, but - like Neanderthals - they couldn't figure how to hack it. I knew each of them was itching for my throat and the opportunity to grab at it. Their resentment seethed: no less, I should add, than mine did for them. I would have dearly loved each of them to have suffered a fatal accident, or been otherwise exterminated.

The final crunch was to come that evening.

I had gone along alone to the ablution block for a quiet shave, and no sooner had I lathered up than Patterson's ugly face suddenly appeared behind me in the bulkhead's steamed-up steel mirror. I don't think he had followed me in there deliberately, but – hey - *que sera, sera.* He swaggered across to the urinal as though trying to stop a pig in a passage, hoiked and spat into the pan for good measure, had a slash, broke wind a couple of times, readjusted some of his scabrous clothing, and turned to face my back. Although tense with prescience, I strove to ignore him, and quietly managed to continue shaving without cutting my throat with fear. He was a tall, gangly, loutish fellow, with a sloppy face and lank and greasy titian coloured hair. He shuffled.

'You're a cunt, George,' he sneered.

I paused, but then measuredly carried on shaving the while. Curiously, my heart wasn't dancing a red hot rhythm number, but seemed to have put itself on hold, as if it, too, was waiting to see what was going to happen. After a theatrically appropriate few seconds, with as much calm as I could, I said matter of factly, but quietly:

'I'm quite sure you're right, Pat.'

'Too fuckin' right I'm right, mate,' he blazed, almost snorting fire from his furiously flared nostrils.

I rinsed my face and whisked my razor in the sink to clear it of soap. Emerging from my towel I turned, and smiled.

'Then what do you propose to do about it?' I asked.

By now he was becoming agitated, starting to shuffle more pointedly.

'Not me, cunt. It's you wants to do something about it,' he sneered, looking happy and vicious, curling his lip like Elvis Presley, but not with such harmless attractiveness.

'All right, Pat,' I replied. 'If you think the time has come for me to do so, then perhaps I will.'

I placed my towel on the side of the basin.

'You mean it?' he grinned, hardly able to conceal his delight. 'What you gonna do then?'

'I'll tell you exactly what I'm going to do, shall I, Pat?' I said, picking up my razor and drying it on the towel. Removing and placing the blade between the index finger and thumb of my right hand I prayed to the great god Gillette and recalled my father, with his upraised cane in the moonlight, and his expression of surprise just before I'd snapped it into pieces across my knee.

Trying to convey an icy stare, I addressed Pat in a slow, measured monotone.

'What I'm going to do is this, Pat,' I said. 'I'm going to give you a warning, and I am going to give you one warning only. The warning, is this: if you don't get it out of your mind that you want to pan me; if you don't forget that I exist; if, after this moment, you dare ever to give me even the slightest indication that you are still looking for aggro, then, lover, I am going to cut out your eyes . . .'

He saw the razor blade I was holding, and I like to think that he did actually flinch. He'd been looking for fisticuffs, not this turn of events.

I allowed about five seconds to elapse while we both thought about what I'd said.

'Do you understand me, Pat?' I asked, and for good measure even tried giving an assassin's smile.

Pat was not at all sure.

I was.

I had already cut a slice out of my thumb from nervously squeezing too tight. All he had to do was call my bluff, take a smack at me, and I was licked. But he hadn't reckoned on the worm turning (neither had I: where ever had it come from?) and wasn't quite sure how to handle me.

'You're a bull-shitter, George,' he leered, giving me the benefit of rotten teeth and the disparaging air-swipe of one hand.

'Think so, Pat?' I raised one eyebrow slightly. 'Try me, baby.'

We were alone.

There was no one for either of us to impress.

He shuffled backwards.

It was getting to me, this game of bluff. Useful bit of lifemanship, I was acquiring. And a vested interest in the potential of amateur dramatics.

'And what's more, Pat,' I added as a rider, 'perhaps you'd care to tell your girlfriend what I've said as well, will you? That way there can be no mistake. He has such pretty blue eyes. It would be a shame to have to cut them out as well.'

Turning on his heel Pat slunk away, muttering oaths and slamming the bulkhead resoundingly with his fists. I picked up my towel and placed it round my neck, cocked my head, grinned with admiration and disbelief at myself in the still steamy steel mirror, quickly rushed across to one of the cubicles, promptly dropped my breeks, and had a serious evacuation. But for the remainder of my time in the regiment I never had a further moment's trouble, either from 'Bumper' Bailey or Pat Patterson.

The sequel to this event was to occur ten years later, when - no longer with the Royal Sussex - I was second-in-command of a unit in Germany. One day, just as I was leaving for lunch, a convoy of trucks rumbled up and rolled through our gates at our Schulenburger Landstrasse dépôt, in Hannover. Who was the convoy leader, driving the first truck? L/Cpl Pat Patterson. Since its amalgamation the dear old Royal Sussex Regiment had by then become 3 Queens, and was now stationed down the road in Lemgo. Leaving his engine running Pat jumped down from his cab, saluted, and handed me his documents. Even more delightful than his response to my threatened razor attack in the East China Sea, was his expression when I returned his salute with a quick embrace, and he suddenly recognised and realised who I was!

Ten years after *that* I was sitting down to dinner in our mess at Camberley, when two officers passing through the garrison and staying there the night, came and sat opposite me.

'You're Mike George, aren't you?' one of them eventually asked, after a few sideways glances.

I confirmed that I was, and in doing so the shrouds of time unfurled to reveal the faces of two erstwhile young Royal Sussex NCOs with whom I had shared a ditch in Korea twenty years before, Len Hart, and Mick Ayling. Both had become RSM's, and then subsequently taken their commissions. I had acquired an earlier veneer, perhaps - they . . . a depth and durability of military knowledge. Len was then serving with the Gurkhas in Hong Kong, and Mick with the Royal Fusiliers. Over dinner I related to them the tale of my razor-blade confrontation and subsequent meeting with Patterson, and they told me that his mate - 'Bumper' Bailey - was still alive, but they'd heard he'd apparently done three years in Pentonville for manslaughter.

Years later I bumped into Mick Ayling again, when he was a civilian, when he told me his hobby had become solo hill trekking, and camping.

'Why do you do that, Mick?' I asked.

'Well,' he said: 'it takes me back in some small way to re-living our old days of boots, puttees and hefting stuff about the place the whole time. Lately, though, no one seems interested in coming along with me anymore, so I have to do it alone.'

*

Meanwhile, back on board *Frederick Clover* we had passed Shanghai on the left, and were just entering the Yellow Sea.

It was 14th February, a crisp, cold, blue, sunlit, crystal-clear day, and so wonderful to be alive, young, and as far down the route to adventure as we were. The horizon was razor sharp and the sea like pale ink. I detached myself from my card-dealing, cigarette smoking companions and went to gaze over the rail. It seemed as if we were the last ship afloat on the final sea at the top of the world, when everyone else had gone away to live in another dimension somewhere. But then three warships went powering south a couple of miles off our starboard bow, and I realised they must be elements of the US 7th Fleet, out of their long established Yokosuka naval base, south of Tokyo.

Then a dot suddenly appeared on the horizon ahead of us . . . no - two dots . . . three . . . four dots had now appeared, like a small squadron of seaborne *kamikazes*. We were closing on a Japanese fishing fleet and the unfolding of a magical, Disney-esque scenario. Cymbals clashed. A hidden quadraphonic orchestra swelled to a crescendo. The curtain rose, the gauze parted and we became the good ship *Buttercup* surrealistically chugging through the bobbing flotilla of gaily-bedecked fishing craft and the smiling, upturned, slant-eyed yellow faces of their crews. I was reminded of *HMS Pinafore*; and from there, hardly surprisingly, Puccini's *Madame Butterfly*.

The Japanese island of Okinawa, or "Loo-Choo" as it was known originally, had been trading for centuries with neighbouring countries: China, Taiwan and Korea - Singapore and the Philippines. It wasn't until the 19th century, however, that Okinawa had first been opened up to the West.

At age 60, Matthew Calbraith Perry, commander of the United States naval forces in the China seas, and a staunch expansionist, had a long and distinguished naval career. Back in 1852 he warned US President Fillmore that the British, who had already taken control of Hong Kong and Singapore, would soon be controlling all trade in the area. Perry recommended that the United States should take 'active measures to secure a number of ports of refuge' in Japan. President Millard Fillmore agreed with Perry. In 1853, having been given command of the East India Squadron, he ordered the Commodore then to proceed with the delicate task of penetrating and initiating trade negotiations with the isolationist Japan, and her 121st Emperor, Komei.

American ships had long been active in the Pacific. The New England whaling fleets scoured the ocean in search of their prey. The China trade had been enriching Yankee merchants since 1784. Japan, however, had effectively closed its doors to outsiders, and it restricted foreign ships to a small part of Nagasaki.

The Tokugawa Shogunate had ruled Japan for 250 years, during 200 years of which no foreigner had been allowed to enter the country at all. Even shipwrecked sailors were forced to remain there, so that no information could leak out. A strict feudal system operated, and no details were available about the place. The Dutch had established trading relations with the Japanese in early 1600, but were then forced, in 1641, to remove themselves and all future trading via an artificial island called Decima, in the Bay of Nagasaki. It was only 600' by 240', with a small stone bridge connecting it to the mainland. A strong guard was constantly placed at this bridge to prevent foreigners entering and Japanese visiting.

That was the situation until the early hours of 8th July 1853 when four black-tar-hulled US Navy steamships, led by the USS *Powhattan* and commanded by Commodore Perry, arrived at Edo Bay (Tokyo), demanding that Japan now open its borders to foreign commerce. Perry knew that the success of this mission to Japan would be his most significant life's accomplishment.

A gentleman called Kayama Yezaimon, *daimyo* (warlord) of Uraga, raced to the Edo Bay battlements, the clash of the warning gong still ringing in his ears. Stopping beside the brass cannon that guarded the bay's entrance, he scanned the horizon. The summer sun flashed high above the blue Pacific, and beneath it he could see the reported four ships approaching with the tide. As they sailed closer, the *daimyo*, his *samurai*, and their retainers watched in silent awe.

While two of the ships waited downwind in support with bright signal flags fluttering from their halyards, the two other steam frigates spouted thick black clouds as they manoeuvred against the wind. With their paddle-wheels churning the water, the frigates came about, bringing their gun-decks to bear upon the shore defences. The Japanese had no idea that such things as steam ships existed. They thought they must be giant dragons puffing smoke, and were shocked by the number and size of guns on board.

Another Japanese worthy, Abe Masahiro, head of the *Roju* (governing council) under Shogun Ieyoshi Kayama, scowled. Through a telescope he studied the ships, which were well beyond the range of his small shore batteries. The ships bristled with cannon much more formidable than his own. Identical flags flapped at the stern of each vessel - red and white stripes, with white stars on a patch of blue. Kayama barked out an order. A *samurai* ran forward and dropped to one knee. The *daimyo* instructed the *samurai* to ride to the castle and to inform the *Shogun* that a barbarian fleet had arrived and was blocking the mouth of Edo Bay.

From the fo'c'sle of the sloop of war *Saratoga*, a Lieutenant John Goldsborough watched as dozens of Japanese galleys approached the American fleet. They were all fantastically decorated with flags and banners. They were propelled by

228

from ten to twenty oars each, with generally two or three men at each oar.

None of these Japanese boats was permitted to come alongside any ship of the Squadron, though all of them appeared quite anxious to go alongside the Flagship. Still none was permitted until the Americans had been fully convinced that a high officer was in one of the boats. Then he alone, with an interpreter who spoke Dutch, was allowed to come over the *Susquehanna 's* side.

On board the *Susquehanna,* Commodore Perry's aide, Lieutenant Contee, informed the official that the Commodore was carrying a letter from the President of the United States to the Emperor of Japan. The Commodore intended to deliver the letter personally to an official representative. Since the Commodore was of the highest rank in the United States Navy, Contee said, he would meet only with a Japanese official of equal status. Two days later, Kayama Yezaimon visited the *Susquehanna.* He informed her captain, Captain Adams, that the Americans must take their message to Nagasaki. In a feat of gamesmanship Perry refused to meet with Kayama, but wrote a message.

'"The Commodore will not go to Nagasaki,"' Adams read on Perry's behalf. '"If this friendly letter of the President to the Emperor is not received and duly replied to, he will consider his country insulted, and will not hold himself accountable for the consequences."'

After several more days of haggling, a suitable representative, 'Prince' Toda, arrived in Uraga. With cannon salutes and a marching band, Perry led a parade of marines to meet this Japanese delegation. He presented Toda with the President's letter, enclosed in a rosewood box trimmed with gold, and announced that he would return for the emperor's answer in the spring.

Perry had impressed the Japanese officials with his diplomacy and with the technological superiority of his ships and weapons. The Japanese *Shogunate* decided to grant the minor trade concessions that President Fillmore had asked for in his letter. Forming a treaty with the Americans, they reasoned, would prevent another European power from imposing even greater concessions.

It is possible that the Japanese feudal system was beginning to collapse at this time anyway, and following the Americans' visit, there were to be 21 years of sweeping reforms.

In February, 1854, Perry returned to Edo with four sailing ships, three steamers and 1,600 men, and on 31st March the long awaited Treaty of Kanagawa was successfully signed. His diplomatic mission had officially established the United States' presence in Asia. Still, the Americans never realized that throughout they had been 'negotiating' with a mere *shogun*, because for the Emperor himself to have consulted with 'barbarians', would have been unthinkable.

After the signing of the treaty, the Japanese invited the Americans to a feast. The Americans admired the courtesy and politeness of their hosts, and thought very highly of the rich Japanese culture. Commodore Perry had broken down the barrier that separated Japan from the rest of the world. He accepted much hospitality and visited several Japanese ports before beginning the long voyage home. Today - despite Pearl Harbour and the horrors of WWII - the Japanese still celebrate Perry's expedition to open up their country to the world, with a ceremony called the annual Black Ship festivals.

*

The Victorian period was a time when gentlemen (and sometimes ladies) of leisure embarked on adventurous escapades around the world. Many of these travellers were avid communicators, writing letters, articles, and keeping journals of their travels. All these personal interpretations of what they witnessed combined to create exotic images of distant lands for those remaining at home. Novels, plays, ballets and operettas were set in foreign locations. Thus it was that after Commodore Perry's successfully concluded treaty with Japan, that nation, too, quickly became a 'must' for travellers.

For example, Lafcadio Hearn, a half-Greek, half-Irish journalist and adventurer, led an impoverished career in

Ireland and the United States before arriving in Japan in 1890. He became infatuated with the country, married a Japanese bride, changed his name to Koizumi Yakumo and eventually became a Japanese citizen. Over 15 years his writings, such as *Japan, an Attempt at an Interpretation* (1904), became popular and were printed in several European languages. He exalted Japan at the expense of the West and helped contribute to the image of Japan as a land of aesthetic accomplishment, peopled with charming, graceful - and complacent - women.

Japan's exotic allure contributed to a vast body of popular literature and fashion. 'Japonisme' was the trend in late 19th and early 20th century Europe. Japanese gardens and interior design became in vogue. Whistler, Ezra Pound and William Butler Yeats, to name a few, drew inspiration from Japanese art and culture. The sense of romance and intrigue fully infiltrated the common imagery of foreign countries.

Exoticism is not too removed from sensualism, so certain Japanese customs such as mixed-bathing and Geisha-houses easily connected into stories of Western man conquering Japanese girl.

Pierre Loti was the *nom de plume* of Julien Viaud (1850 - 1923), a French author of novels mostly set in exotic places visited during his career as a naval officer. In 1887 Loti wrote *Madame Chrysanthème* which set the fashion for stories with a Japanese setting. Loti had actually been to Japan and had a greater sense of the reality of the place than many other writers. His main character, Loti, a naval officer, has two objectives for his stay in Japan: to get a tattoo, and to acquire a temporary Japanese wife. The tattoo is easily come by and pleasing; the 'wife' is a somewhat more complicated story. It was common practice at the time in Japanese treaty ports for girls, often from rural communities, to be hired or sold to city traders for employment as temporary wives. Foreigners were able to look them over, make a selection and negotiate a price. In a straight commercial deal with no romance, Loti acquires a wife ('O-kiku-san', Miss Chrysanthemum). When the time comes for Loti to leave Japan, O-kiku makes a big scene of crying and begging him not to leave which, of course, he must.

Having forgotten something at the house, Loti returns to the touching scene of finding O-kiku counting her money and waiting for her next 'husband'.

This story was made into an opera by Messager in 1893 and was successful for a few decades. Sir Frederick Ashton also choreographed a ballet of this story in 1955.

In 1898 another short story, *Madame Butterfly*, by lawyer/writer John Luther Long, appeared in the *Century Magazine* for January of that year. According to Long his sister had met the real Butterfly's grown son, Tom Glover, in Nagasaki. She learnt that Butterfly's 'husband' had been a British merchant, and that after his departure her subsequent attempted suicide had failed.

In Long's story the principal protagonist, now a US Navy Lieutenant Pinkerton is, in his words, 'banished to the Asiatic station' from the Mediterranean. Opportunistically, he engages a marriage broker to find him a house and a wife; Madame Butterfly. He keeps the less attractive side of his arrangements from her but does convert her to Christianity and banishes her relatives from their lives. Butterfly falls in love with Pinkerton who promises, untruly, to return 'when the robins nest again'. In the meantime Butterfly has a child she names Trouble - meaning Joy. When Pinkerton returns to Nagasaki with his American wife, Adelaide, he does not bother to return to see Butterfly. Adelaide does, however, seek her out and discovers the child, whom she wishes to have for her own. Butterfly attempts suicide, to die with honour, as Pinkerton has taken everything that is precious to her. Suzuki, the maid, cleverly pushes the child into the room, pinching him to make sure he cries. The next day the house is empty when Adelaide returns for the child. This Butterfly is obviously a different type of character than the rather coarse Chrysanthème.

The author, Long, received much criticism for his unfavourable depiction of a U.S. officer.

David Belasco (1853-1931) may only be remembered as a footnote to dance history as having at one time employed American modern dance pioneer, Ruth St Denis, in music hall productions. He actually inserted the 'St' into her name.

However, the Broadway impresario and writer wrote the play of *Madame Butterfly* to fill out an evening featuring the farce *Naughty Anthony* which premiered on 5th March 1900 at the Herald Square Theater, New York. Featuring Blanche Bates as Cho-Cho-San, this one act play scored a great public success. Apart from beginning at the point when Pinkerton has already been gone two years, the play closely follows the story of Long's original. However, Belasco believed there would be more drama if Butterfly succeeded in killing herself. Then Pinkerton would arrive in time to remorsefully cradle the dying body. Adelaide is renamed Kate. Belasco also took a big theatrical risk by taking 14 minutes for Butterfly to stand stationary waiting for Pinkerton, as a lighting effect showed the passing of the night. It was a success.

Later in the same year Belasco's play was presented in London at the Duke of York's Theatre, this time on the programme with Jerome K. Jerome's *Miss Nobbs*.

However . . .

. . . on this occasion there concurrently happened to be in London for the premiere of his own opera *Tosca* at Covent Garden, an Italian gentleman rejoicing in the resounding name Giacomo Antonio Domenico Michele Secondo Maria Puccini. Born on the 22nd December 1858 in the beautiful medieval Tuscan city of Lucca, he died on the 29th November 1924 in Brussels, from a heart attack, after radiation treatment for nicotine-induced throat cancer. Usually referred to just as 'Puccini', he is regarded as one of the great operatic composers of the late 19th and early 20th century. He, also, just happened to catch the opening night of Belasco's *Madame Butterfly*; and the rest, as they say . . .

Even without fully understanding the dialogue that night, Puccini was so moved by the play that he immediately knew he wanted to create an opera of the story, and rushed backstage to meet Belasco.

Puccini turned to Luigi Illica and Giuseppe Giocosa *(La Bohème* and *Tosca)* for his libretto for *Madame Butterfly*. The first act of the opera, Pinkerton's arrival in Japan and setting up house with Cio-Cio-San, is basically their creation. It follows closely the Belasco character of Pinkerton as coarse, rude and patronizing. His character is modified in Act 2 with an extended aria showing his remorse at having to leave Butterfly, and it is Sharpless who urges him to leave. In the play it was Pinkerton who gave Sharpless money to 'pay off' Butterfly. By singing in fluid Italian, Butterfly is finally freed from the pidgin English she had spoken in versions thus far

Between the opera's premiere at La Scala, Milan, on 17th February 1904, and its presentation in Paris in 1906, several changes took place. Most of Pinkerton's slurs of the Japanese were removed, and he became a more likeable and more conventional opera tenor. Kate too was softened. Originally sharing her husband's disdain for the local people, she changes to a sympathetic and compassionate lady who no longer confronts Butterfly, but waits outside in the garden.

As an opera, *Madame Butterfly* is a staple of even the most innovative opera houses, and has been seen practically everywhere opera can be seen. Each director has placed his or her own mark upon it. An unusual example is Ken Russell's staging for the 1993 Spoleto Festival in Charleston, SC. It is set in Nagasaki in the late 30s, Cio Cio San is clearly a prostitute who has opium dreams of giant hamburgers and bottles of ketchup, longing for all things American. The opera ends with the bomb exploding over Nagasaki, after which the stage is filled with the corporate logos of modern Japan - Sony, Honda, Mitsubishi. In his final statement, Russell suggests that perhaps Butterfly's side of the cultural conflict was the winner.

Film versions of *Madame Butterfly* include a 1932 'modernized' Hollywood version of Belasco's play, with Sylvia Sidney and Cary Grant. The opera on film appeared in 1955 in an Italian/Japanese production, with Butterfly being played by a Japanese actress dubbed by an Italian soprano. In 1996 Sony Classical distributed a French sponsored film sung in Italian with English subtitles. It was directed by Frederic Mitterand (nephew of the president) with the *Orchestre de Paris* conducted by James Conlon of the Met . . .

. . . and all this background to the writing and evolution of one such globally renowned opera is what I was determined to find out about, as the Japanese fishing fleet receded behind us and we sailed on through the Yellow Sea towards the Korean port of Inchon, with the famed and magical Top-C of Madame Butterfly's iconic aria *One Fine Day* ringing clearly in my mind.

So there you have it.

That's how it was done.

Because - if like me - you probably thought Puccini had just sat down and rattled it off at his kitchen table one night after supper.

TWENTY-THREE

KOREA.

Land of the Morning Calm.

It has been said that if every hill in Korea was flattened out, the resulting rock, shrub and tree covered turf pancake would cover the world, but whether this was some profound observation posited by a learned geographer, or the deranged fabrication of some disgruntled and footsore infantryman, may never be known.

We still hadn't quite yet reached those hills to discover the veracity of this statement for ourselves, but we were pretty close.

It had now become so cold that the decks and rigging on *Frederick Clover* were iced up, and her winches had to be kept running to prevent them freezing and seizing. Having sighted land a while back, now clad in our string vests, pullovers, combat jackets and parkas for added warmth, we were at last slowly making our way up the curiously named Flying Fish Channel approach roads, passing Walmi-do Island, and inching towards Korea's east coast port - Inchon Harbour.

We dropped anchor at 17.00.

After a two-and-a-half months journey of around 10,000 miles, we had finally arrived.

That night we remained on board.

Reveille next day was at 06.30.

Sunday 17th February 1956

After a light and hurried breakfast, we excitedly scrambled overboard and loaded our gear onto American LCVPs (Landing Craft, Vehicle, Personnel) for the trip across Inchon Harbour's choppy waters, to dry ground. It was a crisp, cold and clear day. As we disembarked from the Higgins boats (the designer of LCVPs) and humped our kit across the pontoons onto terra firma, we were greeted by a giant American banner suspended across our arrival path from two high stanchions, emblazoned with the not entirely reassuring greeting: WELCOME TO HELL.

Inchon was alive with hustle and bustle. US and ROK (Republic of Korea) troops were teeming about all over the place, so I reminded myself of why - and what it was that *we* were now doing here, too.

At the beginning of the mid-20th century's Cold War between the Russian and US Superpowers, in return for certain economic favours, Russia's Uncle Joe Stalin gave his blessing to North Korea's surprise invasion of South Korea, in June 1950, using Russian tanks and weaponry. Following the stunning success of this North Korean attack, United Nations forces resident in South Korea found themselves driven back and trapped in the southeast corner of the peninsula, in an area known as the Pusan Perimeter. While the bulk of the North Korean People's Army (NKPA) was kept occupied there by US General Walton Walker's forces along the Pusan Perimeter, the UN Supreme Commander, General of the Army Douglas MacArthur - the acknowledged Wellington, Napoleon and Montgomery of all-American generalship combined - advocated that a daring amphibious strike should take place on the peninsula's west coast, at Inchon, catching the NKPA off guard, while landing UN troops close to the capital at Seoul and placing them in a position to cut the North Korean's supply lines.

Inchon's harbour possessed a narrow approach channel, a strong current, a 6,000 yard protective moat of impenetrable mudflats at low tide, and wildly fluctuating 32' high tides that crashed against the harbour's easily defended concrete seawalls. In presenting his plan, *Operation Chromite*, MacArthur cited these factors as reasons the NKPA would not anticipate an attack coming at Inchon.

After winning Washington's approval for his bold plan to be executed, MacArthur selected the US Marines to lead the swiftly assembled 70,000-strong 'X' Force attack. Ravaged by President Truman's post-World War II cutbacks, the Marines had to consolidate all available manpower and reactivate much aging equipment to prepare for this sudden amphibious operation that had been thrust upon them.

To pave the way for the invasion, *Operation Trudy Jackson* was launched, a week before the landings were due to take place. This involved putting ashore a joint CIA-military intelligence team on Yonghung-do Island, in the Flying Fish Channel, on the approach to Inchon. Led by an early cross between Rambo and Indiana Jones in the form of one tough US Navy Lieutenant Eugene Clark, this team successfully conducted bloody raids on land and sea, gathered vital information on the approaches and seawalls at the Inchon landing 'beaches', and even managed to turn on the Palmi-do light-house to help the invasion fleet navigate its way in.

As this invasion fleet neared its landing zone, supporting UN cruisers and destroyers closed on Inchon to clear mines from the Flying Fish Channel and lay down a 'softening up' artillery bombardment on the NKPA positions on Wolmi-do Island, in Inchon harbour. Despite these actions making the North Koreans aware that an invasion force was on its way, the commander at Wolmi-do Island still assured the NKPA command that he could repulse any attack.

On the morning of 15th September 1950, the invasion fleet, led by WWII's Normandy and Leyte Gulf veteran, Admiral Arthur Dewey Struble, moved into position. Around 06.30 the first UN troops, led by the 3rd Battalion, 5th US Marines came ashore at 'Green Beach' on Wolmi-do Island.

Supported by nine tanks from the 1st Tank Battalion, the Marines succeeded in capturing the island by noon, suffering only 14 casualties in the process. Through the afternoon they defended the causeway to Inchon proper, while awaiting reinforcements. Due to the extreme tides in the harbour, the second wave did not arrive until 17.30. At 17.31 the first Marines landed and swarmed up the sea wall using wooden scaling ladders, at code-worded landing point 'Red Beach'. Located just north of the Wolmi-do causeway, these Marines on Red Beach quickly reduced the NKPA opposition, allowing forces from Green Beach to enter the battle.

Pressing into Inchon proper, the forces from Green and Red Beaches were able to take the city and compel the NKPA defenders to surrender. As these events were unfolding, the 1st Marine Regiment, under Colonel Lewis 'Chesty' Puller was landing on Blue Beach, to the south of the area. Though one LST was sunk while approaching the beach, the Marines met little opposition once ashore, and quickly moved to help consolidate the UN position.

Believing that the main American invasion would come at Kusan (the result of successful UN disinformation), the NKVA had only sent a small force to defend the Inchon area, so these landings at Inchon caught the NKPA command by complete surprise.

UN casualties during the Inchon landings and subsequent battle for the city were 566 killed and 2,713 wounded. In the fighting the NKPA lost more than 35,000 killed and captured. As additional UN forces came ashore, they were organized into the US X Corps. Attacking inland, they advanced towards the South Korean capital, Seoul, which was taken on 25th September, after brutal house-to-house fighting.

The daring landing at Inchon, coupled with 8th Army's breakout from the Pusan Perimeter, threw the NKPA into a headlong retreat.

The Inchon invasion was the last brilliant operation of General MacArthur's career. One of the most significant amphibious landings in modern history, it was the turning point of the Korean War.

UN troops quickly recovered South Korea and pressed into the north, towards the Yalu River. This advance continued until late November, when Chinese support troops were sent pouring into North Korea, turning the tide again and causing UN forces to withdraw back to the south once more. The war then ebbed and flowed between action and stalemate.

There were some memorable battles took place during the Korean War, the most notable probably being the Americans' struggles for Pork Chop Hill and Old Baldy, and the British and Commonwealth Brigade's famous Gloucester Hill, during the Battle of the River Imjin.

And then on 27th July 1953 there came the long awaited ceasefire agreement. An east-west military demarkation line was established, dividing North from South Korea, with a 1.25 mile deep demilitarised zone (DMZ) running each side of that line, with a central control point at Panmunjom, by the 38th Parallel.

At the cessation of hostilities (and still, today, over 50 years later) the UN continued to retain a peace-keeping and monitoring presence in South Korea. Along with the Americans, participating countries from the Commonwealth Brigade also contributed.

Thus it was that in August 1956 the thousand-strong 1st Battalion The Royal Sussex Regiment had arrived to relieve the 1st Battalion The Queen's Own Cameron Highlanders, to become then the only, and what was to be the last, British fighting unit to serve in Korea.

And now I had come along as well, to help them.

We were based at a place called Kohima Camp, constructed in a valley at the foot of Castle Hill near to where the Glorious Glosters had fought their famous Battle of the River Imjin, which flowed a mile north of our camp. Two miles north of that was the DMZ, following the line of the artificially imposed 155-mile east to west 38th Parallel, and two miles beyond that was North Korea, so we were five miles from the enemy's border, and 60 miles north of our own Commonwealth Forces' HQ, located down in Inchon.

For operational purposes we came under the command of the 24th US Infantry Division, and were attached to the 21st Infantry Regiment: aka 'The Gimlets': their *nom de guerre*

240

being taken from the implement, not the drink.

With no more than 36-hours worth of ammunition at our disposal, we were an expendable suicide force. Our duties were rehabilitative, policing, guarding, vigilance, and patrolling and controlling a border that might still erupt at any moment. In the event of such an occurrence, we were trained to clear camp completely within two hours, lock, stock and all spare barrels, to hit our pre-dug hilltop positions just south of and commanding a pre-coordinated interlocking field-of-fire view of the River Imjin. In short, our role was purely to act as the Americans' point 'suicide battalion', to hold at bay long enough any further North Korean incursion or full out assault across the Imjin, for the Americans further back down the line to rally and get themselves sufficiently organised to assume some sort of retaliatiary posture.

I suppose it would be fair to say that we were 'quite amused by our little lot in life'.

That is what we were doing in Korea.

*

Today the population of South Korea is 50,000,000.

In 1957 it was 20,000,000 - and us.

Hot in summer; cold in winter.

It was now February.

Winter!

Cold.

Very.

Inchon was a corrugated iron and cardboard town of understandably scavenging, make-do-and-mend, war-weary civilians and military, set in a sea of mud and slush.

'Hi, Mike: long time no see.'

I scarcely recognised the speaker, wrapped snugly in his much laundered but still greasy green combat clothing, with half his pinched and swarthy face concealed by a white, dishcloth-like choker wound round his neck, with a misshapen blue beret angled cockily atop his shorn head.

I had last seen Bill Williams propping up the bar at *The*

Gildredge in Eastbourne. I hadn't even known he was in the army, let alone in the same regiment, out here 10,000 miles from home, the proud driver/custodian of one of the convoy of dirty green Army Bedford three-ton trucks that had been sent down from Battalion to collect us, into the back of which we were now humping our kit and jumping up to accompany it.

Most of the time Korean winters crackle along somewhere below zero, occasionally plummeting to minus 40C. The first British troops to arrive there, to assist the US troops during their initial setback at the outbreak of hostilities in 1950, had been the Middlesex Regiment and the Argyll and Sutherland Highlanders. In lightweight cotton jungle-greens they had gone in summer, up from Hong Kong, whilst back in London the then War Office set about forming a Brigade to go out to support them. This Brigade never arrived as such, but was built up gradually, in situ, by Commonwealth reinforcements arriving on the ground piecemeal, while the situation worsened. The first Commander of this initial ad hoc Brigade had to return to UK because his wife fell seriously ill. His pear shaped replacement came from behind a Whitehall desk, and was a mite portly. This gentleman experienced a considerable amount of difficulty getting up the hills each morning and left a lot of his breakfast adhered to the scrub and boulders along the way, but within a month necessity, circumstance and opportunity combined with the inherent guts of the man to make him fit for purpose.

By then it was the start of winter.

The snow was frozen thick upon the landscape and the poor old Jocks and 'Diehards', living in trenches, were still padding about in their tropical jungle-green uniforms. These were fairly hastily supplemented by a motley agglomeration of borrowed American cold weather gear. The Brits who bore the brunt of that first year's offensive were a put-upon Karno's army.

Cold, miserable and inadequately supported, it was not until the following spring of '51 that both these gallant regiments were eventually relieved. Muscularly fit, but worm-ridden and emaciated, they returned thankfully to Hong Kong, where they remained to complete the rest of their Far East tour of duty.

These severe conditions bore only a slight similarity to those which greeted us on our arrival there in '57, but we were still cold and unfit. A few days out of Korea, when the rigging and winches onboard the *Frederick Clover* had begun to ice over and snow lay upon her decks, we had broken out our issue of winter clothing: string vests, heavy duty pullovers, parkas, thick soled boots with innersoles, long-johns, all of them in pristine hue, unbent and stiff. Encumbered now by these new garments, we had clambered with difficulty aboard our small convoy of trucks drawn up on the Inchon quayside that morning, and huddled like so many overweight frogs on the clattering seats in the rear of each truck. The vehicles started up, revved up, and then ground off to pull out of the dockside area and *thrum* us through the black slush and cinders 60 miles through the war torn capital, Seoul, and north towards our new home, Kohima Camp.

Korea that winter still lay numbly gripped in the cold aftermath of its war. Drawn, pallid, weary and wary oriental faces peered covertly at us from their drab backloth of personal devastation. Korean real estate then consisted mainly of petrol cans and cardboard, packing crates and tarpaulin, mud, packed snow and corrugated iron, with a fire beneath the earth floor to keep the whole lot warm. Snotty-nosed kids crawling about with crap-laden kapok romper suits grinned up at us as we passed, having known no other conditions but these, and so with that special adaptability peculiar to children they were happy with their lot. How were they to know or care that in many cases the wherewithal with which the family provided their meagre sustenance, was provided by their older sisters and came from the pockets of lustful young American GIs?

Korea is a land steeped in nearly 5,000 years of history and culture. When she was first occupied by the Japanese, in 1870 - or so the possibly apocryphal story went - in an attempt to evade the rape and pillage meted out by Nippon's warriors, Korean maidenhood first adopted the (to western eyes) asexual mode of dress they were wearing when we first set eyes on them in the 1950s; voluminous frocks gathered into a bunch beneath their breasts, creating a traditional ensemble which rendered the wearer scarcely worthy of a second glance, and yet - although not dissimilar to the dress of a Japanese *geisha* - had the effect of making the girl appear pregnant and the Japanese soldier look the other way. What did they see? Apparently more pregnant ladies, hands tucked in sleeves, demurely shaking their heads and trying not to look too coy. And so the Japanese squaddies looked upon their comrades as supermen, to have thus incapacitated in so short a time the entire female population of this alien land. As supermen they renewed the war effort, wound it up, and returned to their by now own frustrated girls at home, to have a wash, lay them down in the cherry blossom, and set about producing *kamikaze* pilots.

Load of fanciful codswallop.

The Korean maidens, meanwhile, came to appreciate that discretion was the greater part of valour, and adopted their contrived and cumbersome pseudo maternity wear - known as *hanboks* - as the national costume. (More codswallop).

Until the Americans arrived.

Normally avid admirers of culture, history, and oriental charm, there was a fast turnover war in progress; the Americans wanted their bread sliced, instant, and in functional and attractive quick release packaging. Relying upon the Americans for the survival of her family and herself in those parlous times, Miss Korea and her sisters were not slow in switching to accommodate the requirement. Overnight they acquired and assembled the necessary accoutrements with which to accommodate the new wave conquerors. Hence lipsticked, coiffured and wearing a sheath dress and heels, prostitution stalked the land where previously it had been virtually unknown; well - other, that is, than when the Japanese Army had forcibly abducted about 200,000 Asian girls (there being a preponderance of Koreans amongst them) to 'service' their troops in their WWII 'comfort stations'.

Venereal disease followed close behind, and soon the two were swinging their hips along in unison, in early 1950s Korea.

Another story had it that Korea spawned the birth of 'Black

Pox', a particularly virulent strain of venereal disease that responded to no known treatment and struck its recipient dead in his tracks. This macabre scare-rumour was undoubtedly put about by the overworked medical services, but it failed to create the salutary arrest in incidents expected. VD continued to be a rabid and prevalent contagion for many years.

With the Americans came a floodtide of money, yet eager bar girls still contrived to defy the basic law that prices are meant to drop as supply increases. There were oodles of Americans. There were boodles of girls. Yet the going rate remained comparatively high. Eventually it stabilised, and settled at about US$3 a pop. (Then just over £1). US$3 for a Texan was peanuts. For a British National Serviceman from the south east corner of England it was a week's wages, to fulfil a need which in an active service zone is the same as cleaning your teeth; you try to do it as and when and where you can. British troops in Korea were paid in BAFs. These were British Armed Forces notes, which resembled green and red monopoly money. The BAF denominations ranged from threepence, sixpence, through one shilling, to £1. There was no similar US$3 note issued to the Americans at the time. Thus it came about that the British pink threepenny note (marked 3d) made a very good substitute for Englishmen with gall and strange feelings. For a month or so - until the scam was rumbled - the boys of the Royal Sussex Regiment were able to relieve their pent up emotions for threepence a throw, convincing the Korean girls that it was really three dollars. For a while the Brighton, Hove and Horsham swede-bashers gleefully rode the crest of this economic wave. Finally, however, the Americans twigged what was going on and stopped it, just as the whole happy but unstable market was teetering on the brink of an almighty crash on the pebbly beach of minor inflation. Gook 'nooky' then became unfashionable for a short while - but not too long.

Since those early post-war years Korea has surged ahead. The country today houses an industrial and technological society which has a throbbing, pulsating, vital, vibrant and immensely productive economy. Today's Korean businessman

245

has hung up his black, conical hair hat and white shift, in preference for a smart grey suit. Young girls have cast aside their traditional attire for the pill, jeans and T-shirts. Korea today is a cross between Tokyo and America. The US military is still in attendance, but the ROK Army is now a tough and lethally efficient fighting force in its own right.

After the Korean war the US and Australia went on to play their respective parts in the ghastly Vietnam conflagration, while we in Britain had our own Northern Ireland to contend with, leading up to the first and second Gulf wars: but all these events had yet to transpire. Meanwhile . . .

It was 16.00 on Sunday 17th February 1957. We were sick, tired, cold and hungry after the three-hour, bone-juddering truck ride up from Inchon to our new home. As we skirted the rubble-strewn dirt road at the foot of Gloucester Hill, we could see Kohima Camp lying ahead of us, blanketed in snow. The last grey light of day was descending to envelop the camp's serried lines of corrugated steel Quonset huts with darkness. A solitary hooded, faceless, snow and parka-shrouded sentry waved us through the barrier with his multi-gloved hand. The convoy changed down and ground up a steep incline. Finally it stopped to disgorge us onto a small, perma-frosted plateau outside Battalion Headquarters. None of us moved. We were all too numb and soporific from our journey. Suddenly all the vehicles' tailgates were flung down with reverberating crashes. Pick helves clanged against their metalwork.

'Come along, you lot,' raucous voices bellowed. 'Move yourselves, *Chris*sake. Whaddya think this is, some sort of bleedin' holiday camp? Come on, let's be having you. Everybody out. Come along, get *OUT,* I said.'

At last!

We had arrived.

*

Again the pick helves crashed like anti-tank rounds against the lorries' sides.

We got the message.

They wanted us out.

246

We began to move.

Feeling more like prisoners arriving at *Stalag IV* rather than welcome reinforcements for our own county regiment, we tumbled out onto the hard packed snow to gaze dumbly about, as seemingly vicious NCOs herded us into some semblance of order.

Its timbre slicing authoritatively through the hubbub around us, we heard a voice suddenly cut in and intone from on high:

'You are very 'orrible.'

Everything stilled.

It was RSM 'Spud' Houghton, disdainfully surveying his new charges from his elevated stance atop a small snow bluff a few yards distant.

'Yes they are, Mister Houghton,' came the clipped rejoinder of an even more detached and illustrious being, standing with his hands clasped behind his back in front of his Quonset office just at the top of the hill, impatiently tapping his calf, not with a swagger cane, but with a yellow-tasseled, chrome-plated Gimlet-stick, presented to him by the US 21st 'Gimlet' Infantry Regiment, to whom we were attached. The scene might have resembled a well-to-do slave trader displaying his latest consignment to an even better-to-do prospective purchasing gentleman. 'You will now speak to them and rearrange them more to our liking please, Mister Houghton.'

It was Captain Nigel Knocker, the Adjutant.

'The officers to me, please,' he said, turning derisively on his booted heel in the snow, to enter his office.

'Yessir,' replied 2/Lts Broadbent and Day, and RSM Houghton, in unison.

Roger Broadbent and Bob Day slid off uphill to offer their credentials and respects to, and receive a bollocking from, the Adjutant, while RSM Houghton explained to the rest of us the reason for it.

It was us.

We were misshapen.

We had arrived incorrectly dressed.

We were a shambles.

Disregarding the fact that we had barely set foot on this

247

frozen soil, missed our mothers, and hadn't had our tea, we had had the temerity to drive 60 miles looking like pregnant prawns through a blizzard; albeit concealed in the backs of trucks, they were *British* trucks, Royal *Sussex* British trucks as well, and because we had only just come out of training and had spent three months travelling half way round the world to get here on the high seas in a ship and spent three weeks in a Hong Kong transit camp and a week on the China Seas in a tramp steamer and three hours in a convoy of 3-tonners, beating our way up to this frozen and hostile wasteland, there was no reason on earth why we should have arrived before him to stand huddled in the gloaming like this, looking like *shit.*

'DO YOU UNDER*STAND* ME?'

'*YES* SIR.'

'I CAN'T *HEAR* YOU. **_LOUDER._**'

'YESSIR'

After the RSM had told us how ashamed of us he was, and had scrunched away into the snowy darkness to conceal his grin, we slung our kitbags across our shoulders and trudged wearily off to the various locations to which we had been allotted.

1st Battalion The Royal Sussex Regiment then consisted of 'A', 'B', 'C', 'D, 'HQ' and 'Support' Companies; Support Company being comprised of the Mortar Platoon, Recce Platoon, Anti Tank Platoon and Assault Pioneer Platoon, all of which, combined with cooks, bottle-washers, walking wounded, and sutlers, totalled 1,000 men. Each 100-man-strong warrior-company had three platoons, each of these platoons breaking down into sections of ten men each. One's platoon, therefore, was 30 strong, and with its subaltern platoon commander, platoon sergeant and NCOs was one's immediate family within the whole, larger, regimental family.

Jim Davidson, Kevin Flynn, Don Holman, Sam Sampson and I had been assigned to 1 Platoon 'A' Company, which, pride-wise, sounded as if it ought to be just about the prime pick of the Battalion. *1 Platoon 'A' Company.* What a fashionable address for a letterhead: you couldn't get higher up than that!

The Battalion's living and working accommodation was comprised of about 100 corrugated iron Quonset huts, known in the vernacular as 'hoochies', arranged in serried ranks; ten per company, one to each section for sleeping, so there were three for a platoon = nine per company, plus one for use as the company office, with the armoury at the rear = 10.

Having been dismissed by the RSM, Jim, Kevin, Don, Sam and I reached our new home by disconsolately dragging our kitbags along beside us in the unlit dark and snow, whimpering quietly with homesickness, dejection and cold each step of the way of what seemed like almost a mile's trek to get there.

The fashionable address, 1 Platoon 'A' Company, predictably turned out to be just another of those Quonset huts, this one set at the farthest flung corner of the camp, almost beside the perimeter wire, as well as being uncomfortably close to the latrines.

The hut's existing inmates barely stirred as we pushed open the door and went in. In view of the fact that our arrival heralded a serious decline in the oxygen content and quality of their already fuggy interior, and a further crowding of the already overstretched living accommodation, their disinterest can only have been a) contrived affectation, or b) born of tiredness and / or ennui, because our presence was obviously going to affect their lives considerably.

A pot-bellied oil stove glowed and throbbed at each end of the hut. Two-tiered, green, metal bunk beds ranged the concave walls. We paired ourselves off and hassled over who should take the top bunk and who the lower. Jim Davidson and I had teamed-up in England, and in the military pairing system of camaraderie, had become 'muckers'. It may be recalled that Jim came from Hastings, where his parents ran *The Cambridge*. In the fulness of time he would bury his parents, produce Jane and Marcus, tragically lose his lovely wife Diane to post-operative medical negligence, run Rye Museum for many years, hand feed the badgers in his garden each night with home-made peanut butter sandwiches, and work consistently at becoming a recluse, but on that Sunday evening of 17th February 1957 in Korea, he took the top bunk and I had the lower.

Our furniture consisted of one small locker each, a school type tuck box affair with a padlock for stowing personal possessions to be stashed beneath the bed - and a washbowl. Oh, and a bedside mat.

We had already introduced ourselves in desultory fashion to the resident members of the Section, who over the months had become comfortably ensconced in each other's company, and their lifestyle. Cpl George Fry was the Section Commander, assisted by L/Cpl Dick Farrar, an Old Cranleighan who should have been commissioned, but wasn't. 'The lads' were Tom Lish, 'Smudger' Smith, and Dave Prynn: all Old Sweats who had been there for six months already, awaiting our arrival to make up the full section strength. They now lay on their pits comfortably reading and smoking, whilst casting horrific remarks at each other in order to impress us, endeavouring to intimidate us with just how much bloody ruggedness was now lying in store for us for the rest of our lives from tomorrow onwards, but still managing to convey a wealth of useful question-and-answer background information on survival and advancement in that hostile environment - while with blessed relief at having come to rest after months of travel, uncertainty and upheaval, we unpacked and stowed our kit.

Now we could really get stuck in.

Turn in early, have a good night's kip, then get started in earnest in the morning.

Do some laundry.

Write some letters.

Gently start to break in our painful new boots, and winter clothing.

Find our way about the camp.

Start to shake off the slothfulness of these past few months, and train ourselves up to get fit again.

Nice and easy.

I had it all planned as I finally crawled into my sleeping bag at 10.00-o'clock, and completely collapsed with exhaustion.

They do say that if you want to make God laugh, just tell him your plans!

TWENTY-FOUR

THE NORTH KOREANS HAD THEIR NEXT DAY planned as well, and hadn't taken mine into consideration at all.

Whether it was started by a South Korean peasant getting his pants caught in the wire while stealing corrugated shoring from one of our outlying bunkers (which it probably was) or wave after wave of bugle-blowing Chinese and North Korean troops swarming across the River Imjin, at 05.00 that first black Monday morning my deep, deep dreams of Sue were rudely shattered by the wailing of sirens and the sudden eruption of masses of well coordinated activity all around me.

It was a full-blown 'Scram'.

Within the next two hours, fully armed and kitted, we had to be clear of the camp and manning our positions up in the surrounding hills.

Still so dozy I wasn't sure if I was at home, school, summer camp or a troopship, I swung my legs over the side of the bed to find out. First off, I banged my head on the sub-frame of Jim's bed above me, and then fell onto the floor because I'd forgotten I was still done up like a mermaid in my sleeping bag. Jim did exactly the same thing from the top bunk, and came crashing down to land across my shoulders amidst a welter of oaths from us, and misplaced merriment from everybody else.

Jumping about to release ourselves we resembled two large, dark caterpillars, struggling to wriggle free of their dark green carapaces. Succeeding, and climbing to our feet at last, we realised that the hut's old-timers were just placing their steel helmets onto their heads, atop their woollen cap comforters, and were flinging open the door to rush to their positions outside, fully tooled-up and ready to go, as part of 'A' Company's 1 Platoon.

There were gaps between them, which were ours to fill.

'What's up, chaps?' grinned Cpl George Fry, our jovial little Section Leader, whose bandy-legged gait brought him back inside to find out what was detaining us. 'Got your knickers in a twist?'

Yup.

Farting about like hysterical tarts in a tantrum Jim and I, Kevin, Don and Sam were discarding first one gaiter and then the other in an attempt to get them wrapped and strapped sufficiently tautly around our ankles, swollen as they were by our hastily-donned long-johns, thick socks and outer combat trousers. As though getting dressed properly was not bad enough, we had to work out what we should pack to take with us. The old timers had this drill honed to a fine art of course. Like professional fireman ready to leap into action at a moment's notice, their already properly adjusted, pre-assembled pack, pouches and fitted webbing equipment were kept slung across the framework on the backs of their beds. All they had to do was slip quickly into it, clip it on, scoop up their shaving kit and any stray fags or chocolate bars from their locker tops, and they were primed for a month's kill mission.

Next time round, if we lived long enough, we, too, would be just as well organised, but right now . . . we needed George Fry.

'Pay attention, and do as I say NOW,' he snapped. 'It's unfortunate this has happened before you lot're ready, because we haven't really got time to piss about with new girls. But needs must. Put these items on your beds quickly. Two spare pairs socks. Towel. Washing and shaving kit. Boot brushes and polish. Mess tins. Knife, fork and spoon. Mug. Spare shirt . . .'

Fortunately most of the stuff was pretty much ready-to-hand. We hadn't been there long enough yet to have lost, discarded or bartered any of it. No sooner had we slung it onto

252

our beds than George Fry demonstrated with Jim's kit the best way to pack it all. Socks and washing kit were shoved into the mess tins, which went into each other, and were then slipped into their specially designed pocket on the side of our small pack . . . and so on.

'You people should know all this already,' George complained. 'Christ - you're worse than the Marines.'

'What have the Marines got to do with it, Corp?' asked Sam, glancing up from rolling his spare shirt.

'Marines aren't even allowed NAAFI-breaks.'

'Why's that?' Kevin asked.

''Cos they'd have to re-train them again afterwards,' George retorted, neatly finishing his demonstration on Jim's kit. 'You now have exactly twenty seconds to get your horrible bodies outside,' he shouted, and stonked off into the bleakness to organise the rest of the section.

An obdurate protrusion erupted like a hernia through the canvas of my small pack. To flatten it I bashed it smartly against the bed head. It was one of my boot brushes, and gave me cause for reflection. On the parade square I saw every reason for spit and bullshit, but I couldn't understand why soldiers were expected to polish sodden, mud and grime encrusted boots in the field.

Similarly, scraping a blunt blade protestingly across one's chin in a ditch with the aid of cold water and a thumbnail's-worth of tarnished steel mirror at first light each morning used to piss me off a bit, too. In a Korean winter, especially, it wasn't any fun at all. When our breakfast was brought up to the company positions in straw-lined hay boxes, we used to try to drink our tea while it was still hot, but by the time we had traversed the few yards back to our trenches, it was invariably already half frozen in our mugs. All the same, half frozen tea was still better than fully frozen water for shaving in. It made your towel smell something rotten, but mother was 10,000 miles away. Oh, how I longed to retain my bristle in the field, and dispense with pimples and shaver's rash.

One frost encrusted morning, out in my ditch with Kevin, I noticed he was particularly catatonic with exhaustion. How did

I notice? Still wearing his tin-hat, with a glazed expression he was shaving its chin-strap.

Ludicrously perceived minor infringements were another irritation. One day the RSM charged Cpl Richard Farrar for having a twisted bootlace.

'Suppose you were leading an attack and that bootlace snapped on you, laddie; you'd trip, go arse over tit and if they failed to take evasive action the entire battalion would domino into an ignominious pile-up behind you. And behind them, the entire British Army. That twisted bootlace of yours could turn out to be responsible for us losing a whole bloody war. DO YOU UNDERSTAND?'

Now - especially when I see how young men go about their daily business today, wearing unpolished footwear, and unshaven - 'designer stubble'? – *pah* -I appreciate readily enough that such discipline in our day was to prevent standards slipping under adverse conditions. Something to hang on to. When the going gets tough it is all too easy to let things slide, and once the rot sets in there is nothing to hold it. Once you follow that route, next step - you'll be lining up for an earring!

Good enough - isn't.

After the morning's shave, we'd then have the pee ceremony. In 40° below that used to be a bit like firing an intergalactic ray gun. It left its source in a cloud of steam and a split second later zapped the snow like a steel rivet; or a frozen, translucent laser-beam. We all used to pee in a row, and then delicately strum the resultant yellow icicles like crystal tubes before they snapped. We soon discovered who peed what, and next day shuffled about to get the right notes and proper scales into alignment. After a week we could do *God Save The Queen* and *Yankee Doodle Dandy,* but then Pete Charles got posted. He was our A-sharp. After that we concentrated more on eating our porridge while it was still warm, and shovelling down as much compo egg and bacon as we could before that, too, froze over.

My kit was packed and donned; my 20 seconds up.
It was 05.30.

I had tripped sleepily from our hut and fallen in outside with the others.

George Fry marched us round to the armoury, where 2 and 3 Platoons had already drawn their weapons before us.

We formed a queue on a wooden boardwalk, alongside a monsoon ditch of rock-solid sandbags and corrugated-iron shoring supported by steel stakes. It would have given a vampire either a masochistic orgasm or the heebie-jeebies just to look at. Ice had consumed and rigidly packed each stake to its breast, but come the thaw each one would wiggle free, like a tooth from a rotten gum, and have to be re-bedded again before the rains came.

While I stood there musing over the intricacies of monsoon ditch construction, we shuffled slowly forward like a cinema queue. Eventually it was my turn at the issue desk. A guttering, smoke blackened tilly-lamp stood plonked on the wooden counter top, its heat accentuating the smell of gun oil and creosote from the armoury's inner murk.

'Name?'

'George,' I replied.

'George . . .,' came the voice of the armourer, running his pencil down a list of names.

'Yes?'

'Quiet, idiot,' he said to me, 'Ah - yes; *George*, here it is: Three-point-five rocket launcher, and a rifle.'

He yelled this information back to a trogladytic minion in the depths of the racking, who deftly whisked an armful of armament from shelf and aisle, which was quickly brought forward and deposited with a heavy clunk and clatter onto the bashed counter before me.

'Sign here,' I was ordered, and with a chewed pencil stub made an indecipherable squiggle next to my name.

'Next . . .?'

Kevin Flynn took my place to draw up his own consignment of weaponry, while I lurched off back into the night with my goodies crashing about me like a vagrant struck rich. The 10lb Mk IV bolt-action Lee-Enfield .303 rifle had been around for a long time. It was the standard British infantry weapon for target practice, taking out the enemy's soldiers, and, if lucky, by a fluke, the occasional low-flying aircraft as well. The 3.5in rocket launcher, which weighed-in at 15lbs, was for killing tanks. I was only 9st 3lbs and already carrying mess tins, spare socks and a boot brush; oh, and plus a tin hat on top. As I came careening round the corner of the armoury my legs gave way under this unaccustomed overload. In full view of the platoon I went crashing into one of the very monsoon ditches I had been cogitating over earlier. Fortunately its not entirely pleasant rodent quota and usual content of other stuff were dead and frozen, but the impact of my additional weight-assisted ribcage on the crinkly-tin shoring certainly shook up my washing tackle and made me wheeze a bit.

'For God's, fall-in properly,' hissed Cpl Fry.

'I just did,' I panted.

And by Christ, it hurt.

*

One, 2 and 3 Platoons were drawn up on the road outside 'A' Company's office.

Sergeant Peter Crick, 1 Platoon's platoon sergeant, called us up to attention, strolled quickly along the front rank counting heads and scowling, then stood us at ease again. Two and 3 platoon sergeants did the same with their own respective charges.

The whole of 'A' Company proper, a primed killing machine waiting to be unleashed, was now actually 'on parade'.

The CSM, a bad-tempered gentleman called 'Dad' Dunkeld, who, reputedly, through pressure of duty was once obliged to enjoy a period of respite attending a military mental institution, and with humorous pride had a framed discharge certificate above his desk declaring that he was now officially adjudged sane and able to be returned to duty, called us collectively up to attention.

Strolling out from behind the huts, the officers then filtered slowly into view.

Lieutenant Tony Prebble was our 1 Platoon Commander. He was a slight, delicate looking fellow who subsequently turned out to be one of the gutsiest and most robust pocket rockets I ever knew. I shall never forget when we were restoring our hilltop positions up on 'Easy Block' later that spring, and a small bale of barbed wire broke loose to go hurtling down the hill. Tony Prebble was half way up the hill, supervising the manhandling of further engineer stores. Our yells from the top alerted him to the runaway wire, picking up more and more speed as it went lethally bucketing down the steep decline towards him like 150lbs of enraged porcupine with a swiftly revolving stake through its middle. Tony Prebble can't have weighed much more than that himself. He glanced up and saw it coming, bouncing off rocks and tearing through scrub in its wildly accelerating descent. Seemingly without a thought he flung wide both his arms and scrabbled across the scree to intercept it. If he had done so it would have ripped him apart. Realising this just in time, he scurried disappointedly back from its path. He still felt he had to make a futile grab for it as it passed though, like plucking a serrated cannonball out of the air in mid flight, and so lost half his wrist for his trouble in doing so. The wire eventually fetched up embedded in the side of a 3-tonner parked at the bottom of the hill, which juddered visibly from the impact when it was hit.

The driver's eyes watered a bit, as well.

He'd been sitting in his cab reading a comic and hadn't seen it coming.

*

Meanwhile, back on the early morning road outside the company office, glancing to one side of the elevated sidewalk where our officers had assembled as though gathering outside a Wells Fargo office in the Old West, I saw for the first time a man who was going to influence me immensely. Why he should have had such an immediate impact on me I don't know, but if I had been a woman I suspect I might have gone even weaker at the knees than I had with the rocket launcher.

Captain Steve Ellwood, then, was aged 30.

He was 'A' Company's second-in-command.

I had never been especially impressed by any of my masters or prefects at school, but in Steve Ellwood's case I experienced my first case of hero worship. He was everything I had always wanted to be, and wasn't yet. Strong; handsome; enigmatic; able, and self-contained. Plus he was a fully grown man, whereas I was still only really a boy. Up until now I had been striving to emulate John Wayne. Now I started trying to copy Steve Ellwood as well, and the way he walked. Mixing the two played havoc with my deportment. When one or two people started glancing wryly at me, wrinkling their noses like rabbits and calling me Nancy, I decided it was time to revert to being myself.

Major Sam Crouch, 'A' Company's Commander, then wandered out of his office and made a few desultory remarks to none of us in particular about nothing very much, and I realised that although this was to be a whole new adventure for us new boys - Jim, Kevin, Don, Sam and me - it was a commonplace procedure for the others, and so not much to write home about.

'Okay, S'arnt Major. Move 'em out, will you please,' growled Sam Crouch, adjusting his webbing and climbing into his Champ with his radio operator, to go roaring quickly off ahead to recce our positions.

'A' Company moved to the left and filed off, a section at a time, out of the camp, as did - further down the lines - 'B', 'C', 'D', 'Support', and elements of 'HQ' Companies, all heading towards our respective surrounding hilltop positions, collectively known as 'Easy Block'.

For the old timers whose equipment had been worn in and adjusted to fit snugly in all the right places, the five mile march to 'Easy Block' was probably naught but a leisurely stroll.

For me it was an introduction to purgatory.

Despite the below zero temperature, I began to sweat from the unaccustomed effort and the weight of everything I was carrying. My hairy shirt started to itch. The cross straps of my webbing bit mercilessly into my shoulders, which quickly became red and raw. The waist belt had to be worn tightly about the middle to keep one's kit properly in place, hence the laden weight of the small pack, entrenching tool and other paraphernalia dangling about my person yanked the front of the belt up under the ribcage, where it successfully impeded proper breathing, other than in short gasps. This effect was counteracted by the weight of the spare magazines in my front pouches (and I don't mean *Playboy*) striving to push the front of the belt down low onto the hips, where it chafed my pelvis like a gun belt - *and* I was humping an additional 25lbs worth of Mk IV Lee-Enfield rifle, and a rocket launcher. Soldiering wasn't turning out to be too much fun that morning. Dammit, I couldn't even get the gear to hang right, to say nothing of sore ankles, blistering feet and a dull throb spreading from the base of my spine.

1 Platoon was in the lead.

My section was point section.

And I was their first man.

In front.

After being in Korea less than 24 hours, and in very bad condition, I would be the British Commonwealth's, the Americans' and the United Nations' sole representative to be spotted first and shot by any advancing Chinese or North Korean troops.

I didn't feel this was fair, really.

Behind us the rest of the company was a blur in the early morning light.

My world then consisted of the nine men around me, each of us trudging along a frozen paddy field, locked in far away thoughts of his own. Mine were now centred solely on the injustice of having to carry the cumbersome and unwieldy rocket launcher on my first morning out. *Jee*sus - I didn't even know how to fire the wretched thing. Trained soldiers or not, we had never got around to it in basic training, our instructors back at the Dépôt in England knowing that we would get plenty of opportunity to do so once we'd joined the Battalion.

We left the paddy field and crossed the wide, compacted laterite road, which as I was to learn over the coming months was referred to as the MSR (Main Supply Route). This was our lifeline to Inchon and the rest of the world. It was the arterial military highway which winter and summer, hourly, conveyed tonnages of transport, men, ammo and supplies south/north/south. Later the route was to become an arrow straight tarmacadam motorway, with giant concrete slabs suspended at intervals above it, like solid sci-fi flyovers, primed for instant explosive detonation in the event of an armoured enemy blitzkrieg driving south from the north. If dropped, each enormous slab would reduce a squadron of advancing enemy tanks to a wafer thin mash. They appeared to be beautiful pieces of defensive equipment. Chances were that Beijing had a nuke already zeroed on each one of them though, and at Crunch Hour would merely bring them toppling to the ground, disintegrate them with long range lasers, and trundle their tanks right on through to Tokyo. You can't win!

Once across the MSR we clambered down some hefty scree to a small river, about 50' wide. Some time previously some kind soul had gone to great trouble to lay some functional rock stepping stones across it. Bless him. When the snow melted in the spring it would be a different matter of course. The slabs then were washed away and the river became a raging torrent, but sufficient unto the day . . . for the moment we reached the far bank with comparative dryness.

And there before us . . . soaring upward . . . was 'Easy Block'.

'Easy Block' had been so called, obviously, because it wasn't. Steep and forbidding, it rose above us like a small Matterhorn waiting to be scaled. I still suffer sleepless nights, seeing it scowling malevolently at me from the night sky above.

With no pause for respite, or to allow us any introductory appreciation of the natural beauty of the beastly thing, we set our left boots upon it and started to climb.

'Lean in to it, chaps,' Tony Prebble encouraged cheerfully. Lean into it?

Most of us were bent so far double we were almost doing forward up-hill somersaults.

Kevin Flynn struggled along a few paces behind me.

Despite his own hardship, he called out 'Mike, I don't want to concern you, but you're leaving a red trail behind you in the snow.'

'Don't worry; it's only the blood squirting through my lace holes,' I groaned.

Gasping for breath and scrabbling for footholds, I blundered on upwards. What awaited us at the top, I wondered.

A luxury hotel in the sky?

Hot showers; clean sheets; breakfast in bed?

'Okay chaps; well done. Joke's over. Now you can relax. This is Itchy-Won. She will attend to your every need. Wash you all over, massage you with warm oil, and spoon feed you hot chocolate laced with brandy . . .'

Thirty minutes later we reached the top, and staggered forward onto the crude plateau of our second home in Korea.

Kevin and I were given a northwesterly facing, two-man trench to care-take, ankle deep in frozen slush, with a dead rat sloshing about in it with its toothsome mouth in a ghastly rictus. Both still sobbing for air, Kevin and I fell into our allotted hole, and all but collapsed. Flinging our arms across its gun emplacement, we heaved. We glanced at each other, looked cursorily at the derelict winter view, and our faces fell.

'Come along, you two,' hissed Sgt Crick, who had come swiftly up behind us in a cat-like crouch. 'You're not here to admire the scenery. That there's your field of fire. Interlocking arcs with the two trenches to each side of you. This trench you're in was dug by the Jocks last year. Nice of 'em, wasn't it. Since then no one's used it. We've kept it vacant and reserved, just waiting for you two to come out from England to occupy it. Doesn't that make you feel loved, wanted and important'?

It did.

Like accepted members of the team.

For a moment I quite thought he was serious: a nice, kind, thoughtful type, adept at man-management and psychology, tempered with the milk of human kindness and understanding.

'Now get the fucking thing dug out properly,' he snarled. 'I

261

will be back in an hour and shall expect to see this foetid little pit of yours looking like the Kure Hilton. Okay?'

He left.

'One thing's certain,' I told Kevin, as we shrugged off our kit and tried to ease our screaming shoulderblades.'

'What's that?'

'I don't think we'll be seeing hordes of Chinese this morning. This whole thing was just a ruse to get us up here digging holes.'

'They don't need a ruse. All they've got to do is say "Dig holes" and we dig holes.'

'Yeah,' I agreed . . . 'but at 7.00-o'clock in the bloody morning, in the middle of winter'?

'Why not,' argued Kevin, who seemed to have become terribly keen all of a sudden. 'They're our positions, aren't they? We've got to see them sometime. Sooner the better, really. What did you expect? A guided coach tour, with a cup of tea on arrival . . .?'

'That would've been . . . nice,' I muttered.

'Come on,' said Kevin. 'Let's dig. It'll get us warm again.'

*

We sat up on 'Easy Block' for three days and nights.

Our refurbished trench passed muster with Sgt Crick.

The river we had crossed glinted dully below us in the pale wintry sun.

Across the valley floor and up the other side to the west of us, 'C' Company's positions were pointed out, and behind us to the south, 'B' Company's positions as well.

Nigh on 1,000 young men of Sussex, no longer by the sea, 10,000 miles from home and the South Downs, sitting atop three snowy hills in Korea, trusting that their presence there might make communist forces think twice about attacking.

The River Imjin itself flowed like a great grey snake between the folds of the hills just five miles away to our north, and if the communists had decided to remain undeterred by our deterrence and *had* come streaming down that morning, then

Kevin Flynn and I were bunched and ready for 'em.

It was colder than a well digger's ass at night, trying to sleep cramped and huddled for a few hours on the floor of the trench while one's partner kept watch and stamped his feet against the solidly packed shoring to keep his circulation going. During the day, however, it was invigorating. We were not yet as fit as we would become, but we were young, healthy and adaptable. We were filthy, and we smelled. Our hair was matted, and itched. Most of us had boils breaking out like rosebuds. Knuckles became grazed and suppurating. Nail stubs were blacked with grime, but our eyes held a depth and sparkle to them. Our stomachs were plank flat and taut as drum skins, and the screaming aches of Day One were receding.

TWENTY-FIVE

AS A SOURCE OF HUMOUR the Forces are rich beyond compare.

Reader's Digest has always recognised the fact, and pays well for contribution to their *Humour In Uniform* section. I have inundated them with incidents over the years, but to date they seem to have preferred publishing yarns from EMS of Walthamstow, rather than the lucid and amusing outpourings from the pen of M.George.

The Army is aware that when the going gets tough, as it does occasionally, a sense of humour can and often does alleviate the strain a little. When your bomb-blasted and shrapnel-ripped lifeblood is pumping from a shell hole the size of a dustbin lid in your groin, your liver and lights are unfurling prettily into your lap and overflowing down the protruding white bones of both shattered legs, you've run out of ammunition, morphine, and plasters, there're only the two of you, you're a long way from home, your bayonet's snapped into the bargain, and there's an enemy division with flamethrowers ploughing up the hill in front of you about to overrun what's left of your ditch, with what's left of you still in it, there's not a lot else you *can* do but smile. Futile, perhaps, but a gesture that might afford a moment's grateful amusement to your swiftly expiring fellow cohort. Should he - against such odds - just happen to survive and fortunately be repaired and repatriated however, he might then be relied upon to relate to your erstwhile peers at future dinner nights, that you died bravely. So it's something to bear in mind and worth doing, if you can; trying to chuckle to yourself in adversity.

The Army also derives much pleasure from the use of clever code words, and place names. In radio procedure, for instance, the commanding officer's appointment title for identification over the air (no longer so these days, but then) was *Sunray.* The second-in-command was *Seagull.* Apocryphally, an attached female (WRAC) representative answered to *Manhole Cover.* (Not really; I just made that up). Shell-pocked, barbed-wire entangled front line hell-holes have rejoiced in such joyous nomenclature as *Piccadilly, Mayfair,* and *Berkeley Square.* All of which brings us back to Korea.

We had been down from 'Easy Block' for only a week when we learned that we were to take part in an Infantry / Tank cooperation exercise with the Americans. This was due to take place on a romantic sounding plain called *Taro Switch.*

Many years ago, in 1943, the American business and Hollywood tycoon, Howard Hughes, produced a movie called *The Outlaw,* starring a then 22-year-old, bounteously endowed beauty - Jane Russell. A much publicised small fortune had been expended at the time designing an aerodynamically structured bra that would give obtrusive lift-over, up-lift, push-out and spill to that lady's breastworks, whilst contriving to do so within the constraints of certain censorial bounds. It was also a cowboy film.

In 1957 Jane Russell came out on a tour of Korean bases to see us all.

Having then only recently filmed *Gentlemen Prefer Blondes* with the iconic Marilyn Monroe, the 36-year old star was at the height of her fame.

She was scheduled to visit our camp this very night to perform and, so it was rumoured, to raffle her sleeping bag. Now, because of this wretched tank exercise with the Americans, the gig was off.

It was 16.00. We had been on the march since 08.00 that morning.

I was feeling rough.

I was either dying, or had eaten some bad berries.

The wall of my intestine felt as if it had been scrubbed with a brillo pad. Bile, tasting of hard boiled eggs and coca-cola kept rising in my throat. Eventually, however, we reached *Taro Switch*, a large open plain of scrubland similar to Lüneburg Heath, in Germany, and ideally suited for tank ops. Our advance party had arrived in trucks during the day and already pitched camp. Row upon row of neatly lined little two-man bivvies ruffled welcomingly at us in the waning light and chill Siberian breeze. It was almost like coming home to tea and a log fire in winter.

Jim and I slipped off our webbing and allowed ourselves to slump down exhausted onto the hard ground. Nearby, a familiar clattering indicated that tea was up. If I didn't get some now, God only knew when the next chance would be. I rummaged in my small pack to release my mess tins and mug. Clambering wearily to our feet Jim and I scuffed across the peaty violet scrub towards the queue already forming round the steaming hay boxes. Came my turn in the shuffle, I held my receptacles out before me. Tea was ladled into the mug and a dumpling and stew thudded into one proffered mess tin, while a tinned apricot pastry thing landed like a small bomb in the other. No wonder we had blackheads and boils. A doorstep of bread was plonked on top of the stew. I turned to go back to the bivouac to eat. A moment later Jim came to join me, where I was sitting cross legged on the ground.

'Did you hear that?' he asked, shoving half a loaf down his throat.

'What? You fart? Or distant gunfire?'

'No, y'burk. Apparently Jane Russell's now scheduled to turn up here tonight, instead.'

'Where?' I asked, looking vacantly about the tents for a likely spot.

'Not here, y'pillock. At the Yank camp down the road. Anyone who wants to can go. The Yanks are laying on transport, at 18.45. Fancy it?'

The dumpling, stew and apricot thing had started running a red ball of abuse through my plumbing, which seemed to be pulverising everything like a hyperactive waste disposal unit. I half expected the parts to poke through my vest, like the shoe brush through my small pack. I felt rotten.

'Jim, I'm knackered,' I croaked. Really I am. Do you owe me a favour?'

'Prob'ly,' he conceded through a mouthful of apricot. 'It seems I usually do. What is it this time?'

'You wouldn't wash out my mess tins for me, would you? I feel hot, cold and juddery all over. I've just gotta hit the hay.'

'Yeah; sure,' he grinned with a growl.

It was 17.00 now, and almost dark. A light snow had started falling, as had the temperature. Tilley-lamps were bursting into brilliant lights about us as I crawled inside my pup tent. Fully clothed and booted I wriggled into my sleeping bag and zipped it up to my neck. Using my small pack as a pillow I shut my eyes and listened as the gurgling threshings within my stomach alternated with the gentle pad of large snow flakes settling on the roof of the tent just inches from my face. I was almost asleep when Jim came back with my cleaned mess tins.

'Sure you can't make it?' he asked solicitously.

'I've got to be pretty groggy not to, haven't I? Have a good time,' I mumbled, and fell asleep.

Only minutes later, it seemed, the ground heaved and erupted about me and I shot wide awake. My eyes flew open like saucers in the dark. My nostrils tweaked, and having tweaked relayed the message to my recoiling olfactory awareness that all was not well. In fact, sensory perception told me that I was awash in a sea of personal distress. I tried moving my arms to be able to release myself from my sleeping bag, but the zip had jammed. It was horrible. Each time I moved, I squirted. All I was able to do was lie there and moan as my entire person emptied itself inside out, using my bootlace holes, previously employed for evacuating blood, as overflow outlets. I was wearing vest, long-johns, socks, boots, shirt, pullover, combat trousers and jacket. It was pitch black. It must have dropped to 40° below. I was stuck on my own in a pup tent in the middle of the Korean countryside, cocooned to my neck in a sleeping bag, wallowing about in liquid excrement, and couldn't move because I'd got my zip stuck. The boys weren't back from the Jane Russell show yet, so it can only have been about 21.00. There had to be a roving picquet about somewhere.

There was.

I heard him trudging methodically past on his lonely vigil round the tents.

I called out.

Weakly.

The trudging stopped.

There was a pause, so I called meekly to him once again.

'Don't be bloody daft, Sydney,' came the unmistakable Sussex burr of Paddy Holman, shire ploughman *extraordinaire*. 'How can it be a ghost? Y'pillock. It's someone in trouble, ain't it. So what do we do? I'll tell you what we does Sydney, shall I? We opens the flap of the tent from whence the moanin's comin' from, we shines our torch inside of it, an' we sees what's up, don' we. Either 'e's got isself shacked up wiv some wayward Korean bint in there, or else 'e's 'avin' us on, in either case of which we lobs a fire bucket at 'im, don' we, Sydney. Or else 'e's a genuin' case o' dyin' . . . when I don' rightly know what we do. I fink one of us is meant to kiss 'im, sunfink. But I don' reckon I fancy doin' that too much, Sydney. Know what I mean? Perhaps you'd like to 'ave a go at that bit, would ya? That's if it comes to that, o' course. There . . . that's the flap open. *Jeez* . . . it don' 'alf pong in 'ere, you know.'

'Hallo, Paddy,' I croaked. 'I'm awfully sorry. I'm afraid . . . I'm afraid I seem to have shat myself.'

'I should very likely say you 'ave, my son. An' by the look o' what my torch perceives and my nostrils tells me, I'd say you've just about shat your bleedin' sel' half way to Blighty an' back. It smells like a cross between our silage pit and the slurry tank at Burwash. Been at the prunes again, 'ave we? What would you like us to do, then? Fetch you a fire 'ose? Or a bog roll?'

'Bit late for that wouldn't you think, Paddy. Just drag me out of here, will you, please? And get this bloody zip undone. I'll worry about what to do with myself after that.'

Paddy was a stalwart soul, and did as he was bid. He was a son of the soil after all, and well used to farm yards. As soon as he had dragged out and deposited my ignominious carcass in the snow though, and seen the real state of me in the moonlight, battle hardened warrior that he was he suddenly remembered a previous appointment. There was no Sydney, by the way. He was purely a figment of Paddy's imagination, who used to accompany him on night guard occasionally.

With the stars twinkling above I lay there for a while like a soggy wet dishcloth, wallowing in its mire at the side of the sink.

I was drained.

It took me a good 15-minutes to extricate myself from my predicament, to crawl out of the saturated sleeping bag and peel off and discard each item of terminally soiled clothing. Crouching naked and juddering in the moonlight, quickly beginning to die of hypothermia, I tried hard to think what I should do.

Suddenly I was gripped by another searing colic contraction, but through my suffering there rang (albeit muffled) the clarion call of discipline. It was an offence to foul the company lines. Bare-assed and all of a quiver, I clutched my arms about my navel and blundered away from the bivouacs, out into the darkness beyond.

The Jane Russell show had been a terrific success, her renowned *embonpoint* sufficiently apparent to have impressed everyone. She had raffled her sleeping bag, and, well laced and excited, the boys were returning to camp in the backs of the trucks, singing, laughing, and lewdly joking. Dirty beasts. Judging by some of their comments the bromide in their tea must have failed to kick in. The lead truck swung off the MSR. Its main beam stabbed erratically into the night as it bucked and ploughed across the deep tank ruts of *Taro Switch*. Eventually it swung towards our camp area.

That's when I was picked out in its headlights.

A naked, white form outlined in a crude, retching posture in the snow.

The boys screwed up their eyes and squinted, to fathom who I was, all broke into a happy grin when they realised, and then they brutally commenced to capitalise upon it.

'Corr, there she is,' yelled the first illiterate yahoo.

'Quick . . . let me at her. It's her body I want, I tell ya,' cried another.

'I want its body . . . Corrr.'

'Oh, I do feel crude and I wanna get screwed and that body over there in the snow will dooooo,' bellowed the raucous baritone of Bill Harpenden, the company bard.

'Knock it off,' I heard Jim's voice yell from the back of the second truck, when he recognised me and realised what must have happened.

'Sure, okay . . .' retorted the ribald chorus. 'All together - or one at a time?'

'Knock it off, for chrissake,' Jim shouted, leaping from his truck and running through the snow towards me.

The rest of them soon realised the joke was not a joke any longer; that I was in a bad way. I was led hurriedly round to the back of the cookhouse tent where I was given a bowl of hot water to sluice myself down with. A pile of blankets appeared and were wrapped around me, and the next thing I knew I was being bundled into a hastily summoned Champ and driven off back to an American base hospital, to a bed, clean sheets, pills, a book to read and *Radio Kumari* to listen to. Fats Domino's *Blueberry Hill* and Slim Whitman's *Rose Marie* were top of the American pops that week, and it took three days for that virulent bout of dysentery to course through my body, and quit.

*

Next morning my lately discarded ensemble was found stiffly strewn around the entrance to my vacated bivouac.

The picquet who discovered the stuff in the snow at his feet, received the fright of his life. As if the sight alone wasn't enough, he accidentally trod on the frozen left ankle of my long johns. They leapt into the air and saluted him with one leg, whilst slapping him sloppily about the neck with the other. Leaping back in horror, he instinctively belted them in the navel with his rifle butt, making them buckle in the middle and crackle to a final demise upon the ground.

Later, some wit detailed a burial party.

A hole was dug.

The offensive apparel was shoveled quickly in, and covered.

Thus interred, a sort of spoof and sacrilegious service took place, and a small ripple of gunfire was authorised. A note or two of the *Last Post* were sounded, with a deliberately inserted raspberry discord, and that was that.

No rice has been known to grow near that spot since.

*

My sojourn in hospital was brief.

With correctly administered intestinal binders, my drips soon firmed up and clotted, allowing me to be released to rejoin the Platoon in time for another exercise with the Americans.

We loved the Americans, but couldn't help viewing them as a race apart.

Through their good and generous auspices we were enabled to enjoy certain home comforts, which traditionally would never have been forthcoming from our own parsimonious administration. We consumed their food in our cookhouses, for example, which seemed to consist mostly of frozen turkey, ice cream and concentrated fruit juice. We were also able to have our films developed in their PXs (Postal Exchange; the US Forces' equivalent to our Naafi) — and we could stop off for steak suppers in one of their clubs on the way back to our own camp afterwards.

But there the fraternisation seemed to stop.

We were a British infantry regiment, attached to an American infantry regiment, coming under the command of an American infantry division, but we used to resent the way they seemed to do some things. We would march out of camp fully self-sufficient and equipped for war. One hundred and some odd paces to the minute later, over the nearest hilltop, we would dig in, and if asked would be ready to try our hand at repelling anything from a Russian backed invasion to a Martian landing. We considered ourselves fully capable of meeting most of the tasks handed down to us. We became pretty arrogant about it too, I guess – but this was just the attitude that 'helped us through'. Hence the dawn of the phrase 'failure is not an option'.

The American infantry, on the other hand, always managed to overtake us on the way to our respective defensive positions, leaving a choking trail of dust and laughter behind them from the backs of the trucks in which they were being transported. Half of them would have their caps shoved to the backs of their heads, their boots slung round their necks by the laces, and their feet hanging over the tailboard, while the other half would be taking cine films of the countryside . . . and, naturally, the poor old bloody British, us, slogging along in the wake of their mechanised rush like third world *peones* with a grudge, a belief and a secret.

On one memorable occasion, during a thigh-searing flog up the MSR in June, we did actually catch up with one of their trucks. It had toppled off the road and was lying arse over tit in a paddy field, its inmates groggily sprawled about on the dusty verge awaiting their Purple Hearts. As we drew abreast, the driver - the spitting image of Forest Whitaker, with a gash across one eyebrow - was nearly choking himself to death with laughter. Waving his hand vaguely behind him at some mountain on the far side of the valley, he rumbled: 'Man - ah done turned me mah truck off'n the road.'

'Yes,' retorted Lt Prebble. 'It would seem that you have. May we offer you a lift?'

'How you proposin' to do that then, Man?' the negro enquired curiously, with a grin.

Scarcely pausing in his stride, Tony Prebble bent and thrust his right arm between the surprised negro's legs and deftly hoisted and humped him up across his shoulders in a fireman's carry. Tony was slight, and the burger-pumped negro wasn't, but still Tony managed to lope a good ten yards or so further up the MSR with him on his back before the startled, wriggling and writhing negro struggled protestingly back down again.

272

Having successfully managed to disentangle himself from Tony's painful entrenching tool, he hopped about at the side of the road like a small boy dying for a pee, clutching where it hurt most. Strewn about the edge of the paddy field behind him his compadres all roared with laughter. Tony threw them a lovely throw-away mock salute. Re-bonded as never before, an overburdened 1 Platoon 'A' Company, 1st Battalion The Royal Sussex Regiment continued ramrod straight along our way, barely able to suppress our mirth, our pride, and our adoration for our Platoon Commander. After that, Tony Prebble could have committed murder and got away with it.

*

Our mission that day was to defend a particular hilltop against an American attack.

Duly arriving at the duly appointed time at the summit of the to-be-defended hill, we commenced to dig in. Such was our training and inclination in those days, that if we stood still anywhere for more than five minutes, we would instinctively start to dig in.

At 10.30 a red flare shot into the sky, signalling the beginning of the exercise. Secure and confident up there in our defensive positions, we stood-to - and waited.

The attacking American infantry eventually appeared at around mid-day, scrambling about at the foot of a small hillock at the far end of the valley below. In order to attract their attention, and at least get them pointing in the right direction, we loosed off a few gratuitous shots into the air. It was a crystal clear day. Sound carried. We could see the startled Americans turn in surprise, and shield their eyes. Eventually some of them saw us. We had to wave first though.

'Oh, *yeah*: over dere, fellahs. See dem? *Jeeez* - how'd those motherfuckers get all the way up dere, den?'

Regathering their wits, the fitter of them started to pound gleefully up the valley floor towards us. When they had come close enough we began to lob the occasional small boulder at them. The unlucky recipient of one of these could clearly be

273

seen inspecting the dent in his steel helmet, which he'd whipped off in surprise. 'Hey, you guys: d'at's hardly cricket, is it?' he yelled up at us indignantly.

After that, their dander was up and they began to take it more seriously. It was heads down and no further comment, until when they were about seventy yards below us one emboldened voice was moved to sing out: 'Take more'n a few pebbles to keep the Fightin' 21st at bay . . .'

Silly boy.

He should have kept his Arkansas mouth shut.

Tony Prebble's command was passed quietly from trench to trench.

'Fix bayonets.'

Half-a-hundred deadly slivers of shiny steel snicked menacingly home, the sound of them engaging ominously clicking along the crest of our ridge.

'What the hell're those limey bastards up to *now,* chrissake?' demanded a deep Texan drawl, as its perspiring owner almost reached our positions at last.

Apart from a whole load of blundering, crashing about and swearing as they advanced stealthily through the undergrowth, all else was silent. Beside me, I could see that Kevin Flynn was smiling. Overhead a skylark trilled.

Tony Prebble's command, when it came, cut like an incisive diamond along the crest.

He must have been dreaming of a moment like this ever since Sandhurst.

'A' Company. *Take Post.'*

Each one of us leapt out from his trench and up onto the parapet, his bayoneted rifle held stock still at the position of Advance.

A hill in Korea paused.

Above us, even the skylark stilled its trill.

Below us, upturned American faces froze in a frieze of horrified disbelief.

'Advaaaaance . . .' commanded Tony.

Not a man jack of us faltered in his step.

Inexorably, the British line moved forward down the hill.

Epics such as the Peninsular War sprang to mind.

It was a superb piece of play acting.

Sheer bliss.

Tony Prebble must have been giggling with mirth.

'Chaaaaaarge . . . ' he cried.

Where previously we had only impaled and put the boot into straw dummies suspended from beams, now caterwauling terrifyingly and vocalising blood-lust in the prescribed training manual fashion, the fifty filthy members of 1 Platoon 'A' Company gleefully went surging down the hill in hot pursuit of the fleeing Americans, brandishing our cold British steel in a very purposeful manner.

It was heady stuff . . .

. . . those young-blood Glory Days of ours.

TWENTY-SIX

WE HAD BEEN OUT OF THE FIELD FOR A WEEK and settled into a domestic routine about camp, cleaning weapons and kit, maintaining vehicles and radio equipment, and carrying out the myriad other chores that are all part and parcel of a fighting unit's life. Constantly underscoring all these activities, however, was the core need for us to acquire and maintain a constant condition of peak physical fitness. My first few weeks of physical activity had been very uncomfortable. Bloodied boots; strained and torn muscles; screaming calves and thighs; sore back and shoulders, and a cardiovascular respiratory system that still had a very long way to go before it was fully fit for purpose, were par for the course. Then, one day, festooned with a bandolier of bren-gun ammo and a cradle of bazooka bombs, as well as my rifle, webbing equipment and pack, I was clawing my way to the top of a frozen mountain pass, when suddenly - I got there! I'd arrived! To this day I can still remember the moment it happened. I was at God knows how many hundred feet, still ploughing stoically upwards like a beast of burden laden with all those items of armament clanking about my person, thinking there had to be more to my 18-year-old life than this, when suddenly my head popped out above a cloud to startle a passing eagle, the gnarled and engrimed claw that was my fist dragged me by an upward surge and a rock-hold to the summit of that particular hill, there was a distinct tingling like mustard in the top of my skull, my methodically beating heart and lungs filled to full capacity and a loud and clear message flashed jubilantly across my brain . . . *I'M FIT!*

There and then I made a personal vow that from thenceforth on I would never be caught out like that again and would *always* throughout life maintain a certain level of fitness so that I was physically prepared to meet any and every demand at short notice. Now I am in my seventies I can't do quite so many chins to the beam or shins to the bar any more, and my penchant for vodka martinis, combined with my renown for making the best, most potent and man-sized gin and tonic east or west of Suez, have eroded my original good intent rather more than a smidgin, but one or two ladies over the years have been kind enough to comment favourably on my rather nice turn of calf. I never explained how I got them or what civilians need do to follow suit, but I have always been grateful to the Regiment for what's left of my reasonably shapely legs.

We whinged like crazy each time the US infantry used to overtake us in their trucks (only just, mind) but we were deep down chuffed that we knocked them into a cocked hat where strength, stamina and stickability were concerned. The good old Sussex swede-bashers outpaced them every time. Recruits today, apparently, have to wear plimsoles during basic training because their feet are not tough enough for boots, whereas a ten mile march and run in two hours wearing full battle order and carrying weapons was the norm for us.

The Army has always enjoyed undergoing a masochistic annual ritual known as PE (Physical Efficiency) tests, when its athletes, pentathletes, marathon runners, rugger players, cooks, clerks and bottle washers all have to turf out en masse, in most cases to wreck themselves - making sweat. Then along comes each new generation of APTC (Army Physical Training Corps) hierarchy which promptly goes about superseding its predecessors' efforts by devising a more 'updated' test, which incorporates the latest received physical education knowledge, based on facts and figures un*dreamed* of by previous generations of instructors. At some time, in the mid 1970s, the annual PE test became renamed the Basic Fitness test, which was certainly a pretty watered down version of the sort of thing we had to do in Korea.

Subtle and more esoteric fitness routines, like yoga or

transcendental meditation, never caught on in the Army as being good or effective ways to train up and maintain a killing machine. It would not have been infra dig for someone to have tried them out at evening class perhaps, while his wife was in the next room stuffing chairs or basket-weaving, but in the Army it is considered that the only true path to rugged physical fitness, is by making painfully induced sweat.

The SAS, Paras, SBS and Royal Marines apart, to complete the Basic Fitness test a soldier was required to trot along for 1½ miles in his PT vest and boots (and shorts too, of course) and then go flat-out for the next 1½ miles, in nine to 15 minutes, depending upon his age. Old WWII soldiers could doubtless and justifiably pooh-pooh the tests we did in Korea as being namby-pamby . . . but . . . we had to do a 10-mile forced speed march in full battle-order in under two hours, which necessitated periods of running in order to complete the test in the required time.

Full battle-order consisted of our steel helmet, full webbing equipment (with magazines in pouches), the small pack correctly filled and packed, and carrying personal weapons (rifles) and platoon weapons (bren-guns and rocket launchers). These platoon weapons were passed about between us during these marches, as each successive carrier showed signs of flagging. At the completion of the test we then painfully had to bounce one of our muckers and all his kit for 100-yards in a fireman's carry, scale a six-foot wall (no, not with our mucker still aboard for this one), clear a nine-foot ditch, cross a chasm over-hand by rope, then fling ourselves to the ground and commence firing five well aimed rounds at a rifle target . . . *and* score a hit each time. Then we could call it a day, throw up, and light a fag. But if we'd got that far, we had no need to throw up. We were fit. Throwing up would usually have been done five miles back down the road. I threw up. Once.

Flogging ammo boxes up and down 'Easy Block' and chasing Americans round the countryside kept us pretty trim most of the time, but this year's preliminary PE test (just a 'warm up' forced march, without all those ghastly fancy additives at the end, thank God) came round about a week after

I'd come out of hospital with my bout of dysentery, so I was a bit weak about the knees, and failed.

I had started the test with misplaced confidence and determination overriding any misgivings I might or should have had, but I was only able to sustain this attitude for about five miles. After that my efforts became weaker and weaker, until finally I collapsed at the side of the road just a mile from camp, a sodden and shameful wreck of a creature, being grinned at sympathetically by passing Korean farm-hands on their way to work. I was not alone. It had been a tough one. Two thirds of the platoon failed that day. Our masters gave not an inch. The UK taxpayers, although they may not have known or cared very much if they did, were paying for a fit Royal Sussex Regiment to represent their interests in Korea, and that is what they were going to get. If we were 15-seconds late through those camp gates, even with unstoppable nosebleed and blood pumping out of our ears indicating the degree of determination and effort that had been expended, we still failed, and had to do it again. And we loved it. Well – we do now that we've done it; we didn't then.

Would that there was more of it today.

We failures were allowed to pop our blisters and drain our boots, rinse our socks and have a rest, and then we were off again two days later. Failures? *Pah!* Those of us who *failed* could probably have outrun an Olympic team. We were reckoned at the time to be just about the fittest regiment in the whole British Army, worldwide.

The following personnel will parade at 06.00 in full battle-order to complete their PE tests . . . read the Company Order pinned to the notice board next evening.

Spring was in the air.

The snow had melted, and days were becoming warmer.

06.00 was a good time for heavy physical work, before the heat was up. Plus it didn't eat into the working day so much. The Army has always been into its 'value for money, pound of flesh' in a big way.

It was 05.55 next morning.

279

We 20 failures were ready, fully kitted and bearing arms, standing at ease in the dust on the road outside the company office. The usual humorous remarks and ripostes were subdued, shallow, and brittle. We were a chaste little bunch, all slightly wary of just how much unpleasantness the next two hours were holding in store for us.

The CSM was nowhere to be seen.

Nor were any of the platoon sergeants.

This was unusual.

They were normally there, sniffing around to record and comment upon our every nose-blow and twitch.

Had they forgotten us?

It felt like a PoW camp, where all the guards had suddenly upped and done a runner.

Could there have been some sort of foul-up, and we'd all have to psyche ourselves up to come back to do it again tomorrow . . . or was there some more ominous reason for leaving us standing there unattended in the middle of Korea at 05.59 in the morning?

'Good morning.'

As one man we whirled round to see who had spoken.

It was Captain Steve Ellwood.

He had taken the back way down through the long grass from the officers' mess, and was now standing there in the road behind us.

'Turn about properly, would you please?' he said, casually adjusting the holster at his waist. Along with his full battle order he also carried a slung rifle and wore a beige toweling sweat shirt, its crumpled collar peeping surreptitiously out from beneath his combat jacket. It was doubtful whether even one of the regiment's men possessed a single item of civilian kit with him in Korea, hence the glimpse of this sneaky little sweat shirt struck me as being very 'officer like'.

'I understand some of you chaps have been having a bit of difficulty passing this wretched PE test,' he said, speaking quietly, 'and I suspect one or two of you didn't make it because of a lack of gump.' He paused, and slightly raised one eyebrow.

Which of us, did he think, lacked gump? Nobody knew. But one thing was sure. This morning, each of us intended to prove it wasn't him.

'So what we're going to do today,' Steve continued, 'is our utmost to get this damned thing over and done with, once and for all, shall we? Okay. Don't worry. I shall see that most of you pass. Would you move to the right now, please? By the right . . . *Double March.*'

There was no way any of us was going to fail.

Die in the process, perhaps; yes - but not fail.

I had only ever heard of one preamble as persuasive as Steve's.

On the Parachute Brigade's course there is a particularly wicked hill that is expected to be climbed in a similar sort of hurry. Some people have been known to flag half-way up this hill, unable to do ought but gaze hopelessly up at the sky, and in their mind's eye design pink coffins. But, instead, what do they see silhouetted at the top, scowling, with arms folded? They see the Para CSM. And what words of encouragement does the Para CSM whisper down to them?

'If you don't manage to summon sufficient effort to get yourself to the top of this hill immediately . . . YOU WILL BE BEASTED.'

Most Paras found they summoned sufficient effort to get to the top of the hill immediately.

Whilst it was my turn to be carrying the clattering bren-gun, which I had slung like a yoke across my shoulders, Jim was suffering, making quite heavy weather of things pounding along there beside me. I remembered him washing out my mess tins back at *Taro Switch* that day, and so grabbing his sling I pulled his rifle off his shoulder to ease his burden, and slung it across my left shoulder beside my own. Blood pumped, legs churned and sweat bounced as we coursed past the little early morning village of Marjor-ri, leaving a trail of dust in the wake of our outward trip.

One hour later we had turned round at the five mile point, and were surging back again, Steve Ellwood looking so fit and tireless as he doubled up and down our ranks cajoling us on to even greater effort, it appeared he might merely have come along for a pre-breakfast stroll. How the hell did he manage to make it look so easy?

Thanks to Steve pushing us, we all made it successfully back to camp that day, with 10-minutes to spare!

Miraculously, someone (Steve?) had arranged for there to be hot water in the showers for once, and in we all piled, including Steve, whose stripped torso looked like the sort of thing with which poets defended Thermopylae.

He had come unprepared, and wanted to borrow soap, so I lent him mine.

Never washed with it again.

He dropped it down the waste outlet.

I didn't attempt to retrieve it.

Hero worship didn't extend quite that far.

*

During a Korean winter one had to guard against exposure, frostbite, and coughing up lumps of frozen lung.

In summer, nature turned the tables and reversed the process.

All the bugs came out of cold storage.

We took daily dosages of paludrine to ward off malaria, and salt tablets the size of mothballs to replace what we lost sweating.

These were the minnows of the circuit.

The fearsome one? The shark . . .?

Korean haemorrhagic fever (KHF).

KHF was first noted during the Korean War, when 2,300 US troops contracted the disease, 800 of whom died.

The symptoms of KHF include fever, chills, malaise, headache, nausea, abdominal and back pain, which can lead to tachycardia (increased heart rate) and hypoxemia (inadequately oxygenated blood), and then renal failure. Unsurprisingly, flushing of the face, inflammation of the eyes, and petechial rash (red spots caused by the haemorrhaging of subcutaneous capillaries) are also usually present.

It's not a nice thing to catch. Bit of a drag all round, really.

It took a while to establish its cause, too.

Research at the time focused on efforts to isolate the causative agent from the haemorrhaging organs and kidneys of stricken patients.

But to no avail.

British troops who contracted the disease were immediately flown back to UK for excited 'celebrity-case' experimental monitoring at London's School of Tropical Medicine, but then years later it was established that the jostling and effect of lowered atmospheric pressures during airborne evacuation was actually injurious to critically ill KHF patients.

There then entered into the arena a Korean doctor, Lee Ho-Wang, who started to investigate 'outside the box'.

And what did he come up with?

In 1976 Doctor Ho-Wang (since tipped for the Nobel Peace Prize) isolated the KHF virus . . . wait for this . . . in the lungs of striped field mice, living in the vicinity of Korea's Hantaan River.

It transpired that the deadly disease is transmitted by these (and other) infected rodents through their urine, droppings, or saliva. Humans can contract the disease when they breathe in aerosolised virus, or the contaminated dust from the rodents' nests. Transmission may also occur when these infected materials are directly introduced into broken skin, or onto mucous membranes of the eyes, nose or mouth.

Soldiers, crawling about in long grass - beware!

Several hundred cases of KHF occur ever year in Korea.

It can be prevented by the control of rodent populations near human communities and bivouac sites. Grass and shrubbery should be kept well trimmed, and rodents should not be disturbed in their burrows. They should be excluded from homes and other buildings. (They can eat dogs - but no pet mice please, in Korea). Sleeping on the bare ground should be avoided (soldiers, please take note) as should contact with rodent urine, droppings, saliva, nesting materials and other contaminated debris.

Yeah, right. Now they tell us!

Hordes of bivouacking, tramping-about soldiers, sleeping on the ground and suchlike . . . if we'd only known then what they know now.

Since those days a vaccine has been developed, from an inactivated, purified mouse brain, that is now administered liberally to military personnel, farmers - and golfers; but in our day -?

Zilch . . .

. . . except that before we went into the field we had to lay out our kit on open areas where it was sprayed with a particular repellent, the only one we had at the time, which we hoped might go some way to warding off the ghastly KHF.

Apocryphal yarns abounded.

If the bug got you, you started to sweat blood - literally. If you wiped your forearm or any part of your body with a tissue (like, who had tissues) it would come away pink. The blood simply seeped through your pores. It was reckoned one had 24 hours before the full eight pints trickled away completely and you were left a bleached husk of your former self; dead. At the onset of the first ooze, therefore, the victim had to be spoken to gently, knocked on the chin, strapped securely beneath a helicopter, and flown fairly quickly across to Japan where he underwent constant blood transfusions: or, as stated earlier, flown back in vain to London's School of Tropical Medicine, for exploratory poking.

TWENTY-SEVEN

YOUTH IS WASTED ON YOUTH.

Some occasional diary jottings from an active life . . .

<u>Wednesday 24th April 1957</u>
Up at 05.30. Down the firing range all day, letting off brens. Got back to camp at about 16.00 to get ready for that night's Fire Picquet duty. Off duty at 08.30, dismounted and went back to the hut to clean up before going down the range again in battle order to qualify as a classified shot. Back at camp our newly arrived CSM - Charlie Pace by name – just to impress us with his presence and to make a name (a recognised military management technique) got a grip of us for being improperly dressed.

<u>Friday 26th April</u>
Yesterday, down the range all day, loading magazines. We beat the 24th five-nil at football. BHQ Guard duty that night. Today - went down to Icicle Range on trucks. Spent the day doing three section attacks, live-firing the bren, rifle, sten, smoke grenades etc. We set a whole valley alight. I led the attack this afternoon. Result? The new OC said he'd be putting me forward for promotion. We marched back to camp. For the first time in ages my feet seem to be okay, although they are a bit sore. Spent the evening cleaning our weapons.

<u>Saturday 28th April</u>
Loaded up the ammo trucks and went down to Icicle Range to fire off bazookas and mortars. 12.30 lunch break, and then

Lt Prebble briefed us on next week's mammoth 100-mile march.

Monday 29th April

Up at 06.15. Packed gear and paraded at 08.15. Into trucks and off at 09.00. Glorious scenery as we wound our way up and round and over Korea. We shoved all our gear into the trucks and saw them off to the destination, while we took a convenient short cut. It is an exhilarating feeling, being so fit and able to leap from rock to rock, fleet of foot and nimble as mountain goats with nary a thought of snapping an ankle as we went bounding and swarming down the steep, boulder strewn hillsides. Arrived at our overnight camp location at 18.15. Had a meal and laid a bed; three blankets and a bivvy. I am gonking with Pete Goodsall. We are beside a river. It is clear as a millpond, backed by a 500-foot heavily wooded hill rising on the other side. I have just had a wash and a shave in it. Although there is a mist and it is almost dark I am still stripped to the waist, writing this with the aid of a small hurricane lamp. One of the chaps has just braved a quick dip. A few others are fishing with lumps of bread and improvised rods.

Tuesday 30th April

It rained during the night, so everything is fresh this morning. We left this camp at 13.00 and marched for eight miles in three hours to our next camp. It is a treat, located beside a raging torrent. Had a glorious wash and shave in it. I am writing this in the mouth of my tent by the dimmest of light.

Thursday 2nd May

Yesterday - reveille at 06.15. My feet behaved a treat and lasted me for a buckshee march. Felt A-OK, right along the line. Reached the top of a hill, beside a large reservoir. Hit the next camp at 13.15. Had lunch and then a quick wash down in a stream. I heard a hilarious yelp of outrage from behind a bush round a bend just a few yards up-stream behind me. 'Get off me, Sergeant. I don't care. It's my soap and it's my cock, and I'll wash it just as fast as I like.'

This morning we covered 15-miles, which was a bit heavy going. We kept in radio contact with an American plane.

Reached the new campsite about 14.15. I am on guard duty tonight.

Sunday 5th May

Yesterday turned much cooler. I was lugging the 88- radio set. We set a cracking pace up hills and down a steep valley. The whole of 'A' Company are as fit as fiddles now. We can sweat our guts up a hill, but once at the top we soon recover.

Monday 6th May

Reveille at 05.45. Moved out at 07.40. Did one mile as a warm up, and then went straight into a 10-miles bash in two hours. It started off rough, but was then buckshee. We finished right on time, feeling absolutely great. We were picked up by trucks and taken to our next camp site, which was a beauty. Had a glorious wash in a glorious river. I am feeling great, and ready for anything.

Tuesday 10th May

Reveille at 04.45. Moved out at 06.00. Packs were pretty heavy. We had a stiff 15-minutes climb. Rested at the top and then made our own way down the valley to cook breakfast. Pressed on and covered quite a distance. Camped in a pine forest that night.

Wednesday 11th May

Moved out at 07.00 and made a stiff but buckshee climb Rested at the top, and then moved down the valley prior to scaling the steepest of our hills - three hours allowed to complete it. It was really hot. We lost L/Cpl Johnny Guy, 'Dildo' Davies, Wally Grist and Tony Ford, and wasted a couple of hours trying to find them. Lt Prebble and one of the NCOs stayed behind to track them down, and the rest of us pressed on under Sgt Crick. When we finally hit the road it was to find we were seven-and-a-half miles off target. No worries. We bashed on, and were picked up en route by a convoy of trucks which took us on to our next camp. I hit the hay at 21.30. The missing quartet rolled in knackered at midnight.

Thursday 12th May

05.30 reveille. Excruciating foot and groggy tummy, but we moved out at 07.15 on a brief attack. Bit rough at one climb, but otherwise buckshee. We moved out at 11.50 hours and went along a railway line to camp. Some trucks picked us up a few miles off, and were they ever welcome. I never realised I could reach such a depth of sheer soul destroying physical exhaustion and yet still keep going. A Canadian RE Major turned up to take some public relations shots of us *in extremis*.

Friday 10th May

06.45 reveille. Moved off in trucks to look round Chun-Chong, the third most civilised town I've seen in Korea. The journey back was pretty cramped and choked with dust. We were dropped off to *schlep* the last mile to good old Kohima Camp - our 100-mile march now successfully completed.

Nine days later, however . . .

Monday 13th May

Withdrew 20-miles down *Mary Anne II* to *Tomtit II*. Night listening patrol with Flynn, Grist and an 88-set.

Tuesday 14th May

Very hot all day, spent firefighting a forest that was ablaze.

Wednesday 15th May

Moved out and advanced about six miles up a hot, dust choked road. Reserve company for 'D' Company's afternoon attack. Rested up outside a village. Moved out at 02.30 for a dawn attack.

Thursday 16th May

Dawn attack without packs on *Hill 424*. Bit gruelling, but we made it. 1 Platoon carried on along the ridge to clear out the enemy, and we spent the rest of the day up there. Very short on water. We withdrew at 20.30 to rejoin the rest of the company. Three hours kip, and then moved out at 02.30.

Friday 17th May

Dawn found us in position at the foot of a hill. We took the mountain, Kamak-San, by 11.00. Our most gruelling day by far. Then we were pulled out, and returned to Kohima Camp to rest up.

Typically thus were spent the days in the working life of a £5 a week British infantryman in Korea at that time.

That evening I went to watch the movie in the camp cinema
- *It's Good To Be Young* . . .

. . . and thought: they had to be joking, didn't they!

Then again . . . perhaps not.

TWENTY-EIGHT

THE WAR NOW OVER there was a lot of ammunition left still kicking around Korea, and it suddenly befell our lot to dispose of it.

'Our lot', of course, being doughty old 'A' Company again.

We packed a week's supply of kit, and headed off on the two-hour lorry drive from Kohima Camp in the hills, down to Edinburgh Camp, at the port of Inchon. After tea that evening, there not being too much else to do in Korea at that stage of our lives, I took myself off to the Edinburgh Camp cinema to see whatever film it was that happened to be showing.

And just what film did that happen to be?

You've guessed.

Love Is A Many Splendoured Thing.

It seemed strange. I had first seen and been moved by this film in Eastbourne: then visited one of its locations - the tree on the hill in Hong Kong - and now here I was watching it all over again, beyond Hong Kong, out in Korea itself, the land where the film's male lead, Mark Elliot, had lost his life in the opening days of the war. Not such a big deal to a seasoned grown up perhaps, but to an impressionable young lad in his formative years the coincidence seemed amazing . . .

Next morning, dressed in shirt-sleeve order and ready for action we piled onto the trucks and were driven down to Inchon port. The fresh spring breeze came whipping through the gaps in the trucks' awnings and our open shirts, giving us all exhilarating goose pimples. It was a muscle flexing experience. We were young, fit, alive and healthy. Life was great.

At the port we could see the good old *Frederick Clover* again, lying out at anchor, the LST that had brought us up from Hong Kong only a couple of months previously. It was onto her that we were going to load the ammo.

We spent the rest of that day humping 100-tons of mortar bombs onto a flat barge.

That night it rained and I was sleeping beneath a leaky roof, but – hey - what the hell, eh. Next morning we clambered aboard the trucks again at 06.15 and in pouring rain spent the next two hours unloading HE (high explosive) shells from 10 trucks, until 09.15 when we were driven back to camp for some breakfast.

At 09.45 we returned to the docks, where we waited around in a workman's hut till 11.15. Then we went out on a US landing craft to one of their radio barges, where we waited around for an hour before being returned by landing craft, shoved back into our trucks and taken back cold, sopping wet and shivering to Edinburgh Camp once more, work having been postponed because of the inclement weather.

That evening, appropriately, we watched an Abbot and Costello film.

Next day, our clothing now dried - well, sort of - it was work again, as usual. US landing craft shipped us out to the *Frederick Clover* where we spent the day down in the hold stacking boxed .303 rounds and mortar shells. We had a two-hour kip on deck in the afternoon, but then worked again from 16.00-19.45, before returning to camp.

Next day we had an 05.00 reveille, and worked in the hold from 0730-1030; a short break, more humping, and then we had the whole job finally finished by 14.30 that afternoon.

The *Frederick Clover* up-anchored and sailed off to dump the fruits of our labour into the Sea of Japan, while we returned to Kohima Camp to resume soldiering.

Such was the pattern of our daily existence, in those far off halcyon days of our youth.

*

A potential source of disease in summer was the latrines, of course. These had to be constructed soundly, and be well maintained. Rather like any landfill site, eventually an area would reach saturation point, and then a new facility had to be thought about.

One day I had the singular honour to be chosen to join a select party detailed off to build a fresh latrine - or 'bog' as they were affectionately known, to differentiate them from the much simpler downward sloping corrugated iron runnel we used for jimmy-riddling in, known as a desert rose.

Bogs are for the more senior, heavy duty 'long drop' stuff.

There are bogs - and there are bogs, of course.

The fresh 'A' Company bog we had been commissioned to build that day, was far removed from your standard Boy Scout thunderbox.

Ours needed to be a good old 40-seater, multi-turnover, soldier-proof industrial-model bog capable of accommodating a daily throughput of some hundred hairy honkies dropping their kaks and plonking in the pit.

The Cook Sergeant regulated attendance by whim.

Apple increased the turnover.

Compo sausage and chocolate bound you up so tight you had to walk with a wince, and any attempt at slick motion was like revolving on a rusted core. Days like this reduced toilet trade to a minimum, the respite enabling the janker-wallahs to get down and root the place out a bit, slosh the large jerries of disinfectant about and swipe a few mozzies into touch. However -

I am leaping ahead of myself -

How to build a company-sized bog:-

1.   Ask if anyone has built one before. If he has - go get him.

2.   Ask to be shown, and make sure you know exactly where the bog is to be built.

3.   Fetch spade.

4.   Re-assess task; ditch spade; submit indent for mechanical shovel (and operator).

5.   Chat-up operative. Offer him cigarette and

292

ingratiatingly ask him to excavate for you an oblong hole in the ground 20' x 20' x 10' deep.

6. Go for lunch. Come back later, with Holy Man. Before further construction commences, ask Holy Man to bless hole. (There may be nothing in this, but far better safe than sorry; because of the mauling and severe abuse they are being lined up to receive, clods of Korean dirt do appreciate such rites).

7. Sink piles (wooden) into the four corners and centre of your hole. Construct wooden dance-floor arrangement on top, and then, as though cutting tarts from pastry, saw out two back-to-back rows of 20 + 20 sit-upon type openings, for the eventual evacuative egress to the newly consecrated netherworld of great big smelly lumps of squaddies' you-know-whats.

8. Next step: build slat-supported hessian walls to prevent external viewing, a corrugated iron roof to keep low flying vultures at bay, and some steps up from ground zero to your edifice's rickety-hinged door. Manhandle in and install 40 pre-constructed timber bog-stalls from the Chippy's shop, and align same as appropriately and approximately as possible above the thus-far pristine pit below. Nail securely into place with sodding great nails and screws. Erect further hessian half-panelling to create yet another illusion of varying inadequate degrees of semi-privacy between stalls and - hey presto - your bog is ready for its ceremonial opening.

9. Champagne is not wasted at Field Bog Openings. In fact champagne is seldom seen at Field Bog Openings. One of one's game little Korean work party is detailed-off to pour 10 x 10-gallon drums of disinfectant down onto the good old Buddhist earth below, and when that's done . . . creosote everything else. The effect is akin to using the entire annual paint quota for the Firth of Forth Bridge at one go in your drawing room. The mosquitoes didn't know what'd hit 'em. Then the mechanical-shovel operative and the OC Bog Party have a semi-hysterical 'Wetting the Seat' ceremony. This sets in the rot, and The Bog is now 'open for business'.

The mosquitoes re-grouped.

Hessian, shit, disinfectant and urine, concentrated as an aroma-producing plant in one location in winter, in snow, when the ground and its contents were frozen solid and the whole bang-bog was like a subterranean deep-freeze storage pit for turds, was bearable.

In Korea, in summer, it was not.

There was a tendency for the place to hum something rotten.

The bog, in summer, used to hum so much that you could *see* it hum. You could see the mosquitoes and blue-bottles circling lazily in the miasma that shimmererd around it in the heat haze. The bog used to hum so much that if you closed your eyes, or were out of sight behind a building somewhere, you could actually *hear* it hum.

Periodically, if I hit an imbalance between prune intake and stodge stabiliser, a visit to The Bog became inevitable. Sometimes the sense of urgency was such that there was no time even for an anaesthetising belt of alcohol first. To overcome the ordeal I would set myself a small concurrent challenge: number of slow breaths taken to complete task / length of time breath held between times. Once, when the temperature was hovering at 150° in the shade, I managed a whole fortnight's evacuation with three deep inhalations and a giant sob, although I didn't try to reassemble my underpinnings until I had stumbled back outside again.

Remember Alec Guinness being shoved ignominiously into that stinky little Japanese corrugated-iron punishment box in *Bridge on the River Kwai?* Or Omar Sharif riding vaporously towards us out of the heat haze on his camel to meet Lawrence, in Arabia? Remember seeing guys buried up to their necks in hot sand while armies of red ants crawled eagerly up the treacle trail into their eye sockets? Remember how hot you were when you were the hottest you've ever been in your entire life before? Well, combine all this imagery with the largest cabbage water raspberry the world has ever blown, and you're half way to a visit to The Bog.

But it was worse than that.

The best time to visit was early in the morning. It was warm enough then to sit in comfort, but not yet hot enough to have stirred up the denizens breeding in the black-and-tan broth simmering away in the hell's kitchen below, gathering its daily suffusion of strength to pop, bubble and squeak and give off gas like there was no tomorrow.

No one particularly relished the job of cleaning The Bog, so it didn't get cleaned very often. Or for that matter very well. The life of a bog seat, therefore, was relatively short and unpleasant. Bog seat lids were adjoined to their boxes by strips of webbing nailed to the wood. This produced a slack and simple hinge. When these became torn, there were few volunteers to renew them. After a few weeks, therefore, The Bog usually began to show signs of wear and tear. Soon after that it looked quite dilapidated. (Bogs were seldom put on the itinerary of visiting generals). Field bogs contain the seeds of their own demise. Once a bog is deemed to be full (you'll soon know when) its superstructure is removed to house some new hole in the ground 20' x 20' x 10' deep, while the vast open wound of lately vacated effluent is covered over.

Apparently it can grow a mean tomato.

So, built-in obsolescence is aesthetically *de rigeur* and the condition of one's communal bog is expected to deteriorate from the moment the opening ceremony is complete and the traditional 'Wetting the Seat' ceremony has taken place. Thereafter, a considerable amount of wetting the seat occurs, with the result that the bog's crudely constructed timberwork soon begin to shift a bit. The seats become mushy and not particularly nice to sit upon without a ton of loo paper to line them with first, and government issue slip-n-slide did not constitute the most salubrious of sit-upons. The race was then on to fill the pit and close it before deterioration of the superstructure demanded premature closure while the pit was still only half full.

It was on a Sunday such as this, at the half way mark in the Bog's life expectancy cycle, that I decided another of my fortnightly visits was called for.

As was my wont I approached The Bog stealthily from the south east, clutching some purloined personal loo paper and a short novella under my left arm.

It was 07.30.

The entire camp seemed to be lying in that morning.

The Bog and I would be alone.

David and Goliath.

Goliath gurgled and glowered at me malevolently the nearer I drew. His bowels hissed and plopped. I felt like Quatermass approaching his final battle with The Pit. Each footfall thudded puffs of dust from my boots. The Bog's fly-door hung lopsidedly on a broken hinge, like a Depression era privy in the Deep South during a heat wave. There was no plaintive harmonica wailing on the humid air, nor either a big busted southern belle frothing herself up in the bayou, but you get the picture.

I placed my boot gingerly on the first of the three plank steps, and leaned forward to push the fly door open. The entire Bog seemed to shy away from me with a creak, as though it was *I* who had bad breath. Purposefully I wrenched open the door and stamped inside. I felt like a battery hen come back to visit a deserted run. The heat and the flies had a couple of hours to go before hitting fever pitch, but they were tuning up quite nicely in the meantime. I espied my favourite hessianed stall in the far corner, and moved towards it. As I did so, one of the joists below gave a lurch.

Like a hiccup.

A small warning, perhaps?

There is no need for me to go into too much further detail.

You can imagine what followed.

The whole bang shooting works had chosen that moment to give up the ghost and collapse completely around me, so that . . .

. . . cracking timber joists rent asunder, shredded hessian, stall seats, the Lord knows what all else – my short novella and I - all subsided into the triumphantly cackling contents of The Pit together.

Suffice to say that by the time the camp had roused itself sufficiently to hear my cries, to get over its laughter and to make some attempt at retrieving me from the steaming

296

quagmire, an unpleasant hour had elapsed. The sun was now up. What was left of The Bog grinned inanely and snapped at anyone who came too close, but some of the braver of my fellow cohorts eventually drew whips and beat it back sufficiently to have it release me, so that others could lasso and heave me out.

I was not a pretty sight, as with wrinkled nostrils they prodded me off towards the shower block.

I think just at the moment that this is all I want to tell you, about 'A' Company's bog at Kohima Camp, Korea . . .

. . . 'cept that next day we had to set-to again, to start building another one.

*

Having nothing whatsoever at all to do with our new Bog, set into a specially constructed stone plinth at the base of a particular hill in Korea, there can be found four carved stone tablets.

Tablet One reads:

BATTLE OF SOLMA-RI
22ND- 25TH APRIL 1951

THIS MEMORIAL ON GLOSTER HILL COMMEMORATES THE HEROIC STAND OF THE 1ST BATTALION THE GLOUCESTERSHIRE REGIMENT & 'C' TROOP, 170 LIGHT (MORTAR) BATTERY, ROYAL ARTILLERY. SURROUNDED AND GREATLY OUTNUMBERED, THEY FOUGHT VALIANTLY FOR FOUR DAYS IN DEFENCE OF FREEDOM.

Tablet Two reads: The same as above; but in Korean script.
Tablet Three consists of: Carved badges, of the Gloucestershire Regiment and the Royal Artillery.
Tablet Four consists of: A carved outline of the United Nations world map, encircled by its laurel wreath of peace.
And then into the ground just a few paces away, is set a

297

stand-alone tablet which reads:

THIS MEMORIAL WAS CONCEIVED, DESIGNED AND CONSRUCTED BY 1ST BN THE ROYAL SUSSEX REGIMENT ASSISTED BY 24TH FIELD ENGINEER REGIMENT HONG KONG AND 28TH ROK INF DIV. IT WAS UNVEILED BY H.E. THE BRITISH AMBASSADOR AT SEOUL ON 29 JUNE 1957.

I was one of those present that day.

But none of it had been achieved easily.

It will be recalled that my close muckers and I were in 'A' Company.

Further down the Battalion lines, beyond 'B' and 'C', there was located an outfit known as 'D' Company.

'D' Company was commanded by Major H.E.R. Watson, who had Captain Dan Cronin as his 2i/c, Lt Sir William Goring Bt as one of its platoon commanders - and as one of its platoon sergeants, one Sgt Joe Briggs, who spat through the gaps in his teeth whenever he tried to speak the no- known language that he spoke. (His amazing attempts to get his tongue round words of command on parade, were something else).

Oh - and Pte Arnold Schwartzman.

Who he?

Just A.N.Other lowly National Serviceman.

With talent.

Before we left Korea altogether, Britain's last representative infantry battalion, The Royal Sussex Regiment had conceived the rather nice idea of designing, constructing and erecting a monument at the base of Gloucester Hill which adjoined our camp, to commemorate the Glorious Glosters' famous four day Battle of the River Imjin, which had taken place there from 22nd - 25th April 1951.

The designated and now committed day for the completed monument's unveiling ceremony was to be Saturday 29th June 1957.

The four principal tablets described above were being

incised by the 24th Field Regiment Royal Engineers down in Hong Kong, prior to being transported to us up there in Korea.

However, two weeks prior to the scheduled unveiling ceremony, 'D' Company's Pte Schwartzman, otherwise engaged on potato peeling at the time, or perhaps digging a ditch or something equally as constructive, was surprised to receive a summons to report to the Commanding Officer one day, who confided in him that there was no way the commemorative tablets were going to be ready to arrive in time from Hong Kong.

Acquainted with the fact that in civilian life Pte Schwartzman was a burgeoning graphic designer, Colonel Sleeman asked the soldier if he felt he might be up to somehow or other producing four temporary artificial plaques that would not be detected as being anything other than the 'real thing' by the visiting dignitaries and media on the day.

Assuring the Colonel that – yes - he could, Schwartzman went on to request that he be supplied with some sort of smooth-surfaced material with which to work, whereupon the CO's driver was promptly dispatched down to Inchon where he acquired several sheets of rusty metal, which a platoon of men was then deployed to buff down, the purpose of the exercise being kept secret from them so that word of the crafty subterfuge would not leak out.

Using black and white kitbag stencil ink and bamboo-handled calligraphy brushes, Schwartzman set to work stippling a marble effect on the four artificial plaques' frontages. He then took himself off down to the planned memorial site at the same time of day that the ceremony was scheduled to take place, in order to observe the angle of the sun. This intelligence enabled him to create a *trompe d'oeil* effect which made the painted lettering and regimental badges on the four dummy plaques look as though they had been incised into the 'marble'.

No flies on Schwartzman.

But - read on, however . . .

With literary guidance from our Korean camp barber, he carefully lettered the Korean plaque's inscription, and then used our Quartermaster's supply catalogue as reference for the painting of the Gloucestershire Regiment, Royal Artillery and United Nations insignia on the third and fourth plaques.

Nine days later, after very little sleep, working away in secret in a little hut of his own down in 'D' Company's lines, he completed his task.

On the night of Friday 28th June, the day before the ceremony proper, these artificial plaques of his were driven to the memorial location and furtively positioned into the surrounding framework that had been arduously created by the men of our own Assault Pioneer Platoon, ably commanded by 2/Lt John Isaac and the worthy Sgt Hedgecock. Next day - which some report as being brightly sunlit, but I distinctly remember as being humid and drizzly - it's strange how history alters the facts - the Battalion formed up to line the route from Kohima Camp to the memorial site in readiness for the arrival of the invited dignitaries and the commencement of the ceremonial parade, while back at camp Pte Arnold Schwartzman, the saviour of the day, lay gratefully dossed down in his billet for a long, well deserved, and undisturbed sleep.

As the procession of distinguished visitors arrived, the Battalion's street-liners along their route sombrely rested on the funereal Arms Reversed position.

In the first car was Dr Cho Chung Hwan, Foreign Minister of the Republic of Korea, with Maj Gen Pak Yung Bae, representing the Chief of Staff. In the second was General I.D.White, Commanding General, 8th US Army, with Lt Gen A.G.Trudeau, Commanding General 1 US Corps (Group). In the third was HE Hubert Evans, the British Ambassador from Seoul.

The Battalion's Guard of Honour - of which I was one - received each personage upon arrival.

When all were assembled, the proceedings opened with a short address by Col Sleeman, who outlined the purpose of the day's ceremony. He was followed by Gen Bae on behalf of the ROK Army and Gen White for the US 8th Army, who outlined the events of six years previously. The Rev B.E.W.Hobbs, our

Royal Sussex chaplain said a few prayers, followed by Father Krug of the American Forces, on behalf of the RCs. A representative of the Church of Korea concluded. The *Last Post* and a *Long Reveille* were sounded, and the moment of unveiling had arrived.

However . . .

Back at his bunk in Kohima Camp, Pte Schwartzman was to find himself suddenly rudely awakened from his dreams with orders from the CO to get into his battledress a.s.a.p. to be rushed by jeep down to the memorial site where, upon arrival, he found himself quickly, quietly, and appropriately seated alongside the British Ambassador and other dignitaries.

At the appointed juncture in the proceedings the Ambassador mounted and climbed the flight of 13 crudely constructed stone steps, flanked by flowers, to unveil the monument. He pulled a cord, and with the regiment's heraldic trumpets sounding a fanfare the primrose and blue colours of the Gloucestershire Regiment fell away to reveal Schwartzman's brilliantly executed *faux* plaques.

It was a poignant and emotionally significant moment.

The dignitaries quietly *oohed* and *ahaad* with admiration.

One of the more astute of them had been slightly puzzled though, so we learned afterwards, when he saw a fly walk straight across one of the plaques without actually entering any of the 'incised indents' that had been artificially created by Schwartzman's painted *trompe d'oeil* effect.

So far fetched was the original concept though, that even then the ploy wasn't twigged.

Along with the Assault Pioneers who had installed his plaques, our Arnold was quietly introduced to the British Ambassador who – earlier briefed on the artifice - leaned forward, winked at him, and whispered: 'Jolly well done.'

The drapes covering the memorial before the unveiling, deftly, and quite rightly too, perhaps, became the personal souvenirs of the Assault Pioneer commander, 2/Lt Isaac.

The following month the genuine granite plaques arrived by sea from Hong Kong. They were so heavy that a 16-ton Scammell had to be used to carry them along the dried river bed to the nearest point on the memorial for manhandling up the steps and into position. The Scammell actually got stuck and had to winch itself out of trouble with the aid of ground anchors.

After the laying of wreaths on the day of the actual ceremony, the parties then returned to Kohima Camp for lunch, past the street liners who were now at the Present, leaving the memorial to the silence of the Korean valley with its trickling Imjin tributary, the Seoulmachon Stream, where anyone coming along the road cannot fail to see it and pause a while to think.

The sequel is arguably even better.

Today, over half a century on from our original unveiling ceremony, there is a magnificent edifice, the memorial site having received a glorious makeover from our rather crudely constructed affair. There is now a flower and shrub bedecked, brass embellished Gloster Bridge traversing that symbolic little Seoulmachon Stream.

For many years the British Korean Veterans Association has been arranging annual commemorative trips back to *The Land of the Morning Calm*, to coincide with the Battle of the River Imjin memorial service which is organised there at our Gloster Hill Memorial, by the British Embassy, at Seoul, each April.

2007's trip was a more than usual memorable affair however. Because of his pivotal participation, Korea's British Ambassador, Warwick Morris, and Defence Attaché, Brigadier Harry O'Hare got in touch with and invited Pte Arnold Schwartzman to be present.

He accepted.

He flew in from Los Angeles; across the Bering Sea, via Vladivostock and over the Sea of Japan to touch down at Inchon International Airport, only recently then having been voted as 'the world's finest'.

You see, in 1978 Arnold had gone to live in Hollywood, where he pursued a successful career as a film producer and graphic designer, for which, as an Oscar winning documentary movie-maker, designer and author, he was awarded an OBE in 2002 for services to the British film industry in the USA -

- quite a contrast to the mud and corrugated iron that he and we had encountered out there in Korea in 1957.

I never knew Arnold when we were serving in Korea together, but we have met subsequently. He wrote a report of his trip back to the Gloster memorial, which was published in *The Roussillon Gazette,* our regimental magazine. I made contact with him via the internet, and a correspondence ensued. Now in his seventies he lectures periodically on cruise liners about his exciting life on the star-studded Hollywood circuit, where he seems to know absolutely *every*one.

In 2008 he was cruising the Mediterranean, after which he and his charming wife Isolde spent a few weeks in London. It was then I went up and met him there for an Old and Bolds' liquid lunch one day, along with three of his chums from 'D' Coy with whom he'd always stayed in touch.

*

It was the day after the Gloster Memorial unveiling ceremony that I received my long time predictable and almost inevitable *Dear John* letter from Sue.

Most of the guys had had one by now, and reacted in a variety of different ways to them.

Some vociferously contemplated suicide.

Others stormed off to the Naafi, where they got blind roaring drunk.

Some others merely snatched her picture frame from their locker top and hurled it across the room to smash against the opposite wall - or else simply stamped on it, muttering farewell endearments, such as: 'Stupid bitch; who needs her anyway,' or words to that effect.

In my case, I think I was simply philosophically resigned about Sue's well reasoned, difficult, and nicely gentle rejection, which had been to the effect that she didn't think she had quite realised I was going to be away as long as I was - two years - having (typical female) erroneously assumed that it was only going to be for a few weeks.

In other words . . .

. . . various other eminently eligible guys at different social gatherings back home during my absence must have quite naturally managed to persuade her and her busily bubbling hormones that on hot and humid Saturday evening parties in Eastbourne I wasn't really being much use to her where I was - 10,000 miles away on the far side of the world - when they were there beside her now, rampant, ready and willing to place their bids etc. etc. etc.

I guessed that her parents, too, might quite probably have contributed a bit to her decision making.

It was a nicely worded letter, in her best writing, that had obviously been difficult for her to do, and because I was such a reasonable and understanding fellow I appreciated her sentiments entirely.

Bitch.

No - not at all really; and when we did meet again years later, we became the firmest of chums again.

I even flatter myself that she might subsequently have regretted her decision at the time a little bit, too - but we were well removed from her divorce and my first wife's demise and into our respective grandkids by then of course, so the whole issue became purely an academic and fondly nostalgic one.

TWENTY-NINE

AS WORD INVARIABLY DOES word one day filtered down even as far as our hut that the Mother Country was definitely intending to withdraw its last resident British infantry battalion from *The Land of the Morning Calm.*

Our short but memorable sojourn on Korean soil was drawing to its close.

It was then that the Americans decided how much they really liked us, and liked having us around, conveniently located just down the road to get blown up first.

The average age of our battalion must have been about 20, whereas the Americans - although they weren't really of course - seemed much older.

Beside them, most of us looked like a load of kids let into a bar room of adults.

Yet despite our quaint colonial uniforms and apparent immaturity, they respected us a lot.

It was probably the iron discipline of the Royal Sussex, which they had witnessed first hand, allied to the not entirely erroneous 'myth' of the British Tommy in general which combined to create in their minds an image similar, perhaps, to our own long cherished (and fully justified) perception of the Gurkhas.

Rumour had it that negotiations were even then being initiated between The Pentagon and our own War Office, to see if the former could do a temporary take-over bid, in order to retain our services. On the Tuesday it was put about that agreement had been reached on the culinary front (turkey and ice cream), but not on any adjustment or rectification where our pay-rate differential was concerned. The Yanks, apparently, were willing; Whitehall, as always, typically, was not. Precedent and all that. Negotiations (if ever there had been any) fizzled out.

Nothing materialised.

We were pulling out of Korea on 27th July 1957.

*

Meanwhile, the Americans themselves were losing a big name of their own. Since 1955 their 58-year old General Lyman Louis Lemnitzer had been Commander of U.S. Army Forces in the Far East and of the 8th Army, but was now leaving the theatre to become Chief of Staff of the whole US Army.

A farewell parade was to be held for him at the US Headquarters, to which the Royal Sussex had courteously been invited to send along a representative contingent to take part.

Good old 'A' Company, as usual, had duly been detailed to meet this commitment, by providing a dozen soldiers and an officer.

Lt Tony Prebble was that officer.

I was one of the dozen.

Arriving at the American base in our best shiny boots and razor creased jungle green uniforms, we felt slightly precious as we alighted carefully from the back of our 3-ton truck like some clutch of rare and exotic birds of paradise.

'Mind my boots,' was the cry.

Boots that had been designed to plough through shit, shot and shell, up hill and down dale, had now had their ruggedness bulled out of them, and instead reflected the mirror-like gloss of patent leather dance pumps which we treated as gingerly as a lady might protect her full set of carefully varnished nails.

The Americans' parade uniform consisted of a biscuit coloured shirt and slacks, lace-up boots, and chrome helmets - which did look smart. Beside them we still felt like Boy Scouts, in our shorts and puttees.

After we had formed up on the road in front of our vehicle to be inspected for last minute flaws by Tony Prebble,

306

satisfied, he marched us quietly off to our designated position at the far end of the square, tucked into a corner, at the back, out of the way. This was to be a full blown American parade, after all; ours was just a guest appearance. A cameo performance.

Wanna bet . . .!

Around us the Americans were being busily formed into squads and companies, all casting interested looks of wry amusement at us as we marched slowly and quietly past them to take up our position.

Despite our limited strength and arguably funny garb, we really felt that we were representing Great Britain that day, and were so very, very proud to be doing so.

We marched erect with heads held high, almost feeling that we each had our own personalised Union Flag emblazoned across our chest.

Although there were over 300 American troops on parade and only twelve of us, *we* knew who were the best of the bunch all right.

In modern parlance, it was a 'no brainer'.

A public address system crackled to life.

Someone blew down its mike and tapped it with his finger for testing, sounding like some giant farting down a volcano and kicking his heels against the side afterwards to dislodge the embers from its flue.

The parade was 'on'.

The eyes of that particular sector of the US Army were upon us, so we could neither waiver nor glance to left or right, but *God* it was difficult.

Why?

We were unable to believe our ears.

We each riveted our gaze firmly into the back of Tony Prebble's neck, which we knew was bristling.

We knew full well what *he* thought of the whole thing.

The words of command . . . <u>were being issued over a public address system?</u>

Chrissake.

Generations of British RSMs would be revolving in their

graves.

Why - back down the road at Kohima Camp our own RSM - 'Spud' Houghton - was going to have an apoplectic fit when he learned about it.

Tony Prebble, we could sense, was contemplating what course he should take.

British drill movements, after all, were completely different and were executed with different words of command to the Americans.

Tony's dilemma was resolved.

The intelligent American voice over the air appreciated our dilemma (no - that is not oxymoronic sarcasm at all); that we would need to work independently to the rest of the parade.

'Would the British commander please continue under his own instruction,' the voice boomed.

Tony could barely stifle a grin, and visibly grew an inch to accommodate his newly elevated status that had just been publicly bestowed upon him . . . then, having taken a massive intake of air, his Sandhurst accustomed voice rang clearly out across the square for all to hear.

'The Royal Sussex Contingent . . . **Atten** . . . *SHUN.'*

As one man we crashed our feet into the Korean subsoil, as though just having landed by air without parachutes.

'Slooooope . . . ***ARMS.'***

We slammed our .303 Lee Enfields into the first position of the Slope.

We *smashed* our .303 Lee Enfields across our left shoulders into the second position of the Slope.

We nearly dislocated our right arms, whipping them smartly away into the final position of the Slope.

By *Christ* we were good.

Before us - all else was rubbish.

'By the Right . . . Quick ***MARCH.'***

We stepped off together in perfect unison.

Most of the cine film expended that day, we liked to think, was on twelve Sussex men and true, and their young British 'Commander'.

Crisply we marched past the saluting dais, gave an

immaculate *'Eyes **RIGHT'*** to a beaming General Lemnitzer - whose hypnotic gaze followed the glinting point of Tony Prebble's sword as it was flourished, presented and slashingly dipped to him in a respectful and memorable salute - and marched off the American square to climb back into our familiar vehicle to return to camp, beaming with pride for what we knew had been a brief but nevertheless superbly executed affair.

That evening an anonymous crate of beer appeared on the step of our hut.

There were no prizes for knowing it was from one highly chuffed *British Commander*.

*

But the following month . . .

. . . now *there's* a tale to relate . . .

Maj Gen Ralph Zwicker, the US 24th Infantry Division Commander, often remarked that every time the British (i.e. us) appeared on parade somewhere, he would get a rocket from the Corps Commander afterwards, because the US 24th weren't able to drill as well or to appear as smart we did.

As we came under General Zwicker's command at the time, it was perhaps as well that we were soon about to leave Korea.

And yet . . .

The Americans wanted us to remain there.

The then 82-year-old first South Korean President, Syngman Rhee, also wanted us to remain there . . .

. . . but the British government didn't.

So what sort of send-off should we give to everyone?

The British Army has an official and pleasant requirement to observe our Monarch's birthday each year. This may not always be polite when it is a lady on the throne, but in 1957 it suited our purpose particularly well to do so.

Thursday 13th June became the day designated for the combined celebration of Her Majesty Queen Elizabeth II's 31st birthday, and the imminent departure of the Royal Sussex Regiment from South Korea.

Our Farewell Parade.

I will not dwell on the number and intensity of concentrated drill practices and rehearsals which preceded the great day. Many sergeant majors lost their voices and 'idle' soldiers their names in the build up.

But The Day dawned.

It was as if the world had focused its entire attention and that day's quota of sunshine upon us.

From soon after breakfast the sky above us started to fill up with 20 and more incoming helicopters, and the approach roads with an unknown number of pennant-flying staff cars disgorging their passenger manifests of high ranking officers and their wives, to say nothing of several hundred other guests, all of whom had flown in excitedly for this, apparently, very special bean-fest of ours. They had flown up from Inchon; from Seoul; from Pusan — and even across from Japan. It seemed that The Royal Sussex Regiment's Farewell to Korea was the hottest ticket in the Far East's social calendar that month.

Our camp was almost overrun.

As well as the Americans, there were South Koreans, Turks, Swiss, Swedes, French, Australians, New Zealanders, Canadians, Greeks, and — yes — even some Ethiopians.

Among the VIPs present were Lt Gen Arthur G. Trudeau, of the Korean War's *Pork Chop Hill* fame, Commanding General 1 (US) Corps (Group) with Mrs Trudeau; Mr Walter C. Dowling, the American Ambassador, with Mrs Dowling; Mr Choi Hun Kil, the Governor of Kyonggi-do Province; General Sun Yup Paik, Chief of Staff, ROK Army; Doctor Richard Hertz, a German minister; Bishop Quinlan, Regent of the Apostolic Delegation; Bishop Daly, Korea's Anglican bishop, who was to be particularly amused on being told that when the US 24th Infantry Division Commander (the oft' quoted good old Gen Ralph Zwicker, also present) had visited Royal Sussex defensive positions earlier that year and asked a section NCO from Burwash 'What is your mission here, Corporal?' the reply had been 'Church of England, Sir.' Maj Gen Jark, Commanding General, US 7th Infantry Division; Maj Gen

310

Homer L. Litzenburg III, Senior Member of the United Nations Command Military Armistice Commission; Colonel Tore Wigforss, the Senior Member of the Swedish Group — and Consul General Pierre Aubaret, the Senior Member of the Swiss Group - both from the United Nations Supervisory Commission. In short, everyone who was anyone was there that day, except the North Koreans and Chinese.

Through unusually polite and subtle Military Police manoeuvring all the non-VIP guests had been inoffensively edged away from the camp lines towards the large open area of trampled, hard baked, copper coloured earth which constituted our ceremonial parade ground. This they now thronged about with barely suppressed anticipation, the majority of them masticating gum by the hundredweight and whirring expensive movie equipment.

This enabled all of *us* - the star turns - highly polished and gleaming, to pile quietly out onto the road in front of our huts where we quickly shuffled about forming ourselves into proper parade order.

There was not even a need for our moustache-bristling CSM, Charlie Pace, to cajole us into a good performance that day. On such a day as this we were instinctively conditioned and programmed into what was required.

Superfluity.

*

It was 10.30

The temperature was in the 80°s.

'Fall in . . . the Officers,' quietly commanded Major 'Pip' Newton, MBE, 'A' Company's new Commander who had recently arrived to take over from the lately departed Sam Crouch.

Drawing their swords, Captain Ellwood and Lieutenant Prebble took up their positions to our fore.

''A' Company . . . Quick . . . *March.'*

We stepped off gently, to avoid stirring up unnecessary dust. Our gleaming boots creaked. The starch in our freshly

311

laundered green uniforms crackled. With the bleached hairs glistening on our bronzed and muscular forearms, our heavily veined left fists firmly clenched our rifle butts at the Sloped Arms position.

Emerging from their own company lines next to ours, we passed Major Anderson and 'B' Company, marching out slowly to join in behind us. Flanked by Major Walker's 'Support' and Captain Calver's 'HQ' Companies, Major Russell's 'C' and Major Watson's 'D' Companies were also marching equally as sedately up the road to form in behind the rest of us. Only the simplest, most telepathic words of command needed to be given. We had spent months living in adverse conditions, sleeping and working together. We were family. A band of brothers. We knew each others ways. We had rehearsed this parade quite a few times now, and had got it right. We knew what we were all there for, what we were required to do, and that we should do it well.

There was no problem.

All six companies had now quietly coalesced to form the whole.

As one man, 1st Battalion The Royal Sussex Regiment braced itself and to the reverberating beat of the Band's *Susssex By The Sea* blasting out and bouncing back from the surrounding hills, stepped off to enter the arena like victorious conquerors triumphantly returning from afar.

They'd never seen anything like it . . .

. . . the Americans . . .

Every eye and every lens were on us as we marched purposefully forward over the parade ground to form line in file against our already posted right markers, standing rigidly to attention at their pre-appointed places on the square. We were Advanced to face the multitude of spectators, and were then given the command to Right Dress.

Rapidly we shuffled into two straight lines, a third of a mile long, whipped our arms away to our sides, snapped our heads and eyes to the front - and waited.

Our Commanding Officer, Lt Col R.B. de f. Sleeman, OBE, MC, obviously had to be up on the rostrum hosting the dignitaries of the day, so the parade was being commanded by his 2i/c, Major Jack Glennie. It was not for nothing that in his earlier day Major J.A.B. Glennie, DSO, OBE had sometimes been known as 'Bull'. *His* voice needed no assistance from any public address system. The gravel in his tonsils and the force with which he expelled commands would have enabled him to break rocks at Dartmoor from where he stood.

'*Battaaaaaaalion* . . .,' he roared. '*Preeeeeeesent* . . . **ARMS.** '

Several American hats were seen to fly over the stands, and a couple of their ladies' skirts did a Marilyn Monroe above the air vent thing.

As we Presented Arms and the Band struck up a rousing march, the regimental Colour Party - the regiment's two tallest officers, Lts Euan Christian and David Nicholson -and its escort, C/Sgts Barnes, Lewis and Lennox under the eagle eye of RSM Houghton at the rear, resplendent in their gleaming white Number 3-Dress, paraded the Regimental and Queen's Colours onto the square to take their proper place at the centre of the Battalion, where they could be defended from all sides.

Five flags had been hoisted on tall masts to the rear of the Colour Party's position; the Union Flag; the Stars and Stripes; the South Korean flag; the flag of the United Nations -and the Roussillon Plume of The Royal Sussex Regiment, all fluttering side by side contentedly, like proud relatives at a speech day.

We were Stood-At-Ease.

The stage was set.

Brigadier V.W.Barlow, DSO, OBE, Commander Commonwealth Contingent (Korea) together with Lt Gen Charles D. Palmer, Acting Commanding General 8th US Army then arrived, and were received with a General Salute. Similar honours were next accorded to General Lyman L. Lemnitzer himself, who with Mrs Lemnitzer had flown in from Tokyo.

Soon a black Humber glided smoothly up to the stand, which bore Her Britannic Majesty's Minister at Seoul, His Excellency Mr Hubert Evans, the British Ambassador, who suitably attired in morning dress was to take the salute, representing the Queen. It was he, a few moments later, who greeted Syngman Rhee, President of the Republic of Korea when he drew up in his pennant-bedecked limousine, and while our band played *Iktai Ahn* (the Korean national Anthem) the parade once again Presented Arms.

Our Commanding Officer, Colonel Sleeman, then presented the parade to the British Ambassador, who in turn invited President Syngman Rhee to inspect us.

This was done with the aid of two of REME's specially spruced-up ceremonial inspection jeeps, the first carrying Syngman Rhee standing in the back with the British Ambassador and Colonel Sleeman, the second bearing General Lemnitzer, General Palmer and Brigadier Barlow.

Standing there rigidly to attention, the twelfth man along in the front rank, I rather think that the Korean President gave me a wink as he drove slowly by, but I couldn't be sure. He was getting on a bit then, and might just have had a dicky tear duct or something.

When the dignitaries had resumed their places back on the podium, the Battalion Marched Past in Quick Time in Column of Companies - and then re-formed line again.

A Royal Salute was given while the British Royal Standard was broken at the masthead, and we Presented Arms.

Next . . .

. . . there came our amazingly impressive *Feu deJoie.*

A **feu de joie** (French: 'fire of joy') is a gun salute described as a 'running fire of guns', ceremonially unleashed on occasions of the public rejoicing of a nation and / or some ruling dynasty.

During the 18th and 19th centuries it was used to mark a military victory or birthday.

A spectacular *feu de joie* ran up and down double lines of infantrymen at Valley Forge, Pennsylvania, on 6th May 1778, to celebrate America's alliance with France. It is re-enacted yearly.

A Captain Eben Williams witnessed a *feu de joie* during the summer of 1782 at West Point, to celebrate the birth of the Dauphin of France.

Queen Victoria's proclamation as Empress of India in Delhi

on 1st January 1877 was followed with a *feu de joie* described by Marshal Lord Roberts: 'A salute of one hundred and one salvos of artillery was fired, with a *feu-de-joie* from the long line of troops. This was too much for the elephants. As the *feu-de-joie* approached nearer and nearer to them, they became more and more alarmed, and at last scampered off, dispersing the crowd in every direction.'

As part of Queen Elizabeth II's 80th birthday celebrations, a spectacular *feu-de-joie* occurred on the Forecourt of Buckingham Palace, on 17th June 2006, following the RAF flypast after Trooping the Colour. A cascade of rounds was fired by the Old Guard, the New Guard and six Half Companies of Street-Liners in the Forecourt of the Palace. The cascades of blank gunshots were interspersed with the National Anthem, *God Save the Queen.*

Although to mark her coronation there was a *feu-de-joie* outside the Commonwealth buildings in Berlin in 1953, her 80th birthday celebration in London was the first time in the Queen's reign that a *feu de joie* had been given in her presence.

Our own impressive little number out there in Korea that day didn't frighten off any elephants or reach the history books, but it wasn't half good.

It was achieved by snapping all our rifle butts up into our shoulders, pointing their barrels into the air and squeezing the triggers off one after the other to send a wave of gunfire and cordite ripping from left to right along the Battalion's entire third-of-a-mile long front rank, and then searing back again along the rear rank as if each man in the Battalion was a firecracker linked by a giant fuse.

A well executed *feu de joie* takes a lot of spectators completely by surprise, but they always grin and enjoy it alright.

In all, three such volleys were released, sent slashing seamlessly along both files of soldiers like a high speed stick being drawn down a mile-long railing each time, and we then gave up three cheers for The Queen.

A whole regiment Advancing in Review Order can be a pretty awesome sight, as well.

That's what we performed next.

We don't often get to see it done so much these days, and when we do the regiments have usually shrunk a bit in size - but that day in Korea . . . boy, did we pull off a good one.

'The Battalion will Advance . . . in Review Order,' thundered Major Glennie. *'By the Centre . . .* **Quick March.'**

There is no room for error when Advancing In Review Order.

It is a precision exercise.

It has to be got just right.

It is the *pièce de résistance*.

It presages the finale.

With our Band beating out *The British Grenadiers* like there was no tomorrow, we stepped sharply off, completed the mandatory required 15 paces of the Advance forward, and crashed to an earth-booming halt.

'Royaaaal Salute . . . Preeeesent - **ARMS.'**

Five-hundred Royal Sussex rifles flashed forward from our shoulders and in three smart movements were being proffered before us in that proud gesture of respectful supplication - the Present.

The stirring notes of Great Britain's national anthem rolled forth over the heads and over the reciprocal salutes of our guests, and over the hills, and over to China, while the Royal Standard was lowered to briefly kiss Korea's soil.

The Standard was raised, we Sloped Arms, and there then came a short pause while the venerable President Syngman Rhee prepared to give his address. Speaking in English he said he was sorry that the British would not be staying in Korea until the country was re-unified. He expressed the gratitude of his people for all that the British had done for Korea's cause, and then concluded by wishing The Queen many happy returns of her day.

When he had finished speaking, our CO thanked the President for his kind words, and from his position up there on the dais beside him edged his way politely in front of the other dignitaries to come slowly down the steps and out onto the glare of the square, where he was now to take over the parade from Major Glennie.

Both officers' sword blades flashed orange-silver sunlight as they saluted each other.

The Colonel paused until he knew the timing was perfect, and then with a distinctly emotional frog in his throat his command wafted huskily across the expectantly hushed parade ground.

It was a command none of us had ever heard before.

It was one we would never forget.

'The Royal Sussex Regiment will March Past, in Slow Time, and . . . away.'

It seemed he had given the command more as a question, which he himself scarcely believed he had mouthed.

There wasn't a dry eye in the house.

The square drummed as 500 pairs of British boots crashed into the Turn.

'By the Right . . . Sloooooow MARCH.'

The Band throbbed slowly to the beat of the regimental Slow March.

Company after company, the entire Battalion glided forward to pass the saluting dais.

'By the Right . . . Eyeees . . . RIGHT.'

One by one each of the six companies representing Great Britain paid their final respects to Korea, and also wished their Queen a happy birthday, via her personal representative, the British Ambassador on the rostrum.

Bayonets glinted in the hot sun.

Like the elegant curtseying of crinolined ladies, the personal arms of our officers slowly described that deliciously graceful descending and ascending arc of the salute with the sword at the Slow March.

As if on an inspired impulse Drum-Major 'Bomber' Wells tossed his mace high into the air with resplendent flamboyancy and the immediately responsive Band promptly broke out of the tear jerking beat of *Auld Lang Syne*. Instantly switching to the uplifting strains of a jauntily rendered *I'm Getting Married In The Morning,* 1st Battalion The Royal Sussex Regiment marched proudly off parade in Quick Time, out of Korea, and once more into the pages of history.

*

Unlike in the movies, we didn't ride off into the sunset or disappear over the horizon immediately though - just like that.

We didn't have our things packed for a start.

In fact, it was to be another month before we actually pulled out completely.

On the day following the parade, for example, some of us even managed to skive off to spend a few hours swimming in the River Imjin.

Over the remaining few weeks life continued pretty much as usual, with a succession of guard duties, drill parades, cross country runs, marches, swimming in the Imjin, lectures, films, stripping and reassembling our weapons, sending along smartened-up representative drill squads to help say farewell to various home going items of American military hierarchy, and even mounting a further, smaller parade of our own for the visit of General Sir Francis Festing, our own GOC Far East Land Forces who, as part of his parish, just popped in to see how we were getting along one day.

The last few days did finally arrive however, and were spent in clearing the complete camp of all our stores, and the word 'stores' encompassed everything a 1,000-strong battalion of fighting men needed to live and operate. Every muscle and fibre in every body and soul ached from spending days humping iron beds, iron stoves and cookers in from all four corners of our widespread camp to a central storage and collection point, to say nothing of the plethora of lesser items such as bedding, buckets, shovels, sheets of corrugated iron, goal posts, flag masts and general clutter.

The final night before departure (when there was a torrential rainstorm) was passed either on the floors of our empty huts with our fully packed kitbags as pillows, or else sitting in the cinema where an all night show was running. Wherever people were, they were attacked by a memorably infuriating and uncomfortable plague of mosquitoes

318

determined to have their last drop of English blood before its supply source was withdrawn from Korean soil, but although they may not have known it our systems were so riddled with paludrin that if they were thinking of implanting malaria those poor old oriental mozzies were on a fruitless mission from the start.

Reveille next morning - Saturday 27th July 1957, a grey, wet and drizzly day - was at 04.00. At 04.30 we trooped across the muddy soccer pitch to the cookhouse to collect some warmed up tins of American 'C' rations for our breakfast. After this we had to give our huts one final sweep through (I can't remember what happened to the brooms afterwards) and generally tidy up the area prior to handing the camp over to 17 Field Artillery Battalion US Army who, having guarded it for a while, would in their turn hand it over to the South Korean Army, which still maintains it as a military camp to this day.

At 07.00 we were paraded for a final roll call, because it would have been unforgivable if we had inadvertently left someone behind out there: if nothing worse, for one thing he might have bred.

Thirty minutes later a 30-strong convoy of 2½-ton US trucks rolled into camp to transport us to the railhead down at Munsan-ni.

Clambering aboard the trucks, we gazed about for the last time at our erstwhile home. I shall always recall my final picture of Kohima Camp as seeing it set against the magnificent backdrop of a cathedral-like cloud base soaring behind the mountain of Kamak-San and Gloucester Hill - whatever symbolism that might have portrayed.

The small neighbouring village of Marjor-ri which adjoined the camp, was just beginning to stir as we went rumbling through, its peasants preparing to begin their day's agricultural toil in the surrounding fields. I remembered well my introduction to other similar such Korean villages earlier in the year . . .

. . . we had been out on a three week patrol and descended down a steep valley to come across a little mud-thatched

319

community nestling in the heat of mid morning, and its own pungent aroma of waste and dung. There was no sound to be heard as we passed through, except that of our boots clicking and scraping over boulders and loose rocks, and the bayonet scabbards at our hips snicking against our rifle butts slung across our shoulders, their muzzles clanking against the picks and shovels protruding from our back packs. The village possessed an aura of unreality. Small, grubby, ill fed children sat in the dust observing us furtively as they drooled over their filthy fingers. Flowing, white garbed *Papa-sans* in their comical black conical hats squatted outside their hoochies, fingering their straggly wisps of beard like dignified kings on destitute thrones. Small knots of villagers lounged about regarding us with disdainful mistrust; having so recently been overrun and ravaged by war, who were they to know that we really were the good guys. The only sounds to mar an otherwise near perfect silence had been the buzzing of the flies, the croaking of frogs and a peasant in a nearby field chanting to his oxen. It could have been reminiscent of English rural life in the fifteenth century. They were all scenes which we had come to regard ourselves a part of during the course of our stay. Would we miss it all terribly, now that we were going?

At 09.30 we de-bussed at Munsan-ni and started bundling our kit off the trucks and up through the narrow doorways onto the latticed overhead racks of one of the most remarkable little railway trains that any of us had ever seen, parked alongside a railway station platform that resembled more of a Halt somewhere in the middle of the Old Wild West. It was beautiful, unbelievable and straight out of Jules Verne. Whether the French or the British had laid that particular stretch of line and provided the rolling stock sometime in the nineteenth century I don't know, but the livery of that lovely little Victorian train was trimmed with mahogany coachwork and royal blue velour upholstery like something out of fairyland. Most of the lads barely seemed to notice, and promptly stuck their muddy boots straight up onto the meticulously maintained seats, while I sat and wallowed in the incongruity of the setting. The train should have been pottering about some lady's verdant summer estate, delivering cakes to the Duchess and her guests on napkined silver trays instead of conveying a honking infantry battalion half the length of a war-torn active service zone.

Already drawn up awaiting our arrival on the station's hard standing was Company 'D' of the US 6th Tank Battalion, complete with its M46 Patton tanks, APCs, regimental guidons and chrome helmets, forming a much appreciated farewell Guard of Honour to say goodbye and wish us *bon voyage*. The train's officious little Korean guard rose to the occasion and blew his whistle lustily; Company 'D' and its attendant band 'did its thing'; with a hiss and a hoot the little Disneyland train pulled out of Munsan-ni, and within seconds 1st Battalion The Royal Sussex Regiment was asleep to a man, its last glimpses of the Korean countryside chugging by unattended.

After much shunting about and a long wait in Seoul railway station, we finally arrived at Inchon at 12.15, where we promptly encountered our first two hiccups in this particular military operation. Firstly, our troopship - the *MV Asturias* - scheduled to return us to western civilisation, had not yet arrived, and even if it had we would have been unable to get out to board her because - secondly - the US Motor Sea Transport boys, who were going to get us there, were currently busily engaged ferrying ashore a new draft of their own guys who had just arrived in the other direction, from across the Pacific, and were moored off in an American trooper.

The Royal Sussex admin staff were pretty nifty at this sort of thing however, and within minutes another convoy of trucks had arrived to take us to a large RASC (Royal Army Service Corps) warehouse where the whole battalion hunkered down to be fed bully-beef, beans and hot tea. Cigarettes and mouth organs were produced, and yet again - conditioned to do so - we just sat patiently and waited.

At 15.00 the trucks returned to collect us and take us down to the docks.

The clouds dispersed.

The sun broke through.

After land-locked months back there in the up-country mountains, it was glorious to see the clear blue sea once more.

The *Asturias* was anchored about half-a-mile off in the bay, waiting to ship us back home to the western hemisphere.

She was gleaming.

A clean, white ship, and such a joy and an excitement to behold.

The way out to her had to be by American landing craft.

These army-grey amphibians were still ferrying their own boys ashore from the Yankee trooper, so we were obliged to wait until this lift had been completed before we could move.

The Americans had constructed a floating jetty from the quayside out to their landing-craft ramp. It may be recalled from an earlier chapter that as incoming troops we had stepped ashore and looked up to see and be greeted by a giant, sombrely painted banner proclaiming WELCOME TO HELL. Using the same jetty, but walking outwards under the near side of the same banner on the well-earned homeward leg of our journey, this time we were more pleasurably able to read a more garishly hued and optimistic message: YOU'LL SURELY GO TO HEAVEN: YOU'VE SERVED YOUR TIME IN HELL.

As soon as the new draft of Americans had been ferried ashore from their trooper, at 15.30 we Old Sweats received the nod to start embarking.

Humping our kit bags onto our shoulders we strode out hard and tall down onto the floating jetty which was heaving a bit from the choppy sea slopping around it that day. With bevies of American Red Cross girls looking on, none of us dared drop anything or stumble, but with our heads and steely gazes held high and straining out our chests to continue conveying the tough, rugged and impregnable image our reputation had forged for us, while trying to balance a kitbag, two packs, national pride and a rifle as well - it was all a bit touch and go there for a while.

The four designated landing craft started to ferry us out in

322

batches to the *Asturias*, and the closer we drew the wider our mouths fell open.

Not only was it now sunny and we were going to be sailing away on a long sea cruise to new adventures, but the nearer we got to the majestic white ship we saw that up there on board, gazing down gaily smiling and eagerly beckoning us to hurry, were what appeared to be clutches of unattached girls.

Real live *women. WOWEEEEE!!!*

THIRTY

'GOOD GOD,' WE GROANED to a man, staring up from the lighters in disbelief as we drew alongside the *Asturias's* gangplank.

There, waiting squealing at the top, posing and posturing like crazy, tossing their hair, pouting their lips, blowing kisses and waving eagerly to us, stood a whole host of tartily dressed, fabulous looking suntanned blondes in pink, white, red and emerald green mohair stoles, all leaning over the upper rails and calling down excitedly whilst crossing and uncrossing their nylon stockinged legs where they stood.

Had we got to heaven so soon already?

Had the Queen sent us out some companions to play quoits with on the way home?

With an average age of 20 and having just spent a chunk of our young lives on Korea's 38th Parallel, none of us was yet too streetwise.

How were *we* to know that soon that sort of lifestyle would finally became legalised, seemingly almost obligatory at times, even to the extent that most of *us* would soon be made to start feeling like the minority group that should be the ones to have to 'come out' and declare ourselves closet heteros.

Back then in the 1950s though, their proclivity for those kinds of shenanigans, and the ability to indulge them untroubled when off-duty, was one of the reasons that many ships' stewards went to sea.

The den mother of the *Asturias's* clutch was the most attractive of the lot. Rejoicing under the sobriquet *Dixie* it came as even more of a surprise for us when we learned later that he (she / it?) had once been a Royal Marine Commando.

Still not having hoisted-in yet exactly what it was that lay eagerly in wait for us up there at the top of the gangplank though, some of the lads' comments were rife.

'How many times does a thousand go into twelve?' someone behind me yelled out.

'It won't,' was the reply.

'Fuckin' well will,' screamed a third, 'but it'll sure mean a lot of sore meat for someone.'

'Forget it,' growled an elderly corporal. 'It's all rubbish.'

'Looks alright from here, Corp,' piped up Pete Lindsay.

'You get within a stone's throw of any of that lot my son, you'd die of fright,' said the corporal.

'Why, Corp? What's wrong with it? Poxed?'

'I daresay it is, my son. Yeah. But I wouldn't want to find out. Do you really not know who they are?' he grinned, shaking his head in amusement and disbelief.

'American?' I suggested.

'Royalty?' said someone else, and chuckled.

'You're right enough there, lad,' said the corporal, smiling at him. 'First one oo's 'ad a inklin', you are. You're absolutely right. Royalty. That's what they are. Deposed royalty, more like. Whole load o' bleedin' queens, that's what them lot up there are.'

He saw our still puzzled expressions.

'Come on, grow up, f'chrissakes. They're the ship's stewards in drag, aren't they. Gawd's sake. Load of pooftas and trannies, the whole bleedin' lot of 'em. Got theirselves all rigged out in their finery just to wind you lot up something rotten - which is exactly what they've managed to do. Right?'

Still not sure, but starting to grow disillusioned as our euphoria subsided, we clambered up off the landing craft and began scaling the gangplank suspended over the ship's side.

True enough, as we got aboard and drew abreast of *Les Girls* we realised with a shudder that the corporal had been right, and what hideous, blue-jowled travesties of the real thing they were.

In welcome contrast, the raucous voices of the ship-board

MPs directing us to our respective troop decks, was reassuring. The MPs belonged to our world. With them, beasts though they could be at times, we could relate. We knew the rules. They were hetero butch, like us.

By 18.00 we were all aboard, and stowed away.

At 07.00 next day, Sunday 28th July 1957, we upped anchor and set sail away from Korea, heading westward on our new course, set for our new posting - the Rock of Gibraltar.

*

We had only been at sea for a day, when the Captain died.

From cancer.

In his sleep.

Well, that's what we were led to believe, anyway.

It later transpired that what actually happened was that, yes, he had died in his sleep of cancer, but two days previously, while we had still been at anchor at Inchon Harbour. He had then had to be kept on ice for 48-hours until we were sufficiently far out to sea for an appropriate burial to take place.

We were duly appointed to provide the funeral party and a firing detail over the deceased Captain's coffin.

Cpl Richard Farrar and I were two of those appointed to be members of the firing party, commanded by CSM Pace.

We rehearsed the procedure on the Tuesday morning, and committed his body to the deep that evening, while the sun set in a great golden orb over the distant horizon. It only lasted ten minutes, but it was a moving affair. I was 19 and at the threshold of manhood; the Captain, who's name I didn't even know, was probably in his early 50s, so he would have been born shortly after Queen Victoria had died, and what an exciting life I am sure he had led.

The funeral party was formed up on the starboard stern.

The Padre assumed his stance and began intoning his stuff.

'We brought nothing into this world, and it is certain we can carry nothing out. The Lord gave, and the Lord hath taken away.

'The Lord is my shepherd; therefore can I lack nothing, He shall feed me in a green pasture, and lead me forth besides still waters.

'He shall convert my soul; and bring me forth in the paths of righteousness.

'Yea, though I walk in the valley of the shadow of death, I will fear no evil; for thou art with me; thy rod and thy staff comfort me.

'Thou shalt prepare a table before me against them that trouble me; thou hast anointed my head with oil, and my cup shall be full. But thy loving kindness and mercy shall follow me all the days of my life; and I will dwell in the house of the Lord for ever.

'For as much as it hath pleased Almighty God to take unto himself the soul of our dear brother here departed, we therefore commit his body to the deep in sure and certain hopes of the Resurrection to eternal life, through our Lord Jesus Christ.'

For burial at sea the body is laid on a flat surface, the legs and arms straightened, and the fingers interlocked over the thighs. The hair is brushed off the forehead, the face washed, and the jaw secured by passing a bandage under the chin and over the top of the head, where it can either be tied or clipped. The body is then traditionally sewn into a length of canvas of standard width and about 4.5 metres in length, and the Nelsonian practice of putting the last stitch through the nose to ensure that the corpse is actually dead, or that if he isn't he soon will be, should always be adhered to as well. The package is then weighted by fire-bars used in the grate of the ship's boiler being sewn to the canvas on either side of the legs below the knees. The shroud needs to be made of a very strong material and the weights sufficiently heavy to ensure rapid sinking and permanent submersion of the body. There should be three or four slits or openings in the material to allow the gases of decomposition to escape and prevent flotation due to trapped air. Thus prepared, the *Asturias's* late Captain's body had been placed onto an improvised platform that was now resting on the side-rail of the ship's port quarter-deck, covered by a ship's flag secured to the inboard edge of the platform. Wooden blocks had been screwed under the platform and were resting against the side-rail to prevent the platform sliding outboard when the inboard end was raised to allow the body to slide out from under the flag into the sea. It was very important to ensure that the whole operation proceeded smoothly and respectfully without unseemly mishaps. The men allocated to perform the disposal had been carefully briefed. On receipt of the Padre's discreet signal, they now raised the inboard end of the platform and allowed the body to slide from under the flag and plunge with a weighted rush down into the sea.

At the given command the firing party raised our rifles and sent three crashing volleys rolling away over the starboard beam, the sound of them reverberating into eternity, formal outriders to the memory of the departed mariner.

'I heard a voice from heaven saying unto me: from henceforth blessed are the dead which die in the Lord; even so saith the Spirit.

'Most merciful Father we beseech thee of thine infinite goodness to give us grace to live in thy fear and love and to die in thy favour, that when the judgement shall come we may be found acceptable in thy sight through the love of thy Son, our Saviour.

'Our Father which art in heaven, Hallowed be Thy name, Thy Kingdom come, Thy will be done on earth as it is in heaven, give us this day our daily bread. And forgive us our trespasses, as we forgive them that trespass against us. And lead us not into temptation; but deliver us from evil. The power and the glory. For ever and ever. Amen.

'The grace of our Lord, Jesus Christ, and the love of God, and the fellowship of the Holy Ghost, be with us all evermore. Amen.'

Because of the need for a coroner's report burials at sea are very uncommon nowadays, so the majority of corpses are flown home for interment - but that long ago day in the China Sea, job done, the assembled company was then duly dismissed and we all filed off for our tea, the firing party - another unexpected rite of passage having been thrust upon us, undertaken and successfully completed - having cleaned and handed in our rifles first.

Next day we arrived in Hong Kong.

*

Those passengers with contacts, relatives or friends in the colony were soon streaming ashore to mingle happily with them on the quayside. The younger ones of us, those of us not yet fortunate enough to have acquired either friends or contacts anywhere at all much really, and certainly not living in such exotic places as this, contented ourselves with wandering ashore for one last look-see. It was enjoyable enough, and sad to have to return on board again so soon, but nevertheless, to the strains at 18.00 that evening of the band of The Green Howards spirited rendition of *The Royal Sussex Are Going Away* we pulled out from the quayside and headed for the open sea once more.

Sailing down from Korea that first week our masters had very sensibly left us pretty much to our own devices, to become acclimatised, to unwind and generally re-adapt to our new maritime environment. This period of grace had now drawn to a close though, and 'routine' once again reared its unpleasant but necessary head.

At 06.30 each day we were turfed out and trundled up on deck to indulge in shipboard callisthenics. We all agreed it would be nice to be able to retain our Korean standards of fitness, but it seemed unlikely that we would, especially going where we now were, to spend the next two years carrying our ceremonial duties on the two square miles of limestone rock known as Gibraltar.

The Rock of Gibraltar.

None of us seemed to know much about the place, but we had each devised some mental image of it based on personal dreams and portents. I saw the place as a great, dun coloured, crumbling Saracen castle atop a compact sandy mound, with a fishing village at the bottom, a pub, and a catholic cathedral; a sort of sun-baked, miniature *Mont St Michel*, if you will:

certainly not a testing ground of physical endurance, as Korea had been. Our entire tour, we learned, would be taken up with nothing more onerous than guarding the Governor's residence in town, and the colony's border with Spain, down at a place known as Four Corners Frontier Post.

At 10.00 each day we fell-to boat stations where we donned yellow lifejackets and practised queuing up to sink. Maybe the crew knew something we didn't. The *Asturias* had been built by Harland & Wolff in 1925 after all, and this was her final voyage before being scrapped; although at her eleventh hour she did find herself being used as the *Titanic's* stand-in for the 1958 film *A Night To Remember*.

From 10.45-12-noon there were lectures on things, none of which I now recall but were probably about the bren gun, camouflage and the rifle all over again. Occasionally we would don plimsoles and practise guard mounting à la Gibraltar style, but nobody was too impressed with this pastime and after a few days it was put on the back burner till later.

And then from 16.30 to 18.00 once a week, we had shooting off the stern.

Shooting off the stern was not a euphemism for pissing with the wind, nor either some early form of water skiing.

It was exactly what it said it was.

Ordinary, inflated coloured balloons (oh, very well then - and just the occasional contraceptive that like a tracer-round somehow managed to creep its way in there as well) were released from the ship's stern from whence they went bobbing breezily back to Hong Kong, unless we succeeded in atomizing them first with well aimed .303 rounds, which we usually did. A dastardly thing to do perhaps, akin to drawing a sword to kill a mosquito, but it is always open season for balloons at sea and the only way for infantrymen, once they have run round the deck a few times, to keep their professional hand in.

It was while wending our way to the stern one afternoon, hefting our rifles along with us when we started this caper, trailing our bunches of coloured balloons behind us on strings as if we were all off to someone's birthday party, that we really

330

encountered *Les Girls* properly for the first time.

While we lower deck plebeians in steerage had to queue up and fight for our rice, the stewards were kept well away from us, isolated in a different part of the ship. They spent their duty hours serving cornflakes and stuff, and generally fetching and carrying for the officers and other passengers up in First Class. During the afternoons, however, they were allowed a few hours to themselves, and used to take themselves off to sunbathe on a specially designated crew's deck of their own, across which we had to file with our guns and balloons to get where we were going.

It was rather like being a jungle patrol coming in to a clearing to find half the local girls' school sitting round a pool topless. Squeals of delight and flurrying calves slapped the air at our approach. Magazines and bottles of perfumed unguents went skidding unheeded across the deck. Bodies sat upright as though by reflex to preen themselves anew. One particular young thing had had the treatment somewhere along the line and was now the proud possessor of half a left tit, which he fondly caressed and exhibited each time one or other of us bemused boys found our gaze drawn compulsively to his.

Another of them was wearing a cute little pair of pink panties. He stood up to disport himself in them for our supposed delectation, and with one practised flick and flourish tucked his tackle back between his legs in an attempt to look more feminine. When he delightedly pirouetted it looked quite amusing from the front, but from the back resembled rather a bad case of piles.

God - the army chanced its arm at times.

After a whole year in the Ulu with only each other to share a tent with, impressionable young men who had forgotten what the top of a girl's thigh looked like, and here we were being stuck at sea for a month with a boatload of raving poofs.

As already mentioned, the 'Madam' of this shipboard coterie of jungle-bunnies was a six-foot ex-Royal Marine commando called Dixie, who had eschewed the ruggedness of a marine's life when he found the fruit-route more to his liking; stabbing people with hot meat instead of cold steel, so to speak. Dixie was big, broad, beautifully built and must have made many a young steward wince in his day, but he was nice with it also. He would never molest you, and always smiled serenely whenever you happened to find yourself using an adjoining urinal, which was sometimes unavoidable on account of he was usually in there waiting, like a colourful big fish lurking patiently behind a rock to net some unsuspecting little fish.

Dixie had a page-boy crop of lovely titian coloured hair, and smelled gorgeous. Whenever the ship docked he teetered across the cobbled quayside in his lime-green kitten-heel mules with their pink pom-poms and a white mohair stole coquettishly clasped round his shoulders to pop postcards into the nearest letterbox, hoping to attract some secret admirer from the ship's rail viewing him in the romantic harbour lights as he 'put on the Ritz' for us all something rotten.

I don't think Dixie and his mates ever did anyone any harm. They could be banshee hellcats amongst themselves when roused in anger or having some jealous spat or a hissing fit, but it was 1950's society which had obliged them to seek solace at sea, where they could indulge their predilections amongst themselves without hang-up or censure. Thus the cruise liners and troopships became floating havens for them. They served soup well, sun bathed all afternoon, shaved their arms, legs and chests, got to see the world, looked pretty, reeked of poof juice, saved their pennies for when things got better in Blighty, and - who knows - might possibly even have been able to extend an occasional favour or two to the odd passenger from time to time, as well.

*

After we had done our PT, been lectured, shot our balloons and ogled Dixie's boyfriend's tit, the rest of the time was our own to do with as we pleased. Most of it was spent lazing in the sun on the for'ard islands.

Life wasn't bad.

If you didn't mind queuing interminably for it the canteen

provided beer, cider, lemonade, ice cream - and delicious great slabs of industrial-sized fruit cake, which were swung aboard by crane, cut by axe, and consumed by the ton.

At night we used to have the occasional film show, and then turned in.

The majority of us, unable to bear the heat or stench of the troopdeck, would hump our mattresses topside and the decks there, for most of the night, were strewn with prostrate forms huddled behind air vents and hatchways out of the wind. The occasional squall and early morning deluge more than once cooled our ardour for this scheme, but it was still preferable to melting down below.

Four days out of Hong Kong we docked at Singapore to the welcoming blasts of a Gurkha regiment's bugle band giving it almighty stick there on the jetty. We only had time for a few hours ashore here before the same Gurkhas' lilting quayside arrangement of a *My Fair Lady* selection saw us weighing anchor once more. We just caught snatches on the breeze of their bugled version of *Sussex By The Sea* and then the Far East started to hiss swiftly past our stern as we headed for Colombo, Aden - and on up the Red Sea into the Med.

When we sailed for Korea on board *Devonshire* we had done so via Cape Town, the first troopship to do so since WWII, because Egypt's Colonel Nasser had closed the Suez Canal. Now aboard the *Asturias* we were the first troopship since the Suez crisis to go through the Canal since its reopening.

Colombo and Aden were both uneventful stopovers, and then we were in the Red Sea,

It was so hot and humid sailing up the Red Sea that I don't think I have ever been so hot and sticky anywhere else in all the world at any other time either before or since.

Not even in The Bog.

At the top of the Red Sea we had to queue to take our turn entering the Canal, and that was a bit warm as well, but it was interesting to see the sands of Egypt and the desert in such close proximity, without having to get out and walk. Some of our Old Sweats were mildly chuffed when we passed previous camps the regiment had occupied, at Shandur and Ismailia.

Suez was narrower than many of us first timers had imagined.

This enabled us to throw things other than just ribald comments at the toothless Arab with his grubby white *dish-dasha* hoiked up round his loins, who we were amazed to see happily slapping a quick length to his donkey as we passed along the towpath. I suppose if I had been one of the *fellaheen* in that climate with few other worldly possessions but my donkey, I, too, might have fallen in love with it occasionally, on quiet Tuesday afternoons say, when there wasn't much doing up the *wadi* and the fish wouldn't bite. I mean, what else is a fellah to do? Especially if his generation missed out on motor scooters. But it did look very strange to us, to see him thrusting his shiny wog wang up his burro, raising his dirty little embroidered skull cap to us all as we passed, and flashing a yellow-toothed what-a-very-fine-fellow-I-am grin at the officers' wives taking tea in the First Class lounge, all pretending disinterest while trying not to gaze transfixed with popping eyeballs through the window at him. We imagined their collective indignation might even have made the *Asturias* shudder a bit; but it didn't.

At least - not until later, after lights out.

*

Early next morning I lost Jim.

Normally we would have breakfasted together, but he hadn't been in his usual place in the queue at the usual time.

His standee appeared neither tidy nor dishevelled when I checked.

I asked around, but no one seemed to have seen him; nor did they seem particularly perturbed at not having done so.

I circled each deck, twice, in each direction - but to no avail.

There was no familiar sight of his tousled head.

After our morning lecture on the History of Gibraltar, I approached one of our officers and asked if *he* might have any idea of Jim's whereabouts, but he didn't. He didn't seem to think it was especially important at the time, either.

I circled the decks again, but could still find no trace or word of him.

My concern was mounting.

There were clearly defined areas on board to which we did and did not have access. It was not like Jim to have trespassed beyond our domain. His spirit of adventure didn't quite stretch that far. But where could he possibly be?

For all I knew, his life could be in my hands.

If, as you have no doubt realised I thought, he was bobbing about in mid-Med somewhere, it meant he had been doing so for the best part of five hours already. Were there sharks out there? I wasn't sure. In any case, if he had fallen overboard, and by now I felt pretty certain that is what must have happened to him, he would be relying upon me to have the ship turned around to go back and fetch him. By now he would be wondering what had kept me. God - if he didn't lose his life, and was retrieved, I might have lost his friendship forever through my tardiness in taking action. I was becoming frantic. Instead of faffing about like this I knew that I ought to be doing something really positive.

It was 12.30.

In one last vain hope that he would suddenly appear with some simple explanation for his prolonged absence, I joined the lunch queue. No good. He wasn't there, and nor did he show up.

It was definitely time for me to act.

I went to the Purser's office.

It was closed for lunch.

I paced the decks once more.

A Royal Naval medical orderly was leaning over one of the rails, smoking a cigarette.

'Tell me,' I said, leaning alongside him, 'you're in the Navy. How do you go about stopping a ship?'

'Bomb it,' he said, flicking his butt with a silent faraway hiss into the sea. 'Or turn off the ignition.'

'No, seriously.'

'Poison its feed.'

'No, I mean really seriously.'

'Pull the communication cord . . .? What do you want to know for, anyway?'

I told him.

'I've got a stupid suspicion my buddy might have gone overboard,' I said.

'Whatever makes you think that?' He laughed.

I explained.

'In that case, have you tried the Sick Bay?' he asked. 'We had one of your blokes brought in there first thing this morning . . .'

It was Jim.

It had to be.

I just knew it was Jim.

My relief was unbounded.

Dashing to the far end of the ship I rushed up the stairway to the Sick Bay.

There, sitting up in bed in a sea of crisply starched white linen, was a happily grinning Jim.

'Hallo, mate,' he beamed. 'Where've you been? What kept you?'

'Jim,' I blurted, relieved beyond measure and feeling stupid and embarrassed at the anguish I had been through. I wanted to pummel him, but dared not. I didn't know what was wrong with him, or which bits hurt.

'For Chrissake, Jim,' I bellowed. 'I've been going bananas. What happened?'

Apparently the poor old sod had been living for years with an undetected twist in his plumbing. The steadily mounting pressure had suddenly been brought to a head. When he'd gone for a slash that morning he was overly curious to note that he was peeing blood. Curiosity for his unusual predicament waned as the quantity of blood increased, and then he keeled over in the urinal. Fortunately there were some other guys present, also engaged in their early morning evacuations, and having readjusted their dress first they had then carried Jim up to the ship's doctor. The problem was diagnosed, and Jim was successfully operated on straight away. A snick and a stitch in his pipe later he came out of the ether thinking he had died and gone to heaven. A far cry from the steamy depths of the troopdeck in which he had been used to waking each morning, the Sick Bay was stuck right at the top of the ship by the funnel somewhere. There was blue sky, and seagulls circling about outside the porthole. Hence from his new vantage point the *Asturias* must have felt as if it had been transformed into *The Good Ship Lollipop*. He seemed to be suitably touched and impressed by my obvious concern, and reassured me that it wiped the slate clean for the various favours he had done for me in Korea.

Promising that I would pop back and see him again later, I left the Sick Bay and stood for a moment enjoying the view from this part of the ship on-high, to which I had never been before. The Moroccan coast of North Africa lay off to the south. To the right, the southern coast of Spain was melting away from our port side in a haze of north-easterly diminishing perspective as it disappeared on its hot-up-the map climb towards the rest of Europe . . .

*

SPAIN.
   The Alcazar
   The Alhambra
   The bull ring.
   The Civil War.
   El Escorial.
   Flamenco.
   Goya.
   Lorca.
   The Prado.
   Wellington and the Peninsular War.
   Hot sun, and blood be-spattered whitewashed walls.
   Wrought black ironwork.
   Tinkling fountains and cascades of magenta bougainvillaea . . .

The images crowding my mind had not yet been superseded by the grinding cement mixers and clattering, arc-lit birth pangs of the onward marching concrete jungle which the next five decades of tourism would bring.

I would still be able to see Spain as she had always been . . .

. . . and could hardly wait to do so.

THIRTY-ONE

THE ROCK OF GIBRALTAR now hove into view, looming ahead of us like a jewel-encrusted lion lying sentinel at the Gateway to the Mediterranean. Gibraltar still had some of its teeth left in those days. Its tail still twitched when tweaked.

The Royal Sussex Regiment had been sent to Korea to relieve the Cameron Highlanders.

We were now nearing Gibraltar, where this time round we were to relieve the Seaforth Highlanders.

In just four years (1961), in keeping with the times both these fine old regiments were to find themselves being amalgamated to become The Queen's Own Highlanders (Seaforth and Camerons).

Talking 'Jock' I've always loved the positively apocryphal yarn of the two McPhearson brothers, the elder of whom served in the Seaforth Highlanders in WWII, the younger in the Cameron Highlanders. The older brother was awarded four DSOs for bravery, the younger only two, and so for the rest of his life was always referred to as Chicken McPhearson.

*

It was 19.00 on Friday 23rd August 1957.

Asturias was just rounding Gibraltar's Europa Point, the southernmost tip of Europe, and turning gently into the bay.

Above us the huge Rock hung suspended like a giant, slab-sided Mother-ship. The horizon was an orange glow; the sea a midnight blue millpond. Our ship was gliding slowly, gracefully, majestically towards the dockside as though she had cut her engines completely and was being towed on a silver thread by a lone mermaid. There was an all pervasive silence on board. We were all of us lining the ship's rail, gazing up at the lights of our new home as they twinkled and winked at us . . .

. . . then came an unexpected but familiar sound lilting across the still water.

Standing vigil on one of the stone harbour moles a lone Seaforth Highlander in full dress was piping us plaintively in to Gibraltar. It was moving, constituting further memorable affirmation that we belonged to rather an especial brotherhood of men.

Next morning we awoke to a blue sky and a blaze of hot Mediterranean sunshine.

It was Saturday 24th August 1957.

Fully booted and spurred in our best bibs and tuckers we disembarked at 09:00 and with much screaming, shouting and right-dressing our respective CSMs formed us up company by company along the quayside. It made an impressive sight, the frontage of an entire British infantry battalion lined up armed and accoutred awaiting the arrival down the gang plank of its commanding officer and officers to take their posts in front of the battalion. Imagine the delighted grins that broke out on a thousand faces and the heaving shoulders of mirthful disbelief and joy therefore when there first one who pre emptively appeared at the top of the gangplank to commence his electrifying descent to the quay was not our CO, but Dixie, the ship's Royal Marine Commando fairy queen in all his/her glory. Waving to all of us as he/she clip-clopped in heels and a figure hugging lime green dress along our cobblestoned frontage to the harbour gates for his/her own run ashore to The Rock's dives and slash pits, or more probably an early morning shopping spree to restock her makeup box. There is only one word to describe what she had: *chutzpah!* It was deliberate; opportunist; inappropriate, and tainted our approaching glorious next hour with farce, but if it had been on film would have been hilarious.

Our officers eventually appeared and with our Colours

unfurled and flying, the drums beating, the swords of the officers drawn and our bayonets fixed we marched proudly out of the Docks and into the City Fortress of Gibraltar, the Freedom of which had been granted to us when the regiment had last served here at the time of Britain's initial seizure and occupation of the Rock by Admiral Sir George Rooke in 1704.

Troops today are deployed by air, unheeded, in civilian clothes, checking in and out of airports like tourists, but in *those* days . . .

. . . the arrival of one's new regiment was an affair of some considerable moment, not to be passed over at all lightly. In colonial life as it was then, the various echelons of the Garrison's society would be involved closely with us for the ensuing two years. Accordingly, Gibraltar's narrow, bustling Main Street was thronged to capacity with its citizenry who had all turned out to watch and assess us as we went marching by. Gay *señoritas* and colourfully clad and jumping up and down children bobbed excitedly and waved, smiling happily at us as we passed, steely-eyed and macho before them. We did not dare allow our tightly clenched jaws to relax, or our glances to waiver from the neck of the man in front in case we beamed from ear to ear at the delightful and unexpected warmth of the welcome we were receiving. In my own case, and that of some of my colleagues, we would even be going so far as to marry Gibraltarian girls.

Gibraltar's famed and amiable British-style bobbies were controlling the traffic and crowds along the route. The beat of our Band bounced, *whanged* and ricocheted about the walls and windows of the narrow, high-sided historic buildings and shop fronts.

Originally a sixteenth-century convent of Franciscan friars, since 1728 The Convent has been the official residence of Gibraltar's Governor. Its outgoing Seaforth Highlander guard Presented Arms to us as we passed, and cannot fail to have been awed. It was not every day that a full strength British Infantry Regiment of the Line marched past in full regalia, with bayonets fixed, its Colours flying, drums beating *et al.* We had come straight from the hills of Korea, after all. We were hard men. Or we liked to think we were, at least. We were still wearing our jungle green Korean uniforms with our British Commonwealth and US 24th Infantry Division Taro Leaf flashes, which contrasted greatly with Gibraltar Garrison's light coloured Mediterranean khaki drill.

A casemate is a fortified gun emplacement or armoured structure from which guns are fired. Gibraltar's most renowned casemate is situated at the end of its Main Street, but it is the God's Own little acre parade square in the middle of this historic stone battlement which is usually meant when people refer to Gibraltar's Casemates. The Army, the Navy and the Air Force have long since pulled out of Gib which today is manned solely by the home grown Royal Gibraltar Regiment with their own dedicated barracks, so Casemates' former magazines and armouries have become transformed into restaurants, pubs, and boutiques, its parade square now packed with gaily bedecked tables and chairs, which doubtless makes many an expired RSM turn in his grave.

In 1957 about 12,000 Spaniards a day came streaming across from the little border town of La Linea to work in Gibraltar, but then in 1969 General Franco spitefully closed the frontier - for 13 whole years - which meant all those Spaniards lost their livelihoods, and Gibraltar had to import its labour and fresh vegetables from North Africa. Where to accommodate the former? In Casemates of course, whose parade square became a car park and Moroccan slash pit - but for almost 300 years prior to that Casemates had been Gibraltar's answer to London's Horse Guards Parade.

On that fine 1957 July morning we right-wheeled through the throng of spectators onto Casemates' flower-bedecked, immaculately maintained and gleaming white-lined surface, and came to a splendid Halt amidst sporadic outbursts of clapping, waving, and spontaneous cheering. We really were beginning to think that without realising it we must have done something pretty good, instead of just arriving and marching up the high street like we did.

We stood-at-ease, and waited.

At last.

342

We had arrived.

We had sailed to the far side of the world and back, seen some service, and got our knees brown. What had been the 'oft heard taunt to new recruits arriving at the regiment's Chichester Guard Room? *'You wanna get some in, mate.'* We had all of us now 'got some in'. Especially some of the more romantically inclined of our brethren. Once again dripping with the tertiary doses of VD they'd grinningly picked up from the various hot-spots we'd called at along the way, the MO was still exasperatedly but resignedly treating them for what with many seemed to be a chronic condition.

Initially it would have been hard for us to compete with our predecessors, the pipe-skirling, kilt-swirling, tartan-clad Seaforth Highlanders, but as a regiment we had a certain quiet way of our own which we intended to employ in our campaign to win local hearts and minds.

Our CO in Korea, Lt Col Sleeman, had now left us to go farming in Ireland, and for the second time in his life Major John Bedford Arthur 'Jack' Glennie had been promoted to the rank of Lt Col to command us. The first time had been as a 29-year-old promoted temporary Lt Col to command the battalion at the horrific WWII Battle of Monte Cassino, which raged in Italy from January through till May 1944. He had come on ahead from Korea, and was waiting for us now, here in Gibraltar. Later - a keen sailor - he was out in the Far East sailing his yacht off the coast of Borneo when the War Office signalled him with the order that as the man on the ground he should go ashore to get things organised when the Borneo confrontation erupted, in 1962 - prior to the arrival there of Maj Gen Sir Walter Walker. Subsequently, as a brigadier he went on to become the Commandant of Mons Officer Cadet School, and then finished his career as Commander of BAOR's Rhine Area.

While we were serving in Gibraltar a soldier recently demobbed from there reputedly sent out a brown paper package from England, addressed to Colonel Glennie. Such a parcel now would arouse instant suspicion, but under the high, bright Mediterranean sunshine of 1958, bomb scares weren't thought about so much. Jack duly cut the string and unwrapped the parcel, out of which there tumbled a box of toy soldiers, accompanied by a crudely written note, which read: *Now fuck these about, like you did me.*

Not everyone enjoyed their National Service.

*

Meanwhile, back on the square, we broke ranks and dispersed to collect our kit bags from the backs of the trucks which had come on behind us. Casemates was on the Rock's ground floor. Moorish Castle was half way up it. 'A' Company was to live in Moorish Castle Barracks. To get there we had to climb Moorish Castle steps. They were old. They were steep. They were winding. There were lots and lots of them. And there were lots of us. And it was very, very hot.

How are the mighty fallen?

Humping my kitbag onto my shoulder next to my rifle I took my place in the disgruntled queue of parched, overheated, jostling, vertically climbing throng of heavily perspiring soldiery. Having been momentarily made to feel like conquering heroes, this was a somewhat shabby trick I thought, now shoving us out of sight and making us all but crawl up the back stairs to our new home.

After the Lord Mayor's Show - the shit.

Back to earth with a bang.

Still, it was no more than we were used to.

Moorish Castle Barracks consisted of typical redbrick, iron balustraded, Victorian barrack blocks. Ours was the hot clime, early colonial model with high ceilings. There were 24 iron bedsteads in each cavernous room, ranged across heavily timbered floors. Deep sills allowed elbow access for us to open the soaring, solidly framed windows, their woodwork heavily steeped with accumulations of white paint applied by generations of our predecessors. The whole place was instantly redolent of the mid-1800s. I would not have been surprised if Jim, Richard, Kevin, Don, Sam, Pete and all my fellow cohorts had faded before my vision, to return after a couple of blinks

33. We arrive!

Gibraltar viewed from the south, looking at Europa Point.

The hill *(back-right)* is behind La Linea, in Spain; its summit is known as Queen Isabella's Chair

34. In Gibraltar we relieved 1st Bn The Seaforth Highlanders, seen here formed up on Casemates just before our arrival, packed and ready to go off to do a stint in Germany

35. Saturday 25 August 1957: freshly arrived from Korea and just disembarked from *MV Asturias*, A Coy (with the rest of 1st Bn The Royal Sussex Regiment coming along behind them) marching from the dockyard into the City of Gibraltar. Major P.S. Newton leading, with 2Lts Brian Goring and Robin Beckwith

36. Assuming our role as custodians of The Rock for two years; 2Lt Roger Broadbent (and others) marching past The Convent (the Governor's residence) on arrival

37.   Moorish   Castle, Gibraltar,   our   Victorian barrack block

38. L/Cpl The Baron Hans Cristoff von Massenbach *(L)* – with Pete Haffenden

39. Four Corners (1957) – the Gibraltar-Spanish frontier post. The flag shown is the one the author left on the guard room table . . .

40. 1 Royal Sussex on parade on Gibraltar's Naval Ground (now long since a car park) to greet the arrival of the Rock's new Governor, General Sir Charles Keightley, GCB, GBE, DSO - 1958

41. Seat of Power: 'A' Coy Office, Moorish Castle Barracks, Gibraltar

42. Moorish Castle barracks square, where Pte Pete Squires got his salutary 'mauling' from *Gunner*, King of the Apes

43. Four Corners Frontier Guard being dismounted by Cpl Richard Farrar *(by pillar)*

44. Author's American friend Jonathon Evans Harris – hitch-hiking round the world

45. Author with his kit and caboodle – munching bread at the roadside

46. The bringer of bread: the author as the town's star attraction that season

48. Spain, the way she used to be . . .

47. One of Franco's fearsome Guardia Civil

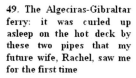

49. The Algeciras-Gibraltar ferry: it was curled up asleep on the hot deck by these two pipes that my future wife, Rachel, saw me for the first time

349

50. Rachel – the mother of his children

51. The author today

52. The author, with Major Steve Ellwood (now a still incredibly fit and virile 81-year-old: *at far right, aged 31, marching into Gibraltar having just returned from North Africa*) - taken in May 2009 at Stephen's lovely 16th century Somerset home

clad in scarlet tunics with little pill-box hats stuck jauntily atop their heads, sporting droopy moustaches and looking like Victorian PT instructors.

Within the following decade Gibraltar's military face was to change forever, both architecturally and geographically. The Army would relinquish its existing historic real estate, married quarters and barracks, and move out of the town completely to the light, modern, airy new custom built Lathbury Barracks (Gen Sir Gerald Lathbury was Governor of Gibraltar 1965-69) at Europa, on the Rock's southernmost tip -and 30 years after *that* even those new Lathbury Barracks would be vacated and converted to civilian accommodation. I repeat: it seems the only thing that's permanent in life, is change.

However, in 1957 we were still enjoying being out there re-living the tail end of the 19th century.

It took me no more than a minute to select a bed, tumble out the sparse but tightly packed contents of my kitbag upon it, sort and arrange the crumpled stuff into my allocated tin broom-cupboard of a personal locker, and after I'd drawn up my bedding and made myself a place to sleep, I was ready for whatever was going to happen next.

What happened next was a terrified scream, the thump of desperately running feet, and the scrabbling of sharp yellow claws across concrete, accompanied by guffaws of laughter.

We all rushed out of our top floor barrack room to gaze intently over the balcony's iron balustrade to see what was happening on the Moorish Castle parade square below us.

One of our number, Pete Squires, had just had an accidental run-in with one of the Gibraltar apes.

Not just any old ape.

But an ape called *Gunner.*

Gibraltar's Barbary apes *(Macaca Sylvanus)* are actually tail-less monkeys and are the only free-roaming semi-primate monkeys in Europe.

Natives of North Africa, their presence in Gibraltar probably dates from the early days of the British garrison when it is presumed that they were imported as pets or even game, inevitably finding the Rock's rough limestone cliffs and scrub vegetation a congenial habitat.

In fact, many legends have grown up around them, one being that originally they travelled from their native Morocco via a subterranean tunnel leading up from underneath the Strait, and exiting at St Michael's Cave, half way to the Upper Rock.

Another legend claims that should the apes ever disappear, the British will leave Gibraltar.

During WWII, through natural causes the number of apes began to decrease alarmingly, and they were in danger of extinction on the Rock. Fortunately Sir Winston Churchill took a personal interest, and being fully cognisant of the legend, from the crucial point of view of morale he ordered that additional animals should quickly be rounded up and brought over from Morocco.

The Gibraltar macaque population was placed under the care of the British Army, and later the Gibraltar Regiment, from 1915 to 1991, who carefully controlled a population that initially consisted of just a single troop. An officer was appointed to supervise their welfare, and a food allowance of fruit, vegetables and nuts was included in the budget. Casualties - the military euphemism for births, marriages and deaths - were gazetted and published on special supplementary orders in true army fashion, and each new arrival was named - usually after governors, brigadiers or high ranking officers.

For many years Sgt Alfred Holmes of the GDF (Gibraltar Defence Force) later the Gibraltar Regiment, and now the Royal Gibraltar Regiment, was well known in and around the Rock as *Officer In Charge Of The Apes*. He was known locally by the nickname of '*El de los monos*' (*He of the monkeys*). Any ill or injured monkey was taken to the Royal Naval Hospital and received the same treatment an enlisted serviceman would have done. Following the withdrawal of the last British infantry regiment in 1992, the Government of Gibraltar then took over responsibility for the monkeys, their welfare now being in the hands of the Gibraltar Ornithological and Natural History Society, and the R.S.P.C.A.

And thereby hangs a tail.

To prevent any public protest, the British Army always denied ever having culled any of the apes under its charge. However, it subsequently transpired that they must secretly have been conducting such a programme, because today (2008), in addition to the pack resident at the Apes Den, the macaques' principal habitat at the top of the Rock, there are now five other packs living wild on Gibraltar's steep slopes, totalling about 250 animals altogether. One of these packs has descended from the Upper Rock to start plaguing Gibraltar's little east coast fishing village of Catalan Bay, breaking and entering properties with impunity to scavenge for food and anything else that takes their fancy. And they have become dangerously vicious. The solution? To commence a culling programme. 'No, no,' cries the outraged citizenry and world wildlife protection enthusiasts. 'Yes, yes,' insist one half of the authorities and the entire population of Catalan Bay. At the time of writing the jury is still out on this one, while the apes continue to run riot and pillage the populace.

But on that long ago August Saturday lunchtime, back in 1957 on Moorish Castle Barracks square, when Pte Pete Squires unwittingly upset one of their apple carts, there were two packs; the Queen's Gate pack, and the Moorish Castle pack.

A venerable old macaque gentleman by the name of *Gunner* was the undisputed king of the latter.

The view from our barrack room's balcony was superb. Sky; sea; Spain; North Africa; shipping and incoming aircraft, all of this was simultaneously within our field of vision. Down below us, the parade square was strewn with regimental packing cases, crates and boxes, all containing QM stores, officers' and sergeants' mess silver and property; clerical equipment for the battalion orderly room and company offices, wireless and signal equipment - in fact all the battalion's domestic goods and chattels which had been conveyed from Korea by sea, and then up from Gibraltar Docks by trucks.

The general public did not have access to Moorish Castle Barracks; but the apes certainly did. Half a dozen of them had been sitting about on the stone walls picking fleas and nibbling bits of stuff off themselves and each other whilst keeping a wary eye on the goings-on of us newcomers to their domain. In honesty, we had already been warned not to tease or play with them, because despite their seeming domesticity they were capable of being extremely unsociable. Forgetting all about this apparently, Pete Squires had been amused by the antics of one particular mother and her baby squatting on the warm bonnet of one of our Landrovers. Putting down his claw hammer on top of the crate he'd been ripping open, he walked over towards them . . .

. . . and that's when *Gunner* had taken his sudden and violent dislike to Pete.

Leaping down from scratching his nuts on a nearby wall, resembling a hunched, mobile, hairy brown dustbin with bared fangs, he had launched himself to hurtle across the square towards Pete, and bowled him over completely, intent either on tearing out his throat with those large simian incisors, or demanding some respect.

He quickly acquired the latter.

His anger spent, his warning now clear and the point made and unquestionably taken, *Gunner* continued to snarl at Pete and to look very annoyed indeed, while the macaque mother and her babe who'd caused all the trouble in the first place went bounding lightly off up the ivy-clad castle wall out of the way.

Great are the tribal names that resound through history: Chaka Zulu; Geronimo; Attila the Hun; Genghis Khan - and now an embarrassed and knocked about Pte Squires of the Royal Sussex Regiment had unwittingly engineered a forceful introduction to *Gunner*, a tetchy old Gibraltarian macaque who obviously didn't like having his womenfolk tampered with.

Neither Pete, nor I, nor anyone else who witnessed what happened that high-noon, has probably ever tried to stroke a monkey again since.

*

That afternoon we were given a tour of the Rock.

The Army calls it acclimatisation.

The thinking is that it's no good being dropped off in a snowdrift with your rifle and being expected to know which way to turn to fight, if all you're preoccupied with are your chilblains; the same as suddenly arriving sweatily in some Middle East desert in mid-summer and being called upon to operate with woolly socks and thick blood. Soldiers must be given time to adapt to their new fighting environment, so that they are on top of it and able to cope with the local elements.

After Korea, Gibraltar was in many ways a holiday camp, so the acclimatisation principle wasn't so essential here - we all slipped in quite effortlessly, but it would still be useful to find out the lie of the land as soon as possible -

At 14.00 we piled eagerly into the backs of the 3-ton trucks that had rolled up, and set off to be shown the sights.

As there are only two square miles of it, the Gibraltar peninsula is not big.

The trip didn't take long.

One road ran right round it.

It was a Mediterranean Saturday afternoon in August.

Eastern Beach; Catalan Bay; Sandy Bay; Rosia Bay - wherever we went was teeming with brown-skinned people making an awful lot of noise dashing gleefully in and out of the sea. Everywhere was jam packed, but it all looked a whole lot of fun.

I was especially interested in Rosia Bay, where after the Battle of Trafalgar in 1805 our naval forbears had brought the body of Admiral Lord Nelson ashore in a barrel of rum. Structural alterations there had obviously been since then, but not too many. Exciting names from the era still lay claim to the ivy-covered bastions surrounding the historic fortress; names like Linewall; Jumper's Bastion; O'Hara's Battery; Ince's Farm; Parson's Lodge - and St Jago's. With its Trafalgar Cemetery, crumbling porticos and waving palm trees silhouetted against choppy blue seas and violet skies, Gibraltar seemed a ready made set for a Hornblower movie.

However -

The *Asturias* had been a troopship; not a cruise liner. For us

Gibraltar was not a holiday resort, but a military garrison. We'd had our march up the High Street to show everyone we'd arrived; had our ride round the Rock; got ourselves bedded in, and now Day One was at an end. We were expected to get on and fulfil our role - i.e. do some work.

*

Whenever a regiment moves somewhere it sends an advance party on ahead to prepare for the arrival of the main party at the new location. At the end of the tour, after everyone's gone on to somewhere else, it then leaves behind a rear party, to clean up, mop up - and hand over.

In battle, the rear party is often prevented by circumstance from achieving these tasks, which are not quite the same in a battlefield scenario anyway, where they consist mainly just of laying down covering fire for the retreating troops - but in peace the clean up, mop up and hand over principle holds good.

The Seaforth Highlanders' rear party still had elements guarding the Governor's Convent residence in Main Street, and the Four Corners guard post, down on the Spanish frontier. The next day, Sunday, we were due to relieve them, so that those poor old tail-end Jocks who had been left behind could pack up and belatedly set off post haste to rejoin their own 'family', who - rather like families moving house - had left the same day we arrived, to go and serve in Münster, in Germany.

I spent 18 months in Gibraltar, and during that time I never once performed a Convent Guard duty; but from Day Two I got to know the Four Corners guard room extremely well. 'A' Company more or less 'inherited' the place.

Our regiment had been one of those who helped to take the Rock from the Spanish in 1704 - hence our having been granted the Freedom of the City, with the right to march through it with bayonets fixed and Colours flying. And now, on the morrow, our 'A' Company guard and I were to be down on the Spanish frontier again, for the first time in 253 years.

Thought provoking stuff.

*

Our 3-tonner deposited us at the rear of the guard room. We tumbled inside and introduced ourselves to the Jocks whom we were to relieve. The hand-over ceremony was a brief one. Our incoming first sentry was simply marched straight outside to relieve his departing Scottish counterpart. Was there a hint of regret behind his barely suppressed glee at leaving Gibraltar? I thought so; but - who knew - perhaps not.

As soon as our truck had driven the Jocks away to meet the next phase of their lives, we set-to blitzing the hutted Victorian guard post and rearranging it to our own Sassenach tastes. There was not much we could do. We threw out the old bottles and newspapers, retained the glamour mags and pinups, swept the place clean, and then crowded the window to watch the first of our number in the heat outside 'acclimatising' himself.

It was the weekend.

A constant stream of traffic crawled to a stop outside. One inmate from each car would gather up a fistful of passports from the others, open the door and either stroll, skip or leap across to the customs post to get them stamped. The car would then go through the gates, pick up the passports from the far window, and then drive off for a day of jollification in Spain. We, meanwhile, stood like prunes in the wilderness, dripping starch and blanco, showing the flag and waiting for something to happen, which - of course - it seldom if ever did. But it was all good for our souls and, I am sure, tempered us to face all manner of future events.

Our self control was admirable. Standing immobile beneath that pounding sun for two hours at a stretch was no easy feat. Flies buzzed around our faces. Sweat bathed our brow, armpits, spine and shoulders. Our feet simmered in their tightly laced boots, woollen socks, hose tops and puttees, while our minds wandered slowly off to consume an ice cold lager somewhere in a riverside pub at home.

Next morning, I did a boo-boo.

There are three prominent positions in Gibraltar from which

the Union Flag is flown: from the top of the Rock; the balcony of the Governor's residence - the Convent; and at the Four Corners frontier post with Spain.

At 06.00 each day it was the responsibility of the Four Corners guard to hoist the frontier post flag. There was quite a little ceremony attached to it, as well. The police stopped all the traffic - both vehicular and pedestrian, which at that time of the morning predominantly included the 12,000 Spanish workers who streamed across daily from La Linea to perform all those mundane domestic, industrial and catering tasks the Gibraltarians considered beneath themselves to do - while the full guard turned itself out to present arms.

Fortuitously it had befallen my lot to be the first member of my regiment since 1704 to hoist the Union Flag over our side of the Spanish frontier post that day.

Being a romantic sort of soul I was quite chuffed at the prospect. My only regret was that my parents were divorced and neither of them could be there to witness the event. Oh, and that there was no one there to film it.

06.00 Monday.

It was time.

The frontier police stepped out onto the road to hold up all the traffic. On the other side of the giant green gates the Spanish police detained the early morning flow of workers. 'A' Company's guard turned out and stood smartly to attention with its rifles. Inside the guard room I pulled my shoulders back, took a deep breath, thought of England, and stepped out onto the verandah, where the air was heavy with the expectant hush of ceremony.

Everyone was waiting - for me.

I loved it.

I alone stood between the smooth running of that part of the albeit waning empire for another day - and a possible international incident.

I came to attention, and stepped off.

Each step bit harshly into the concrete, the echoing squeal of my boots' studs and steel-shod heels *whanging* off the wall of the police post opposite. Thousands of eyes were upon me, focusing on my every move. I drew abreast of the stone plinth that housed the soaring white flag mast and halted. Then . . .

. . . mounting horror clutched at my disbelieving heart.

What had I done?

I had left the flag back there on the guard room table.

'*Sheeeeeeeit* . . .' screamed my brain. *That's* what my colleagues had been hissing at me as I'd swaggered past them so full of swank. I would never live it down. What the *hell* was I going to do? I felt like turning one half of my body round, sticking my thumb in my mouth and grinning. Bruce Forsyth could have done it, but he was not subject to military discipline like me. I had to resolve the situation with as little loss of face as possible, both to myself and the regiment.

It seemed like an hour of deliberation took place, but it was really only seconds. Born of desperation, a ridiculous ploy occurred to me. Without more ado I took one pace backwards, almost broke my neck glancing sharply up into the air, stuck out my right arm like a *Heil Hitler* salute, and aligned and sighted my thumb with the top of the flag mast. Satisfied, I snapped my arm smartly back down to my side, did an abrupt about turn, and marched quickly back into the guard room. Swiping the neatly folded red, white and blue flag from the table I swept it safely under my arm with the same single flourish, and was back outside again before anyone had really realised what had happened. From there on, it all went smoothly. I fastened the toggles to the halyard and started to hoist. The guard presented arms. The police saluted. I broke the flag open and heaved a sigh of relief to see it unfurl correctly; right way up. The guard dismissed; the traffic resumed its flow; 12,000 Spaniards poured into Gibraltar for another day's work; the Foreign Office telex remained undisturbed, and we all filed off for breakfast.

I will not dwell on the ribbing I received from one of the policemen when we had a chance encounter in a local bar the following week.

'What the hell was with the waving the thumb in the air bit?' he asked. 'Were you with the Artists' Rifles, or something?'

'No,' I said. 'It just seemed like a good idea at the time.'

THIRTY-TWO

AFTER OUR FIRST WEEK IN GIBRALTAR Colonel Glennie called a general assembly in Moorish Castle cookhouse.

The gist of his address was to the effect that the Rock was only a small place and we were to do our best. At times things might become claustrophobic and depressing, but we were not to allow this to get the better of us. What he really meant, but restrained himself from saying so, was that we were not to blow our tops, rape the women, shoot the orderly officer or slash our wrists.

In an endeavour to allay these fits of suicidal melancholia, which despite our disciplined self constraint he seemed all of a sudden certain were going to assail his entire battalion by next Thursday, he and his staff were actively negotiating both with the Royal Navy and the RAF to try to get us away periodically on joy rides in their respective modes of transport.

Jack Glennie was no slouch.

A trip in a destroyer had already been arranged.

Thirty members of 'B' Company had been piped aboard and whipped out into the Med for a day, pretending to gun down North Africa. Unfortunately, one of them accidentally did, however. Finding himself back at sea he had momentarily forgotten that he was no longer on *Asturias* shooting at balloons, and had been unable to overcome the urge to take a long distance pot-shot at an African rock. There was a surprised puff of protesting dust from the Moroccan side of the Med upon which the rock had been sitting, one startled Arab farm labourer, and almost a resultant international incident, with much explanation and apology afterwards. After that the number of Royal Sussex joy rides had suddenly become noticeably reduced, and then mostly confined only to submarines.

Actually I made that bit up.

But at his briefing the CO had clearly said the Royal Navy *and* the RAF.

Several months had now elapsed and although half the battalion walked with a gait and was tattooed, none of us yet sported a handlebar moustache.

Daily we heard the growling Rolls-Royce Griffon engines of 224 Squadron's great Mk2 Avro Shackleton bombers as they took off like lumbering eagles from Gibraltar's North Front airfield to bank and go throbbing noisily off into the hazy blue yonder up the coast of Spain. Daily reports filtered out from the Deity via the Adjutant and thence the Battalion Orderly Room clerks that the CO was doing everything in his power to arrange flights for us, but had not yet managed to succeed. Some of the lads who were avid plane spotters and had only got into the Army by mistake, were becoming inconsolable. The least concerned member of the community was Michael George, happily watering the pot plants outside the office, before going to sit up on the roof in the sunshine at lunchtime learning to play his new guitar.

Practising a particularly tricky chord one day my attention became distracted by the shattering revs of one of these long range maritime reconnaissance and anti-submarine Shackletons, running-up its four engines down there on the North Front airstrip. Palming what hair the barber had left at my temples and inspecting my plucking-nail for wear, I returned my attention to the guitar. The pilot released the brakes, let out his clutch and the mighty Shackleton went roaring off down the airstrip and took off, a great glinting grey thing, launching itself into a semicircle and curving up heavily into the sky.

When the resulting sunlit dust particles had stopped reverberating round the rusty Victorian drain cover at my feet, I turned to Alan Linfield who was sitting beside me in his 'relaxed mode' capacity as Orderly Corporal that day, and asked: 'Ever been up in one of those things. Alan?'

'Nope; course not. You know the CO's been trying to arrange it for ages, and can't.'

'Has he? I didn't know that,' I said, idly continuing to strum my guitar. 'All the same . . . I think I'd quite like to go up in one. I've never been in a plane before, so it would be my first ever flight,' and the chord of a fractured A-sharp flowed from my strings: well - a sort of A-sharp; more a Z-flat demolished, really.

Sitting in the *Fox And Hounds* a few days later, sipping a chilled lager whilst waiting for the girl opposite to re-cross her legs, a recently acquired RAF friend of mine called Chris Wise walked in. One of Kipling's ballads was called *Gentlemen Rankers*. It tells of the mental anguish of young men of good lineage who having fouled up somewhere along the line, committed some socially unforgivable misdemeanour or fallen upon straitened circumstances, could find no other recourse than to join the ranks of the Army, as a trooper or private soldier. More romantically perhaps, many went off to join the Foreign Legion, too of course, but Kipling hadn't done time with the French so was not in a position to tell us about that. Anyway, those who served Queen Victoria, and later our respective King(s) Edward(s) and George(s), hairily eked out their days in the Empire's far flung outposts as semi-dissolute barrack room oddities amongst their baser cohorts, and as mild embarrassments maybe, to some of their officers, amongst whose ranks they might more properly have expected to be.

During National Service there were quite a few of these gentleman rankers about, principally those who had either failed or not elected to sit their WOSBy officer selection tests, and each ship, air station or camp inevitably had a fair number of such people on strength. They spoke the Queen's English, even to the extent that they were able to construct and deliver whole sentences without one single use of the F-word; they read books, listened to music, and followed a whole host of other such poofy pursuits, with which the greater majority of effing rank and file was unable to relate. There were several of us in the Royal Sussex Regiment, but the one who springs most readily to mind was L/Cpl The Baron Hans-Cristoff von Massenbach. Hans-Cristoff's mother was English and lived in Lewes, in Sussex, but circa 1939-45 his father just happened to have been a German admiral.

On his 18th birthday Hans-Cristoff had been duly drafted, but under the circumstances the Army didn't seem to think it would be a terribly good idea for him to be commissioned, and yet there were few who were more obviously a born leader of men. In a regiment of fine men there were not many as principled, who could hit as hard, or who stood taller, finer or straighter than Hans-Cristoff von Massenbach, or who could beat seven kinds of shit out of Beethoven on the Naafi piano the way he did.

From today's position as a financially secure grandparent, with a wardrobe of appropriate clothing, a miscellany of other accumulated goods and chattels and a fairly global social circle, it is fun to look back on those early formative years when the most that any of us possessed was our parents, a couple of good mates, a kitbag of army gear, a bedside locker, one casual civvy outfit and about £2 to last us till pay-day. There was at that time only one car in the regiment; a little red three-wheeled Berkeley owned by a National Service subaltern who, it was rumoured, might have had private means. Against this background, the manner in which Hans-Cristoff was able to comport himself rendered the rest of us breathless with admiration, envy, and also a bit of curiosity about how these things were ordained, or worked.

When we were standing-at-ease on Casemates Square waiting to mount guard at 18.00 on a Saturday evening, there would invariably be an empty space beside me. Hans-Cristoff had been unable to make it on time. Where on earth could he be? How could we cover for him? Then scant seconds before the Duty Officer appeared there would be a squeal of car tyres swinging through the stone-arched gateway and a dust covered, insect bespattered Jaguar, all its hot parts *pinging* after the mad dash back from Spain with some titled, bare-legged floozie at the wheel, would screech to a stop beside the square, and out would emerge a smiling Hans-Cristoff, who had already changed in the back seat of the car of course, and was as immaculate as any guardsman as he fell in beside me.

On another occasion I agreed to perform his cookhouse duty for him, because through family connections he had been formally and officially invited to attend the Governor's cocktail party (in battledress and best boots) along with our Adjutant in his service dress, and a host of other ladies and dignitaries in all their finery.

Chris Wise - my new RAF friend for whom I now stood up to buy a beer and had originally met in a bar somewhere - was The Baron Hans-Cristoff von Massenbach's equivalent in blue

'What'll it be? Lager?'

'Fine, Mike; thanks.'

Alphonse, the aged waiter, poured the beer, and the girl opposite successfully managed to re-cross her legs while I wasn't looking, because just then a thought had occurred to me.

'Tell me, Chris; what are the chances of going up for a ride in one of your Shackletons sometime?'

'Well, matter of fact Mike they're not technically mine. I believe they belong to the Station Commander. He's signed for them, or something. But I should think it could be arranged. Where did you want to go exactly?'

'Anywhere.'

'What for?'

'Because it's there? I've never been up in a plane before, so this could be a good opportunity to rectify the matter.'

Chris took a swig from the frosted glass Alphonse had set on a mat beside him.

'They're really awful things to fly, you know,' he said, touching his lips delicately with a spotted snuff rag. 'Hot; noisy; uncomfortable; are you really sure? You'd be much better off on the ground. I could show you round my radar hut sometime instead, if you liked.'

'I'm sure you're right Chris, but I'd love to give it a try - if it can be arranged?'

'Yes, alright,' he said obligingly. 'I'll see what I can do.

Would one afternoon next week suit you?'

'Splendid,' I said. 'Spot on.'

After that our attention was distracted by another girl coming in who would also undoubtedly cross her legs when she sat down. Alphonse brought us two more beers and we started to talk about Wordsworth together. Chris and me that is. We left Alphonse out of it.

*

After tea the following Thursday, I learned that Jim was in the Guard Room.

'What's he doing there?'

'You'd better go and find out, hadn't you. He asked especially to see you as soon as you got back.'

I departed immediately for the Guard Room.

It should be explained that at this stage in our military careers Jim and I (both of whom had acquired the art of joined up writing) were being employed as Battalion Orderly Room clerks.

'I wanna tell y'a story,' said Jim as I sat down beside him on his cell bunk. 'And to do so I shall need to relate it in scenario form. SCENE? Our Battalion Orderly Room . . . earlier this afternoon.

ADJUTANT: 'Corporal Davidson, shouldn't George be in charge of this detail?'

JIM:'Sah.

ADJUTANT:'Then why the bloody hell isn't he? Where's he at?'

JIM:'Malaga, I believe, Sir.'

ADJUTANT: 'I've signed no leave pass for him. What's he doing in Malaga?'

JIM:'Well . . . er . . . he's not actually *in* it, Sir. He's over it. On a bombing raid.'

ADJUTANT:(Slowly) 'Corporal Davidson, explain to me please what it is that you are saying.'

JIM:'Sir - he's gone up on a RAF flight in a Shackleton . . . to Malaga and back.'

366

ADJUTANT:'There are no RAF flights to Malaga.'

JIM:'Begging your pardon, Sir, but I believe there are, Sir. George is on one now, Sir. They go up there three times a week, practise a couple of dummy bombing runs on the bull ring, circle round, and then come back again.'

ADJUTANT:'I know nothing of this, Corporal Davidson. I've organised no such thing.'

JIM:'No, Sir. Well, again begging your pardon, Sir, you're not in the RAF, are you Sir. You're in the Army, Sir. I mean, you wouldn't really expect the RAF to organise or know about one of our Range Days for instance, would you, Sir?'

ADJUTANT:'I mean that we, the Army, have no authority yet to partake in such flights.'

JIM:'No, Sir.'

ADJUTANT:'So how do you account for the fact that George is on one now?'

JIM:'He felt like it, Sir.'

ADJUTANT:'I see. And does he do everything he feels like just because he feels like it, in accordance with whichever whim takes his fancy?'

JIM:'Most of the time, Sir; yes. He does usually seem to. His credos are that life's too short to mess around and that it's usually easier to apologise afterwards than it is to ask permission first: Sir.'

ADJUTANT:'Are you aware, Corporal, that for some weeks now both the CO and I have been carefully nurturing our RAF contacts at North Front to try to get the Battalion up on just such flights?'

JIM:'I believe I did hear something about that, yes Sir.'

ADJUTANT:'And now you're telling me that your friend George has gone and undermined all our good work?'

JIM:'Oh, no Sir. I didn't say that at all, Sir. And I'm quite sure he'd be delighted to make arrangements for you and the Colonel too, if you asked him, Sir: but then, you see, nobody ever does . . .'

Jim was released from pokey an hour later, and nothing more was ever said to either of us about the matter. Perhaps the Adjutant had been too wary of mentioning the incident to the

CO. He didn't even ask if I'd enjoyed myself. I hadn't very much, as it happened. Thinking it might be cold up there I had worn my battledress. In the event it was stifling. The RAF sat me beneath a Perspex cupola. The Mediterranean sun beat down through this so hotly that I felt like an insect being cremated alive by a magnifying glass. The pilot had to show off, of course, knowing he had a pongo on board, even though status-wise I was only a very small pongo. He banked and dived and climbed and turned, and did everything he could to impress and make me throw up. I was impressed. I just hadn't liked it very much. I also got queasy. Queasy as hell. All I could see was glaring expanses of blue sky, clear blue sea and a distorted view of Malaga, once we had reached it and swung round to return to Gib again. How we didn't cause an international incident, abusing Spanish air space like that, I'll never know - but this was then; not now.

The Shackleton lowered its wheels and came roaring in to land. It taxied to a standstill, and cut its engines.

Then I let them have the lot.

'Don't worry,' one of the flight crew said, grimacing slightly as he saw me looking embarrassed at my freshly processed army lunch strewn across the cabin floor. 'It usually happens first time up.'

I could have had no worse experience as an introduction to flying - but even Nelson was sick each time he went to sea, apparently.

Over the years since then I've clocked up a few hours - and more.

One time I even refused my barley sugar.

Back on Earth once more - still in Gib - I entered a phase where I believed that most people seemed to prefer other people to me. I was 19 and still sorting out my plooks, pimples and hang-ups within the institutionalised confines of the military. In those days, of course, the trendy shrinks had not yet come up with 'in' cries like 'hang-ups'. They still strove to practise the real thing. I was merely suffering the ravages and unsureness of late adolescence, and would have to struggle through that malaise as best as possible, with not a little help from that excellent team of benevolent and understanding care assistants, the RSM and senior NCOs.

Emotional highs and lows wafted across my daily life like clouds in an English summer. My burgeoning personality was being arrested and neutered at every turn by the constraints imposed upon me by the Army's petty rule book and the limited *milieu* in which I existed. It reached the stage when I couldn't even look out of the window to judge the weather without someone yelling at me to get my hair cut or have another shave. I didn't know who I was or what part I was meant to be playing in Life's great scheme of things, but I harboured a constantly nagging feeling that I was probably meant to be doing more for myself than was stated on Company Part One Orders each day.

For 15 months I had been soldiering solidly without a break. I felt it was time for me to get away from the regiment for a while, so that I could take stock of myself, discover what was in my soul, find out what made me tick, and learn whether I was actually able to function on my own.

I applied for two weeks' leave. No one was more surprised than me when I got it.

'*Leave,* George. *You?* You've got to be joking,' is what I expected the reaction to be. 'You're with us till hell freezes over. *Leave?* Hasn't anyone told you? You stay with the regiment until you die. Surely you knew that!'

As it was, I expect they were fairly glad to see the back of me, too, for a fortnight.

THIRTY-THREE

IT WAS APRIL, 1958.

One of the first things I had done on arrival in Gib five months before, had been to apply for my first passport. Since acquiring it I had been excitedly across the Spanish border several times to La Linea, where although never acknowledged as being an epicurean centre for gourmets' delight, after army food one could eat there what seemed by comparison to be very well indeed, and drink very well indeed too, for a modest fifteen-bob (75p). Mind you, at that age and in that environment there was an undoubted Zorro-like appeal to be had in quaffing a flagon of *vino tinto* with which to wash down a potato and tomato *tortilla,* that today would no doubt cost thirty-quid or more.

La Linea was all well and good, but it was a little like Newhaven. Now - I wanted to go *further* afield, to discover the Spain of my dreams.

With £25 in my jeans pocket and a rucksack on my back I felt like some timeless adventurer as I climbed aboard the funny little ferry boat that plied across the Bay of Gibraltar to the Spanish port of Algeciras on the other side. My gateway to adventure.

It was a Monday morning.

The regiment and all my buddies would be going about their mundane soldiering matters, and although the officially signed leave pass was folded neatly inside my money, it was still with a sense of foreboding that I was setting off. How could an entire regiment possibly continue to function without me for a whole fortnight? For months they had dinned into me my indispensability. Why - without me there they'd have one less to shout at. Even the great Rock itself albeit benevolently towering above the funny little ferry boat, seemed to be glowering at me with an inquisitive frown, saying: 'Who do you think you are, young fellow, that you can escape my clutches just whenever you choose? You were sent here, and I need you here, to look after me. Me-thinks I shall have to speak to your superiors about you (which at this stage included just about everyone) while you are away, and ensure that you are meted out an es*pecia*lly unpleasant time of it when you return'.

I felt the magnetic pull of the place far out into the Bay, and was certain that the Rock, the regiment, and all the contents of my bedside locker would dissolve like *Brigadoon* before my eyes, and that I would be cast adrift on a sea of nothing, a homeless wanderer all the rest of my days. Either that, or war would be declared somewhere while I was scrabbling dustily about the foothills of the *Sierra Nevada* looking for ice-cream, and I would only hear about it days later, and when I returned all hot and sweaty from my dusty dash back, the regiment would all be gone, posted to a theatre of operations far away, where they'd all be killed, and I would remain forever branded an opportunist coward and deserter.

What a way to start my first ever holiday!

And when I did get back two weeks later, no one but Jim had even noticed I'd been away.

However . . . it was now Day One.

And for the first time in 15 whole long months I had deliberately not shaved that morning.

It was a man thing.

My chin felt disgruntled at the not unpleasant novelty of its neglect, but dammit, if I was going to do this Spanish thing, I wanted to do it properly. I toyed with bits of half-day- old whisker whose forebears had only ever lived long enough to see the light of dawn before disappearing on a blunt razor into a mess tin of filthy foam. Now they struggled for a piece of the action and the chance to enjoy the view of the world from out there on my upper lip and the slopes of my chin, their very own sunlit grassy upland, perhaps sensing that this was only a brief respite from the blade and that generations of their descendants would still never know more than a few seconds of light before terminal extinction.

It was 14.30.

I was sitting scuffing my sandaled feet in the hot dust at a table outside an Algeciras waterfront bar, sipping cognac and coffee after my potato omelette, and smoking a bent, evil coloured cheroot that looked as though it must have been purloined from a drain. Dusty Peugeots and Citroens with French number plates and families in them queued along the quayside in the heat, waiting to board the ferry across to North Africa from whence they would drive to visit grandfather's grave in Algeria; or to Tangier and Casablanca, Rabat or Marrakech. Colourful fishing boats lay set in the glassy sea. A blind and ragged lottery-ticket seller tapped his cane against my chair leg, dislodging his tray against my shoulder. Hesitancy with the language restrained me from negotiating a purchase with my *pesetas*. Suppose I won a prize? I wouldn't know how to claim it, and they would never know how to find me.

Five miles away across the Bay, Gibraltar shimmered in the haze as though being viewed through the wrong end of a telescope. There were people who I knew, sitting in its cafés and restaurants, enjoying their *siestas* or going slowly about their business, but its charisma from where I sat, although still magnetic, was diminishing. I was already detaching myself, and getting a wider view of the world.

My attention was attracted by a stirring of officials at the quayside. The shiny black patent-leather tricorn hat of the green uniformed *Guardia Civil* glinted as he readjusted the carbine on his shoulder. From across the Strait the ferry from Spain's disputed North African enclave, Ceuta, was just nosing its creamy stern round the point of the mole. Within moments it had tied-up and streams of drab coloured humanity swarmed down its plank to spill into the large, cool customs shed, from where - those formalities cursorily completed - they chattered their way animatedly out through the gates to disperse their separate ways to their business.

Suddenly my adrenal gland was undecided whether it should activate, or subside. I felt a nervous sample of the stuff squirt quickly through its tubes - like blowing down a mike to test it. Throughout the fevered disembarkation from the ferry, one group of people had remained aloofly detached, the rest of the crowd having avoided them like a river going round rocks. This select assembly was strolling like comfortably relaxed leopards towards me now. Eight of them. They were Spanish Foreign Legionnaires, from the Sahara. Their soft, light green uniforms were tucked smartly into brown riding boots, the underlying burnish unmistakable, despite its coating of dust. They wore their lime-green shirt collars folded over the outside of their smartly pressed tunics, both garments fashioned low to reveal their sun cooked chests and the gold medallions nestling in the mats of black hair. Their swarthy, vigorously handsome faces were enhanced by the glamorous red and gold tassels which dangled like playful little bell-pulls from the crowns of their light green forage caps. Each man wore a dirk and carried a riding crop. Oh my - I thought, comparing them to my egg-and-chips colleagues who at that moment were guarding Gibraltar in our Benny Hill shorts, puttees and bus conductors' hats. How on earth did we compete? How on earth had we managed to come out on top so often? We must be made of pretty stern stuff for others to have let us succeed and triumph as much as we had. Was there yet such stern stuff in me, I wondered -? - waiting for provocation to release it. Did God implant 'stern stuff' in Britons in pill form at birth, hidden behind a molar somewhere, like a secret cyanide capsule? Crush in emergency, and then surge forward, onward, outwards and up, crying 'God for Harry, England - and Saint George?' A national anabolic steroid only to be fallen back on in time of serious adversity? Whatever it was, I couldn't help feeling I'd missed out on my free issue of it. Or perhaps God wasn't making it for Britons any more. Perhaps our lease on the privilege had expired.

I ordered a coffee.

The latest batch of superheroes lolled elegantly about the two tables adjoining mine, indolently snapping fingers Spanish style for the serving of coñacs. I would love to have taken a photo of them, but daren't in case a dirk flashed from its scabbard and my diced liver and lights were let slip across Algeciras waterfront, to slither amongst the dead and dying fish flopping about there already. Their desultory conversation lisped sibilantly through two coñacs apiece, and then a Spanish army truck ground noisily into the square. The group swung aboard with the fluid languidness of panthers, and drove away to whatever was their destination or purpose.

The square now stilled.

I removed the wrapper from my sugar lump and stirred it into my coffee. Not the wrapper. A Spanish fly, not that sort, the more common or garden sort, settled on the edge of the ashtray, but I moved it keenly away with the dying tip of my cheroot. I wasn't a complete numpty; flies I could handle. The wail of transistorised flamenco wafted tinnily from the open upstairs window of an apartment behind me. The waiter came out to remove the sixteen coñac glasses and wipe down the two tables next to me, before returning to read his paper on the bar stool inside. The sun burrowed into my head like a sabre and I let it and I loved it.

I was in old Spain.

Unwinding.

Simmering contentedly.

Blending with the earth.

A small commotion at the southern corner of the square drew my attention to its cause. A scruffy band of urchins was entering from a side street, dragging along between them an enormous rucksack. Slightly behind them there strolled a tall, fair haired fellow in a navy sweater, faded blue jeans and boots, thus proclaiming himself to be an American. A broad grin lit his copper-tanned face and creased the twin blue pools beneath his bleached eyebrows.

'Hi,' he cried out cheerily as he and his young entourage drew abreast of my table. 'Mind if I join you? You look like a fellow white man. Christ, I'm parched. They do beer around here? *Oiga, camarero,*' he bellowed. *'Una cerveza, por favor.'*

'Si señor,' rang back the acknowledgement from the cool depth of the bar.

He glanced at the five urchins gathered awestruck and silent beside us, like Africans watching Stanley meeting Livingstone. The giant rucksack, this phase of its journey complete, slumped like a corpse at their feet.

'Y cinco limonados,' he yelled out as an afterthought, and grinned.

Tray aloft, the waiter wheeled in his tracks and returned to the bar to supplement the order. The five opened bottles of sugary mineral water with which he reappeared were grasped eagerly by the urchins, who made off giggling when my new found friend clapped his hand and shooed them away. The waiter frowned disinterestedly at the loss of his bottles, and sloshed a head of beer indecorously into a freshly rinsed but undried beaker. On reflection he then made a small addition to the bill, his conscience pricked for his employer's missing empties, placed this beneath the ashtray and went back in to his sports page.

'The name's John Harris,' the American said, as though he wasn't too sure and was asking me. He had already quaffed half the bottle of beer and signalled the long suffering waiter for a replenishment. Wiping his mouth on the frayed blue sleeve of his jumper, he took my proffered hand.

'Mike George,' I said. 'How do you do?'

'All right, I guess. I could use a place to wash and rest up, though. I left Madrid at six-o'clock this morning on a fruit truck.'

'Where are you headed?'

'Calcutta,' he said, and grinned. 'Round the world's the plan.'

I was impressed, but contrived not to appear so. I instinctively liked this chap, but dammit, I was British so couldn't show it.'

'When do you intend to get back?' I asked, still trying to keep the stub of my cheroot alight.

'Next year sometime, I dunno - I guess. I just got out of college before Christmas and worked my way over by sea from New Orleans to Amsterdam on a Norwegian ship. Since then I've come down across Germany and France and now here I am, all set for a summer on the Eyeberian peninsula.' He knocked back half his replacement bottle of beer and poured the remainder more slowly into the beaker. 'Gee, though: I may not stay that long; see what happens. I want to get across to Italy, down through Yugoslavia and Greece, over into Turkey and then straight on to the Far East and home that way. I'm from California. As soon as I get back I'm due a hitch in the military. How about you?'

'I'm in the Army already.'

'You don't say? Is that right? What are you doing here, then? On the run?'

'I'm on leave; sorry - furlough. I'm stationed on that lump of rock over there,' I said, shifting in my seat and nodding across the Bay.

'What's that, then?'

'That's the Rock of Gibraltar,' I replied, suddenly proud of my superior local knowledge and my connection with the place I'd so eagerly been trying to vacate.

'Hey - is that right? I've heard of that place. Well - whaddya know - the Rock of Gibraltar eh, and here I am sitting right here looking at it, without knowing what it was. Yup - ,' he slapped his lips and his thigh and then finished his beer. 'It's a great life, isn't it, Mike. But say, you haven't spent your entire furlough just sitting here, looking there, have you?'

'No.' I laughed. 'I only started today. I've been here about an hour, that's all. I've got two weeks. It's my intention to wander around southern Spain a bit.' I indicated my own, more modest rucksack, which he had not seen hiding behind my chair. When we both looked at it, it seemed to recede a bit, like a Chihuahua under consideration by an Alsation.

'Hey, but that's great,' John enthused. 'Whaddya say we team up for a while?'

'If you like,' I replied, unable to think of any reason not to.

And that is how I met Jonathon Evans Harris.

376

Having scoured the dusty, heat-baked backstreets for a while, we finally settled on an acceptable *pensione* for about fourpence a night (or whatever ridiculous price it was back in those glorious days of old), dumped our rucksacks on the tiled floor and enjoyed a belated *siesta*, before cleaning up in the single wash basin and then going out to hit the teeming, cosmopolitan metropolis of Algeciras again - by night.

Across the Bay, Gibraltar was lit up like a diamante smothered sphinx, or one of those postcard pictures of a city at night when it's been raining, time-exposed so that all the traffic and incoming aircraft appear to have emitted unbroken trails of light across the gloss.

Having stumbled upon and ensconced ourselves in a nearby *bodega* we met a South African biology student in there, from Johannesburg, called Peter du Preez. Peter was going across to Gibraltar next morning to pick up a ship for Southampton, from where it was his intention to walk to Scotland. With heather, kilts and a bag-pipe in his mind's eye, he left us at midnight to go and turn in. I have often wondered since whether he made it - another young adventurer on the threshold of life, learning to smoke a pipe, bed itinerant women, and form and express ideas of his own.

Half-an-hour later John and I left the *bodega* ourselves, and strolled back to our *pensione*. Turning a corner we were suddenly confronted by two exuberant American girls from Munich, whom John had met somewhere along the way on the road, back on their respective treks down through Europe. Their reunion was a joyful one, and with profuse introductions I was immediately drawn into their inner circle, after which most of the rest of that night was spent firmly cementing Anglo-American relations.

Up early next day, after a coffee and bread roll a piece, standing beside the road John and I successfully managed to thumb a lift from, of all people, an out of work Italian school teacher who just happened to be going our way - which was

Cadiz. Neither John nor I understood a word of Italian, but while he bounced his funny little Renault 4CV 'Frog' along at a fearlessly reckless speed across the potholes as if fleeing from the Mafia, we assumed his fervent desire to converse was to take his mind off our two humungous rucksacks that made his now grossly overburdened little vehicle resemble an arse-heavy outboard as the three of us bucketed up the road to Spain's historic sea port.

Historic sea port or not, neither of us found anything overly appealing about Cadiz, so after a cursory stroll about the place we made an early night of it in another *pensione*. It was to be fifty years before I was to visit there again, on which occasion, this time with a car and a bit more small change to jingle, I was able to appreciate the beauty of Cadiz rather more.

Next morning found us pitching about in the back of a cement truck bound for Jerez de la Frontera, the sherry capital of the world. We arrived at midday, when our friendly Spanish driver dropped us off on the pavement just beside the door step of the famous Gonzales Byass Bodega, which consisted of some very fine buildings, one of them even having been designed by Eiffel himself. It was too good an opportunity to miss. We looked at each other, looked at the hot sun overhead, shrugged our shoulders - and went in.

From outside on the road the entrance might have been to some firm of prestigious High Street solicitors, but this was a feature of 19th century Spanish *bodega* architecture, that a sober exterior concealed what was an elegant interior of columns and arches, in the case of Gonzales Byass guarding 80,000 American oak casks, each holding 500 litres of sherry, oh - and more; much more besides.

The seed that grew into Gonzalez Byass was planted in 1835 by Manuel María Gonzalez Angel, with Robert Blake Byass, his English agent, only joining the firm two decades later. The two families remained in partnership through much of the 20th century, and the business has grown to be one of Jerez's most recognisable and important names. In 1988 the Gonzalez family was to buy out the Byass family, thereby taking sole control of the business.

Once inside, the cool, tiled reception area we realised that we were on very hallowed ground indeed. Spotless, immaculate and extremely well run hallowed ground. We endeavoured vainly to conceal our disreputable appearance by being overly charming and trying not to drop too much dust on their gleaming floor, which was so highly polished it even reflected the underside of our scuffed boots' upturned toes. The walls resembled those in some Hall of Fame, being liberally adorned with testimonials and signed photographs of members of royalty and those heads of state and other notable dignitaries who had visited the august establishment at various times. The stunning receptionist behind the deeply burnished, seriously heavy duty mahogany desk was like some up-market movie actress. Everything about the place shrieked out that John and I should not be there.

We need not have worried.

As well as kings, queens and statesmen, Gonzales Byass in its time had entertained far queerer coves than me and John. The radiant receptionist, with whom we had both fallen instantly in love, invited us to sit down. A tour of the *bodega* would be commencing shortly, which if we cared to join we would be more than welcome to do.

She smiled a charming affirmative to us when we asked if we could leave our rucksacks there on her floor.

Over the next ten minutes a trickle of soberly clad, middle-aged tourist couples filtered in to reception to join us. They were doing the whole thing properly. They didn't carry their suitcases with them wherever they went. They weren't sleeping in ditches, but were staying in hotels at night and starting off each day with a shower, and proper breakfast. Oh, how we envied them their financially stable security, and how - I now realise - they must have envied us our unencumbered youth.

In due course a self assured, multi-lingual Gonzales Byass executive strode elegantly into our midst in a pair of highly polished shoes, extravagantly knotted foulard and a faultless Prince of Wales check suit. He was the epitome of a square jawed, international matinée idol incarnate, and really had it made. He burst charmingly into mellow greetings to each of us in French, German, Spanish, English and Dutch. He might even himself have been the possessor of Gonzales or Byass blood and genes. He glanced at his buffed and burnished fingernails; we at our scuffed toe caps. Just from seeing him I realised that before I was going to get anywhere worthwhile in life there was still a broad wasteland of gulfs ahead of me to bridge.

For the next hour or so our group was conducted pleasurably round cool, sherry-filled catacombs to be shown large casks, enormous casks, little casks, old casks - and new. Before today I had only ever seen a normal size English beer barrel. Some of these Spanish monsters were startling, more like ships of the Armada ready to sail. Each turn in the whitewashed stone labyrinth revealed new wonders. *El Cristo* was a sherry butt holding in excess of 157,000 litres, which was purchased for the visit of Queen Isabella II in 1862. That's equivalent to 13,000 crates holding a dozen litre bottles in each. This gigantic butt is accompanied by twelve 6,000 litre butts, representing the twelve apostles, which surround *El Cristo*, except for Judas, which is used to store vinegar! That's another 66,000 litre bottles of the stuff. Sherry, not vinegar. One cask, which looked like King Kong squatting on a trestle throne, had the name Eisenhower stencilled neatly in white across one of the staves of its structure. Another, slightly smaller one *(grrr)* was named after Churchill. But this was no mere sightseeing tour.

It was an exercise in participatory appreciation.

At each bend, each pause, each turn and each excuse, substantial samples of the stuff were offered for us to taste. How skilfully our guide had perfected his art. In his right wrist he loosely held a mahogany cue, with a polished sherry-scoop on the end of it, like a large (very large) English spirit measure, or an oversized candle-snuffer. This he skimmed deftly into an open sherry vat, to fill. Defying gravity he flourished his arm aloft like a preparatory tennis serve to let loose the golden liquid from on high. A finite stream of pure gold arced through the air to thud in perfect unspilled measures just a millimetre from the brim of each of four glasses, till the scoop was empty and each glass had been perfectly filled, their stems clasped between the fingers of his left hand as if nestling in a rack. These he proffered to his guests to sip, and then gathering up and positioning another clutch of glasses between his fingers, repeated the exercise until every one of us was accommodated.

John and I were becoming woozy.

We were young and fit, but neither of us was a practised imbiber. We had not eaten since the previous evening, and then only sparingly. We had spent four hours that morning bouncing about in the back of a cement truck beneath a hot Spanish sun, and within the past hour must have knocked back almost the equivalent of a bottle-and-a-half of sherry a-piece.

We were pooped.

I glanced at my watch. I think it said five-to-three.

We filed into yet another chamber. Here our guide bent down to place a coñac balloon filled with sherry on one of the floor's large flagstones. We each looked at the other, and smiled, wondering what on earth was about to happen. A simple 18th century clock hung majestically on the wall, sonorously ticking its way to the millennium, inexorably continuing the journey it had started when Wellington had been camped without. Our guide glanced fleetingly at its face. We did likewise. It was one minute to 3.0-o'clock. Placing his tanned hand inside the breast pocket of his Savile Row suit he took out not a wallet nor a fountain pen, but a miniature wooden ladder. This he displayed to us like a conjuror, before bending down and placing it carefully up against the lip of the coñac balloon of sherry on the floor.

Standing upright again, with his hands crossed in front of him, he surveyed this handiwork, smiled contentedly to himself, appeared to ignore us completely - and waited.

We also waited, puzzled, having no idea what to expect or what might happen.

In the hush of this expectancy the simple white faced, black handed clock on the wall ticked with the clarity of a water drip. Momentarily it faltered, as though shying away from our attention. Then it regained its breath and on heavy, well turned machinery winched up its chain to chime. Nearly two centuries earlier its bell-hammer had been programmed to inform its owners it was 3.0-o'clock at exactly this time of day each day.

Our guide placed his index finger against pursed lips.

We did as he bade, and with bated breath remained silent.

The clock began to chime.

Once.

Twice.

Thrice.

The third chime wafted across to expire in the dark reaches of one of the far cellars, and as it did so our guide indicated the floor beside one of the nearby casks stacked against the stone wall, from whence there had suddenly appeared . . .

. . . a mouse.

An in*quis*itive little mouse.

Its uplifted nostrils and whiskers were all of a-quiver.

It sniffed the air to assess the situation.

This was obviously a pathfinder mouse. Content with the lay of the land it gave some inaudible mouse signal and was joined immediately by its entire family which gathered all-of-a-similar quiver at its haunches. Still not absolutely sure of itself, slightly wary, it darted daringly forward and then abruptly stopped.

Then it did so again.

Then again.

In this manner, encouraged by the silent cheering of its supportive family it progressed to the foot of the ladder which had been leaned against the coñac glass, which it sniffed before scaling with a well practised wiggle of its haunches, its little pink feet clawing for purchase on each successive rung.

Once it had scaled the top rung it seemed to want to attempt an MGM roar, thought better of it, quickly dunked its little snout into the sherry, and lapped. It came up once for air, shook its whiskers, had another go, lost its footing, fell off the ladder onto the floor and teetered off somewhere behind Eisenhower, to be followed one at a time up the ladder by its father, its mother, its wife, in-laws, some of the neighbours, a couple of aunts and all of their children, the last and smallest of which couldn't quite reach what remained of the sherry without falling into it.

By now we were reeling with delight at the whole charming spectacle.

Our guide stepped forward to tip this last bedraggled little mouse gently out of the glass and back onto the floor. It scrabbled out of its puddle, and even though hurrying to be off still appeared to pause long enough just to say *'Muy muchas gracias'* and give us a cartoon bow and a quick wink before skidding away to rejoin the rest of its mob.

One of the Frenchmen in the party looked ashen.

His wife gently reassured him that they had been real mice and not pink elephants and that the rest of us had enjoyed the same hallucination and weren't falling about with shock so please would he try to pull himself together a bit. This he tried to do, partially succeeded, and when it was adjudged that he was sufficiently recomposed we were led through into a sumptuously appointed antechamber where the Spanish equivalent of two Roedean old-girls on work experience were waiting to present each of us with a small cork pannier of half-a-dozen miniatures. They also indicated that it was possible, should we so wish - and they rather hoped that we would - to purchase a few full-size bottles of the stuff, or even arrange for a large consignment to be sent to our respective homes across Europe and the globe. John and I had the inclination to do so, but not the cash, and our very appearance saved us from any embarrassment by declining. Several of those who did make purchases though, kindly thought to pass their souvenir panniers of miniatures on to us.

Aha . . .

Wrong move -

Leaving the cool of the *bodega* to enter the street outside was like walking from a fridge to a furnace. We were hungry, sick, and our heads throbbed.

We were pissed.

On the opposite side of the road to the *bodega* we espied the lovely green lawn of a well watered park. We sprawled onto its grass and lay there with the world spinning about us.

'That was really something, wasn't it,' John opined, fiddling with the first of the panniers beside him.

'Yup,' I agreed; and giggled.

'I wonder what these miniatures are like?' he said, unscrewing the cap from one of them and taking a small swig. 'Hey, they're just as good as the real stuff, Mike. Try one.'

There were six panniers, with six miniatures in each. Three dozen miniatures equated to a further substantial amount of the real thing.

It was 16.00.

We were awakened at 18.00.

I had flown to Malaysia on the back of a tiger with bells on, and started a hotel for mice in a disused pagoda. One of the natives told me that he had a special gun for curing mice, which he offered for me to see. I grasped hold of it and opened my eyes to find the gun was real, its muzzle poking at my ribs and that it had a Spanish policeman on the end of it, scowling at me like a Goyesque soldier. A mute, semi-circular crowd of about thirty curious people stood gazing down at us, helping to filter the slowly lowering sunlight through the trees behind. Scattered about the grass around us lay six crushed cork panniers, and littered about them thirty-six empty miniatures.

Jerez gaol was cool.

They removed our passports and rucksacks, and put us in a locked cell for two hours to dwell on life in general and the merits of abstinence in particular.

We were released at 20.00 with lots of good natured grins, gruff raillery, finger wagging, and directions to a *pensione* run by the half-sister of one of their wives' aunts. Being a Californian John's Spanish was better than mine, and that's where he said it was we were going. Humping our rucksacks along with us we found the *pensione*, made our mark with Maria, the policeman's wife's aunt's half-sister, booked in, washed off the worst excesses of our day, donned reasonably clean jeans and T-shirts, and went out in quest of food.

On the way we came across a barber's shop still open.

My stubble was now entering its fourth day, and for the first time in its young life as man-growth had become quite a substantial outcrop. I fingered it contemplatively. In our tour round the *bodega* we had become befriended by a Belgian couple and their attractive teenage daughter. Something about us had appealed to them, and it was more than obvious (to the parents too, which was a bit worrying) that their daughter had taken a definite shine to one of us: but neither of us was quite sure which. They were staying the night at *The Swan Hotel* and had offered to drive us with them on the next leg of our journey on to Seville.

'I reckon I might get some of this stubble off,' I told John, nodding at the barber's pole. 'It's neither one thing nor the other at the moment.'

'It never will be, unless you give it a chance,' he replied. 'I thought you said you wanted to grow a beard.'

'Yeah, well, I was,' I said, 'but I'd only have to shave it off before I got back to Gib, so it hardly seems worth it somehow.'

'Have a shave, then,' he said, shrugging his shoulders. 'I'll come in with you and read some magazines.'

If a fearsome couple of gunslingers had wandered in off the street they couldn't have created more of an effect than we did. Five customers were waiting, and there was another already in the chair enjoying having his shave. One side of his face was half done. The rest was still smothered with lather. The barber himself appeared to be about 14-years-old, and was obviously on a learning curve, standing in for his father. Either that, or we had stumbled upon an especially enterprising lad. Or a dwarf. His face turned to disbelief when he looked up and saw us there, the lather-flecked cutthroat razor poised in mid air. With no further ado he whipped the shroud from the shoulders of his half-shaved customer, tapped him on the shoulder, and muttered just one word: *'Americanos.'*

'Si; si; si,' mumbled the ousted customer, a portly local worthy in his mid-50s who slapped the residual lather from his face like spume on the wind and scurried back on dancer's feet to resume his previous place in the queue with the others, who retrogressively shuffled along one. With the broadest of smiles and flourishes the young Sweeney Todd exaggeratedly flicked

clean the chair and indicated it to me like a restaurateur welcoming some Grande Dame to the portals of the nobbiest eatery in town.

'*Por favor,*' I expostulated to the room at large, with hands flung theatrically apart. Then I ran out of Spanish, so turned to John for assistance. 'Please *tell* them . . . *I* don't want preferential treatment, for God's sake.'

'No - but someone else might, one day,' he said, grinning: 'and they think you're American.' Everyone in the shop grinned and nodded their agreement. 'So go on,' John chided mockingly. 'Don't buck the system. Enjoy your new nationality while you can. Just get in the chair and get your darned chin shaved: It shouldn't take long,' he added as an affectionately jibing afterthought, and returned to flicking through a magazine.

The able young barber wielded his gruesome implement with the dexterous finesse of a feather. Within moments my face was smoother than a baby's backside. He probably only charged me something absurd, like a shilling (5p) so I felt obliged to double this amount. Immediately I was the sunshine of his life for a moment.

It wasn't proving too expensive, being an American.

And it was fun.

THIRTY-FOUR

SEVILLE WAS A DREAM OF A CITY.

The Belgian family drove us there in their Buick, both parents and daughter being equally charming. Even at that tender age I was streetwise and cynical enough to know that people seldom did anything for nothing. This meant that for most of the trip I worried about what the expected payoff might be. I thought something would emerge in conversation which would then call forth some shocked accusation of our having been flying under false colours. The worst our host could do would be to stop the car and invite us to leave, but neither event transpired. He, his wife, and their bubbly, personable, and in less restrictive company definitely up-for-it daughter seemed to be nothing more than simply charmed by our company. It was only later, with a wife and daughter of my own who managed to cause me certain degrees of angst and tedium on occasions (however nice I was to them both) that I realised what a welcome breath of fresh air John and I must have been for the poor old fellow (40 then, perhaps?), and why he seemed so loath to see us go when they finally dropped us off with much ceremonious hand-shaking and well-wishing, somewhere in the centre of Seville.

It was coming up for Easter, 1958, the time of the famed *Semana Santa* (Holy Week) celebrations, when bare-footed and be-sheeted Ku-Klux-Klan look-alike penitents shuffle wailing through the streets to muffled drum beats, bearing enormous replicas of the Virgin and her Son across their bowed shoulders.

Hence Seville was crowded.

Our ploy was simple.

While I stood guarding the rucksacks, John hot-footed it round the immediate vicinity searching out beds for the night.

He was back within the hour.

'There's a lovely little *pensione* I've found, just behind the *Alcazar,*' he said. 'Come on; it's quite close by.'

These Spanish *pensiones* were a god-send for the likes of us. They were clean, functional little family-run places with adequate beds, some sort of running water, the occasional shower, and a continental breakfast, all for something like 75p a night. There was no way our budget could have run to a *bona fide* hotel, and on some occasions our sleeping bags by the side of the road would have been inappropriate. We might have got squashed by a bus. That's when the *pensiones* came into their own.

We stayed in Seville for three days, cooking our meagre food over our hexamine burners on the bedroom floor, and then going out later to spend that day's money ration in some semi-fashionable dive or other.

This is how we stumbled upon *La Casa Las Siete Puertas*. (The House of Seven Doors).

Downstairs was like my lurid perception of some 30's Shanghai waterfront bar.

I should explain that I have never actually been to a Shanghai waterfront bar. I have probably got it all wrong and there is no such thing as a Shanghai waterfront bar. Shanghai's waterfront at the time, for all I knew, might have been renowned for its warehousing, schools, convents, squid shops and public buildings, but in *my* book - until I was told otherwise - a Shanghai waterfront bar depicted everything that's nice and sleazy and available at a price, and dangerous about life. Tattooed Dragon Ladies, and muscular, sweat-sheened Mongol bouncers in funny trousers with shaved skulls, top-knots and machetes. Men in off-white suits and shades; hypodermic syringes and wads of greenbacks . . . all of this - plus a fleeing White Russian princess with forged papers, and bumping into a card-playing Billy Manser again there as well - *that's* what a Shanghai waterfront bar was all about.

Downstairs at *La Casa Las Siete Puertas* was like a Shanghai waterfront bar.

Alright?

Heavy, marble-topped tables on wrought-iron legs stood on the square-tiled and saw-dusted floor. In the middle of the room a circular marble-topped bar supported two steam-hissing coffee machines. The aroma of their freshly ground beans mingled with the beer and coñac fumes and heavy tobacco smoke, forming a ground zero cloudbank that spiralled upwards, curling back and under from its slow-motion impact with the yellowed ceiling and suspending itself there in a pall, waiting for one of the establishment's seven doors to open and show it in which direction to eddy.

And then there were the girls.

John and I sat open mouthed round our cheroots and coñac balloons, staring in disbelief and wonderment at their ready availability.

They were everywhere, strolling like indolently seductive panthers on heat round all the seated male customers, certain in the knowledge that by the merest twitch of their tautly encased buttocks each of them would secure a succession of takers through the evening, and on into the early hours.

Even in that sin-Mecca of the universe, Hamburg (with which I was not to become acquainted for another ten years yet) I don't think I ever saw the female of the species assembled in quite such purposeful abundance at one place. Oh, and Thailand too of course, thirty years after that.

None of them was par*ti*cularly attractive, although one or two of them did possess a certain appeal.

John and I had stumbled upon the place purely by chance, in quest of a nightcap.

This slow moving sales line of tarnished pulchritude was an unforeseen and titillating attraction, but we had little inclination to avail ourselves of any of the wares. Surprisingly, in this day and age, contrary to popular belief I was still a virgin, and hadn't planned on having myself de-flowered in a Sevillian back street - even on the eve of Holy Week. I was still suffering the 1950s mantra that pre-marital sexual intercourse was the precursor either to an incurable dose of penicillin-resistant and death-delivering syphilis, or the illegitimacy of an offspring which if they had been conceived in a bed of roses instead, might have borne my name. I am not sure which eventuality it was that concerned me most when fantasising over the possibility of such a liaison: acquiring the pox - or a bastard, having been told by a 20-year-old ex-school friend, after I had just been introduced to his seven-year-old daughter, that condoms did have a tendency to let one down occasionally. The prospect of returning to Seville one day, accompanied by a family of my own and encountering some backstreet filly-of-the-night who bore more than a passing resemblance to both my legitimate daughter and me, although a romantic one, was too fraught too contemplate, and successfully managed to strengthen my resolve to stick just with coffee for the rest of the night.

Temptation still had a trump to play on one member of our party though.

'I've gotta go to the john, John,' I said (quick on the vernacular, me), swilling my coffee grains in the cup and downing them.

I wended my way across the bar to a far corner where the *caballeros* sign pointed its arrow up a very old flight of rickety wooden stairs. At the top I saw the WC located off a small half-landing. When I came out a couple of minutes later it was to collide gently with a girl coming out of the *señoras* opposite. She wore a simple white dress and a pair of white high-heeled sandals. Her bare arms and legs were a delicious smooth olive colour. She paused to observe herself unselfconsciously in a full length mirror affixed to the landing wall. She patted her shoulder length raven hair into place. She was beautiful. What was a girl like that doing in a place like this? Earning a fortune, I should think. I hadn't noticed her among the others downstairs. Sensing my presence she turned her head to allow her dark, lustrous eyes to appraise me slowly. Professionally. Smiling apologetically, she then turned sexily on the toe of one high-heel and sauntered elegantly on up the stairs to a floor above.

I had a compulsion to follow her, so did.

There was no door at the top of the stairs, instead a beaded curtain hung suspended from a lintel. I peered inside and saw a sumptuously carpeted lounge with a deeply polished mahogany bar tended by an immaculately waistcoated factotum, and a stunning redhead with an enormous bust. A lone, middle-aged Spanish businessman sat on a stool with a highball and *tapas* at his elbow - and ranged elegantly about the salon's velour banquettes and sofas lounged a dozen or more of the most beautiful women I had ever seen. Each was perfectly coiffured and attired and, I realised, at twice the price just as available as their downstairs sisters. There and then, if I'd thought about it, I could have coined the phrase 'up market'. Instead, realising that this territory was a bit out of my league, I tiptoed quietly back down the flight of rickety wooden stairs to where at that stage of my life I felt I more properly belonged.

'Where the hell've y'been?' John asked, and I realised his firewater was beginning to bite.

'Do yourself a favour,' I gasped excitedly. 'Upstairs there's a saloon lounge containing the most sumptuous selection of totty you're ever going to see in your life,' I urged him. 'Go and have a look at them. Honestly. They're *fabu*lous.'

'Really?'

'Really.'

'I'd better go and check this out then, hadn't I.'

He grinned, climbed to his feet and weaved his way off through the crowd towards the stairs.

I knew he was on a tight budget, but when fifteen minutes later he still hadn't returned I nipped off back to the *caballeros* again, and on the way back took a peak through the beaded curtain once more. Predictably, I suppose, there was no sign of him in there at all. Nor had he returned to our table when I got back. Shrugging, I left the building and strolled slowly back to our *pensione.*

John got in about an hour later.

He stripped and went to wash certain parts of his anatomy

fairly thoroughly over the edge of the hand basin.

I had already cleaned my teeth.

'You were right,' he said, switching off the light and climbing onto his bed.

'About what?' I asked.

His only reply was one long, draw out, and deeply contented sigh.

*

Ever since my voice broke and I'd had my first beer - and long before that too, of course - the indignant cry in male circles has always been: 'What *me?* Pay for it? Not bloody likely.'

Those who protested most loudly were no different to the rest of us who found normal conquests difficult to come by, and when the hot blood and other stuff was bubbling, if faced with the opportunity to pay for it on a plate, would sometimes succumb.

Man no longer has to defend his homestead daily by force of arms (war zones excluded), nor since the advent of supermarkets is he obliged to hunt his own meat and game as an alternative to starving. He is seldom called upon to cross staves or engage in fisticuffs with an opposing belligerent in a forest glade. Nor is it really expected that he will club women over the head and drag them back to his pad to get some nooky that way.

Although harder and more ruthless in many spheres, life has become a different ballgame to the one we were designed for. The baser predatory instincts of mankind have become suppressed. So ingrained still are those instincts however, that periodically they erupt in war. A great social blood letting and orgasm ensues, and then both sides settle down once more to lick wounds, grow more corn and rebuild and develop a slicker society than the last time.

Then the process re-runs all over again.

So much for man.

Women's animal instincts are in the main generally catered for.

They are seeded; they pod; and they nurture the results; cook, wash, and tend the cave; chatter and moan, and dress up on occasion for parties. Some of the more aggressive ones have started their own Hunt 'n' Forage Clubs for the hell of it, but generally they still like the hearts and flowers thing, and the opening of doors: but none of this chocolate-box superficiality can conceal the fact that - despite their fervent denial and assertions to the contrary of course - deep down in their darkest recesses many of our girls harbour a) the unexpressed (and often unrealised) desire to be scandalised; brutalised; and - I suspect - even secretly enjoy a bit of gentle rape occasionally, and b) indulgence in a night of vanilla prostitution . . . just to see what it's like, you understand.

After Guy, the iconic gorilla, died at London Zoo it was humorously reported in the tabloids that while he was alive the sight of him and the glint in his eye had given many women strange feelings that made them come over all unnecessary.

As man's predatory instincts towards women have become smoothed by urbanity, so *she* has responded by veiling her own secret desires. At least along the high street she has.

Hence one of the reasons for hookers.

What another load of old codswallop.

I agree; but it's fun going there - and I'll bet I've still got your attention.

Hookers offer instant availability, no nonsense lust-assuagement and variety, on those days when the wife's away on holiday, has another headache, or simply doesn't want to play. But how can hooker-dom thrive in such promiscuous times as these, when everybody's doing it with everyone else anyway? In the far back, hardier days of yesteryear, when man's instincts were a well honed daily requirement for survival and woman walked barefoot and pregnant, the oldest profession in the world still flourished. Did early English man, swigging mead from a pewter jar on Sunday in some mud and wattle hostelry also indignantly declaim: 'What *me?* Pay for it?'

Call-girls, whores and hookers don't usually set themselves up just to service hunchbacks, dropouts and the uglier

393

members of the raincoat brigade who can't pull - but, thank God - for whose sakes such ladies do exist.

There are horses for courses, but a high class hooker is usually a pretty classy piece of stuff. She absolutely has to be, or remunerative work would be scarce. But how can she operate . . . if the majority of men would so emphatically rather *die* than pay for it? The reason she can afford a luxury apartment, jewellery, furs and a small Porsche is because her calling does appeal tremendously to the primal urge in a great number of red blooded males who, far from decrying the lady's adopted role in life, heartily support her in it. The men who can afford these top-of-the-league ladies are usually successful people themselves, and appreciate the no nonsense approach and value for money that a high class hooker can provide. She has a business to run and a reputation to maintain. These are not achieved by short-changing clients on quality. She is blessed with and nurtures a Lamborghini body which she can afford to pamper to flawless perfection. She knows what her body is worth and what is expected of it, and delivers that commodity lock, stock and sensuously writhing gift-wrapped barrel on receipt of its hire charge.

I would have thought whoring an ideal calling for emancipated ladies. Instead of settling down with one guy, his name, foibles and underpants, a whore can use all men, turn on or off to them sexually as she pleases, go bra-less if she chooses, be a dyke in her spare time, amass capital and purchase her independence from mankind-at-large before cocking the most monumental snoot at the chauvinist pig in the final tally, if she feels so inclined to do.

She can do this working in an art gallery too of course, but I don't think there's quite so much 'ready' in that.

The concept of whoring is not total anathema to woman's susceptibilities.

Look what they've reverted to in war, when food's been scarce.

There are such things as male brothels too.

Not for men: for women.

On the Continent especially, passed-over but still sexually

oriented spinsters, hard-pressed businesswomen, and others desiring sexual fulfilment from a man but who are disinclined to enter into any emotional entanglement or commitment with one, resort to such establishments for their gratification. Well honed six-packs attached to athletic frames with blue eyes, nice smiles, mouthwash and the ability to maintain a decent on-demand blood supply to certain parts of their anatomy, are available in these places, and can be discreetly hired by the hour, by the room, or as takeaways to the ladies' hotel rooms.

There was once in Holland an ex merchant seaman called Pieter Ros who realised there was a mutually beneficial market to be developed amongst ordinary housewives. He canvassed a few to see how they liked the idea, and found that it was secretly what many of them had been hankering for. Their portfolio of suitably alluring photographs and profiles was compiled, for which punters paid a fee to peruse and select the housewife they thought they fancied; a phone call was made, the meeting was arranged, and off he would excitedly trot to a nice little house in the suburbs to allay the lady's boredom, for which a nice little lunch was thrown in as well, along with some post-prandial coochy-coo.

And a fee.

Win-win.

So there are many indications it is something that perhaps more ladies might like to try, if it didn't mean the traditional lounging round the neighbourhood lamp-post with a cigarette, split skirt, and a poodle in order to clinch their deals.

As for the clients . . . who are they?

You have finally come into your inheritance and would quite like a holiday in the sun. Being a red-blooded fellow you would appreciate some female companionship, but know no one to ask, or who would go with you. You do not trust your ability to hook up with a playmate when you get there - so what do you do? In a holiday environment in the sun, away from her business premises and with the extant arrangement already paid for, the hooker you hire to accompany you will relax, enjoy herself, and probably give you the best time you've ever had in your entire life. Who knows - like Richard

Gere and Julia Roberts you may even end up marrying the girl and living happily ever after.

While I would not necessarily recommend the profession to my daughter, if I'd been a girl and know what I know now – well—— I might have tried giving it a whirl for a while.

I certainly envied my friend John his amorous adventure of the previous hour, there in Seville.

At least he was happily sleeping on it.

THIRTY-FIVE

AFTER THREE DAYS AND NIGHTS the *Giralda,* the *Alcazar,* the shops, streets, clubs and the cafés, the people and the fantastic flamenco evenings at Seville's renowned *Patio Andalusia* were all coming round for the third time, so we decided to press on to pastures new.

Our most frequent mode of transport seemed to be the cement truck, and it was sitting atop the sacked load of one of these that we were now belting eastward out of the historic and beautiful city of Seville, heading for Osuna and then Antequerra, where our friendly driver dropped us off and waved farewell as we trudged up the hill lugging our rucksacks into the little town, looking for something with which to break our fast.

If only I was as effortlessly slim now as I was then!

We were ravenous.

Tortillas con potatos had become our staple diet whenever we ate out. Short of eating earth, there was nothing much cheaper. We ordered two large ones, with tomatoes and a beer each and sat back contentedly while the restaurateur's jolly little wife busied herself with her pots and pans in the café's miniscule kitchen.

The Spanish hinterland in 1958 did not seem as though it could have changed much since Civil War days. It was along the southern coastal belt that the seeds of tourism were being sown, but here in Antequerra, inland, I doubt if anyone ever saw more than a dozen non-Spaniards a year. We were surprised, therefore, to find that our jocular and rotund café owner had lain out on his tables carefully inked menus in

English. Ten marks for initiative and effort, but the English was atrocious of course, and highly amusing, so we rewrote one of them correctly for him to copy, and earned his gratitude and an extra tomato each for our trouble. With an infectious imagination he was probably picturing hordes of British tourists pouring into Antequerra by the coach load, all heading for *Juan's Café* to order one of his internationally famous potato omelettes.

With tomato.

It was night by the time we finished our meal and left. Funds were dwindling a pace, but although overcast it was warm, so we decided to sleep out. It was pitch black. John's torch had run out of battery so we had to grope our way on hands and knees to find a dip on the edge of a field. Laying out our groundsheets we unzipped our sleeping bags, removed our boots, and climbed in. Mine, which had travelled much, still stank of snow-filled Korean ditches . . .

. . . it was getting pretty high - and could tell a tale or two.

We slept like logs.

When we awoke next morning it was to find ourselves surrounded by women.

Without any ambient light, it appeared that in the darkness we had bedded ourselves down outside the main entrance to a factory.

It was 07.30.

The sun was up and hot already.

Our sleeping bags were a good place for mushrooms.

We were both so exhausted we could have slept till lunch, but we had been awakened by this unusual alarm. Our eyes had shot open, and there they were - 50 or 60 gaily laughing girls all merrily ringing their bicycle bells at us. A hooter sounded, the factory gates swung open and the delighted horde of early morning outriders who had so charmingly heralded us to daybreak, happily dispersed to their tasks within, hammering out plough-shares or whatever it was they did in there.

It was a short and silly interlude, but a memorable one.

Wriggling from the pungent folds of my sleeping bag I left it open to steam in the air, stiffly donned my boots and trudged off to a nearby house to purchase some eggs and then on to a police post to cadge some water while John got the fire going.

It was to be our farewell breakfast together.

I had only a couple of days of leave left and needed to head back to Gibraltar. John, quite naturally, did not want to retrace his steps in that direction, especially as Calcutta lay in the opposite direction - so it was *au revoir* time.

After a silent and groggy repast of rice, eggs and potatoes we gathered together our belongings, exchanged the necessary paperwork, battened down and helped each other on with our rucksacks, and with unaccustomed lumps in our young throats, bade each other a sad farewell.

'Great meeting you,' I said. 'Great knowing you. Look after yourself, heh? See you sometime. God bless, and . . . so long.'

My last picture of John was of him shambling along the road towards Granada, weighed down by his enormous world-travelling load, and cursing perhaps, because there was no cement truck immediately in the offing, which we had come to consider our personal 'on call' taxi service round this part of Spain.

He turned once - and we waved.

I was never to see him again.

Periodically over the next year I received letters and postcards scrawled in pencil or runny ball-pen from various corners of foreign fields as he moved inexorably and steadfastly round the globe eastward back to his homeland. When my photographs of our little sector of his trip were developed I sent copies of them to his mother in Los Angeles. When he finally did get home a year later, he joined the US Army, where with his language facility and recent travel experiences he soon found himself on a Russian course at the US Army Language School at Monterey. When subsequently I had met and become engaged to my Gibraltarian fiancée, John wrote to congratulate me on having found 'such a rose in the weed patch of Gibraltar'. Three months after we were married and were living in England, John wrote to say that he was being posted to London the following month. I was elated. We packed up a piece of wedding cake, photos, plans and a proposed itinerary which were despatched post-haste to him out in Monterey. Three weeks later they were returned, accompanied by a curt letter from the adjutant of the US Army Language School to inform me that PFC Johnathon Evans Harris had been killed in a motor cycle accident near the camp.

*

Meanwhile, back in Spain, John was no more than a mile down the road to Granada when a funny little fellow on a Vespa stopped to offer me a lift. This was not like a junction on the A30. These were roughly hewn dirt tracks which could just as easily have been in Katmandu. So it was precariously balanced on the pillion of a bucking Italian scooter that my rucksack and I scaled one side of the mighty *Sierra Nevada*. A few yards from the top, the vociferous Vespa pilot informed me that he had to turn off down a sidetrack to some nearby caves to visit his mother.

Dammit, I thought. What was I going to do now, stuck up on top of a mountain range?

No sooner had I alighted, rubbed my sore thighs and taken two steps nearer the summit, than I nearly lost one of my tail-lights on the front fender of an over sprung Ford Mercury which had come slithering to an uncontrolled stop in a rush of dust and shingle beside me.

'Malaga?' I enquired, sticking my head hopefully through one electrically operated window, which was open.

'Si; Malaga - si.'

The Mercury's swarthy driver, from his hurry he could either have been its rightful owner or a thief, leaned across to unlock the door and allow me to subside gratefully into the plush of the front seat beside him, with my rucksack in the rear. The way the car then took off in a shower of pebbles, gravel, and disturbed scrub I thought either we were being chased, or filmed. Perhaps he was a stunt man and wanted to get a good running jump from the crest. They were filming him from somewhere up there in a helicopter, driving the car in one of those beautiful slow motion shots of a take-off from the soaring peaks of the *Sierra Nevada* out into the Mediterranean below, and I was just ballast.

I was wrong.

It turned out he was simply a Moroccan in a rush to reach Malaga in time for lunch.

He took his great big spongy American cream-puff screeching round one final fir-tree'd bend, and the glittering Mediterranean leapt into view, a sun-sheened, silver-blue metallic strip underscoring the horizon.

Half-an-hour later we were dropping down into the hillside suburbs of Malaga. The way he was driving we almost overshot it, but did manage to stop in time for me to buy my new friend a drink, wave him goodbye, and then check in to a *Pensione Alphonso* where I cleaned myself up briefly, prior to going out to explore.

Malaga harbour stank of fish and ship oil.

Unlike today, back then it was most unfascinating.

The place was a fever of activity preparing for the town's forthcoming *feria*. My time, however, was becoming short and I had to make some serious headway for my return to Gibraltar. That night I turned in early. Next morning I was up at dawn striding merrily out like the Happy Wanderer, along the seven mile route to Torremolinos.

Torremolinos at this time was still a pretty little unspoiled fishing village. When I got there I sat on the edge of a stone well with my rucksack at my feet in the middle of the village square, supping a beer while a scabrous, dun coloured pye-dog with its tail between its legs sniffed at my ankle, but then scant years of hurried development later, the very spot where I sat that day had become the centre point of a death-dealing six lane motorway.

A Gibraltarian friend of mine with local knowledge, business acumen, and oodles of foresight and initiative, had just raised and paid £800 for a stretch of beach there. All he did was lay in a fresh water pipe, erect some rudimentary showers and build a perimeter fence with a gate, and he had himself a ready-made camping site. With a resigned and hopeful shrug of his bronzed shoulders he then left the gate invitingly open and charged five-bob a head (or the *peseta* equivalent) for caravanners to drop anchor there at weekends. The following year he rented out a piece of his beach to a local speculator who wanted to build a bar there. My friend accepted 10% of the bar's takings, and he, his children and grandchildren have been doing so ever since. Within no time at all he had become a very fat, very wealthy and very happy chappie who smoked a lot of Havana cigars and drove round in an ever changing succession of big, sexy cars. I am pleased to say that he is still alive, but pretty much in line for a coronary.

That day in 1958 when I stopped by, he was still slim and in the process of laying the water pipe. He downed tools and we had a beer together, watching the early boom of beautiful people squelching by in their tight white jeans and expensive sun tans. That afternoon, when Jaime had returned to his pipe-laying and I'd hefted my rucksack onto my back once more for the onward journey home, I had cause to reflect: Mike, my boy - I said to myself resignedly: you are a £5 a week (but all found) member of Her Majesty's Armed Forces, serving in an infantry regiment of the line. Your RSM and lesser minions are poised awaiting your return at the barracks gate in Gibraltar. Sitting here in the sun, drinking, on the periphery of the elite, while cluttering up the *plaza* with your rucksack, is the end of a short-lived pipe dream. Now get yourself back to reality.

My feet were killing me and, uncharacteristically, it had started to rain. Feeling depressed I cheated and caught a bus for the two-hour journey back down the coast to Gibraltar. Naturally, I had to stand, but it mattered not because I was young, and fit, and healthy. I was concerned though to see also standing, swaying and barely able to endure their discomfort, an elderly aristocratic looking German lady and her equally distinguished looking daughter, who appeared to be in her mid-30s, and pregnant. The rest of the bus was occupied almost exclusively by men, not one of whom offered to give up his seat for either of these two ladies. Nor did they even seem to notice them or their discomfort. In fairness, they were non car-owning, illiterate Spanish peasants (I think; or else disguised spies who couldn't afford to blow their cover) and possibly knew no better, but as the road became rougher and the going more hazardous and uncomfortable, my anger brewed and bubbled up into a blind but impotent rage. Neither of the German women seemed able to speak Spanish, so as the only other civilised European on board I figured it was up to me to come to their rescue. Despite my unshaven, swarthy, filthy, blue-jeaned state, which made me appear just as Andalusian a peasant as the rest of them, my own Spanish was still in short order and faltering. I spoke enough to get into trouble but not enough to get out of it, so I still fought shy of getting myself into embarrassing situations, but as an English gentleman, albeit a young and heavily disguised one, I felt it incumbent upon me to endeavour to resolve this uncomfortable situation. Dammit: British honour demanded it. Besides, my mother would have been absolutely furious with me if she ever found out I'd done nothing.

The sympathetic and understanding glances I kept flashing to the two ladies, telepathically trying to convey to them the fact that help was at hand and Sir Galahad was at any moment about to leap into action, was probably being misinterpreted by them as just more Spanish lechery. To redress this I started glowering instead at the rest of the passengers, in an attempt to have my wishes fulfilled without confrontation. To no avail. Telepathy did not traverse the language barrier. Or perhaps it was just the bovine lack of receptiveness of this bus load, who all kept jabbering shrilly on about the price of chicken and the rising young star of the bull ring next Sunday.

Then the bus hit a pothole.

I collided into the pregnant German woman, and rebounded against her mother. Both of them teetered and swayed, but managed to hang on fast to the rail.

'Bitte; danke schön,' I said, being the only words I knew in German at the time. With the adrenaline now coursing through my veins I turned to lash our verbally at the nearest unsuspecting Spaniard.

'Señor . . .' I snapped, but was then frustratingly unable to articulate anything further. With my palm I indicated the

intestinal protuberance of the younger German woman, hoping that this would at last do the trick. *'La señora . . .'* I raised my eyebrows enquiringly, willing him to get the picture and leap up apologetically to offer his seat.

Fat chance.

He didn't.

Dumb idiot.

All he did was shy away fractionally, indicating to his bemused companion that he thought I must be cuckoo, or else that I had been implying that he might have fathered the child.

With a wan and pathetic little smile I turned to the two ladies and shrugged hopelessly, as if to say: 'Really; I don't know. I've tried, but these foreigners have absolutely no manners. We from the north at least are aware of how things should be done.'

Once again they misinterpreted my expression of course, and looked blankly and red faced the other way. St George was being left to fight a lone battle this day. Not a soul was interested. Perhaps I was being set some sort of test. But surely these ladies must have realised there was a fervent ally at hand, doing in his nut with the gallantry bit? And because of all this, I was missing the scenery.

It was hell being British.

My dander was really up.

Undeterred, I determinedly selected my next victim. This recipient of my scorn sat there innocently clutching two dead chickens and a loaf of bread, while choking with broken-toothed laughter at the *falsetto* verbal antics of his six-foot companion. Obviously the local comedian. Or simpleton. Broken teeth, be damned. There'd be more broken teeth if I didn't get a couple of seats for these women soon. Probably mine at this rate.

I glowered steadfastly at the inanely cackling chicken-carrier, more intent than ever now on making my thought waves penetrate his thick skull.

At first he remained unaware of my fierce scrutiny, but eventually caught my eye.

Warily.

Dastardly dago coward.

A few seconds later he tried another furtive glance to see if I was still there. Seeing that I was, he rewarded me with just the flicker of a smile.

I was on.

Then he looked away again.

Damn him.

A moment later he stole another sly glance, pleased to find I was still looking at him.

It hit me.

Oh, horror.

He thought he'd pulled.

Even there in rural Spain they'd got them.

When the glint in my eye turned ice cold, nature let him know he'd got it wrong, and I could see him now puzzling over what else it was about him that might have caught my attention. He stole a furtive glance down at his lap to check his fly. Having assured himself that with two missing buttons and one hanging on by a thread they were as intact as they'd ever be, he looked up questioningly again.

Dammit; I *was* going to get a seat for these women.

'*Señora,*' I said, addressing him severely, and realised I'd got that the wrong way round as well. He started, scratched his stomach and belched at my affront. '*La señorita,*' I said, getting that wrong also, as once more I described an arc with my hand to indicate the stomach of the by now even more pregnant German woman, who was obviously getting a bit chocker with this uncalled for attention and being made the object of such vile discussion.

The bus gave another violent lurch.

Once again I reeled headlong into her.

She and her mother regarded me with utter disdain, and alighted.

We had arrived at our destination - La Linea.

It was still raining.

I regained my balance, and now that the self inflicted ordeal was over, some of my composure as well.

Glancing through the steamed-up window of the bus I could

see the dear old Rock looming out of the drizzle on the other side of the frontier, the familiar red, white and blue flag still fluttering unconcernedly at its peak, and I felt triumphant.

Obviously nothing too untoward had taken place during my absence.

Stepping down from the bus I felt something trip me, and I fell headlong into a puddle.

Clawing myself to my feet I found that I was halfway up the leg of Broken Tooth's six-foot companion. Nor did he look like such a comedian as before. The earlier *falsetto* voice was now a rumbling *basso profundo*, like a bulldog defending Dover.

I thought he was going to *hoik* on me.

Tee-hee, I grinned sheepishly, pointing at my head. I wasn't proud. This was survival time. *'Ingles. Loco. Comprende?'*

Oh, what the hell.

Kicking me free of his leg, he snarled, and strode off towards a nearby bar with his stupid, broken-toothed chicken carrier friend scuttling along beside him.

I retrieved my rucksack from the rack atop the bus and strolled falteringly across the cobbles to a café for a coffee and coñac, both of which I felt I deserved, but then looking up from my first sip I was unable to restrain an involuntary heave. The two German ladies were just sitting down at the next table to mine. Now away from the heat of the fray, should I sidle across apologetically and endeavour to explain to them what had gone wrong? I would like to have rounded off the incident satisfactorily.

Arranging and settling themselves, as ladies do, they placed their order with the waiter, looked up, saw me, gently touched each others elbows, grimaced, turned away, and huddled forward in soft discussion.

In English.

'Stop worrying about it, Erica,' the older woman said, patting the younger one's arm. 'Some of these Latin people *are* strange. There's a lot of in-breeding goes on. He's probably a little unbalanced. Now drink your coffee. You'll soon feel better about it. John will be here at any moment and then we

406

can all go home and forget about the whole horrid incident. Ah - here's John now.'

A green Hillman-Minx with Gibraltar number plates had pulled in to the kerbside. Out of it jumped one of the officers of my regiment, who came dashing across towards us.

He passed my table.

I leaped to attention.

'Hallo, Corporal George,' he cried airily. 'Have a good leave?'

I was grateful he didn't wait for a reply.

How was I to know that his German speaking mother and English speaking German wife were travelling overland to join him?

After their joyful embraces, the sun came out.

His wife removed her coat.

I placed some money on the table, and left.

She hadn't been pregnant at all.

She was just fat.

THIRTY-SIX

HUMPING MY RUCKSACK onto my back I strode down the cobbled road to the frontier post.

A Spaniard in a cucumber green uniform stamped my passport with a big red *Salida* to allow me out of Spain. At the other end of the short stretch of no-man's-land between the respective barriers, a Gibraltarian official in blue stamped it to let me back across the border again into Gib.

All this in the space of yards.

No hassle.

Back up at Moorish Castle Guard Room when I checked in, I was greeted by a scowling Cpl Bumstead, who God had put on this earth solely to be a provost corporal. Officers carried swagger canes; soldiers mess tins; Cpl Bumstead? A small black knobkerrie. A self induced fantasy trip at some stage of his development must have convinced him that such an implement would enhance his image.

'You look 'orrible,' he informed me.

'Yes, Corporal,' I agreed, slipping quickly back into the routine and remembering the rules.

''Ow dare you come traipsin' in 'ere into my guard room looking so 'orrid as what you do.'

'Very sorry, Corporal,' I said. 'I'm still technically on leave until tomorrow, you see. It was my intention to clean up and shave as soon as I'd reported in here to you.'

'I should bloody well fink so too,' he said. 'You've always got an excuse, you 'ave, 'aven't you, you smart git. You'd better go an' do it then, 'adn't you.'

'Yes, Corporal,' I answered, turned smartly about and

stepped out into the sunshine of normality once more.

'Bleedin' ponce,' I heard him expostulate, any further rejoinder obliterated by his dragging the little black knobkerrie like a *feu de joie* along the bars of one of the cell doors, just to judder its inmate.

Back in my bunk I was delighted to find an envelope waiting for me on my pillow addressed in my father's familiar hand. Jim must have put it there.

My parents had divorced in 1954, when my brother was twelve and I was sixteen. My father, a bank manager, had gone to live in a bungalow he bought near Shoreham Harbour. For the first time since they were married, mother had had to go out to work to provide food and accommodation for me and my brother. I never knew how she did it, but the ground floor flat we moved in to at number 42, St Leonard's Road, in Eastbourne, was a joy. Its drawing room had wood panelled walls, a showpiece fireplace, and stained glass windows overlooking the garden. She bought a blood red carpet, a Robin Hood style table and chairs, and a honky-tonk piano for us to thump and tinkle on. I loved it. The neighbours didn't so much.

We'd never known such luxury.

Apart from raising us two boys in straitened times, and withstanding WWII German propaganda, bombings and machine-gun fire, the only other thing mother had ever had much inkling about was fashion. So she applied for, got, and took a job on the fashion floor of an Eastbourne department store. After school each day my brother and I used to swing on our front gate talking about girls, homework, school, and provoking each other, waiting for Mother to get home from work to feed us.

'There she is,' we'd mutter, when laden with two full baskets of shopping her familiar figure would appear round the corner at the end of St Leonard's Road. She would always stop when she saw us, put down her two baskets, wave merrily, change hands, and then continue coming on down the road doing an imitation Charlie Chaplin walk for our amusement. God knows what people must have thought. I suppose it should have occurred to us to help her sometimes, but we seldom if ever did. In anything, much. Teenage sons don't seem to do that sort of thing. Indoors she would remove the tacky old raincoat she wore to protect the one good suit she'd bought for work, kick off the scuffed old flatties she walked to and from in each day and place them and the elegant court shoes she took from her basket beside her dressing table ready for the next day. Removing her suit and hanging it carefully in her wardrobe, she would don slacks, slippers and a shirt. 'Right; you chaps must be starving,' she'd say. 'I'll go and get the supper on, shall I?'

'Not half, Mum,' we'd assure her, and then resume bashing each other.

'Supper ready yet, Mum?' we'd holler at five minute intervals. 'We're starving.'

'It's ready,' she'd yell eventually, twenty minutes later, and we'd thunder in to take our places at the kitchen table.

'Pork chops, chips and peas tonight; okay?' she'd grin, plonking a steaming plate of delicious tuck down in front of each of us.

'Great, Mum. Thanks,' we'd say, wolfing down mouthfuls of fodder.

'Aren't you having any, Mum?' one of us might occasionally ask between mouthfuls.

'I don't think so, dear. I'm not hungry tonight.'

'You're never hungry, Mum.'

'That's right,' she'd laugh, ruffling our heads. 'A girl's got to keep her figure, you know. Actually, I had something at work just before I left.'

Good enough for us.

She always seemed to have had something at work just before she'd left, though. I remember once wishing she wouldn't. I thought it would have been so much nicer if she could have waited until she got home, and eaten with us. Then after supper one evening I dashed back in from the garden to get myself a glass of water from the kitchen tap. Mother hadn't heard me. Frozen horror-struck to the spot I watched while she stood at the sink tearing ravenously at the scraps we'd left on

410

our plates.

That's when I knew how we must be placed; and about devotion; and being an adult with the responsibility of children.

Eighteen months later I had joined the Army and mother and my brother went off to South Africa to live, for her to realise a girlhood dream by going there. They set up another little home together, and mother took a job at Garlicks, the Harrods of Cape Town. Within a year she had surprised even herself by her capabilities in the fashion world. Garlicks became very fond of her, and she acquired a good position.

By now I had seen none of my family for a goodly time.

After I had showered, I read my father's letter.

It was a block-buster.

At the end of that week he proposed flying out there to Gibraltar for a holiday, to see me.

*

Latterly the Army was to become so beset with welfare problems that it was sensible for officers to develop some kind of immunity to the anguish and the breast-beating and whingeing of married soldiers with no homes for their families; wives who arrived by public transport to deposit themselves and their kids, kit and caboodle at unit guard rooms, refusing to budge until reconciled in quarters with malcontent husbands; wives demanding money for food because the housekeeping had gone on beer and fags; soldiers who found their wives in bed with other soldiers when they returned unexpectedly early from manoeuvres; soldiers besieged with debt, and soldiers appearing in court for driving untaxed, uninsured vehicles without a licence - with such a stream of miscreants shuffling in hourly to be dealt with it was easy for the poor old regimental officer with only his native wit and the army manual to rely upon, to become cynical and end up giving short shrift to the occasional genuine case he might come across.

Back in the good old days of National Service such a pattern did not exist. Soldiers then were single. Some aged corporals, sergeants and mature officers were married, but almost without exception everyone seemed to be in control of their personal lives, and behaved. In her autobiography *My Nine Lives*, as well as in subsequent interviews on radio and in print, the Australian actress Diane Cilento claimed that her one time husband, Sean Connery, had beaten her on several occasions. Connery vehemently denied the accusations. But then in a December 1987 interview with America's queen of TV, Barbara Walters, he caused an uproar by stating that it was okay for a man to slap a woman with limited force if it was required to calm her down or 'keep her in line'. In *Vanity Fair* in 1993, he said: 'There are women who take it to the wire. That's what they are looking for, the ultimate confrontation. They want a smack.' The vast majority of guys know - other than a little bit of romping chastisement around the boudoir - that it is not the done thing to beat up on their womenfolk, and nor would they ever want to, but as 007 said, some women leave their men no option, and would drive a saint to violence with their provocative taunts and threats: 'If you lay a single hand on me it'll be the last thing you'll ever do . . . 'etc. What should the guy then do? Suffer some sort of cerebral accident of his own, in order to stay his hand from lashing out?

If a wife misbehaved in the army, some husbands would belt her back into line in the privacy of their quarter, and had to be spoken to, and in many cases the wives were more long suffering in those days too, and loyal. The adjutant received a letter once from a lady, who wrote: *My husband, Sergeant Smith, has been away for five years now. I don't want this enquiry to spoil his career prospects in any way, or to get him into any kind of trouble, but I am writing to ask if now that the children are getting a bit older whether he's going to be due some leave soon?* The adjutant was sorely taxed: how to inform this very nice lady that said Sergeant Smith had left the regiment three years before, and to the best of everyone's knowledge was still living in Nicosia with a Greek-Cyrpriot barmaid.

I had just returned from two weeks leave in Spain.

I now had no more leave due to me, and my father was coming out from England on holiday to see me, which in those days was quite an event.

What was I to do?

I had never bothered anyone before with any of my problems.

I'd had none.

I had a bed; food was alright; I got paid.

What problems were there?

I thought about it.

I slept on it, and next morning I thought about it some more.

Then I asked for an interview with Captain Peter Calver, my 'C' Company (to whom for administrative purposes I had recently been transferred) commander.

'What about?' thundered CSM Fred Weymouth in the outer office.

'Personal, sir,' I told him.

'You'd better go and see the doctor then, hadn't you?'

'Not that sort of personal, sir.'

'Padre, then?'

'No, sir.'

There was little in the way of light and shade in those days.

I had just had two weeks leave. If I told my CSM I wanted to ask for more, he would have been rude to me.

'Speak up; what is it lad, Chrissake? I'm busy.' (He was trying to complete the *Reveille* crossword, but I decided it might have been imprudent to notice).

'I'd rather mention it to the OC if you don't mind, sir.'

'Put some bint up the stick, have you?'

'No I haven't, sir.' I bristled with mock indignation, flattered, though, that he'd mentally placed me among the ranks of those whom he thought might have done.

'Getting warm, am I?' he persisted, peering intently at me.

'Well, no - not really, sir.'

'Not turning queer, are you?'

'Most definitely *not*, sir,' I retorted with genuine indignation this time, hurt that he'd mentally placed me among the ranks of those whom he thought might be.

413

'All right; but I can't think what else it could be. I shall clock it up, lad - be warned of that. I shall remember you wouldn't confide your confidence and trust in your CSM. Interview at 14.00 this afternoon.'

*

'What seems to be the trouble then, Corporal?' Captain Calver asked, giving me his otherwise undivided attention as he riffled some papers, signed a letter, referred to a training manual, stirred his tea with his pen, readjusted a fall of wax *agitato* in his left ear on the end of a violently waggled little finger, and then glanced up briefly at me over his *pince-nez*.

'But you haven't got any leave left,' he said, puzzled, after I'd explained my dilemma. 'What do you want me to do? Give you some of mine?'

'Course not, sir.' I could see I was already on a hiding to nothing here.

'Well, you should have foreseen this eventuality, shouldn't you,' he explained sagely, 'and perhaps made allowances for such an occurrence.'

'How could I, sir?' He was responding unthinkingly with standard off-the-cuff retorts in the hope that I would give up and go away. 'I have never been stationed overseas with a regiment before, sir. My father has never had occasion to come to Gibraltar before. I had no way of foretelling that he would be planning to do so now. I assure you sir, his letter is not a fabrication. He's coming. Nor has he timed his letter to coincide with my return from leave in some devious endeavour to wheedle me some more. He doesn't know how much leave a year we get. He doesn't even know I've *been* on leave. I know he will have gone to a great deal of trouble to arrange this trip. It will be very exciting time for him, sir. I'd feel so awful if he came all this way to see me and I wasn't allowed out . . .'

'Allowed *out?* Allowed out? We aren't a penal institution, George. Unless you're on guard duty you'll be able to see him every evening, won't you?'

'Not if Corporal Bumstead has anything to do with it, sir.'

'What's Corporal Bumstead got to do with it?'

'You know me, sir. I'm a ponce. Once Corporal Bumstead hears that my father's coming, he'll make sure I'm on cookhouse fatigues every night.'

'Mmmmmmm; I see what you mean. Well - let me look at that letter, anyway.' He stuck out his hand and flapped it impatiently.

'It *is* a personal letter of course, sir . . . but you'll find the relevant details on page three.'

'Quite so; quite so.' At least he had the decency to flush slightly at my veiled chastisement as I handed it to him. 'Why does your father write on Barclays Bank notepaper?' he asked huffily.

'He usually does sir, if he's writing from his office and not from home.'

'What, you mean . . . is he the *man*ager of this branch, or something?'

'Yes he is, sir.'

'Mmmmmm; but this is *my* branch.'

'*Really* sir? Gosh. Fancy that. That means he probably looks after your account then.'

'Very probably; yes; as a matter of fact, I think he does . . .'

Now is the time to **k-e-e-p y-o-u-r f-a-c-e s-h-u-t, George -** I told myself.

Captain Calver's thought processes were now at work.

Were they ever!

'I'll tell you what, Corporal,' he said, handing me back father's letter. 'What I think we'd better do is this . . .'

He allowed me each afternoon off and a long weekend in the middle, on compassionate grounds, with the gentlemen's understanding that I wouldn't spread it about. Our secret. Just the two of us.

'Oh - and - er . . . you might ask your father if he'd care to call in to say hallo when he gets here,' he suggested.

Course I would. Bless.

I saluted, about turned and marched out.

In the outer office I grinned and gave a thumbs-up to the still perplexed CSM.

Problem solved.

Mother had always said to go straight to the fountainhead.

*

I booked dad into the *Bristol Hotel*, opposite the Anglican Cathedral in the centre of town.

His plane arrived mid-afternoon.

This was April 1958.

I didn't meet him at the airport, knowing that he would prefer to make his own way to the hotel by taxi, unwind, unpack, get the feel of the place, and clean-up at his leisure.

I met him in the *Bristol's* cosy little basement bar at 16.00.

It was good to see him.

He was buoyant, keyed-up and ready to enjoy himself.

Cracking our first beer together in that comparatively far-flung outpost of the empire was a personal adventure we both savoured, recalling that the last time we had done so had been in a downmarket Shoreham boozer 18-months previously. Since then I had been to the far side of the world and back. Standing with dad beside me now in that sun-drenched colonial garrison helped put the world into a new kind of perspective. There was much more to it than just the end of our street, and I was becoming a part of it. Its size, now, was becoming reduced to a manageable level.

That evening we dined quietly at the *Bristol* and caught up on things.

Next day was Saturday.

Each Saturday morning RSM Houghton held a battalion drill parade on Grand Casemates Square.

It practised our drill, showed the flag, reimpressed the personality of his rank and standing in our lives and upon our collective psyche, and must have given the RSM himself a near orgasmic ego trip, which usually sustained him in an equable enough mood right through to the following Wednesday, when he could start preparing all over again for his next fix.

With dad's presence as my excuse, I acquired dispensation

from that week's parade and so was able to stand with him to watch it among the ever-present throng of tourists packing the edges of the square beside the main street.

We had breakfasted well together; not in our cookhouse, but at his hotel.

The hot Mediterranean sun beat down across our shoulders and I could see from his self-satisfied smirk that UK's April showers, and his office, had receded far to the back of his mind.

It was the first time in my life that I had shared my father's company so exclusively or had him in any way dependent upon me, his eldest son. I felt like some first year boy proudly showing his parent over his new school, a boy prince striving manfully to rise to the occasion.

The band struck up with a rousing rendition of *Sussex By The Sea* and came swinging out onto Grand Casemates Square with the whole battalion right behind.

Zulus and Go-Go dancers do it.

There is a need in our lives for drill.

The precise and repetitiously rehearsed co-ordination of meticulous mass-movement has been the lot of the British Army's tarmac technicians for several centuries now. The speedy formation of a British Square in battle? A fully mounted brigade advancing in review order? *Phew.* Stirring stuff. Its participants may not have the thighs of 'Legs & Co' or 'Pan's People' but their choreography is just as gripping. My father and I and a whole load of enthralled tourists thought so anyway, that hot April Saturday morning in Gibraltar in 1958. I was bursting with pride as I stood among them, torn between staying to enjoy the spectacle or dashing out onto the square to take my place and show everyone that I was one of them and could do it too. I had as much pride in my regiment that morning as if I had been its commanding officer showing it off to some visiting dignitary.

When the parade was over and my entire 'family' had marched off, dad and I strolled back to his hotel to pack a valise for him, and then went to catch the ferry across the bay to Algeciras.

Since I was now such a recently updated old Spanish hand, for a few days we were going to 'do' the place together. Some of it, anyway.

At Algeciras we checked in to the *Reina Cristina Hotel.*

Early next day we drove a hire car up to Malaga for dad to take in that burgeoning stretch of the *Costa del Sol,* and catch a bullfight. Sitting there at five-o'clock in the evening as the matadors entered the ring and my ears were being raked by the band's raucous *pasadoble,* I glanced at the sky and wondered at the fact that only a few weeks previously I had been circling up there in a Shackleton.

Next day we caught a coach to Seville. Holy Week was now over and the crowds were thinning, but although dad humoured me by coming to have a look at the *pensione* where John and I had stayed - rather like a Red Cross party inspecting a PoW camp - he seemed to think he might prefer to stop at the *Hotel Cristina.*

The bullfight had been done and dusted, but he had not yet seen *flamenco.*

Conveniently the cellar bar of the *Hotel Cristina* was recommended as a likely locale.

After a day's leisurely sight-seeing tour, dinner and then a coñac a piece, we strolled through the lobby down into the cellar to bag ourselves a table and chairs at which to await the cabaret. There were a few couples smooching their way round the miniscule dance floor, then at 23.30 the show started. As *flamenco* it was typically too glittery and commercialised and lacking the gutsy earthiness of the real thing, so I decided to go upstairs for a breath of fresh air. Once I had left the cellar bar I wondered why the rest of the hotel seemed so quiet, until I glanced at my watch and saw that it was already tomorrow and almost 01.00.

On the far side of the lavishly appointed lounge were some French windows. I strolled across the carpet towards them. There was a small group of three or four continental blades in immaculate tuxedos standing in the centre of the room engaged in desultory and intimate conversation with a stunningly attractive blonde wearing a black cocktail dress. She had her back to me, but my gaze was instinctively drawn to her and compulsively retained. She stood daintily poised on high-heels, pensively swinging on one foot as though waiting to pirouette. There was an unmistakable aura about her. She and her escorts were all beautifully tanned. The men wore frilly-fronted white shirts and lit their cigarettes with high class flames. The whole group looked like some glossy ad for *Cartier*. I continued to stare. I was fascinated. Two of the men flicked the occasional concerned glance at me beneath their hooded Mediterranean lids and I realised that as the only other person in the room I probably appeared to be extremely rude. One of the minders leaned towards the girl and made some slight remark about me, because she turned to look. That's when I got my first full on view - and my heart missed a beat.

It was Brigitte Bardot.

The then 24-year-old French sex goddess of the day.

I could neither close my mouth, conceal my army haircut nor remove my gaze.

I was transfixed.

She inclined her head amusedly and raised one slightly mocking eyebrow in a 'was there something?' enquiry. But she did smile. I bit my tongue, gathered my wits, bowed my head discreetly, and fled. Outside in the foyer I dropped all pretence and rushed back downstairs to the cellar bar.

'De-da . . . de-da . . . Dad . . .' I stammered, pointing wildly behind me, as if reporting enemy hordes advancing over yonder hill. 'You'll never guess what. Ber . . . Ber . . . Brigitte Bardot. There - got it: Brigitte Bardot's upstairs.'

'No she isn't,' he replied, trying to remain cool despite his own heart rate also visibly having quickened through his breast pocket. I turned to follow his gaze. She and her select little entourage were also now descending to the cellar. Perhaps she'd found out who I was and needed to see more of me. Like Michael Angelo's Sistine Chapel depiction of Adam's outstretched finger touching that of God, I was still quiveringly pointing. She stood patiently waiting for me to lower my shaking arm so that she could pass and find a table. My left wrist leapt to grasp my paralysed right and return it to its side.

'Merci, M'sieur,' she purred, sparing me the merest pout as she moved gently to their reserved table beyond.

I slumped exhausted into my chair beside dad, who had ordered himself two more coñacs.

'Pretty girl,' he opined, as though he saw hundreds of her every day and still preferred horses. He leaned forward and sipped with his pinkie out. Dad always was a superb study in assumed nonchalance.

The diamanté-encrusted combo on the rostrum started to play a *cha-cha*, which at that time was the dance popularised by and associated with Brigitte Bardot. As its familiar rhythm crackled into the smoke, she got the tingle. One or two couples already on the floor danced to one side, like motorists allowing an ambulance or police car unimpeded access when they saw B-B kick off her heels and loosen her blonde hair as though something was about to happen. Grabbing number one escort by the wrist she writhed onto the floor with him and started to perform. What price the *flamenco* cabaret now? Twisting sinuously, with her hands clasped in her hair she was *magnifique*. Well, she may not have been, but in the telling it seems that she was.

The music switched from the *cha-cha* and broke into some sort of Spanish *excuse-me* dance. Everyone changed partners. To dad's great amusement I had been inveigled onto the floor by one of the now displaced *flamenco* dancers sitting at the table next to ours. She spoke no English, and as all I could manage in Spanish was 'how much?' and 'can I have another beer please', she soon realised she had made a mistake and would rather have sat down again. Plus she could dance, and I was only good at drill. We had soon reached *impasse*. Each of us was wondering how to bail out politely, when the music changed. She smiled, turned and swept away in relief to do it properly with one of the waiters. I turned, and once more my heart almost stopped as Brigitte Bardot slipped into my arms.

She was in Seville filming *A Woman Like Satan*.

I went to see it about . . . oh . . . several times, actually.

I've often wondered over the years how many times she's related this story.

THIRTY SEVEN

WHEN WE GOT BACK TO GIBRALTAR a couple of days later, dad decided that while I returned to work to continue doing my bit to defend my bit of what was left of the empire, whilst there he would quite like to nip across the strait by ferry to North Africa; to Morocco; to Tangier - for a look-see.

Good idea.

He had a ball there.

One of the things he did tell me was that when he'd gone out for a drink there one evening he had found himself standing at a bar beside another quintessentially blazered Englishman with whom he had got into conversation and later gone out on the town, who turned out to be none other than that great English comedy actor - the gap-toothed Terry Thomas, who was also *en vacance* in the area.

Suntanned, relaxed and healthy, having popped in to the office to have the promised coffee and a chat with my company commander first, and in his son's best interests allowed the former an extension on his overdraft (tee-hee; *got* him), laden down with his duty-frees dad flew back to England the following week and I slipped back once more into the eight months that remained of my contract with Queen and Country, that now somehow seemed to be lacking the lustre that had appealed to me so much as a boy.

In an attempt to allay the tedium of bull, parades, fatigues and off-duty *ennui* I tried to develop a few extra mural activities. I joined Spanish classes at the local adult education centre - for three weeks. Then I decided it might avail me well in the future if I learned to do Pitman's shorthand - for a week. In Korea I had set myself the task (as some might study the Bible) of reading my pocket Oxford dictionary from A-Z, which some have subsequently been rude enough to say is quite apparent. In Gibraltar I began to while away many small hours on duty in the Guard Room, not with the dictionary, but reading the ballads of Rudyard Kipling which portrayed so beautifully the ethos of the army I thought I had joined but found I hadn't. *Boy's Own* heroes, in the light of reality, were dead and gone, it seemed. On the one hand I enjoyed pride in my regimental cap badge and the little of its spirit I was being privileged to savour while the Raj and the Empire were decomposing all around us, but on the other hand I had become disillusioned by my enforced inability to contribute anything to its survival, its on-going-ness or further glory, more tangible than just my presence in it as cannon-fodder. I was just another number, battling with a very small gun, it seemed, a conspiracy by my superiors at all levels to deprive me of ever doing much more than just turning up on parade, and existing. It was time for me to find a larger arena.

Meanwhile, Kipling consoled me.

Creaking saddle-leather; gleaming Sam Brownes; jingling spurs; revolvers; colonial howitzer-fire up the Khyber against the wily Pathan; dust, cordite, rattling sabres . . . *Where East is East and West is West and never the twain shall meet, till earth and sky stand presently at God's great judgement seat. . .* gosh, what a balladeer he was.

I strove to learn one a night by heart. I did well. At one stage I could faultlessly recite a dozen of them. Nobody wanted to hear them of course, nor were they overly impressed when they did, and in due course I forgot them all, but I suppose the exercise must have trained my mind for something.

Three years later I had occasion to visit *Bateman's*, Kipling's beautiful Jacobean house at Burwash in East Sussex. It was a perfectly lovely English spring morning. Birds warbled, brooks babbled, trees sighed and *Puck's* descendants romped happily on *Pook's Hill*.

But *Bateman's* was closed that day.

'I'm sorry sir, we're not open till May,' an old Sussex retainer pruning a privet hedge informed me, but after I had described to him my circumstances and impressed upon him what a true Kipling *aficionado* I really was, he relented and allowed me special and privileged access to the house.

Completely undisturbed by any other 'sightseers' I spent the rest of that memorable morning sitting at Kipling's desk, carefully handling some of his books and pens, looking at his pictures, soaking up the ambience and presence of his spirit and gazing out of the window at nearby Puck's Hill, where Pook romped.

Eventually dragging myself away I strolled dazedly back outside into the sunshine and flowers of his garden.

'Ahhh,' said the old Sussex retainer, stomping one corduroy-legged and army-booted muddy foot on an upturned bucket, pushing his cloth cap to the back of his head and tamping down the dottle in his clay pipe prior to discourse, 'I see you enjoyed yournsel' then? When I was a young man, livin' in the village' . . . he started . . . 'I used to deliver the newspapers to this house, y'know. Sundays I used to hare down that lane on my bike, swirl round in the drive here, and instead of going all the way up to the front door would simply lob the papers to land in the porch there - American style. Well, one day, just as I was about to ride off, the door opened, and there stood Mister Kiplin' himsel'. He was only a little fellah . . . 'bout so high . . ., but looking very stern he snapped out imperiously to me "Boy: boy: you come 'ere." Timorously I walked up this raggedy brick path and stood quakin' before the great man. "Boy," he said to me: "Boy - that is no way to deliver a gentleman's newspapers. You come inside, I will step outside, and then I shall show you how it should be done proper."

'Mister Kiplin' came out, nodded his head, then gave me a little push inside and closed the great oak door as he did so. I didn't know what I was meant to do. Apart from the tickin' of the clock in that great oak beamed hallway the house was in silence. I stood there just staring up in wonderment at all the armorial bearin's draped from the bannisters and walls, the oil paintin's and halberds, swords and flintlocks, and then suddenly I nearly jumped out of my skin when there came a resounding *Bang-Bang-Bang* from the black iron knocker on that great oak door. When I opened it Mister Kiplin' was standin' there with a great big grin on his face, holdin' out *The Times* to me. "Good mornin' sir," he said. "And here are your newspapers."

'Thank you boy,' I said to him. 'And here is a sixpence for your trouble.'

*

In my on-going attempt to evade the army's quest for my soul, I also embraced other literature but Kipling's: novels, classics, paperbacks, various EUPs and tracts on Gibraltar's history absorbed my every leisure hour. In Negley Farson's *Way Of A Transgressor* I was led fascinated into realms far beyond the restrictions of everyday life, yet still not beyond the realms of possibility: probability perhaps, but not possibility. Farson's book led me to begin studying journalism. I fantasized about being driven by fast car from some Fleet Street citadel in a mad dash to Heathrow where a specially chartered plane would be revving up on the tarmac waiting to fly me to Beirut where I would interview premiers, gun-runners and women of intrigue and influence. Secure in the knowledge that I would emerge unscathed from every assignment, I would leap dangerously from front page adventure to newsreel highlight with red hot copy in my inside pocket and a Rolleiflex slung across my shoulder, packed with pictorial sensations. Mine would be the way of a transgressor alright - once I was out of the army.

A tennis ball landed at my feet.

It was a Saturday afternoon.

I was sitting enjoying my reverie on a bench on Gibraltar's Linewall Boulevard, which overlooked the concrete courts. A beautiful, long-legged, suntanned girl in white was staring up at me, her racquet held aloft to signify that if I didn't mind too much she would be grateful for the return of her misplaced shot.

I looked down.

Her fluffy ball seemed to be panting excitedly, wrinkling its fur and winking up at me from between my feet, as though saying: 'I'm onto a far, far better ball game than you are, kiddo: knocks me about reg'lar, she does.'

I had suddenly and very forcibly been made aware of girls once more.

A year later, I was married.

Not to her; but to another one.

I cannot abide delay.

Once an idea has grabbed me, I like to see it through to completion immediately.

Girls there were a'plenty in Gibraltar.

The abundance, throughout their childhood and teens, of sun, sea, fresh fish and fruit, allied to good education, family values, olive oil, and the tenets of Christendom, plus the lack of too much degenerative night life, had contrived to make the majority of them extremely fetching, and the remainder still quite beautiful. They possessed glorious smooth skins, lustrous black hair, and sparkling brown eyes, which depending upon either their breeding or their mood they lowered coyly or else snapped away archly whenever too openly admired.

At fourteen they were well and truly ripe: at sixteen - absolutely over-ready for it, those who hadn't jumped the gun and been there already.

But alien and stringent conditions applied to the courting of any of them.

Gibraltar still lived under the shadow of the chaperone, thus although each regiment stationed there since time immemorial had enjoyed its quota of weddings (the seemingly inevitable result of taking a girl to the cinema) most of the lads shied off that route and opted instead for Main Street's unquestionably sleazy *Suizo Bar*, and its competitor the *Trocadero* for their beer-sodden enertainment, where raddled one-time hookers of dubious origin and excess flesh strutted about in broken heels and garishly tasselled two-pieces, shedding their knackered sequins on the bar tops to the accompanying thump of trumpet music.

I might have been content to do just that (or stick to literature) if it hadn't been for a chance remark made by one of our newly arrived subalterns that very morning. 2/Lt Martin Church had only recently been commissioned and come out to join the regiment from England. A party of us had been rigging Colonel Glennie's yacht together prior to a quick flip round the bay, when he drawled 'Is your name *Michael* George, Corporal?'

'Yes sir,' I said. 'What did you have in mind?'

I was a bit short with him, because I'd just trapped my thumb in a cleat.

'I come from Eastbourne,' he droned. 'Sue Walker has asked to be remembered to you.'

I almost went through the cleat *in toto*, like a shirt-sleeve through a mangle. Regaining my composure with all the aplomb of Norman Wisdom getting up off the floor, I said: 'Oh, that's nice. Do you know her well?' Silly question really.

'Yes, I do actually.' He smiled, and might just as well have added: 'and a damn sight better than you do, too, laddie.'

Dear Sue, who had eventually, sensibly and quite understandably written me the proverbial *Dear John* while I'd been busy building a bog out in Korea: hearing from her directly out of the blue again like that, combined with the tennis ball thudding at my feet, had finally burst my pimples.

The hitherto suppressed sap began to rise and simmer.

Next day, Sunday, I decided to take myself off to Spain.

The sweep of the bay from La Linea round to Algeciras consisted of a glorious swathe of virgin sand. One could strip off and walk naked for miles, roasting in the hot sun and slipping into the gently lapping sea as the whim took one. The occasional *Guardia Civil* could easily be espied sitting smoking atop a sand dune with his carbine between his legs, gazing out to sea as though posted there in 1936 and not having been relieved since. It was then sensible to don trunks. In those days of Franco they'd fix bayonets and charge if they even saw a girl wearing a bikini.

The Bay of Gibraltar was broken by the egress from Spain

426

of two rivers - the *Guadarranque* and the *Palmones*. The *Guadarranque* I forded, as usual, with ease, but the estuary of the *Palmones* was broader, deeper, and its current faster and more strong. There was usually a small ferry on hand, but that day I could see it tied up on the far bank, deserted, with the ferryman nowhere in sight. After waiting in vain for fifteen minutes for his return, I realized I would have to go it alone. The day was closing in. The sun was setting and I had to catch the 18.00 ferry back across the bay from Algeciras to Gibraltar. I jam-packed my shirt, slacks, socks, money and passport into my boots and slipped over the edge of the bank into the swiftly moving current. Holding the knotted boots and their contents above my head with my left arm I started to swim slowly out into mid estuary. All went well until I was three-quarters of the way across. My indefatigable spirit still held, but the strength in my left shoulder had flagged. The boots became heavier and heavier and soon found themselves being lowered closer and closer to the wind-tickled waterline. Suddenly I could sustain them no longer. With a searing burst my shoulder gave in completely and my arm sank beneath the surface, only yards from the far shore. I crawled from the estuary out onto a sandbank, dragging my sodden belongings behind me. If the water had not already been blue I would have sworn I saw the ink from my passport running out to sea. I emptied the boots, wrung out and donned the sodden clothing, squeezed out my money and set off to squelch the remaining two miles through the sand cloying about my heavily dripping trouser bottoms, to Algeciras.

I was quite bedraggled when I finally entered the customs shed and thought of those Spanish Foreign Legionnaires I had seen so elegantly emerging from its portals only five weeks before. The world-weary customs clerk surveyed me disdainfully as I handed him my passport to be stamped. The red ink of that morning's *Entrada* at La Linea mingled wishy-washily with the blue of earlier *Salidas* while my photo now actually bore quite a good likeness. Eventually I was allowed to board the ferry where I immediately slumped exhausted onto a corner of the foredeck like a discarded piece of oily cotton waste. The engines started, and we chugged slowly out into the bay.

And that is where love found me at last.

At first I did not notice the two girls.

The deck beneath my backside was still steeped in residual heat from that day's sun beating upon it, and I was lulled into a doze. My clothes dried. When I awoke they were stiff, crackly and streaked with rime-like salt deposits. I was bathed in an orange glow from the golden orb of the sun setting behind the Algeciras hills. My chin rasped with its bleached stubble. I smelled of sun oil, sweat and salt water; sand, grime and the aftermath of endeavour. I looked like a shipwreck survivor. Slowly I became aware of my surroundings; of the ferry's chugging *pop-pop* sound, and the softly muted voices of people. The clear, fresh hiss of our prow sliced splashes from the deep green waters of the bay. I shook my head to clear it.

It was then that I saw the two girls.

My first view of them was like a film advert for Polaroids.

They were standing conversing at the rail between me and the setting sun, two darkly blurred silhouettes speared by distorting refractions of light and flashes of magnesium intensity when they moved. I wriggled into a sitting position, shielded my eyes, squinted, and appraised them anew.

They were speaking in Spanish.

Both were raven-haired, and tanned.

Their dark eyes sparkled and shone as they flitted expressively from topic to topic. They wore fetching white linen suits, one with navy blue piping, the other with lime green. White handbags and high-heel sling backs completed an ensemble which if it hadn't been a hot evening in the Bay of Gibraltar might have suggested two Californian tennis tournament hostesses.

I licked my lips.

Not lustfully.

More like a Bowery wino deciding to move away from his doorstep for another stab at life.

Phase one of my appraisal was complete.

Both girls were attractive.

428

But at that tender age I possessed insufficient panache just to be able to stroll up and break into some gauche chat routine with two stunning young ladies who were obviously returning from some ritzy lunchtime drinks party in Spain.

They might have been amused.

More likely they would have been embarrassed and annoyed.

They might have been anything but inclined to converse, with a view to eventual marriage, with what at first sight appeared to be the seventh Moroccan mate on a Spanish ferry boat with a crew of six.

I thought better of it, and stayed where I was.

Twenty minutes later we docked in Gibraltar.

I still lay sprawled indecorously on the deck. The girls picked their way daintily over me, like high bred fillies stepping over a cowpat.

'Byeee,' I said, grinning inanely and curling my fingers in a weak wave, limply registering my presence. I was so parched that my tongue cloyed to my palate, making my *byeee* sound pretty loony. Not surprisingly, they ignored me, smiled at each other, stuck their noses pertly in the air and bobbed lightly down the slatted ramp onto the quayside. Dragging myself to my feet I re-tied the piece of string that was holding my trousers up, and loped after them. Chris Wise, my RAF friend who had arranged my earlier Shackleton flight, was waiting for me at the port gates looking immaculate in his blazer and neatly pressed flannels.

'Hallo, sir,' he cried. We always called each other sir. It was mutual consolation for the lack of respect we suffered elsewhere. Chris was the epitome of an aristocrat. He had no chin, and the two front teeth hung over. But, good old Chris. He'd unwittingly done the trick. Two pretty heads snapped back with suddenly awakened interest. Two pairs of dusky brown eyes softened curiously. We must have been mistaken. Who is this dashing corsair just returned from some death-defying mission in Iberia to be met by someone who must surely be the British pro-consul in person as the sun sets on the bay and twilight envelops the Rock?

Oh, God: was Walter Mitty ever alive and well and living in Michael George.

The girls flounced off one way, while Chris and I repaired to *The Fox & Hounds* for a couple of beers.

Next evening, showered, shaved and ponced, the more presentable version of me was walking back to camp down Gibraltar's Main Street after some important small mission or other in town, like buying ink, when I saw one of the girls again. The one who had been wearing green piping on her suit. Now she was wearing jeans and a delightfully filled T-shirt and was walking unsuspectingly along the pavement towards me. Mentally I stroked the moustache I didn't have. What should I say to her? My brain screeched through its panic gears. Then I wondered why I had to say anything at all. We hadn't met. We didn't know one another. On the ferry she had made it quite clear that I was nothing but dross. I could easily and justifiably ignore her and pass by without even a glance. Why all this fuss?

Then realization waved at me through the fog.

There were forces at work.

Cupid - that amorous emissary of fate had selected this particular creature to be the subject of Michael George's chase in this week's edition of The Love Game.

I regarded her afresh.

She was a voluptuous and exotic piece of goods all right, possessing a classic Spanish beauty with finely stretched facial features, to say nothing of a gorgeous pair of boobs.

Yes, I thought.

She'll do.

She recognized me.

While we were still five yards apart the most radiant smile lit her lively face and her eyes sparkled. The smile slowly faltered and died, and I was disappointed. Perhaps she'd thought I was someone else and had just realized her mistake. She seemed to be pouting. Then I sensed why. It was me. I had been scowling. I had been told about my scowl. I did it unwittingly to cover shyness, and still do.

We had drawn abreast of each other, trying to slow our pace

430

to prolong the encounter without making it apparent. I knew now I would have to acknowledge her. Cupid had obviously sent her a memo as well. I was home and dry. I was on to a winner. I gave her one of my wan little half-smiles for which I am renowned, and then she'd passed, gone on by, lost in the crowd. It was my own fault.

Damn.

I didn't see her again until four days later.

It was 22.30. I was walking past The Convent when I saw her strolling elegantly along on her own in front of me. There was no one else around. Unless I turned purposely up a side road to avoid her I would inevitably catch her up. Steeling my resolve and placing my hand over my heart to stop it jumping out I strode up alongside her, jovial as you like, just as if I'd known her all my life.

'Hallo,' I said. 'Do you mind if I walk you home?'

'Not very original, but I suppose it'll do' she said. 'Alright, if you'd like to.' She smiled, perhaps a little taken aback by my sudden appearance and effrontery, as if I'd just come overhead through the trees to cut her off, and had swung down onto the jungle path on a branch from above.

'My name's Michael,' I told her. 'What's yours?' (Hey; this was smooth, man; but *smooooth*).

'Mine's Raquel,' she replied. 'Rachel in English. Rachel Gabay: although my family calls me Fudge.'

'Fudge? Why Fudge?' I asked.

'Take your pick,' she laughed. 'The book says it's either a soft sweetmeat, or, I believe — a piece of nonsense.'

In the event the book proved right. Of the former.

People seem shocked when they ask and I tell them I picked my wife up on the street.

Apparently she'd fancied me on first sight though; and who could blame her for that?

The rest of that week we went to the cinema a couple of times, and for a few coffees and stuff, but then the following Sunday I was invited to lunch to meet her family. I didn't realize until afterwards that this was quite an accelerated occasion in the Gibraltarian way of things. Apparently my acceptance indicated that my intentions were quite serious, but nobody thought to inform me of this at the time. All I went along for really was to get a square meal and have a shirt button sewn on.

Obviously I passed muster, because the same thing happened the following two Sundays as well.

By then, of course, they 'had' me.

I was in up to my neck.

'Was there anything you wanted to say to me, Michael?' Rachel's father asked when the table had been cleared and the girls were washing up after that third Sunday meal.

'No, I don't think so,' I said, all innocence and charm. 'I enjoyed my lunch very much, thank you. It was nice.'

He *hurrumphed* and turned to his newspaper, rustling it meaningfully, although I still hadn't fathomed the drift.

I sat there with my knees together for a while, hands clasped in lap, and then got up to look at the goldfish.

I think it winked at me.

Perhaps it knew something I didn't.

I wandered out into the kitchen.

The women pretended I wasn't there.

Something was definitely awry.

'What have I done?' I asked Rachel as we strolled arm-in-arm through the Alameda Gardens together later that evening.

'Nothing,' she said. 'It's more to do with what you haven't done.'

'I know,' I said, snapping my fingers as realisation dawned. She turned eagerly to face me. 'I should have brought some chocolates for your mother.'

On the way back to camp later I stopped off for a beer at the Gibraltar Football Club.

'Hi, Mike,' Pepe the barman called. 'Have this one on the house. I gather congratulations are in order.'

'Thanks, Pepe,' I said, gratefully accepting the beer I was handed. What he had said then registered. 'Congratulations?' I queried. 'Why congratulations?' I looked over the top of my tankard as I drank.

'I heard you got engaged today.'

'En*gaged*? I spluttered. My beer spilled. What are you talking about?'

'Heard you got engaged to Raquel Gabay. It's all round town that today was the day.'

'That's right,' came a chorus of male Gibraltarian voices from the billiard table.

'Fellahs,' I pleaded. 'Do me a *favour*, please? I don't know what you're talking about. Engaged? Me? Why, I've only known the girl three weeks.'

'We know that, yes, but you had lunch there today, didn't you,' stated Pepe.

'Yes. So?' I replied, warily.

'And you had lunch there last Sunday, as well,' someone else offered. (Gibraltar is a *very* small place).

'Yes,' I agreed, hesitantly.

'*And* the Sunday before that, too,' Pepe roared.

'Yes,' I thundered back, 'but just what the hell has any of this got to do with the price of bread?'

A silence fell across the room like a hand. Someone scraped a chair leg on the tiles. Pepe polished a glass and softly whistled. Others I looked at raised their eyes to consider specks on the flyblown ceiling. I began imagining Sicily and sharp knives.

'Mike?'

I glanced over into the far corner of the club. A kindly old fruit seller was sitting there for whom I had bought the occasional beer on some of my more expansive evenings. He beckoned me over. Glancing behind me furtively, I shuffled off towards him and bowed to lend him my ear.

'It's like this, you see, Mike,' he said - 'every country has its own funny little rules, customs and traditions. Here in Gibraltar we seem to have more than our fair share of them, considering what a small place we are. One of them, it just so happens, is that if a fellow takes lunch with a girl's family on three consecutive Sundays, it is fairly commonly accepted that his intentions towards her are more than just a little serious. In fact it is tantamount to a public announcement that they have plighted their troth to one another. Get it?'

I got it.

Even though that hadn't been his exact phraseology, I'd certainly got it alright.

He grinned, smacked his toothless gums and proffered his glass for its refill.

Sheeeeit.

I'd been let down by ignorance, my stomach and a shirt button.

I contemplated the options.

Rachel was delightful.

If she wanted me that badly, who was I to refuse?

Besides, having got myself into it, I didn't know how to get out of it, so supposed I'd go along with it. My mother hated people who welshed on things. Besides, she did have rather a nice body. Rachel. Not mother. Well, mother too of course - and at the time I had a nice body as well, for that matter. We should be able to make nice children togeter.

The whole thing was beginning to seem like quite a good idea after all.

Accordingly, I accepted the situation, and lay back to enjoy it.

Since I had got my feet under the table, my shirts washed and ironed and someone to hold hands with in the cinema, life assumed a whole new lustre. The army still struggled valiantly for the total capitulation of my soul, but it received less and less of my attention as Rachel received more and more. My duties became easy, and authority became uneasy.

L/Cpl George seems to be very happy with himself these days, S'arnt Major. Has he discovered religion all of a sudden? Gone of his rocker, or something?'

'In a manner of speaking sir, yes. Rumour has it there's a young lady wot has wheedled her sorry way into his rotten little life and he thinks all his birthdays have come at once. Would you like me to rift him, sir? We could always post the bas ... the little sh ... Corporal George back to the depot, sir.'

'No, don't let's do that S'arnt Major. Let him have his fun. We need him for fatigues. Keep an eye on him, though.'

'You mean 'arass him a little bit, sir?'

'Not necessarily that S'arnt Major; no.'

'Shame about that sir, but very well.'

It was now July 1958. Students of world affairs may recall that this was when one of the first of the many crises in Lebanon blew up. This necessitated the battalion's operational move from Gibraltar to Benghazi from then until October. Just how marching about in the North African desert for three months was meant to help avert a crisis in the Lebanon, I do not now recall, but it was deemed by our Whitehall masters to be an expedient step for the battalion to take at the time.

On the fateful day of our departure - Friday 18th July - we were drawn up on Grand Casemates Square in FSMO (Full Service Marching Order) with towels, toothbrush and a spare pair of socks, waiting to be lifted to the docks where the Royal Navy was standing by to swish us across the Med to Libya in one of their ships, the county class heavy cruiser *HMS Cumberland.* In 1951 the Lords of the Admiralty had decided to turn *Cumberland* into the first and only trials cruiser, a duty she continued to carry out until 1958, testing everything from atomic warfare defences to plastic hats! She also tested out new gunnery techniques, radar, and fibre-glass boats, some of which are still used in the modern Navy today. Very few warships had attained the distinction of still being in full commission after 30 years active service, one of *Cumberland's* commissions having been the acceptance of the Japanese surrender at Java in 1945. In November 1959 she left the Med for the final time, for her birthplace at Barrow-in-Furness, for decommissioning and to be broken up, the oldest serving ship in the Royal Navy. When she finally paid off, her paying off pennant was over 600-feet long!

In August 1956, at the start of the Suez crisis, *Cumberland* was deployed in trooping reinforcements to Cyprus. Engaged on similar missions, Captain H.G.T. Padfield and his jolly Jack Tars had been zotting about the Med in this high speed troop transporter of theirs ever since. Now they were moored at Gibraltar dockside waiting to take 1RSussex across to the desert. Rachel, thinking I had deliberately arranged the whole Middle East crisis myself, was quite upset of course.

Nevertheless we bade each other a sloppy farewell the previous evening and promised to write hourly.

An emissary had detached himself from the orderly room and was scurrying across the square towards a group of officers *haw-hawing* politely in the corner, flicking fly-whisks against their calves they'd dug up from somewhere, and thinking of Rommel. The emissary squeaked to a halt in his hobnails, threw up a salute and handed the adjutant a communiqué. He read it, cursed, and I just knew it had to do with me. He gave the piece of paper to my company commander who in turn beckoned to the CSM. The two of them engaged in a brief conflab and then, as I knew it would, my name rang clearly across the square.

'C'orl George?'

'Sah.'

I alone crashed to attention and took one pace forward from the rest of the battalion which was standing easy. My knife, fork, spoon, mess tins, mouth-organ and shaving brush rattled like a broken Christmas parcel in the pack on my back. It seemed a shame to have disturbed them. I could see one of my Naafi Mars Bars trickling through the brass eyelet in my left-hand ammunition pouch, beginning to stain my shirt front.

'Fall out, and report to the orderly room, C'orl George.'

'Sah.'

Turning to the right I saluted smartly and marched quickly off the square towards the orderly room. Clumping inside I unslung my rifle and leaned it against the counter. It was nice and cool in there.

'What's up, Syd?' I asked the orderly room clerk.

'Dunno, mate,' replied that self-styled fount of all knowledge. 'Operational secrecy, I guess; but I know the OC Rear Party wants to see you.'

The adjutant's officer door was open. A voice boomed from within: 'If that's you, C'orl George, step forth within.'

Pompous twit.

'Sah'.

The Major, OC Rear Party, had been suffering a bit from angina lately, and was being left behind for that reason. Hot sand and deprivation weren't good for angina apparently, according to the doctor who was a friend of his and knew his wife. He was to command the camp, the married families and the skeleton company which was to be retained in Gibraltar to perform all duties.

I skidded to a halt on the mat on the highly polished lino before the gap in his desk, crashed to the floor and fetched up clutching his ankle.

'F'chrissake man, what do you think you're doing?' he yelped, peering down beneath the desk at me from his side.

'Sorry, sir. I tripped.'

I stood and faced him, flicking my burning wrist where I'd banged it on his chair leg. He gave me a funny look, removed his glasses, rubbed his eyes and then sneaked another peek at me to see if I was still there.

I was.

Resigned to his task, he spoke:

'C'orl George; Parsons, the laundry store man, has broken his leg. . . .'

'On this floor, sir? I'm not surprised; but I'm very sorry to hear it,' I added, hoping the quickly summoned sentiment would stand me in good stead in heaven.

'Quite so; quite so,' he murmured. 'Apart from that, though, L/Cpl Johnson, the mail NCO, has had to be flown back to England on compassionate grounds. His mother's dying, and . . .'

'I'm very . . .'

'Yes, I'm quite sure you are, C'orl George. We'll take that as read, shall we? Now - I shall need someone who can read and write and tie up bundles to take over both duties. With the battalion gone neither will be a particularly onerous task and should easily be handled by one person. You.'

'You mean . . . you mean . . . I won't be going to Benghazi with the rest of the battalion, sir?' (I wanted to make sure I'd got this absolutely right).

'I'm sorry, Corporal; I'm afraid not. I can understand your disappointment, but these things happen sometimes, you know. Your company commander asked especially that you be elected to remain behind, so obviously he thinks highly of you. Come along now, don't look so crestfallen. You're young. You've got the rest of your life ahead of you. There'll still be plenty of time for you to go to Benghazi.'

'Yes, sir,' I sniffed, trying not to emit a *whoop* and kick my heels in the air with joy.

We heard a whine and a rumble outside. A convoy of three-tonners had just come roaring through the gates from the MT park. The familiar crash of tailboards, cries and thumps indicated that several hundred bodies with their kit and caboodle were clambering aboard. The sand. The flies. The heat. Oh, God; I'd be missing them all. There I'd be, stuck behind on my own in my bunk here in Gibraltar with the communal shower all to myself, my books, and Rachel every night, oh . . . and the laundry and the mail to look after for an hour or so each day too, of course. God - life was so unfair.

In the first week alone I was so overcome with euphoria that I sent the battalion three loads of dirty smalls from the WRAC camp up the road, and their clean socks and mail back with a draft of troops to the regimental depot in Chichester. The following Thursday someone else was appointed NCOi/c laundry, and now with only the mail to look after I had even more time to laze on the beach with Rachel and plan our future. I felt awful about it - but life's like that.

By now I had only four months left to serve before being flown back to England for demob, although by now my relationship with the army had degenerated to such an extent that it wouldn't have surprised me if they'd told me to walk.

But what would I do as a civilian?

My mother and brother had just gone out to South Africa, so thinking it might be rather nice to see them again I thought I would apply to join the British South Africa Police, not realising that they operated in Rhodesia, not South Africa. Once back in England I would stick all my photos in an album, hitch-hike to South Africa via Gibraltar and the Sahara, work like stink until I had saved enough to fly back to marry Rachel, and . . . oh well . . . it was fun to plan.

*Some*thing would turn up.

Then in October, suntanned and fit, the battalion returned to Gibraltar, and after three months of idyllic idleness, on my final month's countdown to demob I found myself being harshly thrust back into the rigours of regimental soldiering once more, getting rollocked and bollocked by all and sundry from arseholes to breakfast time for twisted bootlaces, dirty brasses, flowing hair, and not having shaved for half-an-hour . . . what a swan-song . . .

. . . but then -

- the fateful day dawned at last.

I was called before the CO, Lt Col J.B.A. Glennie himself to bid my adieu.

The old boy looked quite relieved as I was marched in front of him. He almost rose from his chair to greet me, but a discreet cough and raised eyebrow from the RSM and adjutant respectively reminded him of his station, and he sat down again. But he forgot he'd pushed his chair back. His *veldschoen* shoes refused to grip on that damn lino and his hat fell over his eyes. With the adjutant's hurried assistance and much blowing and puffing, and 'Oh, my goodness me's, and 'Keerists' from the RSM, he regained his chair, composure was restored, and normal service resumed.

The RSM introduced me.

'23463195 L/Cpl George, sir.'

'Well, Corporal. You're finally going to leave us.' (Big nods; grins all round).

'Yes, sir. I believe so. My time's up'

'Any idea what you're going to do?'

I didn't have a clue really, but thought the British South Africa Police bit might impress. Briefly I outlined my plan, but the CO interjected —

'Have you considered the possibility that they might not accept you?' he asked.

'No, sir.'

'Oh, I see.'

'Im 5' 8", sir, single, and don't wear glasses.'

'Yes, I'm sure that's all very well, but . . . look, I don't want to dampen your spirits, but have you stopped to consider the effect my final end-of-service report about you might have on future job prospects?'

'No, sir.'

'You haven't?'

'No, sir.'

'Oh; I see. Well look, you must appreciate that I am hardly in a position to give you a glowing testimonial, am I? Everyone I've spoken to is under the impression that you seem to consider the army a bit of a lark.'

'Isn't it, sir?'

'No, it's not at all a lark. The army is a very serious profession.'

'Yes, sir.' I grinned, not wishing to expound my and most of the battalion's reasons for disagreeing with him. He had devoted his life to it. It would be unfair of me to set him wondering now'

'However,' he continued charitably, much to the annoyance of the RSM, who if he'd had his way would have had me gibbeted - 'apart from one or two occasions when you seem to have preferred natural flora as a means of recognition (he was referring to the time I'd stuck a feather in my tin-hat) you have worn the regiment's cap badge for three years, so I'll tell you what I'm prepared to do . . .'

'What's that, sir?'

'What's what?' He swung round in his chair to see.

'What is it that you are prepared to do, sir?'

'Oh. I see. Yes, well, I was just going to tell you, so don't interrupt.'

'No, sir. Sorry, sir.'

'If you promise you *will* go to South Africa, and stay there, I am prepared to perjure myself and write you a reasonable report.'

'That's very kind of you, sir. Thank you.'

Silence fell.

Nobody spoke.

The CO suddenly looked embarrassed and shuffled some papers.

He cleared his throat.

He paused, steepled his fingers contemplatively, and looked from the adjutant to the RSM who each looked at each other and raised their eyes.

Oh, God; there wasn't going to be some 11th hour hitch, was there?

The CO spoke again.

'Now look, C'orl George. There is just one other thing that I am officially commanded to ask you before you leave us. As you know, National Service is drawing to a close, and we're soon going to have to start building up and strengthening the regular army . . . you've . . . er . . . you've never actually thought of signing on as a regular, have you?'

'Oh no, sir.' I laughed.

'Oh, good,' he said with enormous and obvious relief, and I saw the adjutant and RSM emit large exhalations of breath, too. 'Well that's that, then. It only remains for me now to wish you all the best for the future.'

He beamed, and the RSM let him stand up properly this time to shake my hand. Even the RSM smiled.

I saluted, turned to the right and marched out.

That evening I left Rachel in tearful abeyance, pending some firm development regarding the next phase of our life, and returned to camp in a thunderstorm to crush three lockersful of accumulated gear into a kitbag, and a shopping basket I'd borrowed from my prospective mother-in-law.

At 04.00 I arose, bade farewell to Jim, made my way to the airport and flew home to England for the first time in two years.

*

So it was December 1958 and my three years with the regiment were finally up. I had said my farewells, flown back to Blighty and reported once more to Roussillon Barracks in Chichester to do the discharge business. There I had the ill-advised temerity to use a phrase that had been used so often on me as a rookie. Unfortunately I chose the wrong bloke to use it on.

The cookhouse that teatime was crowded with a new intake

of raw recruits, and there I was, tanned, done Korea, just got in from Gibraltar . . . I was made up with myself.

'No, you can't have another slice of bread and jam,' the wizened cook sergeant said to me.

'You want to get some in, mate,' I retorted foolishly, fully expecting to impress the surrounding queue of new recruits by a phrase I'd waited three years to be in a position to use.

It was not to be.

'So do you, sonny,' the cook sergeant retorted. '*I've* been in since 1936. Now put the bread back please, there's a good lad.'

Blushing furiously I considered myself suitably chastened and - mortified - never forgot the lesson.

Next day I handed in my kit, received my final pay, phoned dad to say I was on my way, caught the train to Shoreham in the rain, and commenced sleeping on the floor of his spare room while I planned the next stage of my life.

It was off with the puttees and out to purchase a new suit.

A pinstripe, perhaps.

At last I was a civvy again.

EPILOGUE

THIS EPILOGUE AFFIRMS my belief that although army life as I knew it is no more, regimental life (from those days) is still a continuum.

Let me explain why.

Although there were many aspects of my early military life that were mind-numbingly tedious and the universal cry of most National Servicemen was 'Roll On' (to demob), the account of my final farewell interview with the regiment's then CO, for example, was flippant and exaggerated. There are few of us who do not harbour a great and lifelong pride in our regiment and in the tremendous and unforgettable camaraderie that we enjoyed.

In June 1959 I flew back to The Rock to marry my Gibraltarian fiancée, Rachel. The Prince of Wales Own Regiment of Yorkshire was now the resident battalion, 1RSUSSEX by then having returned to Lingfield for a spot of home duty.

Over the next four years Rachel and I lived in Brighton, produced the first of our offspring and I earned my crust in advertising, but then I felt I wanted more out of life than civvy street seemed able to offer. Although, as stated above, throughout the whole of my three years with the Colours the 'in' cry had always been 'Roll On', in 1963 - having been to Westbury where I sat and this time passed an RCB (Regular Commission Board - what had earlier been WOSBy) I sent Rachel and our then eight-month-old daughter, Natalia, back to Gibraltar to her parents, while I went to Mons OCS (Officer Cadet School) in Aldershot for four months officer training.

Having left L/Cpl The Baron Hans Cristoff Von Massenbach behind in Gibraltar, at Mons I found myself sleeping in the next bed to a 19-year-old Officer Cadet just up from Eton, one Sir Ranulph Twistleton Wykeham-Fiennes, whose potential even then was glaringly self apparent. 'There's only one thing for you to do in life, and that's to become an explorer,' I said to him one day; which turned out to be the most prescient remark I've ever made in my life. Ran was the toughest person I have ever met. At final Battle Camp in the Brecons I 'did' my knee in a bad way on one of the final endurance marches. Only two weeks away from our commissioning parade by Her Majesty The Queen herself, a back-squadding seemed imminent. *'No way,'* said Ran, and as well as his own kit he immediately insisted in divesting me of mine and hefting it for me over the rest of that morning's obstacles.

In July 1963 I was commissioned into the RASC. In 1965 I was absorbed into the RAOC after the McLeod 'Reorganisation of The Q Services.' (The first of many). That same year I took my lieutenant to captain practical promotion exam. Where? In Windsor Great Park. Who turned out to be my examining officer on the day? None other than Major Steve Ellwood, my 1RSUSSEX boyhood hero from Korea days. 'I'm not going to be the one to fail you, he said with a twinkle in his bright blue eyes. 'Go and try that chap over there.' Promptly I was handed over to an unsuspecting Guards officer leaning on his shooting stick beneath a bushy-topped tree, who was kind enough to give me a pass.

Whilst running a military supply depot in Hannover in 1968 I had to undergo an infantry attachment in order to 'bone up' for my captain to major promotion exam. To which infantry regiment was I allotted? Right. 1st Battalion The Royal Sussex Regiment (which by now had become 3 Queens) then stationed at Lemgo. I duly reported to a given grid reference in a German wood on a Sunday afternoon to be met by CSM Len Hart of 'A' Company. Len and I had been hoppoes, corporals together in adjoining platoon ditches in Korea. 'Good afternoon, Sir.' He grinned broadly as he tabbed in and smacked one up, both delighted and taking the rise out of me at the same time. 'Welcome back to your old regiment and especially to your old company, 'A' Company, Major Nigel Knocker commanding: Sah.'

'Knock it off, Len,' I grinned back happily, warmly pumping his hand.

Sitting on a log at last-light addressing his 'O' Group Nigel Knocker, too, kindly referred to my previous service with the regiment and welcomed me back, albeit only for a week but albeit also a week of unremittingly sustained nostalgia and joy. Recollections of my attachment? Major Mike Johnson pouring over a map in his carpeted and designer decorated APC command vehicle, and - no longer in Windsor Great Park, but now back with 'our' regiment in Germany once more - the perennially gung-ho Major Steve Ellwood again, bucketing flat out across the Heath in *his* APC as if chasing a cheetah on safari. (He still rode point-to-point at age-65, on one memorable occasion completing the course with a broken stirrup leather).

I subsequently passed my promotion exam.

Some weeks later a convoy of three-tonners came rumbling into my Hannover depot to collect some kit. The NCO i/c? Cpl Pat Patterson, the bully with whom I'd had my near razor fight in the ablutions of the LST *Frederick Clover* in the China Sea, sailing from Hong Kong up to Korea 10 years earlier. My then unknowing RAOC CO seemed to consider it a tad unseemly that on this occasion Pat and I all but embraced each other.

The next encounter was in 1973 when I took my son to meet his housemaster for the first time at his new prep school. He turned out to be none other than cricketing Lt David Nicholson from Korea and Gibraltar days, who over the ensuing years then became an occasional drinking companion at Eastbourne's *Pilot Inn* when I was home in the town on leave. It was extremely sad then to attend David's untimely funeral at Eastbourne College (his *alma mater)* in the early '90s, at which blue and orange ties prevailed because so many of the 'old crowd' had so loyally attended the occasion.

When finally I resigned from the British Army in 1978 I

went to spend a sabbatical year in Portugal and then California, but then my bank manager suggested that if I wanted to sustain my lifestyle and keep the children at their respective schools he would be grateful for a further infusion of funds. As a succession of pustular 19-year-old personnel directors had informed me that at my age (then 40) I was far too old ever to be considered for gainful employment in Britain again, I realised that I would have to try to hire out my sword for a living.

In March 1980 I arrived in Muscat as a contract officer for the Sultan of Oman's Army. Who was the first person I should meet walking along the beach there one afternoon the week I arrived? The British Military Attaché. Who he? Colonel Nigel Knocker. Who was the next person to arrive in Oman as a mercenary? Major Mike Johnson. And the next? Ex-Cpl, ex-CSM, ex-RSM - but now Captain Len Hart. I couldn't get away from The Royal Sussex if I *tried*.

Nigel Knocker eventually departed from Oman. (He had previously had a very good war there against the communist-fuelled *Adoo* some years earlier, as CO of The Desert Regiment). Who turns up there again two years later, though? Colonel Nigel Knocker once more - this time round as a contract officer.

In 1986 Len Hart left Oman to become the Coroner's Clerk for Northampton Police, and sadly died on 5th June 1995.

I left Oman in 1985. Some years later I applied for the job of Emergency Planning Officer for East Sussex. Who was the then Emergency Planning Officer for Wiltshire? Colonel (Retd) Nigel Knocker, who was kind enough to give me sufficient tips to come second in the pecking order, beaten to the post by a sailor who was younger and had only more recently hung up his anchor.

In 1986 cancer was to steal Rachel away from me, my dear Gibraltarian wife of 27 years. Some years later I remarried, but from Army life and what you have been reading here, my new lady, Diane, knew nothing. One evening I took her to an Anglo-Omani Society meeting in London where the speaker was to talk about the history and development of the Oman

Forces. Who was the speaker? You've guessed it. Colonel (Retd) Nigel Knocker again! The erstwhile Royal Sussex adjutant who'd thought my draft and I were scruffs when we had first arrived in Korea as private soldiers to join the regiment over 40 years before.

Now the three-hundred-year-old Royal Sussex Regiment is no more, of course. These days it constitutes part of the newly formed The Princess of Wales Royal Regiment. At an Eastbourne Old Grammarians' Lunch recently I met a young Old Boy who was the then new Regiment's CO. I'd left the school in 1956. He'd started there in the '70s.

Then in June 2007 I flew out to Gibraltar for a niece's wedding. Whilst there I went into King's Chapel one afternoon to pay respects to our regimental colours, which are laid up there. When I signed the visitors' book I was 'gob smacked' to see that the previous entry, its ink still hardly dry on the page, was that of Sgt Peter Crick, our 24-year-old 'A' Coy platoon sergeant out in Korea. He, too, had married a Gibraltarian girl, back in 1958, and was obviously there now on a concurrent visit with mine. I worked it out. He was 74!

I photographed the book's page with both our entries on it.

Back in England I went to pains to track him down, and did so. I acquired his address and sent him the photograph with our names, and an explanatory letter.

Two days later my telephone rang. When I picked it up, a well remembered voice at the other end . . . *'Come along, you two, you're not here to admire the scenery. That there's your field of fire. Interlocking arcs with the two trenches to each side of you. This trench you're in was dug by the Jocks last year. Nice of 'em, wasn't it. Since then no one's used it. We've kept it vacant and reserved, just waiting for you two to come out from England to occupy it. Doesn't that make you feel loved, wanted and important? Now get the fucking thing properly dug out. I will be back in an hour and shall expect to see this foetid little pit of yours looking like the Kure Hilton. Okay?'* . . . this time simply uttered two equally gob smacked words at the fateful coincidence of it all:

'*Fuck*in' *ell.*'

447

There had by now arrived the miraculous internet.

In Korea and Gibraltar I had a particularly close friend, called Richard Farrar. After he left the regiment we lost touch with each other completely, although ever since then I harboured a strong prescience that one day our paths would cross once more. Doing research during the writing of this book, I stumbled across a Royal Sussex website I had not seen before. Scrolling down - lo and behold - there leapt onto the screen a photograph of Richard and me in Korea together. Immediately I got onto the website, and later that same day I received an excited e-mail from Richard himself, who was then (and hopefully still is) a retired Grant Thornton partner, living in Toronto. 'This is amazing,' his e-mail shrieked. 'Next week I shall be back in UK on my annual visit.' So within just one week of touching base again, we were having lunch together at the *King's Head* in East Hoathley, where the conversation carried on exactly where it had left off fifty years earlier.

On Richard's annual UK visit the following year, he was instructed to come for lunch - instead of at the *King's Head*, East Hoathley - this time at our home in Eastbourne. What I didn't tell him was that Jim Davidson had also been asked. But I didn't tell Jim about Richard. I also invited along Lt Col David McAllister, our attached RAEC Sgt in Gibraltar, who was later commissioned and was the guy most instrumental in getting me to rejoin the army myself, and after having attempted several business ventures in civvy street had *also* later served with me as a contract officer out in Oman; but I didn't tell *him* about the others coming along, either. Result? As each young-at-heart old soldier arrived and recognised the other after half a century, unbelievingly delighted great arm-punching cries of 'You Old *Bugger*' went up. The dining room had been done out in our blue and orange regimental colours, and I had suitably captioned blown-up photographs of all of us sellotaped round the walls, aged 20. Additionally what I had was a blown-up photograph of our hero there as well, the then 30-year-old Captain Steve Ellwood.

'What a guy he was,' they all agreed. 'You really ought to try to get in touch with him Mike,' they suggested, when I mentioned that in a few weeks time I would be making a trip down to the west country, where we knew he lived. So I summoned the requisite courage and determination to write the Great Man a letter, reintroducing myself after all those years, and telling him about our reunion lunch and what had transpired; and so – 'might I pop in for coffee, on my way through Somerset in a couple of weeks time?'

Two days later the telephone rang.

It was himself . . .

. . . like having the Duke of Edinburgh, or Charlton Heston, or even God on the line.

'Coffee's no bloody good,' he said: 'Come for some lunch.'

I did.

It was a delight.

He was now 81, and living with his still lovely wife, Pat, in a sixteenth century farmhouse down a muddy medieval lane which meandered back right into the middle of Olde England, and - as hoped for and expected - just about the fittest and finest looking 81-year-old I had ever seen in my life. I mean, dammit, he had even just got back from a blue water fishing trip in Cuba!

These days my reunions are coming round like belt-fed mortars.

There's the Royal Sussex Annual Dinner at Lewes Town Hall each April; my old school lunch at the Royal Eastbourne Golf Club every November; the RCT, RAOC (now RLC) dinner at Deepcut's HQ Officers' Mess near Camberley, and the Sultan's Armed Forces dinner at the Army and Navy Club in St James's, all also held in November . . . Life definitely seems to be completing full circle, and I am sponging more soup off ties than I can shake a stick at, but I would not have it any other way.

The snag is, although instinctively I now read all my magazines' obituaries first, having just celebrated my 70th birthday I still feel 17 inside, and ready to embark on the *Devonshire* for Korea all over again - but then, don't we all.

Get some in?

I think most of us have.

And there you have it!

THE END

. . . of the beginning

Lightning Source UK Ltd.
Milton Keynes UK
11 October 2009

144818UK00001B/4/P